One Last Dance

JUDITH LENNOX

One Last Dance

headline
review

First published in 2014 by HEADLINE REVIEW
An imprint of HEADLINE PUBLISHING GROUP

1

Cataloguing in Publication Data is
available from the British Library

ISBN 978 0 7553 8412 9 (Hardback)
ISBN 978 0 7553 8413 6 (Trade paperback)

Typeset in Joanna MT Std by Palimpsest Book Production Limited,
Falkirk, Stirlingshire

Printed and bound in Great Britain by
CPI Group (UK) Ltd, Croydon, CR0 4YY

Headline's policy is to use papers that are natural, renewable and recyclable
products and made from wood grown in sustainable forests. The logging
and manufacturing processes are expected to conform to the
environmental regulations of the country of origin.

HEADLINE PUBLISHING GROUP
An Hachette UK Company
338 Euston Road
London NW1 3BH

www.headline.co.uk
www.hachette.co.uk

To Dominic and Victoria, with love

Esme

18 September 1974

And in the distance, the sound of the sea.

Her eyes closed, she listens to the rush and pull of the waves. She pictures the swell breaking on the beach, leaving a frill of foam as the emerald water draws back, heaving with it a hundred shiny pink and amber pebbles. She sees the heavy blackish-green heads of the pine trees on the cliff tossing back and forth and the wind rippling through the gorse.

Esme opens her eyes. She is in her bedroom in Little Coxwell, eighty miles from the coast. There is no wind, no storm, and yet she can still hear the sea. Is she, perhaps, going mad, demented – or could she in fact be dying, her poor tired heart giving out as she heads for Paradise?

Not today, she thinks. I have things to do.

The crash of the waves is fading now, and she remembers that she was dreaming of the sea. In her dream, she was running along the beach with her sister, Camilla. She still feels the hard, compacted sand beneath her bare feet, the scratch of the grains caught between her toes and a knobbly shell cutting into her instep. She is running as fast as she can, her lungs straining as she tries to catch up with Camilla, who, flaxen plaits streaming like banners, seems to shrink as she pulls ahead. By the time Esme reaches the far end of the bay, her sister has scrambled

1

up the jagged rocks and is standing where they jut out into the water, laughing as the waves' white spray soaks her, laughing at silly little Esme, who is scared of heights and the sea.

It is memory, this. She recalls how Tom ran in and out of the white-tipped waves, and how she upturned her bucket to make a perfect dome of sand. The nursemaid spreading out the picnic on the beach. The chauffeur dozing in the Daimler, parked in the shade of the trees.

She must have been five or six years old. A few years later, her mother or the nursemaid would have told them off for behaving like hoydens. *Hoyden*, she thinks, lying in bed, fully awake now, her gaze settling on the grey line of light between the curtains. She hasn't heard that word for years. Are there any hoydens these days? Times change, she thinks. She remembers the summer clothing she and Camilla wore, the layers of vest, knickers, petticoat, frilled voile frock and pinafore deemed suitable for a day at the beach. She thinks of Coral's jeans and sleeveless T-shirt. Yes, times change, and sometimes for the better.

The sound of the sea recedes, then is gone. She looks at the clock and sighs. It's twenty past five: so many hours to get through before Zoe arrives. She feels a mixture of impatience and dread, the needing-to-get-it-over-with sensation that one endures before an aeroplane takes off. Or before a dance. The plainer, less favoured daughter, she was the sort of girl who hovered on the perimeter of the ballroom, self-conscious, wondering what people thought of her. It is one of the great advantages of old age, she thinks, that she no longer cares.

Her apprehension, the coiling in the stomach as she considers this evening's summer party, comes, she knows, from a fear that she might fail. She has planned carefully, but there is always the possibility that what she has set out to do will be thwarted, that her arrangements may prove inadequate, or that her fractious, fractured family will refuse to do as she wants. Will refuse, even, to turn up. *This may be my last birthday, one never knows at my age.* She has used emotional blackmail, played the frail old lady card, more than once these past weeks.

The day may still slip away from her, receding into the distance like Camilla's running figure. She is afraid that she will falter, that she will lack the grit to confront the past, and that she will be left standing on the sand while Camilla looks down at her and laughs her last triumphant laugh. She is afraid that her heart, which her doctor, who is young and tactless, describes as 'flabby', will not hold out, and she will never know the truth.

She feels anxiety surging through her like the waves of the sea and she closes her eyes and tries to breathe deeply. She has taken to going once a week to yoga classes at the village hall – herself and half a dozen young mothers, trying to lose their baby weight – and she recites in her head the instructions of her bouncy young instructress, to relax each muscle in turn, to breathe from the diaphragm, not the chest, to empty the mind.

Her mind drifts, and she is at Rosindell again. She is walking through the garden, away from the guests who spill on to the loggia and the terrace. The music, some old song, becomes distant as she follows the path of the stream towards the trees. A hard white moon has turned the grass to iron shreds and the purple candles of the rhododendrons seem luminous. The lights of the house recede, and now, in the disjointed manner of dreams, she is walking beneath the holm oaks, and the wet ferns are brushing against her ankles. There is the sound of the sea, the rich, salty smell of it, and she is standing on the clifftop, and dizzyingly far below her the waves are pounding against the rocks.

She must have slept, because she is woken by the phone ringing. Her heart beating fast – *flabbily*, Esme thinks crossly – she pulls on her dressing gown and hurries downstairs. Zoe nags her to have a second telephone installed in the bedroom, but Esme won't hear of it: the expense, and besides, she is of a generation that regards the telephone with respect and a little dread, to be used sparingly, or in cases of urgency.

She is breathing hard by the time she reaches the foot of the stairs and her right hip hurts. She picks up the receiver and says her name.

'Mum, it's only me, nothing to worry about.' Zoe's voice. 'Happy birthday.'

'Thank you, darling.'

'Sorry to ring so early, but I've a lot to get through today. By the way, Philippe's coming.'

'Philippe?'

'You remember, Coral's father.' The patronising tone of the young prompting the unreliable recollection of the old. 'He telephoned last night, asking if he could come to the party. It's going to be a surprise, so we mustn't tell Melissa or Coral.' Zoe sounds distracted.

Esme imagines her daughter running her eyes over a row of figures as she talks, the telephone receiver jammed between shoulder and chin.

'Of course, darling.' Tired and apprehensive, Esme remembers to say, 'It's good of you to do this, Zoe.'

'It's no trouble. Three o'clock, then, Mum.'

Esme is about to make her farewells when Zoe says suddenly, 'I'm still surprised – surprised you wanted it at *Rosindell*!'

'Are you?' says Esme vaguely. 'Well, no matter. I'd better go and pick out some clothes.'

'Haven't you packed?'

Esme knows that Zoe will have planned her weekend outfits days in advance, will have organised her suitcase after finishing work on Friday, and will have folded her party frock between layers of tissue paper so that it does not crease.

She says soothingly, 'It won't take me a minute. I'll be standing on the doorstep, case in hand, I promise.'

She ends the call. It is a quarter past seven in the morning and the garden is at its most beautiful early in the day, so she puts on a mackintosh over her nightdress and dressing gown, sticks her feet into a pair of wellies, and goes outside.

Sunshine makes diamonds out of the dewdrops on the grass. There is only a small square of grass – she dislikes lawns; all that tedious business of mowing and feeding – but she has naturalised cowslips and fritillaries, and in spring the little green square reminds her of the Devon meadows of her childhood, which sparkled with flowers. Esme's home stands in the centre of a quarter of an acre of garden. The cottage, with its small windows and low ceilings, is inconvenient and old-fashioned, but she bought it for the garden, which is her private paradise. The garden walls her off from the rest of the village. It was Rosindell, of course, that bred in her the habit of solitude.

Narrow gravel paths divide the beds and bees hum around the sedums, which are in flower. She likes September, her birthday month: it still holds the possibility of opulence and yet it lacks the oppressiveness of the dry August heatwave, which always seems unnatural in a cool, rainy country.

Esme's hens, pert and handsome Buff Orpingtons, forage in the undergrowth. A thrush sings, perched on an apple bough. She knows why she dreamed of Camilla, yet the dream has recalled to her something she has not thought about for years: the jealousy that as a child she felt towards her elder sister, in all its destabilising intensity. Extraordinary, she thinks, how the old insecurities remain, even after so long, and with such a forgotten power. The joys and miseries of childhood are so easily dismissed, and yet their consequences have remained with her throughout her life. She knows now that it is too easy, the creation of a favoured child. She has her own guilt. Loss and longing will always paw at her heart. Jealousy and longing, she thinks: these are the emotions that have shaped my life.

She turns back to the house. Upstairs, she takes a simple black frock from her wardrobe, a pair of black low heels and her pearls. She picks up the small sheaf of paperwork – the *evidence*, she calls it to herself – from the top of the chest of drawers and, sitting down on the bed, leafs through it. The *Country Life* photographs, and a much older picture of Rosindell's servants, lined up outside the front door of the house. An illustration stolen from a library book, of a beach party at Cannes. Esme can tell, studying it, that the subjects consider themselves louche, stylish and modern, and yet their old-fashioned swimsuits look ridiculous now and the hairstyles are stiff and unflattering.

Old secrets, long and sour in the plotting. But she feels calmer now. She thinks, today I will know the truth. But when did the truth begin? You have to go far, far back. To the war, the first war, which ran a harrow over her generation, leaving it crushed and bleeding. No one who did not live through it can understand the tidal force of that war, or that it left nothing unchanged. Afterwards, she and her contemporaries carried a darkness in their hearts. Perhaps the darkness eats at her even now. Perhaps it ate away at Camilla, who nursed during the war. And now she wonders whether that was how Camilla was able to do what she did, because she had seen so much of death and betrayal that they no longer seemed important to her.

If you want to discover the truth, she thinks, you have to go back to 1917. To London, and to Devlin Reddaway, on leave from his regiment at the Western Front.

Part One

Inheritance

1917–1932

Chapter One

London, January 1917

A maid showed Devlin Reddaway into the drawing room of the Belgrave Square mansion. Half a dozen people were sitting on the armchairs and sofas. He saw Camilla Langdon immediately. She was wearing a light green dress, white stockings and low-heeled white shoes, and her hair, which was a pale, silvery blond, was pinned up at the back of her head.

She rose, smiling, taking his hand. 'Devlin, how lovely to see you. How are you?'

'I'm very well. And you?'

'Thank you, I'm in perfect health. Lady Clare, Captain Reddaway is a friend from home.'

Lady Clare was seated on the central sofa. Shrewd grey eyes surveyed Devlin and greetings were murmured. She had seen Rosindell a long time ago, Lady Clare mused, when she had been a girl. Hadn't the house once been famous for its summer ball? So sad when the old traditions fell away. Still, one must move with the times.

Camilla introduced Devlin to the woman seated beside Lady Clare, a Mrs Sheridan, round-faced and pretty, her cheeks the smooth pale pink of dog roses. The girl in a blue frock on the sofa beside Camilla was Edna Clare, Lady Clare's daughter. Besides Devlin himself, there were two other army officers present, one with his arm in a sling, the other curly-haired, freckled, very young.

Tea was poured, cake offered. At first Lady Clare directed the conversation, but after a while she left the room and Mrs Sheridan took centre stage. The talk was light, of the cold weather, of the recent Christmas and of a film Mrs Sheridan had seen. Devlin's gaze was drawn constantly to Camilla. It seemed to him that there was a challenge in her eyes, a recklessness in her smile. Her boyish, earthy laugh startled.

Camilla's enquiry to the curly-haired officer resulted in blushes and stammering.

'I'm g-going home tomorrow, Miss Langdon. S-see my parents in S-Suffolk.'

Camilla turned to Devlin. 'Will you go home this leave?'

'I should do. It's been more than a year. If we only have to put up with each other for a couple of days, perhaps my father and I won't fall out.'

Edna Clare spoke. She had a low, attractive voice. 'Family squabbles become unimportant at times like this, don't they?'

Their last quarrel had been of such a bitter nature that Devlin doubted that, but he said, 'Yes, I expect you're right, Miss Clare.'

'Darling Edna, you have a more forgiving nature than I have.' Camilla smiled at her friend. 'To me, a quarrel is a quarrel, and neither time nor war nor anything else will heal it.'

'You don't mean that,' said Edna.

'I do, but let it be. I won't quarrel with you.' She turned to Devlin. 'How is your father?'

Walter Reddaway had been in poor health for some years. 'No worse, as far as I know,' Devlin said. 'And your parents? And Tom? And . . .' There was a sister: he must be tired, Devlin thought as he scoured his memory, because he had forgotten her name and could recall nothing of her but a mass of amber-coloured hair. A tall, thin girl, weighted down by her hair.

'Esme? She's well, I believe. And Tom is stationed at Portsmouth, land-bound, which he hates.' Camilla was frowning at him. 'I wasn't sure you'd come. I'm such a hopeless correspondent. I thought you might be cross with me.'

At five o'clock the party began to break up. As Devlin rose to go, he spoke to Camilla.

'May I see you again?'

'I have an engagement tonight. Tomorrow, if you like.'

'I'm visiting a friend of mine in Derbyshire tomorrow.'

'Will you be back by the evening?'

He expected to be. Camilla turned to Mrs Sheridan. 'Captain Reddaway may join us tomorrow evening, mayn't he, Sally?'

'Yes, that would be delightful.' Mrs Sheridan bestowed on him a smile. 'The more the merrier.'

Devlin Reddaway had arrived in London that morning, having left the front in northern France two days earlier. A slow, stuttering train had drawn him from the battle lines across grey and brown countryside to Le Havre, from where he had sailed overnight to Southampton. A second train had crawled between English fields and woodland. Arriving in London, he had taken the Underground to Victoria, and from there, needing fresh air, he had walked to Marble Arch, where a fellow officer had lent him his flat. The flat was masculine in taste, furnished with leather armchairs and Indian rugs. As he unpacked his kitbag, the four unfamiliar rooms had seemed chilly and unwelcoming. Only the letter that the porter had handed him in the foyer, the letter from Camilla, inviting him to tea in Belgrave Square that afternoon, had lightened his mood.

Camilla Langdon's family lived in Dartmouth, in south Devon. Charles Langdon, Camilla's father, owned a boatyard on the river Dart. Charles's wife, Annette, was fair, fat, pretty and socially ambitious. You took a ferry from Dartmouth across the mouth of the Dart to reach the village of Kingswear. Three miles from Kingswear was Rosindell, Devlin's home, marooned on its blustery headland.

Rosindell's history was written in timber and stone. The first buildings on the site had been a hospice and a chapel, constructed in the fourteenth century. Later, a great hall had been added, along with farm buildings. In Tudor times the house had been further enlarged, but the family had clung to the old religion, had chosen the wrong side during the Civil War, and then the estate had fallen into a long decline. Cattle had lived within the confines of the buildings, and brambles and ivy had woven their long tentacles over the walls. Rosindell had been close to ruin when, in the nineteenth century, George Reddaway had restored the house, doubling it in size. Since then, Reddaways had lived and died and prospered and wasted. Now, Rosindell had fallen into decline once more.

Devlin's father, Walter Reddaway, and Camilla's father, Charles Langdon, held each other in mild contempt. The Langdons had built a large, brash new house in Dartmouth; Rosindell had stood in the same isolated valley, among the same acres of fertile farmland, for centuries. But Devlin had been to the same prep school as Tom, Camilla's brother, and they had liked each other well enough. Tom was lazy and affable, good company when they were younger for a day's boating or bird's-nesting. A secretive and moody adolescent, Devlin had admired Camilla Langdon's looks.

Shortly after the outbreak of war in 1914, he had joined up. He had been sent to France in the summer of 1915, and in September he had been wounded at the battle of Loos. After he had been discharged from hospital, he had gone home to Rosindell. There he had quarrelled with his father and done what he could to shore up the estate. One afternoon in Dartmouth, he had encountered Camilla by the harbour. There had been a sudden rainstorm, the skies had opened, and she had put up her face to the heavens and laughed. In that moment, attraction had become compulsion and admiration had turned to desire. Her blonde prettiness, even the perfection of her features, might have seemed insipid in a different woman, but Camilla's beauty was that of a pale flame, light-reflecting and restless, her small, curving mouth and speedwell-blue eyes informed by rapidly changing emotions: amusement, anger, excitement.

She had turned to leave, the shoulders of her coat darkened by the rain, when he had said, 'Write to me, won't you, Camilla?'

'Yes, I will, if you like,' she had replied. And then she had added, 'But don't be cross with me if I forget.'

In the year that had followed his return to France, four letters from Camilla had reached Devlin at the front. The last had been posted from London. Camilla had written to him that she had left home to work as a nurse in a hospital in Belgrave Square. The hospital was housed in the ballroom of a mansion belonging to the mother of her school friend, Edna Clare. It *has taken me months to persuade my mother to let me go to London. Fortunately, Edna's mother is Lady Clare and Mummy is such a snob.*

After Devlin left Lady Clare's house, the London streets in the blackout seemed gloomy, dim and mysterious. But for the bright, narrow wand of a searchlight, dancing in the charcoal sky, he might have slipped back in time. The pubs had opened and Devlin bought a glass of watery beer, then found a quiet restaurant, where he ordered supper. A gluey drowsiness came over him as he drank his coffee, and so he headed back to the flat.

As soon as he lay down in bed, he drifted instantly into a dream in which he had tumbled from the cliffs at Rosindell to the sea below. He would reach out, grab a rock and try to haul himself out of the water, but the rock was always needle sharp, tearing his hands, or slippery with seaweed and impossible to grip.

* * *

The following morning, the Sheffield train was crowded. Devlin gave his seat up to a woman and child and stood in the corridor, looking out at the wintry fields. Leaning a shoulder against the window pane, he dozed on and off until the train drew into Sheffield station. There, he changed trains, sitting in a carriage that jolted between the majestic, snow-topped hills of the Peak District. He alighted at Hathersage and walked up the steeply sloping road to the Hutchinsons' house. The route was familiar; he had stayed there two or three times when he was a boy, in the school holidays.

He steeled himself before knocking on the door. Mrs Hutchinson opened it. 'Devlin, how good of you to come.' She embraced him. 'My dear boy. We've all been so looking forward to seeing you.'

Devlin hung his greatcoat on the hall stand and put his cap and gloves on a table. 'How is Eddie?'

'He had a bad night, I'm afraid. You mustn't mind if . . .' Her voice fluttered away.

She was a kind, motherly woman, and he had been fond of her as a boy. Edward's father had been a vicar, but was now retired. The Hutchinsons had married late in life and had only the one son.

Mrs Hutchinson patted Devlin's sleeve. 'It's so good to see you. And looking so well. Come and say hello to Edward. He's in the snug, catching the sun.'

Devlin followed Mrs Hutchinson through the house. A large window framed a view of the hills. Edward's wheelchair was beside the window. A tartan blanket was tucked over the stumps of his legs, which had been blown off above the knees.

'Hello, Eddie,' said Devlin.

Edward turned a scarred face towards him. 'You shouldn't have come.'

'Dearest,' said Mrs Hutchinson gently, but Edward looked away to the window.

'I could do with a cup of tea, if you have a moment, Mrs Hutchinson,' said Devlin. 'There wasn't any to be had on the train.'

'Tea,' said Mrs Hutchinson with a breathless gasp. 'Yes, of course. I'm so sorry, you poor boy, you must be parched! And a piece of cake – you'll have some fruit cake, won't you?'

She left the room. Devlin drew up a chair and sat down opposite Edward. Before he could speak, Edward said, 'I meant it, you shouldn't have come. I'm as dull as ditchwater and you'll only have, what? A week's leave?'

'Five days, because of travelling.'

'Then you shouldn't have wasted it on me.'

'I'm not wasting it. I wanted to see how you were.'

'I am as you see.' Edward gave a twisted smile. 'I'm three fifths of a man. I've worked it out. Two legs and half my face gone, so minus one fifth for each leg and the hole in my face makes up for the stumps. Don't say it,' he said roughly, as Devlin began to speak.

'Don't say what?'

'That I'm still the same person underneath or some rot like that. Because I'm not.' He nodded to the hills. 'I'll never walk there again. I'll never be there on my own, looking down the valley from the peaks, seeing the whole world around me. I'd rather be dead. *She* knows I'd rather be dead. That's why she never leaves me alone, that's why she sends my father to the shops instead. Annie, the maid, has gone, you know. Couldn't stand the sight of me. She used to flirt with me, when I was in one piece.'

There was a clinking of cups and plates. Devlin took the tray from Edward's mother and set it down on a table. The pouring of tea and the handing round of cake allowed some light remarks. Edward's cup jittered against his saucer; as his mother mopped up the spills, he glared at her, his expression a mixture of contempt and resentment.

Devlin searched for a topic of conversation, rejecting in rapid succession London, Camilla, the war as hopelessly tactless or unsuitable. Rosindell: but then he had never invited Edward to Rosindell, too embarrassed as a schoolboy to expose his friend to its dereliction or his father's oddities and tempers.

His gaze alighted on a library book on the windowsill. He asked Edward about it and Edward made some grudging reply, then Mrs Hutchinson supplied a few bright comments and Devlin talked about a book he had read, and so the conversation limped on for an hour or so, Eddie taking little part, that expression of viperous outrage often naked in his eye.

Devlin left shortly after lunch, pleading his evening engagement in London, promising to return on his next leave. He took a window seat on the Hathersage train. *I'll never walk there again:* he turned away from the view and concentrated on lighting a cigarette. On the train from Sheffield, he sat in the corner of a carriage, closing his eyes. He didn't sleep, though. He found it almost impossible now to remember the Edward he had once known, with whom he had played at school and walked and climbed in the Peak District. It was as if the man he had seen that day had erased those memories, as if they had never been. It was not only Edward who had been destroyed, but his family also, who had once seemed to him the ideal of the happy family, an exemplar, almost, of what might have been, had his own mother lived. Since her death when Devlin had been five, his father had cut himself off from the world. Visitors had stopped calling at the house, deterred by Walter Reddaway's rudeness and moroseness. His father had neglected Rosindell and now the roof on the oldest part of the building let in water and in winter the cellars were awash.

More passengers piled on at Doncaster and then the train rattled off again. His exchange with Camilla the previous day now seemed one of politeness, holding no promise. An acquaintance from home, adrift in London; what else could she have done but allow him to tag along with her? What did he hope for? He did not want to want Camilla Langdon. In

16

Flanders he had lost the habit of wanting. Out there, you desired the absence of things – cold, rain, fear, mud. And then yesterday, he had glimpsed desire itself, rushing into the void.

The train drew into London at a quarter past seven. He had time to kill before meeting Camilla and her friends, so he ate an indifferent supper in a café and then found a pub. As he walked to Piccadilly, girls with painted faces smiled at him, huddled in their thin coats in doorways. London was clamorous, frenzied and hollow. If you picked at the surface, you would find nothing beneath.

In the nightclub, he ordered another drink. Already he could see how the evening would turn out and already it bored him. He would be an intrusive and unwanted extra to Camilla's circle, tolerated for pity's sake. He would compete with her more favoured friends for time alone with her.

Half an hour passed before they arrived, the bright silks of the women's dresses contrasting with the dull khaki of the men's uniforms. Camilla was wearing a simple white gown, so that she seemed luminously pale, almost ghostlike. Round her shoulders rested a stole of white fur, which gleamed as it caught the light. In his mind's eye, Devlin imagined a creature, an ermine or an arctic hare, running across a snowfield, free, alone, swerving this way and that, leaving a looping trace on a blanched hill.

He was introduced to Mrs Sheridan's husband, a sandy-haired man with a nervous tic that caused his head to jerk sideways every few minutes, and to another couple, the Crowthers, the woman darkly vivid and thick-browed, her husband twice her age. Edna Clare was accompanied by a cousin who was in the Guards.

There was a tall man with a neatly trimmed moustache, who ran bored eyes over Devlin as Camilla introduced them.

'Devlin, let me introduce you to Major de Grey. Victor, this is Captain Reddaway, a friend of mine.'

Seats were found, drinks were ordered. Devlin sat between

17

Captain Sheridan and Mrs Crowther. Mrs Sheridan talked about her nieces, while her husband remained silent, staring at the dance floor. Camilla and de Grey sat opposite Devlin. Camilla was talking to de Grey but her words came to Devlin only patchily, drowned out by Mrs Sheridan's voice and the music of the three-piece band. The major had an aloof look and his occasional smiles were compressed and brief.

Interrupting Mrs Sheridan's monologue, Devlin glanced across the table. 'Have they known each other long?'

'I don't believe so, Captain Reddaway. Major de Grey's sister is married to my cousin. Greenwell, the de Greys' estate, is in Gloucestershire. Do you know it? Reggie and I stayed there one summer before the war. The gardens are famous for their allées of pleached limes.'

Watching de Grey lead Camilla on to the dance floor, Devlin felt the savage bite of jealousy. Was she keen on de Grey? Surely not – the man seemed a cold fish.

A voice hailed him; looking up, Devlin saw an officer he had known at training camp. 'Hello, Bridges,' he said.

'Good to see you, Reddaway. Let's have a drink.'

Camilla's friends showed no inclination to move up and allow Bridges to join them, so he and Devlin sat at another table. Bridges was an unprepossessing man, short, snub-nosed and wet-lipped. Devlin remembered that he had a mild, agreeable nature, unsuited for war. He was someone you would have assumed would have been pointlessly wiped out in an early futile skirmish.

He was teaching at a training camp in Hertfordshire, Bridges told him. 'I'm good at maps,' he said.

'Good for you.'

'Envious of you fellows on the front line, of course.'

'Are you?'

Bridges' head dipped. 'Feel I should say I am. It seems cowardly, to be glad to be stuck at home.'

'Rot. I should make the most of it.'

'That's what Louisa says.'

'Louisa?'

'My wife.' A photograph was unearthed from a wallet and a wedding portrait of a heavy-jawed woman overburdened with white lace offered to Devlin.

'Pretty girl,' said Devlin. 'Congratulations.'

'She's in Lancashire, worse luck, with her mother, because she's going to have a baby, or I'd be with her tonight. Don't awfully care for these places, but I needed a drink.'

The dance came to an end. Devlin saw Camilla and de Grey separate and murmured an excuse to Bridges. The band struck up 'If You Were the Only Girl (In the World)', the syrupy rhythms soaring as Devlin asked Camilla to dance.

'I knew you'd be a good dancer,' she said after they had circled the floor a couple of times. 'I can always tell. Victor hates dancing. He can be such a bore.'

Devlin felt beneath his hand the broad, straight sweep of her back, with its strong musculature. A lock of hair clung to her cheek like a curling golden wave on white sand. His fingers slid on the satin of her dress as they had slipped on the seaweed-covered rock in his dream.

'I thought you seemed close,' he said.

'Did you? I doubt if Victor's close to anyone. There's something distant about him. He doesn't try to please. How was your friend in Derbyshire?'

'Pretty awful, I'm afraid.'

'What happened to him?'

'His legs were blown off on the first day of the Somme.'

He felt her shudder; he said, 'I'm sorry, that was crude of me.'

'You'd think I'd have got used to it, working at the hospital. But you don't, at all. If anything, I hate it more.'

'I felt guilty not staying the night. His mother wanted me to. I don't think they have much company. But I was desperate to get away. I was glad I had the excuse of meeting you this evening.'

19

'Is that what I am, an excuse?' Her teasing smile faded. 'I can hardly bear to look at some of them. We're supposed to be a convalescent hospital, so we used to get only the more presentable ones, but now they seem to send us anyone at all.'

'Will you throw it in?'

'No, certainly not. If I did, I'd have to go home. Devlin, I'm trying to explain to you why I didn't write very often. I was afraid that something might happen to you. Lots of men ask me to write to them, you see.'

He felt resentful of them, these unknown, importunate men. 'And do you?'

'No, I usually put them off. You start to like someone and then something unspeakable happens to them. The other girls write to soldiers and they're always waiting for letters. I'd hate that. I hate waiting for anything.'

'But you wrote to me.'

'There are always exceptions, don't you find?'

'Was I an exception?'

'Yes.' She laughed. 'Do you want me to flatter you, to tell you why?'

'If your reason is flattering, then yes.'

'I don't know that you'll think it is. That last time we met in Dartmouth, I thought you had a wild look. Wild and unpredictable and only pretending to be civilised. The Reddaways have a reputation, you know.'

He pulled her closer. 'I thought you were the most beautiful woman I'd ever seen.' Her head fitted neatly under his chin and he could feel the quick rise and fall of her breath.

The dance came to an end and there was a flutter of applause. As they walked back to the table, she said, 'When are you planning to go to Rosindell?'

'Tomorrow.'

'Don't go.' Again their gazes locked together, and then she returned to her seat next to de Grey.

20

A girl joined the band and began to sing 'Roses of Picardy'. Mrs Sheridan seemed to have talked herself out at last because the silence stretched until Mrs Crowther said quietly, 'Pray God the war will end this year.'

'Surely it must,' said Mrs Sheridan.

'Why?' Her husband's head jerked sideways. 'Why must it?'

'It can't go on for ever.'

Sheridan ran a palm down the crease of his trousers. 'I don't see why not. We've tumbled into a pit and can't find our way out.'

De Grey said, 'This year, next year, there'll be a breakthrough. It's a question of wearing the enemy down.'

'*We're* worn down,' said Sheridan. 'We're worn down almost to nothing.'

'Come, come, you're exaggerating, man. We've held the line for two years. Sooner or later our fortunes will turn.'

'Trench warfare favours the defending army,' said Crowther. 'You can't deny that Sheridan has a point. We charge at them and they repulse us and nothing changes.'

'You're wrong, dear fellow.' Captain Sheridan's palm moved faster and faster, as if he was rubbing something away, and he gave a high-pitched, guttering laugh. '*Something* changes. A few thousand more men put through the mincing machine. It'll go on for ever, I tell you, or at least until there are none of us left.' His voice had risen to a shrill, reedy pitch and people seated at the other tables were staring at him.

'I say, steady on, old chap,' said Crowther.

'Here.' Devlin pushed Sheridan's drink towards him.

'Let's go home, Reggie,' said Mrs Sheridan. Her face had collapsed like a wilted flower.

The Sheridans left the room. A few conversational skirmishes followed their exit, all fading into silence. The soloist's voice had a harsh edge to it and the dance floor had emptied. Devlin felt depressed by Sheridan's outburst, the more so because he agreed with everything he had said.

21

'It's late,' said Camilla. 'Are you coming, Edna?'

Devlin offered to see the two young women home.

'It's on my way, I'll go,' said de Grey.

'No thank you, Victor.' Camilla rearranged her fur stole. 'I'm sure Captain Reddaway is capable of finding a cab.'

The three of them left the nightclub. During the short cab ride, Camilla sat between Devlin and Edna Clare and the two women talked about their work. The muted lights of the street lamps raced past, counting out the moments. In the pit of his stomach Devlin felt a knot of excitement. Now and then Camilla's shoulder brushed against his. Something was going to happen. He knew that he needed only to give events a push.

Outside the house in Belgrave Square, Edna Clare thanked him for escorting her home.

'You go on in, Edna.' Camilla smiled at her friend. 'I'll be there in half a mo.'

As soon as Miss Clare was out of earshot, Devlin said, 'I have to see you again.'

'I thought you were going home to Rosindell.'

'That can wait. On your own, Camilla. Not with the others. Is that possible?'

'Yes,' she murmured.

'Do you know the Long Bar at the Criterion? I'll wait for you there tomorrow evening.'

Her lips, soft and warm and velvety, brushed against his cheek, and then she was gone.

Sitting in the burnished opulence of the Long Bar the following evening, Devlin's gaze darted over an infantry major, blaring about the French railways, and a huddle of fat, grey-haired men in evening dress.

Light multiplied in the metallic sheen on the walls, and he saw her, framed in the doorway. Beneath the white fur stole she was wearing a black dress with lace round the neckline. Two cream-coloured roses were tucked into her waist and a third rose was pinned on to the heap of fair hair on the back of her head.

'You look lovely,' he said.

'I feel quite cheap. Artificial flowers . . .'

'I thought they were real.'

'Did you? How sweet of you. They are silk, I'm afraid. There are no hothouse blooms to be had for love or money.' She ran the back of her fingers over the fur stole. 'We're not supposed to dress extravagantly in wartime, are we? But I couldn't resist wearing my loveliest things.'

'Thank you for coming, Camilla.'

'You shouldn't thank me.' Her expression was a mixture of excitement and mockery. 'I only ever do things that please me. It pleased me to see you, Devlin, that's all.'

'I've booked a table in the restaurant,' Devlin said. 'I wasn't sure how long you would be able to stay.'

'I'll stay as long as I like. Lady Clare watches me like a hawk. I don't think she approves of me. I tried to pass you off as an old family friend, but old family friends aren't often so handsome, I'm afraid. But I'm a hard worker, so she puts up with me. I have to keep on the right side of her or she'll send me home.'

'And you wouldn't want that?'

'Certainly not.'

'Weren't you happy there?'

'Devlin. Were you?'

'Happy enough.'

'You mean when you weren't quarrelling with your father. What did you quarrel about?'

'The house, mostly. My father seems content to let it crumble into the sea.'

'And you don't care to inherit a romantic ruin?'

'Not much, no. How did you escape from Lady Clare?'

Camilla made a swooning expression. 'I have a sick headache and have taken to my bed. Do I look very unwell, darling?'

'You look the picture of health, as you always do. Won't your friend look in on you?'

'Edna? Oh yes, she'll try to make a fuss of me. She can be tiresome like that.'

'It's kind of her to be concerned.'

'Perhaps, but it's a nuisance on occasions like this. Jane Fox will fend her off.'

'Jane Fox?'

'She came with me to the hospital. She helps me with my clothes and hair when she isn't slaving away as a ward maid. She's a sweet girl, very clever with her hands, and she does whatever I ask her to. You know her, don't you?'

'A little.' Jane Fox's elder sister, Sarah, was a maid at Rosindell. Jane had also worked there briefly a few years ago. Devlin recalled a lean-faced girl, as tawny-red as her surname implied.

He said, 'How was your day?'

'Pretty rotten. I overslept, I'm afraid, and the Clare tore me off a strip. She has a way of treating one like a housemaid. I long for the day when I can tell the silly bitch what I think of her.' Camilla gave him a sideways look. 'I shouldn't have said that. What must you think of me?'

'That you're tired and you work too hard.'

'A dozen new patients arrived this morning. It's always such a rush when when there are so many, and some of them were in an awful state.' Her mouth twisted. 'If I get through this, I shall never do anything frightful again, I shall just have fun.'

'Good idea.'

'You don't disapprove?'

'No, not a bit. Dance and carouse as much as you like.'

'I shall. I shall go to parties and I shall buy myself a motor car and drive very fast.'

While she spoke, he admired the curve of her jaw, the long,

slender column of her neck and the fierce glint of humour in her eyes.

She said, 'When the war's over, what will you do, Devlin?'

It was unimaginable, not worth considering, and to do so would be to tempt fate, but he said, surprising himself, 'I shall go home. And I'll never go away again.'

'Is that what you most want? In the whole world?'

'It's one of the things I most want.'

'What else?'

'You. I want you, Camilla.'

'You're very forward, Captain Reddaway.'

'I'm short of time,' he said bluntly. 'You must see that.'

The waiter arrived to tell them that their table was ready. She was ravenous, Camilla told Devlin as they rose and walked to the restaurant, and then she gave her great throaty laugh and heads turned to look at her.

'You must forgive me,' she said. 'I can't go along with that business of pretending to have the appetite of a bird. I expect those women go to the larder at night and stuff themselves silly.'

Dining at the Criterion was like being enclosed in a jewellery box. The gilt, mirrors and mosaics seemed a fitting setting for Camilla, who, like the room, glittered and gleamed. Their food had been served when she leaned across the table, as if about to impart a secret.

'Jane Fox told me she saw a ghost at Rosindell.'

'Jane was little more than a child when she worked for us. A child with a vivid imagination.'

'No headless nuns, then?'

'I'm afraid not.'

'You're disappointing me, Devlin. You'll have to make it up to me, if you've no ghost stories to entertain me with. Or I won't forgive you.'

'Won't you?' He held her gaze.

'I told you, I don't forgive easily.'

25

'Then I'll try harder. Rosindell's an old house. There are always stories about old houses. People from the towns and villages find the place too remote and they let their imaginations run away with them. The timbers creak and groan in the wind and perhaps they mistake the sounds for footsteps. Or maybe a lamp casts a shadow and people think . . . Well, you know the sort of thing they think. All sorts of nonsense.'

'Tell me what it's like. I've sailed once or twice into the bay, but I couldn't see the house.'

'You can't, from the sea. It's hidden in a valley that runs down to the cliff. You might say that architecturally it's rather a hotchpotch, but I think it's quite perfect.' In his mind's eye he saw the house, storm-lashed and solitary, the Reddaways' fiefdom.

'You're making me feel ashamed of myself, persuading you to stay in London instead of going home.'

He took her hand. 'I know what I want, Camilla.'

'I imagine you do. And I expect, most of the time, you get it. You are a man and the world is made by men.' Her tone had become bitter.

'That may be true, but women have their own power.'

'And you're so afraid of it, you bind us about with rules and regulations so we can hardly use it. Shall I tell you when I was happiest? I can remember the exact moment. I was on a friend's yacht and the wind was in the sails and we flew across the sea. It was magnificent and glorious. And yet I had to beg my mother to be allowed to sail. Every time, some dreary old relative or friend of the family must come along too. If no one could be found, there I was, imprisoned at home with my sister.' Devlin was surprised to see a flicker of fear in Camilla's expression. 'Sometimes,' she finished with a short laugh, 'I'm afraid I'll end up all alone in some poky room in Bayswater.'

'I don't think so. Do I have to spell it out to you?'

'I want you to.'

'Camilla, I think – I know – that I've fallen in love with you.'

Her lips parted. She said nothing, but gave a small nod.

At eleven o'clock that evening, he saw her back to Belgrave Square. In the moonlight her skin had the iridescent sheen of pearls and her hair was a web of frosted threads.

Outside the mansion, Camilla gave a thin whistle. In an upstairs window, curtains moved and a pale face appeared, like the moon showing between clouds. Devlin's hands encircled her waist and his lips found hers, and they kissed and kissed. Then a side door opened and Camilla slipped into the house.

He spent the next morning searching for flowers for her. Camilla had been right, there were few to be had, but he scoured London until he came across a girl outside Waterloo station, come up on the train from Hampshire with a basket of snowdrops.

From Waterloo Bridge he watched the ships that crowded the Thames. Half a dozen coal barges, strung together like a necklace, glided beneath the span, and there was the tang of salt and rotting vegetation. He felt a stab of homesickness for a greener, better-loved river, and he seemed to jolt away from the city to Devon and the river Dart, and from there to the isolation of the peninsula on which Rosindell stood. The roar of traffic was replaced by the crashing of waves in the cove and the scream of the wind tearing across cliff and combe. Exhaust fumes gave way to wood smoke, sea salt and roses.

He met Camilla at midday. She pressed her face into the snowdrops, closing her eyes. They had lunch in a café, a brief half-hour together before she had to return to work. Walking away, exhaustion smothered him like a blanket, and the crowds seemed to impede his progress as he made for Marble Arch. In the flat, he lay down on the sofa and, without so much as loosening his bootlaces, fell asleep.

He was part of a long file of men, walking on duckboards through no-man's-land. Snowdrops flowered in the mud, a great field of them. A mist came down, hiding the remainder of his platoon, but when the clouds thinned he found that he was alone and on the road to Rosindell. He walked on, up the narrow, high-hedged lane. The sun gleamed through the shreds of mist and light glinted on the ploughed furrows in the fields. A brightness in the sky showed him where the sea was, over the hill to the south. But when he reached the top of the rise and looked down to the hollow where the house should have been, there was nothing there.

He woke and looked at his wristwatch. He had slept for three hours. His mind drifted back to Rosindell; not the vanished Rosindell of his dream, but the living house, familiar yet mysterious, tucked into its remote corner of Devon. He saw with perfect clarity, almost as if he had come across it in the pages of a book, what he would do to transform it into a fitting home for Camilla.

That evening, as they dined, he told her about his plans. How he would take down the old barns and outbuildings that lay close to the house. How he would build on the land that he had cleared, flying out from the existing structure, a new Rosindell. The rooms would be modern and spacious and their tall windows would face out to the narrow valley in which his mother had planted a garden.

Later, walking back to Belgrave Square, he took her into the shelter of a doorway and kissed her. She seemed to melt into his arms and pushed herself hard against him, and he felt the swell of her breasts and her jutting hip bones. *Touch me*, she murmured, and he ran his hand beneath the soft fur of her cape, his fingertips tracing out the hardness of her collarbones and the hollow of her throat. When he pushed aside lace and pressed against flesh, she flung back her head, her eyes closed and her lips parted. His mouth found the smooth, pale curve of her breast, his palm shaped the round-ness of her hip. He felt her strain against him and heard the rapid rise and fall of her breath. She rose to meet him, passionate and demanding.

A middle-aged couple, complaining of the cost of their hotel, headed down the pavement towards them. Camilla tidied her clothing and they walked on. At the Clares' mansion, the same routine as the night before. The whistle, the face at the window like the moon rising through clouds, and then she slipped inside the house.

On the morning of his last day in London, Devlin called at his bank, then bought essentials at the Army & Navy Stores. In the afternoon he packed his kitbag. Without his belongings, the flat returned to the state in which he had moved into it a week earlier, a resting place for the transient.

The minutes ticked away until he saw her again, but also counted off the moments before they were to part. If being with her left him light-headed and exhilarated, made breathless by her beauty and brilliance, Devlin found himself unable to contemplate the thought of not seeing her for months or even years. He shoved to the back of his mind the possibility that he might never her again.

He shouldered his kitbag and left the flat, handing the keys to the porter. His train was due to leave Victoria at five o'clock. As he walked to Belgrave Square, the trees and lawns of Hyde Park had a vivid familiarity and the mansion houses he passed seemed to have become a part of him. Time fell through his fingers like sand.

She had told him to wait for her on the far side of the square. She was on duty that afternoon but had promised to slip out to say goodbye to him. He took up position near a corner of the railings, from where he could see the front door. It was four o'clock, and as he waited, the first specks of snow began to fall, washed with gold as they danced through the dimmed glow of the street lamps.

He glanced at his watch. It was a quarter past four. The snow was whirling, icing the tops of the railings and the branches of the trees. The door to the Clares' mansion opened and Devlin tensed. But it was not Camilla; the woman who came down the steps was shorter and stouter than she. He felt a heavy disappointment, a premonition of a much deeper grief.

Half past four. He walked quickly to the house and knocked on the door. The maid opened it.

'May I speak to Miss Langdon?'

Waiting in the hallway, Devlin's gaze raked over the oil paintings on the walls and the blots of water his boots made on the black and white tiles.

Footsteps: his heart leaped. But it was Edna Clare, not Camilla.

'Captain Reddaway, I'm so sorry, but Camilla is busy, I'm afraid.'

'Five minutes,' he said. 'I need to say goodbye.'

Miss Clare ran a hand down her apron. For the first time, he noticed the streaks of red on the white cloth. 'You see, another half-dozen patients have just arrived.' Her voice was kind. 'We really are all so busy.'

'Yes, of course,' he said. 'I'm sorry to have troubled you, Miss Clare.'

'I'll tell her you said goodbye. And God bless you and keep you safe, Captain Reddaway.'

He walked away from the house. When he reached the corner of the square, he looked back, but the snow and the darkness had already erased the building. As he made his way through the crowds inside Victoria station, he peered now and then towards the entrance. People poured in and out and he cursed every one of them for not being Camilla.

On the platform, soldiers were saying goodbye to their wives and mothers. One leaned out of a door, smoking; another shouted to his mate to hurry up. Carriage doors slammed shut. Beyond the station, above the rails, snow rushed and danced in a circle of ochre light.

Over the hubbub, he heard a voice calling out his name. Whipping round, he saw Camilla. He forced his way through the crowds towards where her white cap bobbed as she ran.

She threw herself into his arms. 'I'm so sorry – I couldn't get away – Edna told me you'd come to the house!'

'It doesn't matter.' He kissed her, crushing her to him, breathing in her perfume, making himself memorise the softness of her skin and the way she stood straight and strong, like a birch tree. 'Nothing else matters, only that you came.'

'I was afraid you'd already be on the train and I wouldn't be able to find you! I was afraid you wouldn't have waited!' She was laughing and crying at the same time.

'I'd wait for you for ever. Will you wait for me?' He looked down at her tenderly. 'Camilla, I want you to marry me. You will, won't you?'

Her lips parted; she said something, but the shriek of the guard's whistle blotted out her words. Smoke billowed from the funnel of the engine.

He said fiercely, 'Marry me, Camilla. Marry me, and I'll build a new Rosindell for you. I shall bring the house back to life for you.'

'Yes,' she murmured.

As the train began to pull away from the platform, the door to the nearest carriage was flung open and a voice called out, 'Here you are, sir!'

Camilla took a step back and Devlin swung into the carriage. The train gathered speed and he leaned out of the window, a hand raised in farewell, his gaze fixed on her, a blur of blue and white, until she merged into the crowds.

Chapter Two

Autumn 1917

Devlin's battalion was moved into the Ypres Salient in the autumn. Rain fell unceasingly from a bruised sky. Some trenches had been blasted into the mud by the force of the bombardment; others were filled waist-deep with brown water. You lost your bearings out there in the wasteland, and depression clung to you like the mud.

One night in mid December, Devlin was detailed to take a dozen men through the trenches to a different part of the battle-field. Now and then the red sparks of a shell showed against the black sky, illuminating the scars and debris. He led the men along a sunken road, the sergeant major at the rear. The road, little more than a foot wide, was awash with water. Where it crossed a track, the remains of a gun carriage blocked their way and they had to clamber over the bloated, mud-stiffened bodies of the horses. When the shellfire crackled they crouched in the icy water until the bombardment died down. A party of stretcher-bearers appeared and they flattened themselves against the earth wall to allow them to pass. One of the wounded lay on his front, blood flowering over the back of his tunic. Another, a young, fair-haired boy, had a head injury. His hair was red and brown with mud and blood except for a single flaxen curl that hung over his forehead like a stalk of wheat in a ploughed field.

The shellfire died away and they walked on. A full moon, streaked with ragged clouds, showed in the sky. They came to a German trench, where the dead sheltered from the storm. Men lay in the hollow, one with an arm raised to cover his eyes, as if to protect him from the brightness of the flares. Another man had lost his legs; they were a short distance away, giving the body the look of a jointed doll that had been roughly handled. Rats were gnawing at the dismembered limbs. Behind Devlin, the men were gathering watches, tins of chocolate, water flasks and medallions. A loud burst of firing made them stoop again, forcing on them a greater intimacy with the dead. A private muttered a string of curses that had the monotonous rhythm of a prayer.

Silence as the guns died away. Without the gunfire, the battlefield became a void. Earth and sky were inseparable and featureless. They were walking through an absence; this, Devlin thought, was what Hell must be, a terrible nothingness, a dark journey that had no end. He could hear the moans of the wounded and the squelch of his own boots.

They found themselves in the shallow earth declivity of a bomb crater, where duckboards had been slung loosely over the ground. Devlin passed back word for the men to string themselves out. He heard cries from behind him.

'Buchan's gone into the mud, the stupid bugger.'

'Give him your rifle, Richards,' Devlin ordered.

Buchan clung on to the rifle and two men hauled. The ground gave a contemptuous gasp as he was pulled free. He was covered in mud to his chest and was shaking visibly. Mud flailed from his shuddering limbs as he walked, as if he was shedding skin. The quiet from the enemy lines persisted, and Devlin was relieved when they reached the shelter of another trench.

Ten minutes later, the barrage broke the silence, an intolerable crashing and roaring. They took cover, fumbling with gas masks and rifles. The earth juddered; nothing was solid any more. When Devlin looked over the parapet, a wave of grey was pouring towards them. The Lewis guns crackled, picking off the enemy soldiers. After a while, the grey men didn't come any more. More wounded were brought along the line, stretcher after stretcher, some of the men groaning, some cursing, some weeping for their mothers, others silent, their eyes open.

There was a crash and a flash of light. A shell had landed in the trench. When he gathered his platoon together, Devlin discovered that only three men had survived the blast. The stretcher-bearers and the wounded were all dead. The explosion had affected Devlin's hearing. Buchan had been wounded but his yells seemed deadened. Devlin hooked him over his shoulder and they ran for cover.

Half an hour later they reached another battalion's trench. Buchan was patched up and sent off down the line to a dressing station, prattling rather than screaming, knowing that his wound would send him back to England. The barrage died away and the dawn came. Someone found Devlin something to eat. He sat in the dugout, his trembling hands wrapped round an enamel cup in which tea cooled, watching the liquid swirl and slop against the sides.

After that night, he couldn't picture Rosindell any more. He tried, but it wasn't there in his head. The shell blast in the trench seemed to have wiped it away, along with some of the hearing in his right ear. When he closed his eyes, he saw instead the mesh of roads and railway lines that criss-crossed Europe, taking men and weapons to the front, entraining the injured to the hospitals and the dead to the cemeteries. He saw the factories that made the armaments, the fires of their forges and the smoke and steam that gouted from their chimneys. He saw those things as part of a huge machine that ground on, taking men in and spitting them out. They were fuel for the machine, that was all.

I long for the day when we walk through the valley together with only the

34

wind and the sea for company, he wrote to Camilla. *Did I tell you why the house is called Rosindell? It's because of the roses that grow in the valley. In June, their perfume is intoxicating.*

He took out her letters and read them through, but he couldn't see her any more either. When he tried to recall the night he had kissed her in the doorway, the scratch of lace against his fingertips and the soft, erotic brush of fur on the palm of his hand, it seemed as if all that had happened to another man. He had not heard from her for six months; she had not replied to his letters. He wondered why. She was busy, and she had warned him that she wasn't much of a correspondent. He imagined her impatient, restless, scowling at pen and paper, unable to express the vivacity and spontaneity that defined her, crumpling up the paper and throwing it away. She had promised to wait for him and that was all that mattered.

In February, he wrote to Edna Clare. A week later he received a letter from her telling him that Camilla had left the Belgrave Square house. The last time Edna had seen her she had been working for a charity that supplied ambulances to the front. She had not stayed there long, however, and Edna regretted that she and Camilla had since lost touch.

He wrote to Camilla's family in Dartmouth but had no reply. As the days passed, he knew that he was teetering on an edge. One night, boiling up water for tea on the spirit burner, he thought of putting his hand in the flames. He had the idea that it wouldn't hurt. But then Vickers, the second lieutenant, came into the dugout, so he didn't, because he knew it wouldn't look right, him putting his hand in the fire. Vickers, a cocky type, might think he was doing it for a Blighty wound, and in spite of everything he baulked at that.

The letter telling Devlin of his father's death had arrived on 18 March. Jessie Tapp, who had once been his nanny, had written. Walter Reddaway had been unwell for some time but had refused to call the doctor – if Jessie had been living in the house she would have sent for Dr Spry, but she was now lodging in Kingswear. His father had died peacefully in his sleep, Jessie claimed, though Devlin doubted this: his father had done nothing peacefully. Jessie hoped he would be able to come home for the funeral a week hence. He was needed at Rosindell.

Vickers came into the dugout and began to brew tea. Devlin found an errand for him. Why had Jessie been living in Kingswear and not, as before, at Rosindell? What did she mean when she wrote that he was needed at Rosindell? As with Edna Clare's letter, he sensed things not said. The more troubling thought, that his father was dead and that what had been broken between them could now never be repaired, he put to the back of his mind. Regret had become a luxury and death so everyday that it was hard to be troubled much by the loss of a parent who had shown him little affection or concern.

He put in for leave and was granted it. The day before he was due to go, a new German offensive was launched and all leave was cancelled. The mist that passed through the British lines that morning was made of poison gas. Shells screamed and there was the crash of explosions; flashes of light showed through the mist. There was a stream of wounded men, their bodies pierced by fragments of shell and blistered by the gas.

The bombardment lasted for five hours. At dawn, dazed and numbed, they fumbled to load their guns and peer over the parapet. A sea of field grey swept towards them. As the attackers cut the barbed wire, the Allied soldiers opened fire with the Lewis guns. The enemy was beaten back, only to advance again. There were eight onslaughts that day, and on the ninth, a gap opened up in the Allied wire and the enemy troops poured through. After bitter hand-to-hand fighting the order was given for the Allied front-line troops to fall back to the reserve line.

The advance trenches were lost; the retreat had begun. The attack continued, of a pulverising force, and the days became a confusion of marching, deploying, digging in, holding the enemy back for a few days, and then moving south again. They passed civilians fleeing the battlefield, their belongings loaded into prams and wheelbarrows or tied up in a handkerchief and slung over a shoulder. Children cried and old people hobbled, crouched and shivering in the damp, cold dawns. A hen squawked in a cage; a pig had escaped from its owner and ambled through woodland, snuffling at acorns.

April: they came to an orchard trembling with blossom. They dropped their packs and lay on the grass beneath the trees. The guns had died away and they could hear the birds again. Some of the men fell asleep. The grass was an impossibly bright green, the unfolding buds like silk. Devlin felt a homesickness so intense he could have cried aloud. What would happen to Rosindell if he died? He had no brothers, no sisters, no cousins. No wife, no children. What distant, greedy relative would fabricate a claim to the house, knowing nothing of what it had meant to him?

He took out a piece of paper and a pen and wrote a few sentences, leaving Rosindell to Camilla. He had Lieutenant Richards, a schoolmaster in civilian life, witness it. He let the paper dry in the sun before folding it and putting it inside his cigarette case for safe keeping, and then the bombardment started up again and they moved out of the orchard.

During the retreat through France in the spring and summer of 1918, the Allied front line became the main street of a village or a trench dug through a garden. Word came to them that German guns were pounding the outskirts of Paris, as they had during the first months of the war, four years earlier. They had gone round in a circle and had come back to the beginning. They would go round in the same circle over and over again. Attack, retreat, counterattack, stalemate. Devlin remembered the Piccadilly nightclub and Captain Sheridan saying, *It'll go on for ever, or at least until there are none of us left.*

The ragged, exhausted remains of his battalion struggled to hold together. Retreat, deploy, retreat again. March for eighteen hours without break, with little food and scarcely any water to drink, and then dig into some field or village. The soles had come off the men's boots and their feet were blistered and torn, and they had worn the same filthy uniforms for weeks. But it was the lack of sleep that did for them. More than the cold, more even than the thirst, sleeplessness disjointed time, dragging out minutes or compressing hours. The month told Devlin summer was coming, but in his heart winter had never ended.

Once, crossing a field, he heard phrases in German from over a hedge. His men flattened themselves on the grass. There was the drumbeat of boots on a road; overhead, an aeroplane puttered. When the enemy had gone, the British soldiers silently turned back the way they had come.

Now and then they chose a defensible position and made a stand. Sheltering in a farmhouse, they held off an attack for three days. In the cellar were dried sausages, beer and champagne. In quieter moments, they feasted. Then a mortar shell landed in the orchard and they abandoned the farmhouse and retreated again.

By the time the enemy attack petered out in mid July, the Allies had been reinforced by fresh American troops and were pushing the German army back over the ground they had recently gained. Devlin was the only member of his original platoon to have survived the last three months unscathed. Everyone else was dead or wounded or sick with dysentery. He couldn't think why he was all right when he wasn't particularly careful any more. He was tired and sometimes didn't care whether he lived or died. Indeed dying, which he thought of as a long sleep, had a certain attraction. Only the thought that he would never see Camilla or Rosindell again made him hang on to some sense of self-preservation.

Forcing a path north, the army reached Amiens. On the battlefield, bones, tin hats and mangled weaponry were mixed into the earth, like currants in a pudding. You dug your trench and the walls were shored up with other men's bones. The smell of death pervaded the soil.

The Allied offensive took the German lines by surprise. In a break from former tactics, there was no forward bombardment to warn of the attack. Tanks lumbered forward, and after a sharp exchange of fire and a dash over the pocked landscape, Devlin found himself lying on his stomach in a shell hole. He was alone, and for a few moments he watched the planes scribble their warning against the sky and a tank plunge through the earth, leaving tracks like a mollusc's trail.

Mortars threw up their red and white flowers and there was the crash and crump of bombs. Not far away, a man was groaning. Devlin crawled out of the shell hole to the wounded man, then dragged him back into the hollow, where he bandaged the laceration in his thigh. Other casualties were scattered over the battlefield. Crouching, Devlin shepherded them one by one back to the crater. There were five in all, and after he had given them brandy from his hip flask, he led them out of the shell hole in search of a first-aid post. Four of the men were walking wounded; the fifth, a small, wizened fellow, he slung over his shoulder. A white flag with a red cross pointed out to them a canvas tent where a medical officer was stitching and bandaging by the light of an oil lamp. 'Good show,' the MO said as Devlin ushered in his charges.

Devlin left them to it and set off in search of the rest of his battalion. He must have been five hundred yards away when the shell hit the first-aid post. The force of the blast threw him to the ground. Wreckage – fragments of flesh and canvas and khaki cloth – showered through the air. There was a crater where the post had been.

He walked on. He heard a *crack-crack* and felt a searing pain in his leg. Foolishly, he turned, as if to see the sniper who had fired at him. Something struck him on the head, an obliterating force, and he collapsed.

Time passed. He had used his first-aid kit on the wounded men and had nothing with which to bandage the wound in his leg. He watched his blood mingle with the earth. After a while, stretcher-bearers turned up and hauled him away. They took him to another first-aid post, where he was patched up and then sent down the lines.

Later that night he arrived at the casualty clearing station, where surgeons operated, stripped to the waist, by the light of generators. The Stations of the Cross – the phrase came to him from nowhere. The stretchers lay side by side on the ground, close-packed like floor tiles, each one with an unconscious or groaning man. The nurses moved between them, wetting lips, holding a hand. The men's uniforms were torn, muddied and bloodied, their faces pulped and their limbs ragged. Screens hid the operating tables from those who were waiting their turn.

He must have cried out, because a nurse said something to him and gently smoothed back his hair. Devlin closed his eyes and slept.

He lay, hovering between life and death, at a military hospital at Étaples for three weeks before they judged him strong enough to survive the journey to London and a hospital in Wandsworth. There, he endured two operations on his leg. Five weeks later he was moved on once more, to a convalescent hospital in Kent, where he learned to walk again.

He had a scar on his temple from where the sniper's bullet had glanced off his head. He must have a thick skull, the doctor had commented, to have survived the shot with only concussion and a propensity to headaches. But his leg had been a mess of shattered bone and flesh. Again he had been fortunate. It had been touch and go, a nurse told him bluntly when once he expressed impatience at the length of time he must spend in hospital, whether the surgeons would have to amputate. After that, he endured the pain and lack of privacy without complaint.

He was discharged from hospital on 12 November, the day after the signing of the armistice that announced the end of the war. He telegraphed ahead to instruct Josiah to meet the train at Kingswear station. During the last part of his journey, the railway line ran along the steep, sloping bank of the Dart. Flashes of light from the boats on the river showed between the trees, but most of the time there was only the darkness and the drizzle. Passing the bend in the river that sheltered Langdon's boatyard, Devlin craned his head, but could see nothing.

With a screech of brakes, the train pulled into Kingswear. The young curate with whom he had been sharing the compartment since Totnes reached down Devlin's bag and held open the door. Devlin thanked him, then climbed out on to the platform.

An oil lamp lit up a tattered newspaper hoarding headlining the signing of the armistice. Soon, the bustle of people on the platform, meeting passengers off the train, thinned out. Though the pony and trap stood outside the station, there was no sign of Josiah. Devlin left his bag on the trap and returned to the platform.

Inside the refreshment room a fire burned in the grate and a handful of passengers sat at the tables. The girl behind the counter said, 'Mr Reddaway? It is you, isn't it? Don't you remember me, sir?'

She was young and chestnut-haired and had a soft Devon accent. When he did not respond, she said, 'I'm Hannah Brown. My mother used to do the laundry up at Rosindell. Welcome home, sir.'

'Hannah — yes, of course. Have you seen Josiah?'

41

She tilted her head in the direction of the higher part of town. 'No doubt you'll find him in the Ship, sir.'

Devlin leaned on his stick as he headed up the steep incline to the pub. Rain gleamed on the cobbles. The cottages were closed up, the inhabitants indoors on this cold, wet November evening. Just as Hannah had changed, the village too seemed altered. Streets that he had once known so well now felt foreign to him.

The pub was beside the church. Josiah was more familiar with the one building than the other. Light shone through the windows, and through the thick stone walls Devlin heard a howl of voices.

He opened the door and went inside. The low, beamed ceiling of the barroom was browned by tobacco smoke. He made out Josiah, standing in the centre of the room, pouring a pint of ale down his throat, cheered on by a dozen men.

'Josiah,' he snapped, and the room fell silent.

Josiah turned towards him, running the back of his hand over the grey stubble on his chin. He gave a tottering bow and raised his tankard.

'Drinking to your homecoming, Mr Devlin.'

'Out.' Devlin jerked his head towards the door.

Someone sniggered. 'Off you go, Josiah.'

'But sir . . .'

'Now.'

Devlin grabbed the older man and hauled him towards the door. There were jeers and a smattering of applause.

'I was drinking for my health.' Josiah gave a theatrical shudder at the cold air outside and made to sit down on a wall. 'I've been poorly.'

Devlin seized his matted grey curls and thrust his head into a nearby horse trough. There was a howl of protest and a stream of curses as Josiah emerged, spluttering and dripping freezing water.

'That should wake you up. Now get a move on.'

The complaints continued as they drove along the road that led out of town. He'd likely get that Spanish flu that was going round, whined Josiah as he flicked the reins and the horse moved to a trot. The lamps on the trap picked out the tall hedgerows to either side of them. It was raining more steadily now and Devlin put up the collar of his greatcoat. Every lurch and bump of the wheels on the stony, rutted surface jarred his leg.

As they climbed higher, he knew each twist and turn of the road. Over there was Nethway House, and over there the hamlet of Boohay. The hedgerow fell away and they came to an expanse of grassland. The lamplight flickered and he was back in Flanders, surrounded by a sea of mud and bones, crouching at the sound of mortar fire, blinded by streaks of light. In spite of the cold, sweat washed over him and he had to fight the urge to jump from the trap and run for cover.

The vision faded; he took a gulp of air and said to Josiah, 'How are the servants?'

'They've took off.' Josiah made an expression of pious disapproval.

'Took off? Mrs Satterley . . . and Sarah Fox?'

'Yes, sir. Always a grumbler, that Sarah.'

'Why?'

Josiah gave him an innocent look. 'I don't know, sir. Perhaps it was Mr Walter. He was never an easy man.'

'Who's looking after the house now?'

'I found a girl from the village. Molly. She's a good girl.'

The road sloped down towards the valley. The gate was open and they sped through it. Devlin felt the sense of familiarity, of ownership, for which he had thirsted. This was his land, this was where he belonged.

Josiah drew the trap to a halt outside the house. Devlin climbed out. Rosindell stood before him, sensed rather than seen, veiled by the night. The ancient manor house hid among the wild landscape that surrounded it, long and low and black, crouching against the ragged darkness of the sky.

His stick dug into the gravel as he walked to the front door. Inside, the hallway was bitterly cold. He flicked a switch, but the electric lights, fed by a petrol generator, were dead. An oil lamp stood on a side table, its small beam illuminating the black and white tiled floor and the broad carved oak staircase that swept up to the first-floor landing. Shadows pooled there; the clock, high on the wall in its plaster frame, showed Devlin that it was past nine. On a side table stood a beer flagon, and someone had slung a pink jacket and a pink woollen hat, ornamented with artificial cherries, over the newel post.

Inside the great hall the remains of a fire smouldered in the grate and the candles on the mantelpiece had burned down to stubs. The lamplight glided over the massive wooden beams that supported the high arched roof and then swept along the walls. Rainwater issuing through a cracked window pane had left a dark stain, and mould flowered on blown patches of plaster. A wine bottle stood on his mother's grand piano, eating a dark ring into the rosewood; dirty glasses and plates cluttered the hearth and table. A pair of laced boots, thick with mud, lay on their side on the Persian rug.

A hen roosting in an armchair squawked, rising in panic and scattering feathers as Devlin shooed it away with a furious sweep of his hand. As he stood, taking in the devastation of this, Rosindell's most magnificent room, he became aware of the sound of music, a tinny rendition of a Viennese waltz, issuing from the adjacent library.

He flung open the door. Sitting in a leather armchair by the fire was a girl. 'The Blue Danube', scratched out on his father's gramophone, came to an end. His father's dog, an old black and white spaniel, lay on the rug, gnawing a bone. Books, not coals, were burning in the grate, and the astrakhan-collared coat the girl was wearing had once belonged to Walter Reddaway.

He said, 'Molly, I presume.'

She was young, black-haired and bold-eyed; her gaze raked over him. 'What if I am? Who are you?'

'I'm Devlin Reddaway.' He kept his voice civil, for now. 'And I think you should leave.'

She leaned forward in the chair, letting the coat fall open, revealing plump breasts inadequately covered by a dirty white blouse.

'I don't mind staying if you like, lovey.'

'Get out.'

Molly gave a sulky pout and began with deliberate slowness to climb out of the chair. Devlin seized her hand and dragged her out of the room and through the great hall. As he pushed her out of the front door and threw the pink jacket, hat and boots after her, she gave a vicious snarl and said, 'Horrible house anyway. I wouldn't stay if you paid me.'

Devlin slammed the door shut. Pain gripped his head in a vice. The dog ambled up to him, paws tip-tapping on the floor, and he stooped to stroke her.

'Hello, Dido, old girl. Unfaithful to me, were you?'

The spaniel pattered by his side as he surveyed the rest of the house. In the ballroom, a spray of dead leaves made a copper swirl on the floor and the threadbare curtains moved in the wind that whistled through broken window panes. His heart was filled with bitterness as he walked back through the great hall and library towards the oldest part of the house. The medieval dining room, with its vaulted ceiling supported by pillars, was a place of intense cold and shadows. Other medieval rooms were now used as a kitchen and for storage. Here, in what had once been the original house, Rosindell's old bones showed through the overlay of plaster and paint, and there was a sour, damp smell, which reminded Devlin of the charnel-house stench that had clung to the Somme. Men had died here: centuries ago this part of the house had served as a hospice. He found himself wanting to turn back, to leave this for daylight. But the compulsion to reacquaint himself with his home, as well as a grim determination to know the worst, made him press on.

A gust of icy wet air as he opened a final door made him raise the lamp high. Rain was hammering through a hole in the roof; stepping forward, he saw that part of the end wall had collapsed, weakened presumably by the rainwater, leaving the structure open to the elements. A section of roof was unsupported and the floor was awash with water. Outside, the heap of tumbled shale and limestone that had once formed the wall spilled across the grass. As Devlin swung the lamp up, he cried out with rage at the ruin of his home.

Stooping, he picked a stone out of the rubble. He felt the weight of it, its roughness and heft. The last hands that had touched it had belonged to Rosindell's medieval builders; the thought calmed him. The chunk of rubble cradled to his chest, he limped to the far side of the lawn. There, he laid the stone on the wet grass to mark out the line of the foundations for the new house that he would one day build.

The wind howled, changing direction with savage frequency, hurling the rain against him. Returning to the collapsed wall, he picked up another stone, and then, when he had laid that down, another. His progress was slow and his breath was laboured as he fought his way through the storm. Words repeated themselves through his head like an incantation. *For you, Camilla, for you.*

Only when exhaustion threatened to fell him did he give up and straighten, swaying, and return to the kitchen. There he found the end of a loaf and a hunk of cheese. He ate in the library, the only warm room. The fire had almost burned out and there were no coals, so he added *Payne's History of the Reform of the Devon Magistrates' Courts* to the embers.

Sometime in the night, a door slammed, waking him. It was his father, he thought, returning from one of his midnight prowls round the estate. Then he remembered that his father was dead, had been dead eight months, and was taking his rest, or otherwise, in the churchyard at Kingswear. Yet he lay awake, straining to hear the creak of floorboards, half expecting to feel a rush of cold air as the door opened.

It took him a long time to fall back to sleep. He lacked the strength to fight off the despair that lived inside him, deep and dark and persistent. Memories bobbed and broke through the thin skin that in daylight covered over horrors, memories of mutilation, loss and abandonment. He shivered, though he had heaped the bed with blankets. Dawn seeped greyly through the windows when at last he drifted off.

During the next two days Devlin was sick with a fever. He left his bed only to fetch water from the kitchen. Josiah was there; Devlin gave him his marching orders and he left the house, grumbling. The dog lay at the foot of the bed, raising her head now and then to peer at him with a concerned expression.

On the third morning the fever lifted. Devlin rose, bathed and dressed. His hand shook too much to shave. Outside, the rain had stopped and the clouds had cleared away and the first rays of light made the dew on the grass sparkle. In the dawn light, the valley looked washed clean, the house free of whatever had haunted it during his illness. He went to check on the horses and found them cared for, fed and groomed. Josiah had been dismissed many times but he always came back to Rosindell. Though he was slovenly and dishonest, he was good with the horses.

Above the dark line of pines to the south, the sky was luminescent. The path to the cliff was slick with mud and Devlin took it slowly, stopping frequently to rest on his stick. The damp brown fronds of the ferns brushed against his legs and a branch shed its droplets as he reached out a hand for support. He felt weak, emptied out, but his heart rose as he made his way to the sea.

He had come home.

Trees – oaks and birches – cast their shadows. Drops of sunlight came and went on a path that had a copper patina of dead leaves. He tasted the salt tang of the breeze and breathed in the cold resin of the pine trees. From the clifftop he looked down to a bay where the sea ebbed and flowed like a rumpled length of blue-grey satin. The high cliffs surrounding it seemed like outstretched arms, sheltering and secluding. An islet floated on a soft mist, and in the distance the horizon seemed to melt into the sky.

Soon, when he walked down this path through the valley, Camilla would walk beside him. They would take the boat out for the day and, in the evening, moor in Rosindell Bay. He pictured them taking in the sails, stepping out on to the small stone jetty. He saw her turning towards him, the breeze tugging at her bright hair, and that look in her eyes, that mixture of excitement, desire and private merriment. They would bathe in the sea, then build a fire of driftwood and cook the fish they had caught that day and drink from the bottle of wine they had cooled in a rock pool. Afterwards, they would make love on the sand.

I'll make Rosindell glorious again for you, he promised her, there and then. *I'll do it somehow, whatever it takes, even if it destroys me.*

He turned and headed back to the house. Tomorrow he would go to Dartmouth, call on the Langdons and find out where Camilla was living. Today he must see to the house and begin to look into his father's affairs. He doubted whether they would make good reading, but then you needed money to marry.

Chapter Three

November 1918

Esme Langdon's bedroom window looked down to South Town, the road that ran out of Dartmouth towards the castle perched on a rock at the mouth of the estuary. When there was a storm, Esme sometimes walked there to watch the waves pounding the rocks.

From her bedroom window she liked to look out at the people in the street below. Perhaps that girl in a cloak was hurrying to meet her lover; perhaps that overcoated man, with his cold, sardonic face, had kidnapped an heiress and was planning to carry her off to Gretna Green. These imaginings nourished her, compensating for the routines of St Petrox Lodge, the Langdon family home.

She had been sent to her bedroom to tidy her hair. That it so rarely behaved, her mother seemed to regard as a personal affront. Esme twisted and knotted and pinned until her head bristled like a porcupine. The pins would fall out as soon as she went downstairs; they always did. One of Camilla's friends had picked up a hairpin and handed it to her. *I say, is this yours?* Esme had blushed. She found Camilla's friends daunting, their conversation a fast, spiteful chatter about people and places of which she knew nothing.

From the other side of the house you could see the estuary,

with its bobbing flotilla of yachts and sailing ships. The guest bedrooms and Camilla's and her parents' rooms were on that side of the house, while Tom's and Esme's were on the road side. Esme loved the sea, but was not a good sailor. Though she pictured herself boldly reefing sails and steering a path through rocks, she tended to find herself flopped over the handrail, limp and green-faced. *Oh dear, we really should have left you at home, shouldn't we?* Camilla had once said when Esme had been horribly ill sailing on Father's friend's yacht. Esme had hated her then.

She checked her reflection in the glass. She was wearing a white frock, chosen by Mama. It made her look like a stork, she thought, a tall, skinny, beaky stork. She would have preferred to look dramatic in purple, crimson or bronze. Camilla loved to wear white; Esme had seen her looking in the glass, stroking her blond hair into curls so that they tumbled on white silk. The Langdons might be handsome, but they were also vain. The many mirrors at St Petrox Lodge reflected the family's images back at them. Sometimes, when she had a spot, Esme went around squinting, so as not to see herself.

She should go downstairs. But she loathed the thought of it, picturing herself sitting on the sofa next to her mother, back straight, ankles crossed, hands folded. Mummy would nudge her and whisper, too loudly, *Why don't you go and talk to that nice boy?* And the nice boy's eyes would examine her, bored, and then drift back to Camilla.

Five minutes more. No one would notice. Leaning her forehead against a pane of glass, Esme looked out again. The girl in the cloak and the overcoated gentleman had gone. Instead, a blue-uniformed nanny pushed a pram and two boys careened down the hill, their hobnailed boots clattering on the paving stones. Further along the street, closer to the town, a man stepped into the protective shadow of the wall as they hurtled past.

Esme became very still. Was it him? Could it be? Her heart pounded as she stared through the glass. The man was tall, broad-shouldered and dark-haired. He was limping. Esme chewed her lower lip. Months ago, Tom had told her that Devlin Reddaway had been wounded in France. The news had worried her for ages.

He was coming up the hill, towards St Petrox Lodge. As Esme watched him, his features, which had been blurred by distance, coalesced.

It *was* him. Devlin Reddaway had come home.

Now the day was transformed – now the hours to be endured had become moments to be treasured. Three years had passed since she had last seen him. She had mentioned him in all her prayers. *I don't mind if he never speaks to me and I won't mind if he never notices me, so long as you keep him safe* – this had been her bargain with God. Now she murmured thanks for Devlin's return from the war, and when her breath misted the glass she quickly wiped it clear, so as not to lose a single second of him. His stride was laboured, and as a coal dray came along the road he paused as if the climb up the hill had tired him. *Oh poor Devlin*: tears sprang to her eyes.

He was almost level with her window. The dray rattled past and Devlin crossed the road, and Esme realised that he intended to call at the house. She stepped back towards the curtain, afraid that he might see her.

The doorbell rang. Esme opened her bedroom door and heard voices. Then she tiptoed to the landing and peered over the banister.

Devlin asked to speak to Mrs Langdon. The maid told him that she would see whether her mistress was free.

But then, Tom Langdon's voice: 'Who's that, Hetty? Is that you, Reddaway?'

'Tom, I'm sorry to turn up uninvited.'

51

'Oh, puff and piffle.' Tom was in the doorway, blond, jovial, red-cheeked. 'Let him in, Hetty.' He thrust out a hand. 'Good to see you in one piece, old fellow. Heard you'd got yourself bashed about a bit. Are you well now?'

'Perfectly. And you?'

'Oh, top-hole,' said Tom cheerfully. 'Missing the navy. Father's got my nose to the grindstone again. Come and join in the celebrations.'

'Celebrations?'

'Camilla's got herself engaged.'

Camilla's got herself engaged. Bewilderment, then shock, then disbelief tumbled on each other like the collapsing stones of a wall as Devlin followed Tom through the house. Ludicrous to hope that he had misheard. Ludicrous to allow the thought to cross his mind that Camilla had told her parents about their engagement, and that they had welcomed it.

Tom was still talking. 'Her chap's staying with us. He's brought down some of his friends. I never thought she'd do it. Hundreds of the poor saps throw themselves at her feet and she gives them all hell. Are you all right, old man? Am I going too fast for you?'

'Just need to catch my breath.'

Devlin stood in a corridor, fighting to regain control. Tom murmured concern; there was a hum of voices from a room ahead of them. Devlin's reflection stared back at him from a giltwood looking-glass, pale, grim-faced, humiliated.

He said, 'Who is he?'

'Who?'

'Camilla's fiancé.'

'He's called de Grey, Victor de Grey.'

They went into the drawing room. Three pairs of French windows looked out on to a paved terrace high above the Dart, so that the room seemed to teeter vertiginously over the estuary. The walls were papered in pale blue and cream and the furniture was upholstered in the same colours. On the marble mantelpiece were photographs, candlesticks, a gilt clock, vases with sprays of berries. Guests were sitting on the sofas and chairs.

Tom said, 'Mother, look who's here.'

Annette Langdon was sitting on a sofa. Devlin found the presence of mind to wish her good afternoon.

'We weren't expecting you, Mr Reddaway.' Her tone said, *We didn't want you.*

'I apologise if I'm intruding.'

A voice said, 'Devlin', and looking up, he saw, with a mixture of shock, pain and pleasure, Camilla, standing in the open French window.

Her dress was the colour of the winter's sky, a very pale icy blue. A smile fluttered across her face, then died.

The smile re-established itself. 'I'm glad to see you, Devlin. I heard you had been wounded. I hope you've made a full recovery. You must be so pleased to be home.' She looked over her shoulder, calling, 'Victor, you must come in now, we're letting the cold in.'

A man came up the steps to the terrace and into the room. 'Victor,' said Camilla, turning to him, 'Captain Reddaway is here. Devlin, this is my fiancé, Victor de Grey. You remember, don't you; you met in London a few years ago.'

'Last year,' said Devlin. 'Only last year, Camilla.'

'Of course. Last year.' Her flush was almost imperceptible. 'Not so long ago. But you must see these things differently.'

Camilla frowned. De Grey took her arm, drawing her away to a group of people on the other side of the room.

'Do have a sherry, old man.'

Devlin forced his attention back to Tom. 'No thanks.' He watched Camilla out of the corner of his eye as he asked Tom about his work.

'You'd think building boats would be fun,' said Tom self-pityingly. 'But it's the chaps who do the work, while I'm stuck in an office, pushing paper around.'

Charles Langdon had claimed Victor de Grey's attention. Devlin saw his opportunity and made his excuses to Tom.

Camilla gave a strained smile. 'I hope you haven't come here to scold me.'

'I wouldn't presume. But I need to speak to you in private.'

'You're not seriously suggesting I leave my guests?'

'We need to talk.'

'Do we?' Her lids lowered; she murmured, 'I'm not sure that we do, Devlin.'

'Anything up?' De Grey's voice.

'Nothing at all, darling,' said Camilla.

De Grey's glance slid to Devlin. He drawled, 'Perhaps a drink.'

Devlin suppressed his anger. 'I was hoping that Camilla might spare me a few moments of her time.'

'I don't think she wants to, there's a good chap.'

'A few minutes,' said Camilla unexpectedly. 'Excuse me, Victor.'

There was a small room, papered with roses and trellises, at the end of a corridor. After Devlin had closed the door, Camilla said furiously, 'I won't be told what to do. I won't be *spoken for*.'

The room was furnished with small, fussy chairs and a small, fussy writing desk. The flashes of low winter sunlight on the river hurt Devlin's head. Camilla stood in an attitude of impatience, hands folded, brows raised.

Devlin said, 'I went back to France believing us engaged to be married. Now I come home to find you engaged to someone else. What do you expect me to do, Camilla? Offer you my congratulations?'

'It wasn't really an engagement.'

'I asked you to marry me and you said yes. It was an engagement.'

'You were going off to the war. It was perfectly possible that I might never see you again. It was all too much of a rush. I needed more time to think.'

'What are you telling me? That you agreed to marry me out of pity?'

'No, not exactly.' Her mouth pursed. 'I liked you . . . I was fond of you.'

'I loved you, Camilla.' Seizing her hand, he felt the narrowness of bone, the beat of her pulse. 'I still love you.'

'Don't, please.' She snatched it back.

'If, as you say, you were fond of me, then why are you marrying de Grey?'

'I can't explain.'

'Try, Camilla. You owe me that, surely?'

'I owe you nothing! It was rash and overhasty! Can't you see that?'

As if the outburst had tired her, she sat down on one of the little chairs. Devlin, too, sat.

She said, after a silence, 'Does it hurt?'

'My leg? Yes.'

'I'm sorry.'

'The doctors say it will get better.'

'I'm glad of that.'

'Camilla, it may have been rash.' He was calmer now. 'And it was certainly hasty. But that doesn't mean it wasn't heartfelt.'

'Times change, people change. These last years have changed all of us. Are you really the same person I said goodbye to at Victoria station? I find that hard to believe. I don't think I'm the same person at all.' She spoke soberly.

'The past can't be changed. What we had between us can't be changed.'

'There was nothing between us, Devlin!'

'Is that what you honestly believe, or what you feel obliged to say? I remember kissing you after we walked back to Belgrave Square. I remember your perfume. I remember that your hair felt like silk and that the air was frosty and that my lips fitted just so into the hollow of your throat. And I remember the taste of your mouth.'

'You shouldn't.' She turned away, but not before he had seen her flinch. 'Memories . . . what are they? Nothing solid. You can't live on memories.'

'I understand if you felt discouraged – I understand if you lost hope—'

'I warned you!' she cried. 'I told you I hated waiting!'

'You can't marry de Grey. Be sensible, Camilla.'

'Sensible?' She gave a wild laugh. 'You can't possibly think that marrying you would be *sensible*? You are extraordinary, do you know that?'

'In London, you told me that de Grey bored you.'

'I love Victor. Did you hear that? I'll repeat it, just in case. I love him!'

'Do you?'

He seized her hand, pressing it to his mouth. When she did not pull away, he took her in his arms and kissed her. For a moment she seemed to yield, her eyes closing and her lips parting.

She spun aside. 'Devlin, no.'

'Tell me why you are doing this, Camilla. Tell me the truth.'

'The truth?' There were tears in her eyes. 'Then here it is. That time in London, yes, it was wonderful for a while, but as soon as you'd gone, I saw that it was impossible. We're too different – or too similar, I'm never quite sure. We both *want* things, but they don't happen to be the same things. I want the city, I want life, I want fun, I want pleasure. And I don't want to wait any more. So tell me, Devlin, would you give up Rosindell for me?'

The question took him by surprise. Seconds passed during which he could not answer, and then she said bitterly:

'I knew you would not.'

'I didn't say that.'

'You didn't have to. You've made your priorities perfectly clear.'

'Camilla, you're being unreasonable.'

'No, you are unreasonable. You don't love me, Devlin, you love your acres of land and you love that house. Did you seriously think I'd bury myself in the middle of nowhere for you? Good God, Jane Fox told me you used to keep pigs in the drawing room! You can call me cold and practical if you like, but I don't want squalor, I never have.'

He said furiously, 'I hadn't realised you could be so mercenary.'

She gasped. 'How dare you?'

'De Grey came along and you saw a better opportunity. Isn't that about the gist of it?'

'I hate you!'

'You're marrying him for his money, for his position. But then what else would I expect from a Langdon?'

'And what else should I have expected from a Reddaway?' Her eyes flashed. 'Not civility, nor respect. You are arrogant, insulting and boorish. Perhaps you are a drunkard, like your father. Perhaps that's why you're speaking to me like this. Have you been drinking, Devlin? I should have guessed – like father, like son!'

The ice-blue frock, he thought, did not suit her. It took away what little colour she had, so that her skin looked waxen.

He said slowly, cuttingly, 'My father never thought much of the Langdons. Arrivistes with an eye to the main chance, that's what he called you.'

'I think you should leave.' Camilla flung open the door. 'If I felt anything at all for you, then I was a fool. I hope I never see you again.'

* * *

57

The door slammed. Devlin went to stand by the window, breathing hard. A sound: he whipped round, but it was the younger sister, Esme, peering into the room.

'Are you all right?' she said. 'You look awfully pale.'

What had she heard? He said sharply, 'I'm fine,' and saw her take a step back.

What had Camilla called him? Arrogant, insulting and boorish. 'I'm sorry,' he said. 'I've a headache, that's all. Please forgive me.'

'I'll get you a cup of tea. Wait there.'

Esme Langdon vanished. He expected – hoped – that she would not come back, but a few moments later she returned with a cup and saucer in one hand and a sherry glass in the other.

'The others are drinking this. I wasn't sure which you would prefer.'

He took the glass from her. 'You have the tea, Miss Langdon.'

'You can call me Esme if you like. We've known each other for ages, haven't we?'

'I suppose so.' His response was mechanical. The sherry was sweet and sticky, but he drank it, and it steadied him.

Esme Langdon said, 'Is your headache very bad?'

'It's better now,' he lied.

'And your leg?'

Her eyes, blue mixed with grey in equal quantities, were kinder than Camilla's. The concern he saw in them surprised him.

He made an effort. 'It's fine. By which I mean that it's the same as usual.'

'Does it hurt a lot?'

'It stops me doing the things I want to do. I've always to take it into account, to think whether it will last out. I'm sorry, you don't want to hear all this.'

'I don't mind, honestly.'

'When people ask you how you are, they generally want you to tell them that you're very well.'

'Do they?'

'Yes, most of them do.'

He sensed her working up to saying something, but was too strung out to make it easy for her. She was a strange-looking child, her face too long and narrow for beauty, her lightly drawn features swamped by that astonishing heap of hair, trussed up in a style too old for her. Her eyes were framed by brows and lashes of a pale sandy colour that made them almost invisible, giving her face an open, unguarded appearance. He wondered whether the Langdons acquired their handsomeness at a flick of a wand when they turned twenty-one.

She said suddenly, 'You mustn't mind about Camilla. She's always had an awful temper. Tom and I are used to it. I expect it's the wedding, that she's nervous about the wedding. It's all they talk about now.'

He said softly, 'I shouldn't have come here.'

'I'm so glad you did, Devlin.' Blushing deeply, she adopted a polite, formal tone. 'Please accept my condolences for your loss. You must miss your father.'

Did he? More than he had expected to, perhaps. Sometimes Rosindell seemed poised, as if waiting for the return of Walter Reddaway's dominating spirit.

She said, 'What are your plans?'

'Plans?' His loss tore at him. He had no plans now. He had planned to marry Camilla Langdon. He had planned to rebuild Rosindell for her. All that lay in ruins.

But this child was sitting beside him trying to make conversation, which he recognised as generous of her, and so he said, 'My father didn't leave Rosindell in a good situation, I'm afraid. I have to work out what best to do.'

'Rosindell . . .' Esme gave a little sigh. 'I always think it sounds so romantic.'

'I doubt if that's the general opinion.'

'But you love it, don't you?'

'I do, it's true, but then it's a part of me. It's my home. You can't help loving your home, can you?'

'I suppose not,' she said, rather doubtfully.

Her clumsy efforts to be a good hostess amused him, but then he crashed back into the darkness of Camilla's rejection. 'I mustn't take up any more of your time,' he said. 'You'll want to get back to your sister's party.'

'No, not at all.' She looked at him, big-eyed. 'They're all very clever and sophisticated. Very London.'

Devlin stood up. 'I must pay my respects to your mother.'

In the drawing room, Annette Langdon was still seated on the pale blue sofa. Dusk had fallen and they had put on the electric lights. The furniture had been moved against the walls and couples were dancing, Camilla and Victor de Grey among them.

Camilla flung Devlin a furious glance, then turned back to her fiancé. She murmured something; de Grey laughed.

Esme Langdon was still at his shoulder. Devlin said, 'Do you dance, Esme?'

'Not very well, I'm afraid.'

'Then we should suit each other.'

He held out a hand to her and she made a small sound but let him take her in his arms. He held her close, a little closer than was necessary, and smiled down at her. You could hardly call it dancing, he murmured, more stumbling; he hoped she would forgive him. He kept his voice low and tender as he made enquiries about her pastimes, her interests. She liked to sketch, she told him, and to play the piano.

'My mother was a keen pianist,' he said, loudly enough for Camilla to hear. 'You should come to Rosindell and try our piano. It doesn't get played a great deal these days.'

Let Camilla taste how it felt, he thought savagely. Let her see how easily she passed from his mind. Let her see that he had already forgotten her.

Yet he could not help but be aware of her proximity. The scent of her perfume as she passed, the hem of her ice-blue gown brushing against his leg. You could long for and hate someone both at the same time.

The music came to an end. The desire to torment, to hurt, vanished, and he was left exhausted, the ache in his leg worsened by the exercise. He thanked Esme for the dance and took his leave of Charles and Annette Langdon.

Outside, the cold air soothed him as he walked to the quayside where the Kingswear ferry was waiting. Water lapped against the green-fringed stones, and in the centre of the estuary the moon and stars trembled and split and joined themselves together again. There would be a hard frost tonight.

Disembarking at Kingswear, Devlin retrieved the pony and trap from the inn where he had left them earlier that day. Driving out of town, he was bitterly aware of his own folly. That he should have continued, in spite of all the evidence, to hope. The signs should have been so easy to read. Camilla had warned him that she did not like to wait. Now, when he remembered their kiss, it seemed to him hungry, responsive, *practised*.

The trap jolted over the hills. Mentally and physically depleted, he was relieved when the house came into sight. He heard footsteps on the gravel and tossed Josiah the reins.

Indoors, a fire heaped with coals and the spaniel's warm body resting against his. A glass and a bottle of brandy. The company of inky shadows, falling from cupboard and settle, and his own brooding thoughts. The piece of paper on which, in France, he had written his will, leaving Rosindell to Camilla, smouldered to ashes in the fire. Camilla had only pointed out to him a truth. What had he to offer her? A crippled body, a comfortless house and a mountain of debt.

Her voice again. *Tell me, Devlin, would you give up Rosindell for me?* Yes, yes and a thousand times yes, he would have said, had he a second chance.

Chapter Four

December 1918

Esme Langdon had been thirteen years old when she had fallen in love with Devlin Reddaway. People thought that little girls of thirteen weren't capable of falling in love, but what else could you call the way he had keyed himself into her mind, so that a glimpse of him or even the mention of his name gave her a startling delight? She had liked to write his name in her diary, twirling the 'D', precisely dotting the 'i'. She had dreamed of improbable encounters, at a masked ball or on a cliff path.

What had made her pick him out from the other friends that convivial Tom had brought home? His looks, of course, his severely handsome features, his irises of so dark a brown the pupils were absorbed in them. But there was something more: a capacity for stillness and a contained energy, a touch of irony in those fathomless eyes. He was alien, complicated, a different being entirely from the complacent blond Langdons, and she had been drawn to that.

Sixteen-year-old boys did not notice thirteen-year-old girls. When, occasionally, he had spoken to her, she had been mute, as empty of thought and word as a baby, even a simple hello beyond her. Any small attention from him she had treasured like a pearl, rolling it gleaming in her palm, searching for meaning. Had he meant to convey liking? Did he think her pretty? Or had his smile been one of mere politeness? What?

Nineteen years old now, and if she was still, on occasion, wretchedly shy, at last she had acquired a measure of certainty. She watched Camilla and her admirers, how they courted her sister, showing their interest in her, murmuring to her, their voices low and soft, the more sleekly confident holding her gaze as they smiled their slow, amused smiles.

That evening Devlin Reddaway had danced with her. He had talked to her, had smiled at her. This was undeniable. More than that, miracle of miracles, he had invited her to Rosindell. Esme imagined calling at Devlin Reddaway's house. Something would grow of it. The sadness she saw in him would lift as she played the piano in his elegant drawing room. She recalled the weight of his hand on her waist, her bliss as he guided her round the room.

Victor de Grey and his friends went back to London. Days passed. Every ring of the doorbell gave her hope; every time the caller was only a Langdon relative or an employee with a message for her father, her happiness and optimism were punctured. After a couple of days she began to wonder whether she had imagined it, his particular attention to her. After a week she wondered whether she would ever see him again. Perhaps he was unwell, perhaps he was unhappy or lonely. Perhaps, after Mummy had been so unwelcoming and Camilla so horrible, he would never visit the Langdons again.

Her Langdon and Salter aunts and cousins visited one afternoon for cake and the divulging of news. The terrible boredom of family life, the conversations that seemed merely repetitions of what had been said countless times before, oppressed Esme. The air seemed stale, as if every breath of it had been drawn in and exhaled already. She yearned for adventure, and for true feeling: to live.

Her mother was complaining about the sandwiches, that

they were ham when she had particularly asked for tongue. Her aunts were talking of the price of satin. Esme carried a cousin's teething baby round the house, trying to distract her with a looking-glass, a rattle.

From the dining room, Camilla's amused drawl, talking to a friend.

'Mummy's planning a lunch. So tedious, all these things to be endured when one is engaged.'

Esme went into the room. 'Here?'

'Naturally, where else?' Camilla eyed the baby without enthusiasm. 'That infant's making a frightful noise.'

'Who's coming?'

'Everyone. The Arnolds, the Pearses, the Donaldsons . . .'

'Devlin?'

'Devlin?' said Camilla. 'No, certainly not.' She gave Esme an up-and-down look, then laughed loudly. 'I've heard that Devlin Reddaway spends most of his time in the inn at Lethwiston. You should give that child to its nanny.'

Esme sat on the stairs, patting and soothing until the baby's eyes began to close. Did Devlin miss her? Did he think of her, wait for her? Was that why he sought solace in drinking?

You should come to Rosindell and try our piano. Her mother, who disapproved of the Reddaways, would never take her. Tom would agree to but would not get round to it. Pointless to ask Camilla, who never put herself out to oblige anyone, and who was perpetually bad-tempered since Mr de Grey had gone home.

And she couldn't possibly go alone, could she?

At the beginning of December, Camilla and her parents left Dartmouth to stay with the de Greys in Gloucestershire. The Dartmouth house seemed to quiver with relief as the front door closed behind them. Aunt Julie, brought in to look after Tom and Esme, sat on the drawing room sofa, eating chocolates and leafing through a novel.

'We're going out!' Esme called, grabbing her mackintosh and hat from a peg. There was a bleat from Aunt Julie; they escaped.

The rain had cleared, but the roads and buildings were sheened with water, dripping with it, as if the town had hauled itself out of the river.

'Are you going to the boatyard?' Esme asked Tom.

'Later. Ned and I are taking the launch upriver for a while. What about you?'

'I told Aunt Julia that Caroline had invited me to lunch.' Caroline Blake was Esme's best friend. They walked on, brother and sister, understanding each other.

They passed the slipway. The ferry was pulling out into the centre of the river and a queue for the next crossing had begun to form. A woman carried a hen in a wicker basket; workmen in navy overalls leaned against the wall, smoking. Across the water at Kingswear, the tall oblong of the Royal Dart Hotel shimmered greyly in the wet air.

'That's where Devlin Reddaway lives, isn't it?' Esme said, pointing.

'Not Kingswear. A few miles to the east.'

'Have you been to Rosindell, Tom?'

'To the bay, never the house.' They had reached the quay. 'Ned!' Tom called out. 'Hey there, Ned!' He turned to Esme. 'Sure you won't come?'

'No thanks.'

'What will you do?'

'Go for a walk, I expect.'

She headed quickly away from Tom, afraid that he might read her intention in her eyes. Waves cracked against the harbour walls and the fishing boats jostled, creaking as they bobbed up and down on the tide. Esme walked back towards Bayard's Cove. She stood alone on the wet cobbles, looking across the estuary. The ferry, which was now in the slipway at Kingswear, was small against the black bulk of the town. Not far beyond Kingswear was Rosindell, and Devlin.

The ferry started off on its way back to Dartmouth. It was mid morning. Five minutes to cross the Dart to Kingswear, and half an hour, Esme estimated, to walk to Rosindell. A short visit and then she would return to Kingswear. Devlin might offer to drive her. Concern in his eyes: *Did you come all this way by yourself?* She would be home by mid afternoon. No one need ever know.

She took her place in the queue behind a man with a leather portfolio tucked under his arm. Ahead of her, the hen squawked and the ferry circled, nudging the flat stubby platform on to the slipway. A cyclist wheeled off first, the foot passengers following him. Esme felt in her coat pocket for her purse, took out a sixpence and handed it to the ferryman as she boarded the boat.

A cold wind struck her face. The ferry pulled away from the shore and she felt a moment's panic as Dartmouth grew smaller. Resolutely changing the direction of her gaze, she focused on the far side of the river.

It took her a surprisingly long time to find her way out of Kingswear. The steeply sloping road threaded round church and cottage, doubling back on itself before pressing on once more. A light rain sheened the cobbles. Esme passed cramped courtyards where women took in washing, looking up at the sky for rain, and a narrow cul-de-sac where a maid of all work mopped the slabs and a butcher's boy perched on a low wall, smoking a cigarette.

At last the road spat her out high above the town. The woodland fell sharply away, down to a valley. Ferns grew from the high rocky bank to one side of her; a last red campion was still in flower. She walked with a sense of elation because she was putting an end to the waiting, the wondering, and in a short time she would see him again. The countryside was grey-brown and tremulous and the ploughed earth glistened. Raindrops shivered on the bare blackthorn hedges.

This was an empty land, devoid of cottages and farmsteads, and when the hedgerows fell away Esme saw the pastures to either side of her, their sage-green slopes dotted with sheep. Somewhere, she supposed, over the hills, was the sea. The racing clouds had sped up since she had first noticed them in Dartmouth, as if in competition with each other, and here on the higher ground the wind had found its voice and howled and moaned as it flattened the grasses and wrinkled the water in the ditches.

She had enquired at a shop in Kingswear for directions to Rosindell. *Stay on the road, lovey, and don't turn off till after Pepper Lane, or you'll end up in the middle of nowhere and a long road back to town.* The middle of nowhere was a good name for this place, in Esme's opinion. Nowhere, nothing: it might have been a different country to the friendly bustle of Dartmouth. The only living creatures she passed were a trio of ragged black crows perched on the roof of a derelict barn, and a flock of sheep, huddling together for warmth beside a trough.

As she walked, she rehearsed their conversation. Her enquiries after his health, his delight that she had taken up his suggestion to come to Rosindell. He might offer to show her round the house: what a glorious view, she imagined herself saying, such a splendid room.

Entering a stand of trees, she saw that a road branched off to the left. Had she passed Pepper Lane? She thought she remembered seeing a track by the ruined barn. And had the grocer instructed her to turn right or left? Poised beneath dripping branches, she was almost sure it had been left.

Puddles had formed in the ruts in the mud. Where her path dipped down, coffee-coloured water had gathered in the hollow, spreading the width of the road, and she had to climb on to the verge, clutching clumps of rusty ferns as her gumboots slithered. A short distance ahead of her she made out the outlines of buildings, shimmering in the drizzle, as if they too were made of water: a barn, a shippon, and a run of cottages slumping wetly, not far from a crossroads. Rain rang into a tin bath in a garden; a billy goat, tethered by a rope to a post, chewed at a soggy cardboard packet. The door to one of the cottages lay open and a small child, bundled up in dirty rags, squatted on the doorstep.

Esme peered down the three branches of the crossroads. Rosindell must be an imposing house – might it be hidden by those distant trees? Yet she could not see the sea, which she had thought must be close to hand.

She went back to the cottage. She smiled at the infant, tapped on the door and called out a good morning. There was the muggy smell of laundry; the small, gloomy interior was festooned with drying clothes.

An old man came to the door. He was wearing patched trousers and a threadbare jacket open over his bare, grizzled chest. Esme asked for directions to Rosindell. The man put a hand to his ear and Esme repeated her question in a louder voice.

A stout woman in a blue dress appeared out of the gloom. 'He can't hear you, my lover. Deaf as a post.'

There was a roll of knitted blanket at the woman's breast; Esme realised there was a baby inside it. 'Please, I wondered whether you could direct me to Rosindell.'

'Rosindell? Get back inside, Dad, and sit 'ee down, you're not decent.' The woman gave the old man a shove, hauled the infant on the doorstep on to her hip, then pointed back down the muddy track along which Esme had just walked.

Esme plodded off, skirting the puddle once more and heading back through the trees. She was tired, cold and wet and rather hungry. She saw how easy it would be to lose her way, and it frightened her. She walked up a slope to where a few stunted trees crouched and flinched from the wind. The earth track was slick with mud and the wind whipped the rain into silvery sheets; a crackle of lightning made a luminous white vein on the livid skin of the sky.

The path wound down through a hamlet. Ahead of her she saw trees and a gate; above the trees were the peaks of a slate roof. For the first time, doubt washed over her. Devlin might have gone away. He might have forgotten her, he might not want her there. He might be entertaining: she imagined a party, the women with short skirts and long ropes of pearls like Camilla's London friends, the men casting an eye over her as she entered the room in her soaked mackintosh.

Rosindell came to her out of the rain, against a backcloth of storm clouds. Dark trees grew to one side of the house and to the other lay a ragged, wintry garden, nebulous in the gloom. The roof of the house was a jagged series of gables, and the pale stone of the frontage was incised by black oblongs of windows. Esme would have liked to have seen lights in the windows. She would have liked the door to have opened and a voice to have called out to her. But she understood nevertheless in that first sight why Devlin loved it so, because the house seemed to have risen out of the wild countryside that surrounded it, formed of earth and stone and tree and sea, never an interloper, rooted in history and landscape and family in a way that made her own home seem temporary and without solidity.

She rang the bell-push, then waited, not wishing to seem importunate, counting to fifty before ringing again. Might the bell not be working? Rain lashed the courtyard. Clinging to the shelter provided by the house, Esme walked round to the back. The far end of the building appeared to be in ruins. Heaps of rubble lay on the grass and roof beams were exposed like black ribs. What had Devlin said to her? *My father didn't leave Rosindell in a good situation.* She had thought: a coat of paint, some gambling debts.

She returned to the courtyard. Where were the servants? Had everyone gone away? It appalled her to think that she might have to turn round and endure that dreadful walk back to Kingswear without respite. With a rising sense of desperation, she rang the bell-push half a dozen times.

Then she tried the handle and the door swung open.

Beyond was a tiled hallway with doors leading off it. Inside the hallway there was a shallow marble-topped table, a knobbly wooden bench and a coat stand. A staircase with barley-sugar banisters swept up to a landing.

Esme stepped inside, dripping rainwater on the tiles. 'Hello?' she called. 'Is anyone there?'

No answer. On the wall beside the landing a clock was set among plaster swags of fruit, flowers and cherubs. The Roman numerals told her that it was past two o'clock.

Which meant that it was two and a half hours since she had left Dartmouth. Even if she visited for only half an hour, scarcely long enough to dry out, she would not reach home until late afternoon. She would not reach home before darkness fell.

It seemed even colder inside the house than out. 'Hello?' she called again. 'Is anyone at home?'

Her voice sounded small and lost. She thought she saw a movement in the shadows on the landing and there was a rush of icy air. She tensed – but no one came.

An army greatcoat was hanging on the stand beside the front door. When she ran a hand over a sleeve, she found that it was damp. This was the first wet day in a dry week. Not so long ago, then – only this morning, perhaps – Devlin Reddaway had marched into the house and flung his wet coat on the stand.

Cautiously, Esme opened one of the doors that led off from the hall. A long, high-ceilinged room, dotted with large, unwieldy pieces of furniture, lay before her. Embers in a grate inside a massive stone fireplace gave off warmth. Standing in front of the fire, Esme warmed her hands. She saw that curious marks were carved into the mantel, a series of incised inter-locking circles.

The room itself was noticeably dusty and untidy. Muddy footprints surrounded the grate, cigarette stubs overflowed from an ashtray, and a cup, flecked with tea leaves, stood on the table. Esme cradled the cup in her palms, searching for the imprint of his lips. A knitted jersey was rolled up on one end of the sofa, as if he had lain there, using it as a pillow. She ran the back of her hand over the khaki wool. Then she pressed her face into it, closing her eyes, breathing in its scent.

She added a few coals to the fire, then peeled off her wet mackintosh and draped it over the back of a chair. She knew that in doing these things she was invading Devlin's privacy, and that felt both dangerous and delightful. Rain hurled itself against the windows and the house whispered and creaked. When she lay down on the sofa, drowsy from the exertion of the walk, her head cushioned on the khaki jersey, she looked up and saw that from the ends of the roof beams, impish wooden faces were staring down at her, their features distorted, pop-eyed, open-mouthed, grinning.

That morning, Devlin had called on one of his tenant farmers and offered him the farmhouse and land for purchase. On his way back, he stopped at the inn at Lethwiston, a low, rowdy establish-ment, sufficiently remote to be able to ignore, by and large, the licensing restrictions imposed during the war. Sensing the coming gale that morning, he had walked rather than take the horse out in the bad weather, and now his leg hurt.

He drank alone at first, but then the Adams brothers, thieves and liars the three of them, came into the pub and they played cards. He was sober enough − just − to leave while he was in profit. While he had been inside the pub, the storm had rolled in from the sea. Wild and angry, it seemed to echo his mood, reducing sky and field to an ominous, ash-coloured uniformity.

Walking back to the house, he had to lean heavily on his stick. Sometimes the mud was reluctant to give it back to him and threatened to topple him to the ground. His vulnerability, coupled with the fact that he had that morning sold off a part of his birthright, intensified his resentment.

Inside the house, he pulled off his oilskin and threw it on the settle. Then he limped into the great hall, where he unstoppered a decanter of whisky.

A sound made him turn round. He saw that on the sofa, someone was raising herself into a sitting position. *Camilla* – his heart skipped a beat.

Then he recognised Esme Langdon from the hanks of honey-coloured hair that tumbled round her face.

'What the hell are you doing here?' he said.

'I'm so sorry . . . I must have fallen asleep.' She was scooping back hair as she scrambled to her feet.

'I asked you what you are doing here.'

'I thought I'd pay you a visit.' Her voice was an alarmed bleat. 'No one was in. I let myself into the house. I know it was impolite of me, but it was so wet, you see. I hope you don't mind.'

Devlin poured Scotch into a glass. 'I do, actually. Where's your mother?'

'In Gloucestershire.'

'Gloucestershire?'

'Mummy and Father and Camilla are visiting the de Greys.'

He took a mouthful of whisky while he considered this. 'Are you telling me that you came here by yourself?'

'Yes.'

'How?'

'I walked.'

'Why?'

She swallowed. 'I wanted to make sure you were all right.'

'Did Camilla put you up to this?'

'Of course not!'

He crossed the room to her. 'Perhaps it was amusing to you both.'

'No!'

'I don't believe you. I think the two of you thought you'd see just how great a fool I was.'

He was standing close to her. There wasn't much of Camilla in her – a spark of blue in the eyes, a way of holding her head – but it was enough to make him hate her.

'So shall we find out?' he said softly. 'Is this what you came here for?'

Pulling her to him, he kissed her. Her lips were soft and warm and her hair was scented by the rain and fresh air. She gave a muffled squawk and stiffened, trying to raise her arms.

He felt her tug away from him, her route impeded by the sofa, and he released her.

'*Please!*' She looked frightened and close to tears. 'Please don't! Camilla doesn't know I'm here. It was my idea, no one else's!'

Her clothes were wet, backing up her story that she had walked from Kingswear. But why? He said roughly, 'Tell me why you *really* came.'

'Because you asked me!'

'Me?' He stared at her. 'Nonsense!'

'You did! That evening you danced with me! Don't you remember? You said that I should come here. You asked me to come and play your mother's piano!'

He shook his head. 'I was being polite.'

'Polite?'

'It's the sort of thing one says. You can't have thought I meant you to turn up on my doorstep.'

'But yes, I did.' She looked distraught.

'On your own . . .'

'No one would have taken me.'

'No, I shouldn't have thought they would.'

She dipped her head. 'You talked to me,' she murmured. 'You listened to me. Didn't you mean it at all?'

Good God, he thought wearily, the girl is in love with me. He threw out his hands. 'I was making conversation, that's all.'

'You seemed so unhappy!'

'And you thought you'd save me?'

Her silence told him that his guess was correct. What a mess, he thought, what a complete bloody mess. And what complications her foolishness would cause. He felt a certain guilt for his own role, guilt that tried his patience more.

'If you knew that your mother would refuse to bring you here,' he said, 'then you must also know that our families are barely on civil terms.'

'That's just Mummy. She takes against people.'

'But it isn't only your mother, is it? I'm sure you also know that Camilla and I quarrelled. How much did you hear?'

'Nothing!' She gave him a horrified stare. 'I wouldn't . . . I didn't . . . I put my fingers in my ears, honestly, Devlin!' She moved towards the door. 'I'd better go.'

'You can't.'

'What do you mean?'

'I mean that you'll have to stay here overnight.'

'No.' A high squeak. 'You won't make me!'

'I won't make you stay, you ridiculous girl. But this storm will.'

'I can't possibly stay here overnight!'

'You should have thought of that before you came here. If it was remotely feasible, I'd bundle you off to Dartmouth in two ticks. But I won't take the horse out in this weather. Besides, I'm too tired.'

She glared at his empty glass. 'Drunk,' she said tartly.

'Yes, that too. Drunk. But even if I were as sober as a judge, I wouldn't risk the horse.'

'I'm not asking you to! I'll walk!' And she dashed out of the room.

By the time he caught up with her, hobbling on a leg that by now ached unendurably, she had opened the front door. Outside, the wind howled, blowing rain and dead leaves on to the flagstones in the hall. Dusk had fallen and it was impossible to see to the far side of the courtyard.

'Oh!' She stared out at the darkness.

He hauled her back indoors, slamming the door shut. 'You wouldn't last half an hour in that. You may as well make the best of it. I'll take you back to Dartmouth in the morning.'

'But what will Mummy say?' She put a hand to her mouth, looking wretched. 'And *Father*?'

Devlin was all too aware of the consequences that must follow Esme Langdon staying the night under his roof. Any explanation of his would be disbelieved by the Langdons. Every assumption on their part would be coloured by outrage.

'I can't think they'll be best pleased,' he said curtly. 'You're a damnable nuisance and that's the truth of it.'

He limped back into the great hall and poured himself another drink. He heard a sound: looking back, he saw that she had sat down, and had covered her face with her hands and was weeping.

With a sigh, he sat opposite her. 'Esme, crying won't solve anything.'

Such a platitude: you cried for sorrow, not resolution. She gave no indication that she had heard him. She cried like a child, unrestrainedly, tears pouring down her face, gulping for breath, no letting up, only tears and despair. He felt a flicker of self-loathing. It was hardly her fault that she was Camilla's sister.

'I'm sorry if I was rather brusque,' he said, but she went on crying. Her loud sobs disturbed him; he remembered Jessie Tapp once telling him of a child who had cried herself into a fit.

He moved to the sofa beside her. 'Esme, please,' he said, and put a tentative hand on her shoulder, and she flung herself on him, still weeping, pressing her face against his shirt. He stroked her hair and tried to think of soothing things to say. His shirt was wet with her tears. She was only a girl, he thought, and who was he to condemn her for falling in love with the wrong person?

'Look, I'll think of something,' he said. 'I'll make it all right with your parents, I promise.'

She tilted up her head, her eyes swimming, and he found himself wanting to kiss her again. He moved away from her, as if she was dangerous. What was wrong with him? She was right, he had drunk too much. He felt a pressing need to return the situation to something more normal, if that were possible.

He said, 'Have you eaten?'

She wiped her hand across her face and scooped back her hair again. 'I'm not hungry.'

'You need to eat.'

'Please don't leave me alone.'

'I'm only going to the kitchen.' He caught sight of her expression. 'Is it the storm? Are you afraid of the storm? There's no need to be, Rosindell has survived far worse than this.' Suppressing another sigh, he added, 'Come with me, if you wish. But you'll need this, the rooms are cold.'

He passed her a blanket from the back of a chair and she wrapped it round her shoulders. In the kitchen, which was warmed by the iron stove, he took out a loaf of bread, a chunk of cheese and the remains of a ham and egg pie. He offered her tea or milk and she chose milk. Then he put everything, along with cutlery and plates, on a tray and carried it back to the great hall. It was unsettling to have her padding behind him through the house, a pink-eyed, snuffling shadow. He had become used to his solitude.

At first they ate in silence. The wind rattled the window panes and made the flames in the grate leap and spark. They would lose more roof slates tonight, Devlin thought grimly. He doubted whether what was left of the chapel roof would survive the gale. He must check the horses and the poultry before he went to bed.

Esme said, 'Where are your servants?'

'My servants?' Devlin cut the cheese. 'You mean Josiah.'

'Is he your valet?'

'Hardly. Josiah takes care of the horses. And this and that, repairs and suchlike. He is probably at the inn in Lethwiston. Drunk, no doubt, as well.'

She looked down, chewing her lip, fiddling with her hair. He had noticed that these were the things she did when she was embarrassed.

'But your cook?' she said. 'And your housemaids?'

'Mrs Satterley, my cook, and Sarah, my housemaid, moved out of Rosindell several months ago, after Josiah installed his mistress here. I daresay I'll get round to begging them to return by and by. Mrs Satterley is a Methodist, you understand, and disapproves of immorality, and Sarah is a Fox, and thus permanently at war with the Adamses. Molly, Josiah's mistress, is an Adams.'

'How complicated.'

'I suppose it might seem so. I sometimes think life is really quite simple, a straightforward battling against the elements, as well as other people's greed and stupidity.'

'You sound angry.'

'Do I?'

'I expect it's because of the war,' she said kindly. 'I'm sure that now you are home you'll soon feel better.'

He was about to say something sarcastic, but stopped himself, suddenly sharply aware of her innocence. Instead, he said, 'Josiah may make his way home during the night, or he may fall down senseless in a ditch, I don't know. But I doubt if his presence would make our situation any more respectable.'

Adding quickly, afraid that she might howl again, 'I meant it when I said that I would speak to your father. Don't worry.'

'Aren't you awfully lonely here, Devlin?'

Good God, she felt sorry for him too. Was he such a pitiful figure? 'I have Dido for company,' he said. 'Dido is my spaniel. She must be with Josiah; she's not a faithful creature. Besides, I'm used to solitude, it doesn't trouble me. At least no one's shooting at me here. And you? Why aren't you with your family in Gloucestershire?'

'Oh no.' She smiled. 'They wouldn't have wanted me. Camilla thinks I'm a nuisance. She always has.' More hair-fiddling. 'Everyone likes Camilla best because she's pretty, not ordinary like me.'

Esme was sitting in a corner of the sofa, her feet tucked beneath her. Her hair had dried into curls, bright and opulent against her white blouse. The thought occurred to Devlin that she did not look like a Langdon. She looked wild, reckless and unpredictable. Pretty – no, not exactly. But not forgettable, either. And certainly not ordinary.

The bedroom to which Devlin escorted her that night was large and oak-panelled and shockingly cold. Don't go, Esme longed to say to him, as he wished her good night and walked away down the corridor. Don't leave me here alone. But that would have been even more improper than all the other improper things she had done that day.

Fear filled in the space left by his absence. Fear of what must be happening at home: Aunt Julie would have sent to Caroline's house to see why she had not yet come back. Then Tom would have been questioned. Esme had told Tom that she was going for a walk. Were men at this moment scouring the cliffs round Dartmouth, shouting her name?

Fear of her parents. She couldn't think of a good way of explaining to them why she had gone to Rosindell. *He asked me to come and play his piano:* it would sound like an assignation. As for, *I thought I'd be home by mid afternoon and no one would know,* this would hardly help.

And then there was the room. She wasn't at all afraid of the storm, as Devlin had assumed, but she was so afraid of the bedroom she could hardly bear to look closely at it. The kerosene lamp that Devlin had put on a small table beside the bed, with many admonitions about being careful, as if she were a child, threw menacing shadows. A large wardrobe became an ominous portal, concealing who knows what, and the candelabra cast black, spidery fingers on the walls. The wind that rattled the window frames made the fingers move. The door latch jiggled, making scratchy little sounds, as if someone was trying to get in.

The walls were covered in a pink moiré fabric. Lighter squares showed where pictures had once hung and there was water damage beneath the windows. The bed was a four-poster, curtained with dusty pink brocade. Esme stood in the shelter of one of the curtains while she took off her outer garments. As if something might be watching her. The doorknob was still jiggling, the window still rattling. She knew that the sounds were caused by the storm, but still.

She clambered up on to the high, domed, slithery mattress. There, she was in bed now and all she had to do was fall asleep. Her mind jangled, overfilled by the events of the day: the walk across the headland in the storm; the dark, empty house; Devlin's arrival. Wriggling her feet down into the icy sheets would have to be done cautiously. Although Devlin had instructed her to extinguish the lamp before she went to sleep, leaving her a candle and matches if she needed a light during the night, she could not bear to do it yet.

There was a pretty little dressing table opposite the bed, of dark wood with blond inlays. The oval cheval looking-glass on top of the dressing table was framed with the same light-coloured material as the inlays. Esme wished that the mirror did not face the bed. Her eyes were drawn towards it. If she closed them, it troubled her, the thought that the reflection of the room must still be there, unwitnessed in the glass. If she were to put out the light, there would be no reflection, only darkness, and that thought troubled her more.

Think of something else. Think of what had happened in that strange room with the impish figures on the roof beams. Devlin had kissed her. It had been alarming, not at all romantic or lovely, as she had imagined a first kiss would be, but vengeful and contemptuous. And yet his embrace, when she had cried, had been warm and delightful. She had wanted him to hold her like that for ever. She had wanted him to kiss her again.

Her gaze went back to the mirror and it crossed her mind that something existed within the reflection, just out of sight. Once the idea came into her head it was impossible to get rid of. Her eyes kept sliding back to the mirror, checking. Perhaps if she forced herself to look at it properly and saw that it was just an ordinary looking-glass, like those at home, she would be able to put off the light and go to sleep.

The glass oval was sliced in two: one half light, containing the lamp and her own reflection; and the other half, which mirrored the unilluminated part of the room, dark. It was the dark side of the glass that frightened her. She saw nothing odd when she looked straight at it, but when she turned away, she seemed to glimpse out of the corner of her eye a flicker, as if someone had dipped a hand into the still water of a pond. Silly of her; how could anything be there? Mirrors reflected only what they saw: the sway of a curtain within a draught, the drift of shadows within shadows.

She sat up suddenly, her breath drawn in a silent scream of open-mouthed gasps, her eyes, wide and unblinking, fixed on the mirror. At first she was frozen by terror, and then she grabbed the lamp and thrust it towards the dark side of the room.

Nothing. There was nothing there. A chest of drawers, a clothes stand, a row of books, a painting. The light shivered. Inside the mirror, there was now only the outline of the bed, the white of the pillows, the pale oval of her own face.

Sliding off the bed, she swung the mirror round, so that the wooden backing faced into the room. She threw her blouse over it for good measure. Then she jumped back into bed, extinguished the lamp and pulled the eiderdown over her head. The sound of her breathing filled the void.

When Devlin woke, the storm had blown itself out, leaving in its wake an unclouded sky that shimmered as if it had not quite dried out.

He shaved and dressed. The door to Esme Langdon's room was ajar; he knocked, and when there was no reply, opened it. The room was empty. Standing at the window, he looked out. Josiah was scratching at the gravel with a rake, gathering fallen twigs and branches, and Esme was emerging from the woodland between the garden and the cliff. He watched her as she continued along the path, towards the house, and then he went downstairs.

As he opened the front door, voices came to him from across the courtyard. Esme was remarking on the beauty of the day.

'Some might think so,' Josiah responded gloomily. 'The cellar's awash and the old chapel roof's fallen through.'

'Oh dear, how awful.'

'No doubt he'll expect me to risk life and limb putting the slates back. But then Rosindell was always an unlucky house.'

'Miss Langdon!' Devlin hailed Esme as he crossed the gravel. 'I was beginning to think you might have set off on another of your solo expeditions.'

She looked abashed. 'I didn't want to disturb you. I walked down the path to the sea. It's so beautiful there.'

'Isn't it? It's my morning stroll. Did you sleep well?'

'Yes thank you.'

'We should leave as soon as possible. How long will it take you to be ready?'

'No time at all.'

Ten minutes later, the pony and trap was driving through Rosindell's gates. As they passed the hamlet of Lethwiston and headed up the hill, Devlin spoke.

'It would be better if you told your family that you went out for a walk and became lost, and ended up at Rosindell by chance.'

'Yes.'

'You only intended to walk for half a mile. The storm set in, you mistook your way.'

'Yes,' she murmured. 'If you think so.'

The trap rattled on. Esme tucked the travelling rug over her and began to eat the apple Devlin had given her for her breakfast. Sunlight glittered on the water in the ruts and the headland had made itself calm and pretty, as if in penance for the excesses of the previous night.

Chapter Five

December 1918

Devlin hunted out Rosindell's former servants. Jessie Tapp, who had been his nanny, was living in a terraced house in Kingswear. She received him in a small parlour. A meagre fire burned in the grate and a collection of framed photographs, mostly of children, stood on the mantelpiece.

Jessie was wearing a tweed skirt and a hand-knitted jersey and cardigan. Her brown hair was coiled in earphones, her unvarying style. 'You're looking thin,' was her opening remark.

'I've had to fend for myself. But Mrs Satterley has agreed to come back to Rosindell. Sarah Fox, too.'

'Why haven't you come to see me before?'

'I wasn't sure what you would say to me.'

'You knew what I would say to you and you chose not to hear it.' Jessie poured out tea. 'I expect you've come here to ask me to return to Rosindell, but I have a position here, in Kingswear. They're a pleasant family, two children under five and a baby. I don't live in. I chose not to, I wanted a place of my own.'

'Jessie, please, we need you.'

'You know why I left. Your father was bedridden, his last few months. Josiah took advantage of that.'

'I've sent Molly Adams away. It won't happen again.'

Jessie handed him a cup and saucer and the sugar bowl. 'I stayed on at Rosindell after you had grown up out of loyalty to the family, and to honour your mother's memory. I turned a blind eye to certain goings-on when your father was alive, but I won't do that any more. I won't watch you destroy yourself, as he did.'

'I have no intention of destroying myself.'

'Is it true that you go to the inn at Lethwiston?'

'I have the occasional drink there, yes.' Containing his irritation, Devlin added, 'I'll stop.'

'And is it true that there was a woman at the house?'

'A woman?' he repeated, shocked.

'A young woman from Dartmouth.'

He said angrily, 'I assume that the gossip concerns Miss Langdon.'

'I never listen to gossip, Mr Devlin.'

'I'm sorry. Forgive me. Esme's just a girl. There was nothing wrong in it.'

Jessie said nothing. Devlin reflected on his last few phrases and said, 'I hadn't realised it would be all over the county.'

'Hadn't you? A girl like that, did you really think such a thing would pass without remark?'

A fortnight ago, he had escorted Esme Langdon back to her home in Dartmouth, where he had spoken to her aunt, a flustered, tearful creature, who had imagined the worst and who had fallen on Esme, weeping. He had then returned to Rosindell and had not thought of her since.

Jessie spoke again. 'I don't like to think of you alone in that big house.'

'I won't be alone. You'll be there.'

'You should marry.'

'I daresay I will, sometime.'

'Soon.' Jessie stirred her tea. 'There will always be talk otherwise. You must find a good girl, a strong girl who'll give you a family. That's what Rosindell needs. It's too quiet there, and the mind plays tricks. That house needs half a dozen children running round the rooms.' She put her hand on his sleeve. 'You're a solitary soul, like your father, but it isn't good for you. You're living too much alone.'

Devlin said goodbye to Jessie a quarter of an hour later. Before he left Kingswear, he walked along the road that ran parallel to the river. The walk was easier than it would have been a month earlier, when he had first come home. He limped less and he no longer needed the stick. Eventually he was able to look down on to the river, and Langdon's boatyard. A boat lay on the slipway and there was the tapping of hammers, the whine of a saw. Signs of industry, and yet Devlin noticed workmen lounging against a wall, smoking, and empty berths beside the pier. He wondered whether Charles Langdon had left Tom in charge during his absence.

The sun was setting and the sky and river were washed with apricot and lilac. He was glad of the ride home, of the concentration required to swing into the saddle and head out of Kingswear, even of the ache in his leg, which provided a distraction from his uneasy thoughts. It had not occurred to him that Esme Langdon's visit would have become public knowledge. But then he had not cared to find out. It was easy, of course, to work out the source of the gossip. He would have liked to kick Josiah out of Rosindell, using a well-aimed boot on his scrawny rear, but if he were to do that, who would look after the horses?

Any rumours would die down, he told himself; rumours always did as soon as the next scandal came along. And even if they did not, what could he do? It was not his responsibility. He had not asked the wretched girl to come to Rosindell. He had not invited her to ruin her reputation.

But he had. *You should come to Rosindell and try our piano.* A careless, throwaway remark, but she had thought him sincere. Naive of her, no doubt — but then how old was she? Eighteen or nineteen, little more than a child, a child who must have led a sheltered life, moving from nursery to school to drawing room with no exposure to the world. Esme was not like Camilla; he knew in his heart that she was not. Her spirit was quieter, gentler, kinder. Camilla challenged, Esme trusted. Camilla would have known his conversation to be no more than flirtatious flummery. She would have played the game. Esme could not.

He had used her. He had used her to taunt Camilla, to pay her back for her rejection of him, and he disliked himself for that. He had not paused to consider that his words might have unintended consequences. He had thought only of his own need to wound Camilla as she had wounded him.

Neither was it true that, as he had told Jessie Tapp, nothing wrong had happened at Rosindell. He had kissed Esme. He had kissed her to punish her for coming to Rosindell, and in spite of the fact that he was in love with her sister. When, later, she had thrown herself into his arms, weeping, he had wanted to kiss her again. Was it true that he lived too much alone? Was he so desperate for company that he had seized on any human contact, regardless of the harm it might do?

A lamp burned in the window of the pub at Lethwiston, but he passed by without stopping. Dusk was creeping along ditch and gully. At Rosindell, there was no sign of Josiah, so Devlin stabled the horse before going indoors. Lamps were lit in the hallway and letters had been stacked neatly on the table. In the great hall, logs burned in the grate and someone had swept the hearth and plumped up the cushions.

He heard voices and, following their source, went into the library. Sarah Fox, a pleasant-faced girl of twenty, was polishing the brass candlesticks.

'Who was that?' he asked.

'My sister, Jane,' said Sarah. 'She was just leaving. She can find her way in the dark, our Jane. You don't mind, do you, sir?'

'No, not at all.'

He had last glimpsed Jane Fox almost two years ago, at the window of the mansion in Belgrave Square. The frosty night, the brush of Camilla's lips against his cheek – he had to turn away from Sarah to hide the spasm of pain that he knew must have crossed his face.

'The Langdons have returned to Dartmouth, then?'

'Yes, sir, they came home this morning. Miss Langdon is going to London next week to order her trousseau. Our Jane's going with her. Are you feeling well, sir?'

'A little tired, that's all.'

'I'll bring you something to eat. I can make a Welsh rarebit, if that would do.'

'Thank you, you're very kind, Sarah.'

He sat down by the fire in the great hall. Sarah brought him supper and he opened a bottle of wine and lit a cigarette. So the Langdons had come back to Dartmouth. Esme's aunt would have to tell her brother-in-law of Esme's disappearance, and then Charles must equally surely speak to Esme. Charles was no fool, and Esme, Devlin suspected, no liar. Charles Langdon would come home to find that his unmarried daughter had slept the night in Devlin Reddaway's house.

The flames in the fire caught a piece of green ash. Red sparks spat and smouldered on the stone flags. Esme had come to Rosindell out of love for him. However little he wanted her love, and however much he loathed being an object of pity, he could not condemn her for that. She was a quiet, sweet girl, likely to be overlooked in a household that contained handsome, charming Tom and beautiful, brilliant Camilla. Annette Langdon was shallow and ambitious and Charles was a businessman through and through. Both saw the value of possessions, both liked to put on a show. Esme lacked glitter and her value would now be diminished. Her reputation might never recover. She might, in the drawing rooms of Dartmouth, always be the girl who had stayed the night at Rosindell. Charles might send her away or marry her off to the first dullard who would have her. Devlin found that he disliked that thought.

As for him, he knew that Jessie had been right, and that rumours would always fly around Rosindell, because they always had. His father had sought solace for his loneliness over the years. There were people who would not visit the Reddaways' house, Annette Langdon among them. His father, who had loathed callers, had not given a damn, but did he feel the same? Again, Jessie Tapp had been right: he knew that he found it too easy to slip into misanthropy and isolation. The past haunted him, the war haunted him. Did he intend to live alone here, with his ghosts, repeating the patterns his father had set?

In spite of all he had endured, something inside him still cried out for life. The life that he had thought he would have with Camilla – marriage and their children – had slipped from his grasp. Would he mourn that loss for the rest of his days?

He would not love again. Of this he was certain. What else had Jessie said? *You must find a good girl, a strong girl who'll give you a family.* Into his mind came an image of Esme Langdon, walking out of the pines that fringed the cliffs, her long strides taking with ease the steep path back to the house, her complexion rosy in the cold, and her glorious hair, which was her claim to beauty, tumbling over her shoulders.

At midnight, he went upstairs. Sarah had lit a fire in the bedroom and Devlin sat in the armchair beside it, though he did not turn the pages of the book open on his knee.

Yet he must have dozed, because he dreamed. He was at Rosindell, but it was a different Rosindell. French doors led out on to a wide veranda, and through the glass roof he could see the stars. He was dancing with Esme Langdon, moving with such speed and grace it was almost as if he was flying. Music played, faster and faster, and from the bay he heard the crash of waves. As he circled, his feet hardly touching the ground, he looked down and saw that he was no longer dancing with Esme. Instead he held Camilla in his arms, and her smile was one of triumph.

Devlin woke. Sweat beaded his forehead; he felt hot and feverish. Knowing that he would not sleep again, he went downstairs to the parlour. The papers spread out on the table, papers compiled during the weeks since he had returned home, all told the same story: that without money he would lose Rosindell. Not immediately, maybe not for years, but some day. And if he lost Rosindell, he would have lost everything – the woman he loved, his home, his future.

There was a solution. If it discomfited him that through taking action he would, like Camilla, be muddying the boundaries between love and money, then he was too weary, too burned out to feel shame. Besides, though his mind twisted and turned for the remainder of the night, he could see no better answer.

Esme opened a drawer and began to pair stockings. On the other side of the house, Camilla was also packing. Camilla was to go to London, to order her trousseau from a Bond Street fashion house, while she, Esme, was to be packaged off, like a parcel of second-hand goods no one wanted any more, to a cousin in Leeds who kept budgerigars. Thelma liked to open the cage and let them fly round the room. Esme was always afraid that a bird would fly into her hair. Thinking of that made her sit down on the bed, stockings knotted in her hands, and start to cry again.

'Oh for heaven's sake, turn the taps off,' Camilla had said to her at breakfast that morning. Camilla had been sharp-tongued ever since she had come home from Gloucestershire, ever since Aunt Julie had told Father what had happened.

The doorbell rang. Esme heard from below a murmur of voices. She opened the door an inch.

Her father was saying, 'I should have you horsewhipped.'

'How is Esme?'

Devlin Reddaway's voice. Esme pressed her fingertips against her mouth.

'She has been, not surprisingly, distraught. Why have you come here? To beg my forgiveness for seducing my daughter?'

'No, I should imagine you would think that beyond forgiveness. Not that I did seduce her, as I'm sure Esme herself must have made clear.'

'What you did or did not do makes little difference. Esme stayed the night under your roof.'

During this exchange, Esme tiptoed along the corridor to the top of the stairs. Below, her mother had emerged from the morning room, a Christmas glass bauble in her hand, and the maid who had opened the door to Devlin lurked in a doorway, listening. The Langdons did not often conduct their quarrels so publicly.

Esme called down, 'Are you well, Devlin?'

'Yes thank you. And you?'

Her father, red-faced, looked up. 'Go back to your room.'

'What I have to say concerns Esme,' said Devlin. 'I've come here to try to put things right.'

'Too late for that!' Purple, now.

'What's all the noise about?'

A cool, dry voice from the other side of the landing. Camilla was standing there, head cocked to one side, eyebrows raised. Stagey, thought Esme critically. Contrived.

Charles Langdon snarled at his audience of women, 'Get along with you all! Have you nothing else to do but listen in corners? Hetty!' he bawled at the maid. 'Fetch me coffee. I must have coffee.' Then he stamped down the corridor to his study, Devlin following behind him.

Esme went back to her room. Camilla came after her. 'What's he doing here?'

'I don't know.'

Camilla pursed her mouth. 'He hasn't come to see *you*, if that's what you're thinking.'

'Why do you care, Camilla?' Esme scrutinised her sister. 'You're marrying Mr de Grey.'

'Thank God for that. I wouldn't stay here a day longer if you paid me.' The door slammed.

Looking in the mirror, Esme seemed to watch herself grow up. She wouldn't cry any more for him, because Camilla had been wrong: Devlin had come here for her, instinctively she knew this. The waiting, the tedium was almost over, and her life could begin at last. And if whatever was to happen next was not on the terms she would have chosen, then she would learn to live with that.

In Charles Langdon's study there was a globe, tide tables and papers piled on the desk. And the ashy reek of bridges burning. Devlin felt an ache of regret as well as a grain of pleasure in witnessing the rapid procession of emotions – shock, outrage, cunning – that crossed the older man's face.

Outrage won for now. 'Marriage,' Charles repeated after Devlin stated his business. 'You have the nerve to come here to ask me if you may marry my daughter?'

'Please,' said Devlin tiredly. 'Let's try to avoid melodrama. I haven't come here empty-handed. I have a name and a home to offer Esme.'

'A tarnished name and a house that is, from what I hear, falling round your ears. I detest your kind,' went on Charles bluntly. 'I detest the pampered landed gentry who think it beneath them to do an honest day's work.'

Quietly Devlin pointed out that he had spent the last four years fighting for his country. Charles's discomfiture was relieved by the maid arriving with the coffee tray.

Devlin's leg hurt and he shifted his weight. Charles seemed to notice, because he said abruptly, 'Sit down. I must have

coffee. That girl's howls kept me awake half the night.'
He poured out two cups of coffee.

Devlin spoke again. 'You're right, my kind won't survive
without changing. Land values have collapsed and our income
along with them. But I won't give up Rosindell and thus I
have to find a way of raising money elsewhere. So there's a
condition to the marriage.'

'A condition?' Charles glowered at him. 'Do you think you're
in any position to demand *conditions*?'

'I want to work for you at the boatyard.'

'At Langdon's? You?'

'Yes, why not?'

'Because you know nothing about boatbuilding. What can
you do?'

'Anything.'

'Anything except behave like a gentleman, it seems.'

The coffee was strong and jolted the nerves. 'I can learn,'
said Devlin. 'I can start at the bottom. Running a business can't
be all that different from running an estate like Rosindell. My
father was ill during his latter years, while I was in France,
and neglected the place, so I need to earn money. The house
is, as you pointed out, in disrepair.'

'Ruin, I've heard.'

'I'm going to rebuild it.' The remark took even him by
surprise: he had thought that ambition abandoned, gone with
Camilla. 'I'll make it into a fit home for Esme, I promise you,
a place she'll be proud of.'

'Why should I believe your promises?' muttered Charles.

Devlin sensed a weakening in him, the beginning of an
awareness of a bargain to be struck. 'Give me six months' trial
at Langdon's, and if at the end of it you think me of no use,
then I'll go without a fuss.'

'I have Tom. Why should I want two of you under my feet?'

'Tom detests the job, you must know that.'

Charles glared at him. Then he sighed. 'He's an idle devil and that's the truth of it. I look for him in the office only to find he's gone fishing. Why do children not come out as you want them to? One daughter a flirt – not that it seems to have done her any harm – the other a fool, and a son with his head in the clouds.'

'And I would want shares in the company.'

'Is that all?' Charles's anger flared. 'Are you sure there's nothing else? My wife, perhaps, or the rug under my feet?'

'Twenty-five per cent after a year, say, if I meet your expectations.'

'I no longer have expectations,' said Charles with acid self-pity. 'Only disappointment and regret.' A flicker of another emotion: self-interest, perhaps. 'Marriage . . .' he murmured. 'She wouldn't be doing as well as her sister, but then she hasn't Camilla's looks.'

Devlin felt pity for Esme along with dislike for Charles.

'I suppose you have debts,' said Charles. 'Your sort always does.'

Reluctantly he admitted, 'Yes.'

'Old money, no money, that's what I always say. If you were to marry my daughter, I would pay them off. I won't have a child of mine start married life indebted. Is that why you're here, Reddaway?' Charles's eyes, the same grey-blue as Esme's but completely lacking in their kindness, studied him.

'I believe that Esme is fond of me,' Devlin said. 'I believe that she would make me a good wife. I need to marry. Rosindell's been too long without a mistress. I would do my best to make her happy.'

'Aye, you had better,' growled Charles, 'because if you don't, never doubt that I'll do my best to make your life hell. But a little of my money wouldn't go amiss, you'll admit?'

'Money never does.' He did not turn aside from Charles's knowing gaze.

Charles refilled their coffee cups. Devlin detected in the action a trade carried out.

'I prefer a modern house myself,' Charles said, as he sat back in his seat, cup in hand. 'A place that's comfortable and easy to look after. You'll draw up a list of your debts and let me see it by Monday. If there's to be a marriage between you and Esme then it had better be as soon as it takes to call the banns, though some, no doubt, will infer the worst from that. You can start at Langdon's after Christmas, if you've the stomach for it. We'll see how long you last.'

'So I have your permission to speak to Esme?'

Charles's head inclined. 'It would seem so.'

The maid tapped on the door and told her that she was needed downstairs. In the drawing room, Devlin Reddaway was standing by the fireplace. He looked tired and ill; Esme suspected that she, who had cried for a day and a night, looked worse. For a moment neither of them spoke, and it crossed her mind that they were disappointed in each other.

Then he said, 'I seem to have made difficulties for you.'

'No, I made them for myself.'

'I should have called before, to see how you were.'

'You were under no obligation.'

'Still, I had a responsibility.'

'No.' She poked out her chin. 'I am not your responsibility. I'm to be sent away, to stay with my cousin in Leeds; did my father tell you?'

'Do you want to go?'

'Not at all.'

'Because I wondered whether you would consider marrying me instead.'

His words seemed to strike the walls and windows like bright particles of light. How easy and how miraculous it would be to say yes. But she had learned a little these past weeks, and intuition and a sense of self-preservation made her say:

'Why are you asking me?'

'Because I need a wife. I need a wife for Rosindell. And you appear to need a husband.'

'Do you like me at all, Devlin?'

'I admire your fortitude, your perseverance.'

Such old-fashioned qualities, and she detected a certain irony in his words, as though he felt these characteristics to be double-edged. 'Because,' she said, 'I love you.'

In spite of everything, a small part of her dared to hope that he might say, *And I love you too.* But he was silent, and that small part died, having taken only a breath or two of life.

'I've always loved you,' she said. 'Since I was thirteen.'

'Good God, I can't think why. I was a sulky, obnoxious youth.'

'A good day was a day when I saw you. A wonderful day was a day you spoke to me. Do you think that some day you might love me too?'

In the silence, she heard a ship's whistle on the river and the distant high-pitched grate of her mother scolding the maid.

'I'm not sure I'm capable of falling in love with anyone any more,' Devlin said. 'I've seen too much; I've seen terrible things, things I shall never tell you about. I sometimes feel that my heart has dried to the size of a nut.' He curled up his hand, as if holding something inside it. 'I can give you a home and a position and I can give you independence from your family. Esme, I realise that what I'm offering you is of limited value, and if this is not enough for you then I'll go away and not trouble you again.'

No, she thought, what he was offering her was of inestimable value. He was offering her hope. But she could not speak, and instead took his folded hand in hers. Teasing open his fingers, inclining her head in assent, she pressed them against her face.

Shortly afterwards, Devlin left the Langdons' house. He had almost reached the old castle steps when he heard a voice from behind him call out his name.

Though it was a cold December day, Camilla had left the house without coat or hat. He waited for her to catch up with him.

She cried out, 'You can't marry her!'

'Why not?'

'Because you love *me!*'

The wind whipped red into her cheeks and pulled at her pale hair. She was out of breath from her run, and trembling, but whether from cold or fury Devlin could not tell.

'No,' he said. 'Not any more.'

'I don't believe you!'

'I wanted you for a while, that's all.'

'Why are you doing this?' Her voice shook with emotion. 'Is it to hurt me?'

He turned away from her and began to walk towards the town. Her words followed him, carried by the wind along with the cries of the gulls.

'You don't love her! You'll never love her! You know that – never!'

The rain spat as he headed past Bayard's Cove. Across the river, the ferry was leaving Kingswear. Devlin fumbled in his pocket for his cigarette case and, sheltering by the sea wall, struck a match as he took his place in the queue.

Esme and Devlin were married in St Saviour's church in Dartmouth at the end of February. Esme's wedding dress had been made by her mother's dressmaker. 'I think, Lily,' her mother said, fingering samples of satin and lace, 'a nice cream fabric.' A small Langdon cousin held her bouquet of early spring flowers while she and Devlin exchanged their vows.

After the service there was a reception at St Petrox Lodge for family and friends. Devlin had no family and invited only his solicitor from Totnes, Mr Hendricks, and his wife, and a Major Morris, under whom he had served in France, to act as his best man. They made up the shortfall of guests with Langdons and Salters. A cousin drank too much champagne and was rather ill, and Charles Langdon, no orator, spoke for too long. The cake was small and mean-looking, because of rationing, and the eyes of the women, as they travelled over Esme's middle, were curious. Camilla wore a matching frock and coat of scarlet shot silk; she and Victor de Grey stood apart from the other guests, as though they had already set off on their different, London life.

Devlin's expression throughout the day was one of strained endurance. When they were alone at last, on the Langdon launch, crossing the Dart, he looked beyond the water to Kingswear and said, 'Thank God that's over.'

'Have you a headache?'

'A little. Did you enjoy it?'

'Oh Devlin, no. It was awful. How could I?'

'Women are supposed to enjoy weddings.'

'I hate people looking at me. I always have.' She smoothed his hair, which was ruffled by the wind, back from his fore-head. She wanted to smooth the frown lines away but he turned aside.

'When we get to Rosindell,' she said, 'we'll sit down and have a cup of tea and everything will be ordinary again.'

'Will it?' he said.

Of course, he was right. No part of her life would be ordinary ever again. That night, in bed, seeing the scars on her husband's body, she wept. He thought she was crying because she was frightened. No, she sobbed, it's because of what they have done to you. As she kissed the reddened, pitted flesh, her tears washed his wounds with salt. When he made love to her — that act that had been whispered about with fascinated, horrified inaccuracy at school, and had been alluded to with much distaste by her mother the night before her wedding — really, it wasn't so bad, and afterwards he held

97

her in his arms. And then with, she suspected, similar feelings of relief, they both fell asleep.

Later in the night, he woke gasping for breath, fighting off horrors. He sat on the edge of the bed and lit a cigarette. She heard the raw, unsteady in and out of his breathing.

'Sorry,' he murmured. 'Sorry. Go back to sleep.'

When Esme woke in the morning, she was alone. She lay in bed looking round the room. It was much larger than her bedroom at St Petrox Lodge, with gold curtains and rugs and large, dark pieces of furniture. She climbed out of bed, flinching at the cold, and peered into the dressing table mirror to find out whether she looked any different now that she was a married woman, now that she had done *that*. Her hair was tangled and her features had a blurred quality, as if they were undergoing some sort of metamorphosis.

There was nothing on or in the dressing table. That suggested to her that Devlin had imported it into the room for her use, which was thoughtful of him. She was trying to remember where she had put her hairbrush when the door opened and the maid, Sarah, came in with a tea tray. Esme glanced at her wristwatch, a wedding present from her father, and saw that it was almost ten o'clock. She slid back beneath the warm covers while Sarah put the tray on the side table and knelt in front of the grate to light the fire.

Esme drank her tea, then washed and dressed. She still could not find her brush, so she tidied her hair with her hands. Then she went downstairs. It took her a while to work out *how* to go downstairs, because Rosindell was all winding corridors and rooms that led unhelpfully into other similar rooms. Through misted windows, dark grey trees loomed out of a light grey sky, as if a cloud was smothering the headland.

In the gloomy dining room, the windows showed only more grey. Covered dishes stood on a sideboard: opening them, Esme found curls of brown bacon, somewhat solid yellow scrambled eggs, and sausages. She wondered whether she was supposed to wait for Devlin or the maid, or to help herself. She did not know how they did things at Rosindell. It was as if she had arrived at a seaside hotel with no staff or other guests. Eventually hunger won out and she put some eggs and bacon on a plate and sat down. Then Sarah came in with a rack of toast and asked her whether she could fetch her anything else. Esme asked for coffee and enquired about the whereabouts of − what should she call him? Devlin? My husband? Mr Reddaway? She settled for 'my husband', because she liked the sound of it.

Sarah expected that Mr Reddaway had taken the horse out. He always walked or rode first thing in the morning. Then: 'Mrs Satterley would like to talk to you about the menus, madam.'

Mrs Satterley was the cook. At home, Mummy discussed the day's menus with the cook each morning. Esme had been to the Rosindell kitchens once before, on the night of the storm, but could not remember their direction. By the time she had finished her breakfast, Sarah had disappeared, so there was no one to ask. Esme explored methodically until she reached a part of the house where the walls were made of rough stone. A clanking and clattering and a raised female voice, scolding someone, reassured her that she had found the kitchen.

Mrs Satterley was older than Sarah, short and fat and red-faced.

'Good morning, madam.' She gave Esme an exasperated look. 'I need to get on with my menus. Sarah must set off for the farm.'

'Have I held you up?' said Esme guiltily. 'I'm so sorry.'

Mrs Satterley thumbed through a notebook, licked a pencil and waited. Esme, calling on her limited knowledge of cuisine, suggested devilled kidneys, perhaps, followed by turbot.

'Won't that be too rich for luncheon, madam? Mr Devlin's always preferred plain food.'

'Oh! Yes. What would you suggest, Mrs Satterley?'

'Leek soup and a nice pork cutlet. Unless you're wanting fowl.'

Esme assured Mrs Satterley that pork cutlet would be lovely. A chocolate blancmange was agreed on for pudding and then the dinner menu was discussed. Mrs Satterley remained rigidly to attention until Esme remembered to thank her and left the room. She blundered her way back through the house until she came to the hallway, where she found Devlin, his hair curled by the damp, removing a greatcoat beaded with raindrops.

He looked at her as if he was surprised to see her – as if he had forgotten she was there. 'Good morning, Esme,' he said. 'Have you found everything you need?'

'Yes thank you.'

'I have to go and see Fawcett about the rents. Will you be all right?'

'I shall go for a walk,' she said, with a burst of inspiration.

'Don't go on the cliff path in this mist. Oh, and I should like to invite Fawcett for lunch, if you don't mind.'

'Yes, of course.'

Devlin frowned. 'You may see my gardener, Philips. If he seems shy or unfriendly, it's because he suffers from a facial disfigurement. He was in my regiment during the war.'

He limped off, leaving Esme standing in the hall. She put on her coat and hat and went outside. The mist had shrouded Rosindell so that the hills of the interior and the trees on the cliff might have vanished during the night. In the damp garden, brown seedheads drooped, made heavy by drops of moisture. The stream ran through the valley silently, as if muffled by the low cloud.

A man was working in the kitchen garden, pushing a spade into the clogged soil. When Esme called out a greeting, he turned towards her. She saw that his features were immobile, without expression, and she realised that his face was covered by a metal mask. He went back to his digging and Esme walked on.

The valley broadened, sloping down to the cliff. Purple and gold crocuses pushed their heads through the grass and pearls of water rolled from the dark green leaves of magnolias and laurels. It was the sort of place, Esme thought, where one might expect to find a delightful little bench, except that Rosindell did not seem the sort of house that provided delightful little benches. The path became muddier as it approached a gate, which led into dense woodland. The gnarled, shadowed bark of the oaks seemed to form into faces, elfin, wizened, as inexpressive as Mr Philips' mask.

Esme heard the soft hush of the sea and smelled salt in the air. Here the mist was thicker, and she reached the precipice before she realised it. The cliff tumbled down steeply, Rosindell Bay lost somewhere at its foot. Looking down, she felt a momentary dizziness and took a step back.

A few paces away, steps were cut into the rock. As she set off down the cliff, Esme marvelled at the way she seemed poised in the air, like a seabird. The sound of the sea was louder here, the push and pull of the tide against the shore clearly distinguishable. Down and down until she heard the crunch of pebbles, tugged over the sand by the waves. The steps beside the beach had crumbled away, requiring her to crouch, holding on to clumps of spiky grass so as not to lose her footing.

The bay, with its pleat of sand, curved round to either side of her. Streaks of rose quartz threaded through the rocks and pink pebbles glistened on the shoreline, as if someone had scattered handfuls of sweets. Esme looked out to the mist-strewn sea. The discouragement she had felt in the house was forgotten, replaced by exhilaration as she walked along the shore in the shadow of the cliff. This glorious, secret place was hers. In time, Devlin would look at her with affection instead of doubt. She imagined them running down the cliff steps together, peeling off their clothes to swim in the sea, or climbing into the wooden boat moored to the small concrete jetty.

After a while, she headed back up the stone steps. The upward climb was harder, the rocks slippery and wet, steep in places. When she looked back, she saw the sea swimming muzzily beneath her.

As she went inside the house, she heard men's voices. She prised off her muddy shoes. In the great hall, Devlin was talking to a weather-beaten, tweed-jacketed man. They both turned to look at her as she came into the room.

'Esme, this is Mr Fawcett, from Lethwiston,' said Devlin. 'Fawcett, this is my wife.'

'Congratulations, Mrs Reddaway.' They shook hands. 'How are you settling in to Rosindell?'

'Very well, thank you. Look.' Esme scooped pink pebbles from her pockets and held out her palms to the two men. The stones had dried and had lost their sugary gleam. 'I found them on the beach,' she said. 'Aren't they beautiful?'

'The beach?' said Devlin.

'Yes, the cove's so pretty.'

'You climbed down the steps in this fog?'

'Yes.' She realised that he was angry with her and said quickly, 'I was very careful.'

She saw him bite back whatever he had wanted to say and murmur instead, 'Lunch is ready. Don't you need to change?'

Excusing herself, she hurried upstairs to put on clean shoes. She still could not find her hairbrush. On her way down, she found Mrs Satterley standing at the foot of the stairs.

The cook said, 'How am I meant to divide four cutlets between three people, madam?'

Guilt made a blush rise to Esme's face. 'I'm so sorry, I forgot to tell you there would be three of us for lunch. I would be perfectly happy with a piece of cheese, Mrs Satterley.' She dashed into the dining room, where the men were waiting.

The talk over lunch was almost entirely of estate business. Mr Fawcett was a pleasant, reticent, plain-spoken man, who let Devlin guide the conversation. Neither man mentioned the wedding or the fact that this was Esme's first day as a new bride at Rosindell. Indeed, as the discussion of crop yields and the slow demobilisation of farm labourers from the army continued, she began to feel doubtful herself, and the events of the previous day took on an increasingly unreal cast, as if they were some overripe fantasy in which she had indulged. It was almost as if she had taken on employment at Rosindell as a rather inept housekeeper – the cutlets arrived supplemented by breakfast sausages – instead of a contract of marriage. *I need a wife for Rosindell*, Devlin had said when he had proposed to her. For Rosindell, not for himself. It was a business transaction, an exchange of services, like those undertaken by the tenant farmers the two men were debating. She felt a heaviness around her eyes and thought that in other circumstances she might have cried.

After coffee, Mr Fawcett took his leave. When the door had closed behind him, Devlin said, 'I told you to keep away from the cliff path.'

'I thought you meant the path to Kingswear, not the steps to the beach.'

There was a dreadful blankness in his eyes. 'My mother slipped and fell on those steps,' he said. 'A day later she died giving birth to a premature infant.'

She said, appalled, 'I'm so sorry. I didn't realise.'

He gave a slight nod, then took his coat from the stand.

'Where are you going?' she murmured.

'To Boohay, to call on one of my tenant farmers. You had better stay indoors this afternoon. Sarah has lit a fire in the library. You'll find everything you need there – notepaper, envelopes, and there are some novels, if you wish to read.'

He went outside. Esme stumbled upstairs. Sarah was dusting the pictures on the landing. Esme had to bite her lip to stop the hot tears falling before she enclosed herself privately in the first room she found.

She cried for a while, fearful that every day would go on like this one, underpinned by the nagging suspicion that the house did not want her here, that Devlin did not want her here. Looking out of the window, she saw Devlin and Josiah standing outside the stable block. She had no place here, she thought miserably. Devlin did, Josiah did, even Sarah did. Devlin had taken her on because he had felt obliged to do so, and because he needed a woman to look after his house and sit at his dinner table. Perhaps he would have preferred another sort of wife — a little older, much more beautiful, skilful and confident and sophisticated. Perhaps he would have preferred a woman like Camilla.

She knew so little about him: that his father had been a difficult and unapproachable man, that his mother had died when he was a small child; a few tales about his schooling from Tom, almost nothing about the war. She did not know, for instance, whether he minded talking about the friends he must have lost, whether it would comfort or rake up painful memories. His feelings had only occasionally been visible to her. She had seen him as a schoolboy look down his long, aristocratic nose at a friend who had tried to cheat at cricket. Yesterday, at the reception, she had seen much the same expression on his face as he had talked to her mother.

She had chosen this, Esme reminded herself sternly. This marriage had been her choice, not her parents', not really Devlin's, no one but hers, the first true choice she had ever made. So, if this muddling, untidy house and the acres of garden that surrounded it were to be run by herself and four servants, all of whom would have gone on scrubbing and peeling and digging regardless of whether she was there or not, scarcely noticing if she were to tumble over the cliff or lose herself for ever in some hitherto undiscovered corridor, then she must learn to live with that.

And she must learn to make herself useful to Devlin. Just as she must stop looking over her shoulder, searching for this improbable person, whenever someone said 'Mrs Reddaway'.

Outside, Josiah was saddling up a horse. Esme watched Devlin caress the animal's glossy black neck. She longed for him to touch her with equal tenderness. He had told her that he was incapable of love, but she did not believe him. The capacity was inside him somewhere, she knew it was. It was a question of finding the key, and the key to Devlin was Rosindell. Devlin's heart was shut away in Rosindell.

She went downstairs to the library. She wrote a letter to a schoolfriend in Bath, telling her of her marriage, and a note to her mother, giving her an edited version of her first day at Rosindell. Then she tidied up the room, using her pocket handkerchief as a duster, organising the books on the shelf and straightening out the scattered items on the desk. Poor Devlin, she thought, all alone for so long in this big house with no one to look after him. Well, he wouldn't be alone any longer. *She* would look after him; *she* would make him happy.

When, several hours later, Devlin returned to the house, he went to the library to look out documents connected with the farm in Boohay. But the room, which had been his comfortable retreat since he had returned to Rosindell, had altered. Now, nothing was to hand. Books were in a different order on the shelves and the papers he had been working on earlier that day had been put away. With rising impatience he opened drawers until he found them.

The desk furniture had also been rearranged. His fountain pen had been placed with careful precision by his blotter, and a vase containing sprigs of winter honeysuckle stood on a corner of the desk. He knew that Esme had done this, not Sarah, who knew better than to touch his things, and in a rush of regret it occurred to him how happy he would have felt had it been Camilla who had thought of tidying his desk for him, Camilla who had walked through his garden searching for flowers at this unpromising time of year. And then disquiet followed closely on regret, because he knew that in thinking so, he was betraying Esme, his wife of only one day.

The mist was thickening, the afternoon darkening, and already he could not see through the window as far as the trees on the other side of the courtyard. Though his body had begun to recover, he knew that the deadness at the heart of him persisted, and that safety and sanity were to be found only in his own acres of red Devon soil.

Chapter Six

August 1919

A series of postcards arrived at Rosindell throughout the summer of 1919. Sarah Fox arranged them on the narrow shelf in her attic room, where they made, she thought, a nice colourful splash. The postcards were from her sister Jane, who was travelling with the de Greys on their honeymoon in Europe. The first cards, which reached Sarah in May, had been posted from France. As the summer lengthened, postcards with pictures of mountains, lakes and beaches were delivered to Rosindell, their stamps from Switzerland, Italy and Spain. Jane's scribbled notes described parties that Victor and Camilla de Grey had attended, famous people they had met, gifts that Mr de Grey had bought his wife on their honeymoon. *Mrs de Grey has a bracelet with emeralds as big as robin's eggs. She let me try it on. Mrs de Grey looks like a princess when she wears it.*

Rosindell was less than a mile from Lethwiston, where both Sarah and Jane had been born, so it suited Sarah, and Mr and Mrs Reddaway were easy enough to work for, a lot less trouble than the old man. Sarah had sometimes wondered whether it was because of old Mr Walter that Jane had taken against Rosindell, whether the old devil had ever tried it on with her. Jane disliked men. She had cause to; their own father was a brute and a bully, and what Jane had endured at his hands had poisoned her view of the entire sex.

Jane had worked at Rosindell for a scant three months before leaving. She claimed to have been scared off by a ghost, but then she had always made up stories. There were, of course, ghosts at Rosindell; Sarah believed that there were ghosts in most old houses. If you didn't bother them, they didn't bother you. You didn't go down to the cellars after dark — even Josiah took the dog for company when Mr Reddaway sent him for a bottle of wine — and Sarah had always disliked one of the bedrooms. In the ruined rooms in which Mr Reddaway and his guest Mr Ellison had been poking around that morning, there was a feeling of sadness that clung to the stones along with the damp and the cold.

But Sarah had seen a baby sister die of scarlet fever, and her father had beaten her mother to within an inch of her life, and compared to that, ghosts held no terrors for her. She liked working at Rosindell well enough. Mr Reddaway had a temper, but he didn't take it out on the servants, except for Josiah, who was an idle so-and-so and deserved it. Neither Mr or Mrs Reddaway seemed to notice a little dust on a mantelpiece, which was just as well as the house was far too big for Sarah to do much more than skim round, cleaning the parts that showed the dirt most. When Mr Devlin's mother had been alive they had had ten servants at Rosindell, including three housemaids.

The temperature had been rising for several days. In the fields, the crops had been brought in, leaving only the shaven, dusty stubble. Flies buzzed in the kitchen, and the attic where Sarah slept was like an oven. Mr and Mrs Reddaway and Mr Ellison were spending the afternoon at the cove. In the kitchen, Mrs Satterley, her face glistening with sweat, was packing the picnic. A cold roast chicken, slices of ham, a tin box of salad, hard-boiled eggs, tomatoes fresh from the garden, smelling of summer, a raspberry tart and white rolls, fruit, a bottle of wine, a flask of lemonade and another flask of tea were all wrapped in tea cloths and napkins and placed in the wicker basket. Mrs Satterley was complaining about her swollen ankles and Josiah had taken the horse to the blacksmith, so Sarah offered to carry the picnic down to the beach. The basket was heavy, but Sarah, who had been in service since she was twelve years old, had strong arms.

As she walked outside, the midday sun struck her, its light blinding and its concentrated heat enveloping her like a blanket. Looking up, she saw that a man was coming down the drive towards the house. He was shabbily dressed in a worn shirt and corduroy trousers, workman's blue jacket and a cloth cap. A stream of unemployed labourers had turned up at Rosindell over the summer, driven by the scarcity of work. Mrs Satterley's response to them varied according to her mood. Her mood was irritable today because of the hot weather.

After Sarah had explained that there was no work to be had, the man begged a cup of tea. Stooping, Sarah opened the picnic basket, poured a long draught of lemonade into a tumbler and offered it to him. As he gulped it down, she wrapped rolls, fruit and hard-boiled eggs in a napkin.

'Here, take this,' she said, passing the bundle to him.

'Thank you, miss.' He touched his cap. 'I won't forget your kindness.'

Sarah wiped the tumbler dry on her apron as he headed off towards Brixham. Then she put it back in the basket and started off for the cove.

The heat brought out the scent of the roses in the garden. Mr Philips, who had recently returned from hospital after an operation on his face, kept it nice, she thought approvingly. It wasn't so bad, working at Rosindell. At least she *had* work, unlike that poor fellow. Sarah had no wish to become a lady's maid like Jane. Jane was ambitious, and had seen it as a step up. Too much fussing around one person, thought Sarah privately, though she didn't mind helping Mrs Reddaway with her clothes and hair.

As she stepped beneath the laurels, the air became cooler. There was the whine of a bee, and, from high above, a louder, more insistent buzzing. Gazing upwards, Sarah saw between the silhouetted branches of the shrubs an aeroplane tracing a path through the hard blue crystal of the sky. She stood motionless, watching it. What would it be like to fly like a bird, looking down on the people on the ground as they scurried around?

The aeroplane flew out of sight. Sarah continued along the path, through the gate and beneath the deep shade of the oaks and pines. She could smell the sea before she emerged from the cover of branches back into the heat and the sun. Here, the cliffs tumbled down to the bay and light glared on the water. On this sheltered part of the coast sea pinks sprang from between the tufts of grass, and if you were lucky, you might, even in August, find pockets of violets in unseasonal flower.

On the beach below, Mr Reddaway and Mr Ellison were walking along the sand. Mrs Reddaway was sitting on the concrete rim of the bathing pool, her feet dangling in the water. Sarah tutted disapprovingly. Mrs Reddaway was wearing a bathing suit – and her expecting a baby at Christmas!

Shading his eyes, looking up to the sky, Conrad Ellison said, 'Perfect day for it.'

Devlin watched the aircraft swoop and jitter out to sea. 'Have you ever flown?'

'I had a friend in the RFC who took me up for a spin when I was in France. What about you, Reddaway?'

The plane became a speck of dust in the distance. 'No, never,' said Devlin.

The two men continued their stroll along the beach. Ellison, an architect, had before the war worked as an assistant to Edwin

Lutyens. He and Devlin had met by chance in a restaurant in London. Overhearing Devlin's name, Ellison had introduced himself. 'Are you a Reddaway of Rosindell?' he had asked after apologising for the intrusion. 'When I was nineteen,' he had explained, 'I spent a summer biking round England, taking a look at all the country houses I came across. I tried to get a glimpse of Rosindell, but a pack of hounds chased me away, so all I saw was a roof and some chimneys.'

A conversation had ensued: Walter Reddaway's dislike of visitors; their mutual admiration for Lutyens; the importance of unity in any architectural project. At the end of it, Devlin had invited Ellison to Rosindell.

That morning, Devlin had shown the architect round the house. Ellison was thin and dark-haired, his jaw slightly prominent and his smile on the toothy side. But his hazel eyes were coolly intelligent and he had a dry sense of humour along with a certain reticence. Devlin had found himself watching him, trying to read his reaction to the house, but Ellison had given little away.

Now he said, 'What did you think of it?'

'It's breathtaking.' Catching Devlin's look, Ellison said, 'I mean it. The building, of course, is in poor condition but the setting is unparalleled.'

'Tactfully expressed.' Devlin spoke with a dry irony. 'If the house were sited in some dull field or suburb I could wash my hands of it, but as it is . . .'

'I must admit, I had some trepidation in coming here. I was afraid I might find you attached, by reason of sentiment, to a monstrosity.'

Devlin laughed. 'You're very frank.'

'Men up and down the land have come home to impoverished estates. Some are worth saving and some are not.'

The wavelets, warmed by the sun, licked at their toes, and the sea was a flat, unbroken skin that shifted back and forth.

The tall cliffs muffled sound, so that when they spoke, it was as if they stood on either side of a sheet of glass. They were approaching the part of the cove where the beach narrowed. They scrambled over rocks clefted by long pools in which crabs and sea anemones took refuge from the heat.

'Permit me to be frank again,' said Ellison. 'The oldest parts of the house, the early medieval rooms, are, I believe, beyond repair. I fear that the chapel and hospice were poorly sited in the first place, without much consideration given to aspect. Even this morning they seemed cold and dark. And the Victorian additions are of no particular merit.'

'Are you telling me that I should pull the place down?'

Ellison smiled and shook his head. 'No, not at all. It would be a tragedy to lose the great hall and the Tudor rooms. They are exquisite.'

'It's like dragging a damaged limb around,' said Devlin ruefully. 'I can't cut myself off from the place but I can't cure it either.'

'Let me draw up some plans. I'll have to stay a couple more days to take measurements and get to know the site, but I promise I won't get in the way. I've an idea of what I'd like to do to Rosindell, and I want to get it down on paper and let you see it.'

'That's good of you, Ellison, but unfortunately I'm not yet in a position to make improvements to the house.'

The architect took off his spectacles and rubbed the lenses, squinting at the sunlight. 'I don't intend to suggest improvements. My recommendations will be far more radical, so you may dismiss them out of hand. I have a suggestion to make: that we agree to defer payment for my services, on condition that if you like my ideas then you make a commitment to employ me as your architect when you are able to do so.'

'I hadn't thought to do anything other than some necessary repair work.'

'Is that true? Forgive me, but in your position I would want to do so much more.'

Devlin recalled his first night at Rosindell after he had returned from the war, his grief and anger at discovering the ruin of his home. He had hauled the stones from the collapsed wall one at a time, through the rain, as if by doing so he might single-handedly restore the house to what it had once been.

'You'll have a child soon,' Ellison reminded him. 'You must think of the future. Look, Reddaway, every architect hopes to come across a project that will establish his style. Lutyens has Castle Drogo and Marsh Court. I need to make my mark, and I know that, given the opportunity, I can do that with Rosindell.'

Shortly afterwards, the two men dived into the turquoise sea. Devlin made for the jagged rock that formed an island perch for seabirds, concentrating on swimming the distance in the shortest time possible while making his bad leg do equal work with the good. He knew that he would not have had the strength for the swim when he had first come home. His body was recovering.

The enthusiasm he had felt talking to Ellison remained. He already wished he had taken the conversation further, that he had asked Ellison to describe his plans for the house. Langdon's boatyard was prospering and he could see that there would come a time when he had money to spare for Rosindell.

He had been working for Charles Langdon for the last seven months. He enjoyed the work and had discovered that he had an aptitude for it. The yard had been founded in the previous century, when Dartmouth had been at the height of its success as a coaling station. After a period of poor management the business had fallen into decline until Charles Langdon, leaving his native Leeds to marry Annette Salter, had bought it and rechristened it. Charles had rid himself of the failing parts of the enterprise and had constructed a new boathouse, offices and another slipway. In time, Langdon's had made enough money to allow Charles to build his showy new house on one of Dartmouth's most pleasant streets.

Devlin had started work at the bottom, in the yard itself. He liked the smell of wood-shavings, the soft lap of the river, and the sense of purpose. The boats grew before his eyes, a spine and ribs acquiring skin and flesh until it became a trawler or launch. He liked to see the hull slice through the water when they took a new boat out for trials, to feel it rear and dance as it reached the place where the river mouth met the sea.

After six weeks he had been transferred to the office, to become acquainted with the firm's record-keeping and account books. He had learned how to keep track of the progress of an order and how to chase up suppliers and late payments. Sometimes he accompanied Tom or Charles on their visits to customers. Tom's calls involved long lunches and frequent diversions to see a girl in Brixham, a Miss Reeves. By now, Devlin knew that there was spare capacity at the boatyard and that he must find cheaper suppliers. He needed the yard to make a profit. He needed it for Rosindell, which swallowed up money.

After six months, Charles had called him into his office to invite him to stay on at the firm. 'You're a practical man,' he said. 'I like that. And you haven't done as badly as I thought you would.' This, from Charles, was a compliment. 'I seem to remember you asking for a twenty-five per cent share in the business,' he had gone on. 'I won't give you twenty-five – Tom has twenty-five, and I'll be damned if the two of you will be able to block me – but I will give you twenty. If you put your mind to it, you'll be able to make something of that.'

Charles Langdon had paid off the debts on the Rosindell estate on Devlin's marriage to Esme. This had allowed him to start with a clean slate, but had also left him permanently obliged to his father-in-law. Devlin had a certain respect for Charles, for his ambition and his capacity for work, but he found Annette irredeemably vulgar. His mother-in-law saw the world through a prism of money. She ran her small blue eyes over Rosindell's prints and china and demanded to know their worth. Devlin knew that Annette looked at him with the same assessing eye – was he a presentable husband; did his blood run true enough to father a healthy child? Perhaps all women looked at their sons-in-law so. Devlin's gaze trawled along the beach. Esme's bright blue hat was abandoned on a rock; Esme herself was sitting on the wall of the bathing pool.

He put his heart into his work at Langdon's and so felt no prickling of conscience about the manner in which he had come to it. But with Esme living in it, Rosindell had changed. Devlin would come home from work and catch sight of her talking to Philips in the garden, all long, angular limbs and a head made too heavy by her hair, and it would bewilder him how he had somehow come to share his home with her. Her unpredictability, the fact that he could not tell what she might do or say, unsettled him. She was often shy, sometimes gauche, and yet she had a reckless streak. She did not appear to fear storms, solitariness or the tall cliffs of Rosindell Bay. She was only on her guard with other people, fearing their opinion of her, or perhaps her opinion of them. He had come to think that her shyness was a sort of snobbery, one that he himself shared; a dislike of the commonplace, the second-rate.

Her love was a burden to him, a love he had neither sought nor deserved, nor was able to give back. It reminded him of his own deficiences, of expectations he could not meet. And yet he could lose himself in the soft hollows and curves of her body, erasing memory and consciousness, escaping from thought and responsibility.

He watched her slide into the pool. The baby was expected in mid December. 'You certainly didn't waste any time,' Annette had said, when they had told her about the coming child. You could never overestimate Annette Langdon's capacity for coarseness. Well, so be it. Marriage to Esme Langdon might have tied him to her family, but it had also saved Rosindell from financial ruin.

Esme was young and strong, and he had made arrangements for her to have the baby in the best nursing home in Exeter. But he was out of the habit of trusting in the future, and it was only now, as he struck out from the islet, that he recognised that he had begun to feel the first shoots of optimism, white and feeble and deprived of light, but alive nevertheless.

The bathing pool, walled in concrete, jutted out from the shore and filled up with seawater with the tide, protecting the swimmer from the strong currents in the bay. Esme's limbs were outspread like a starfish as she floated. Now and then she covered her eyes with her hand and then, slowly parting her fingers, watched the rays of the sun pierce between them, in flashes of white.

The previous day, sorting through the bedroom in which the architect Conrad Ellison was to sleep, Esme had found a photograph inside a drawer. The sepia print had been of a man and a woman, the man dressed in tailcoat, white bow tie and winged collar, the woman with plumes in her hair and wearing a narrow-waisted, puff-sleeved gown. The photograph had been taken in Rosindell's ballroom, the couple standing in front of one of the painted *trompe l'oeil* pillars. When, later that afternoon, Esme had unlocked one of the tall double doors in the ballroom, a curtain had danced in the breeze and the perfumes of summer had seeped into the musty space.

In her imagination, Rosindell's windows were lit up and the house shone like a beacon on the headland. Guests filled the rooms and music drifted from the ballroom, where couples swirled round the floor, the women's diamond necklaces catching the light from the chandeliers. She was dancing with Devlin, handsome in evening dress. She herself was wearing gold lace, perhaps, or old rose. When the dance came to an

116

end, Devlin kissed her, a kiss born of love and passion rather than duty.

She ran a palm over the curve of her belly. Sometimes she was afraid she would not have love enough to spare for a child. Sometimes she was afraid she might look at her baby and feel nothing, that in some complicated way she could hardly express she might need Devlin to love her before she was able to love another person. As if love were circular, one person's adoration fuelling another's.

But Devlin did not love her. His strongest feelings were for his home. Driving back with him from Kingswear, she had often mentally remarked on the expression on his face as the house had come to him hazily out of the mist, or brightly gilded with sunshine. She would have given anything to see such passion in his eyes when he looked at her. Touch was the only language they shared: in bed, he buried his fingers in her hair and she heard his breath catch. His kisses were urgent and his hands and mouth explored every inch of her body as if he wished to own it. She sensed that she gave him something he needed, and yet during the day they stumbled over words, she afraid of asking too much of him, he incapable of talking of feelings.

Looking up, she saw that further along the beach, Devlin was wading through the shallow water. Who could say why you loved someone? As a girl, she had loved Devlin Reddaway for the curve of his mouth and the black, consuming fire of his eyes. Now it seemed to her that she did not love him for anything other than himself, and the knowledge that the loss of him would, she could see quite clearly, destroy her made her life precarious.

The sun had moved, and now the bathing pool lay inside the shadow of the cliff. Esme shivered. With an effort, she hauled herself out of the water, wrapped herself in a towel, and headed for the hamper that Sarah had left on the sand.

Chapter Seven

May 1920

In the great hall, Esme ran a fingertip over the mantelpiece to check for dust and then let it drift down to trace the circles incised into the stone surround. Sarah Fox had told her they were witches' marks, carved by the masons who had built the house. She ran a final glance round the room before taking a jacket from the hall stand and going outside.

The breeze swayed the crimson heads of the tulips in their stone pots. Sunlight shimmered on the sage-green hills, and the dark branches of the fringe of pines on the cliffs bobbed and waved. Esme had pictured her guests roaming round the garden for half an hour before it was time to come in for drinks, but weeks of stormy weather meant that the garden had a ragged look. The irises and peonies that grew against the front wall appeared bruised by the wind.

Inside the stables the horses turned their great liquid dark eyes to her as she peered into the tack room, looking for Josiah. They were nervy creatures; only Josiah and Devlin could control them, and only Devlin could control Josiah. 'Josiah?' she called out, but the room was empty.

She headed down through the valley to where Devlin and Conrad Ellison were inspecting the site where the new house was to be built. The plans that Conrad Ellison had drawn up showed two wings branching out at an angle from the rooms that he intended to retain: the Tudor bedrooms and the medieval great hall, dining room, library and stairs. The new Rosindell would be laid out in the shape of a Y, an unconventional arrangement but one that would make the most of the views across the valley.

Mostly the men's voices were obliterated by the wind, but now and then Esme caught a word or a phrase.

'. . . shale beneath the topsoil . . .'

'. . . God-awful job . . .'

Conrad glanced up as she approached. 'We're building castles in the air, Esme.'

'I hope not.' She smiled at him. 'I hope you're going to build me a wonderful new house that will be the envy of all Devon.'

'Too many damned underground streams.' Devlin scanned the site. 'God knows why the house was ever built here in the first place.'

'Because your ancestors were unsociable recluses, I expect,' said Esme. 'Do you think it's possible?'

'The house? Oh yes, I like a challenge.' Conrad's hand sketched out a wall, a roof line. 'Do you see that hollow? That will be the covered terrace. Next to it will be the dining room, and there' – a broad sweep up the valley – 'is where the drawing room will be.'

'It'll be magnificent.' There was in Devlin's eyes an expression that Esme had come to know, that she glimpsed only when he was talking about the house. An expression of complete absorption. Obsession, almost.

'But since,' added Conrad lightly, blinking through the lenses of his glasses, 'I suspect that magnificence isn't what you most value, Esme, the house will also be a retreat from the world, a private haven for you and Devlin.'

'Hot running water and electricity . . . I can't wait.'

'I'm afraid you may have to, for a year or two at least. But it will be worth it, I promise you.'

Esme turned to Devlin. 'I can't find Josiah. Mrs Satterley needs more cream and no one else is free to go to the farm.'

'I'll go,' Ellison offered.

'No, no, Con, there's no need.'

'I should like to. I could do with the walk.'

'Then thank you.'

'The wretched fellow has made an art of never being there when you want him. Excuse me, Esme, Conrad.' Devlin headed quickly back to the house.

As Esme and Conrad also started back, Conrad asked her when her dinner guests were to arrive.

She glanced at her wristwatch. 'The Hendrickses and Mr Fawcett and his sister will arrive fairly soon, I should think. Devlin will collect Caroline from Kingswear at four. Tom will be late, he always is, though perhaps Miss West will hurry him up. My sister and her friends should be here at around five, though it depends on the roads.'

'Are they driving down from London?'

'No, from Greenwell, Victor's place in Gloucestershire.'

They walked back to the house. As they reached the courtyard, Esme saw that Mr Petherick, one of the clerks from Langdon's boatyard, was propping his bicycle outside the front door. She excused herself to Conrad and crossed the gravel to speak to him. Conrad Ellison strode off over the fields towards the farm.

Indoors, Esme sent Sarah to find Devlin. Then she went to the kitchen to check on the arrangements with Mrs Satterley. The agency maid she had engaged to help with the serving of dinner had turned up on time, saucepans were steaming and rattling on the stove, and Mrs Satterley was twirling a pie dish on a fingertip as she slashed away excess pastry, snap, snap, the pallid ribbons flopping on to the kitchen table.

'Them flowers in my sink,' she said accusingly to Esme. 'White lilac, everyone knows it's unlucky. I wouldn't have it in

120

the house.' Esme rushed into the scullery and dealt swiftly with the flowers, whirling the creamy blossoms into vases, which she carried to the great hall.

Then to the nursery. In the small kitchen, Jessie Tapp was preparing the baby's bottle. Esme offered to give the feed and settled herself into the low nursing chair. Zoe's eyes, which were darkening from blue to brown, fixed on her with intent concentration as she fed. The haze of fine black hair on the baby's head confirmed Esme's suspicion that her daughter was a reserved, stormy Reddaway rather than a fair, commonplace Langdon.

She had been born five months earlier, a fortnight before Christmas. They had called her Zoe Mary; Mary after Devlin's mother, and Zoe because they had both agreed it to be a modern and original name, suitable for a girl born on the cusp of the new decade. After a two-day labour, Esme had felt that the effort of turning her head to look at the baby that the midwife had placed on the pillow beside her was almost beyond her. The infant had been tightly bound up in a blanket, like a moth in a cocoon. Esme had sensed that the nurse expected her to pull back the blanket and look properly at the little face, and so, fighting exhaustion, she had done so. The baby's features had been red and swollen, her eyes closed, and tufts of dark hair had been matted to her head, reminding Esme of an otter's pelt.

The nurse had said, 'Would you like to hold her, Mrs Reddaway?' and Esme, to be obliging, had said yes. The nurse had plonked the baby on her chest, a surprisingly substantial bundle. It had been too much, all she had endured: the indignities, the unimaginable pain – far worse than she had anticipated – the dreadful tearing as the baby's head had emerged and the stitches that had resulted, and now this weight on her. All this, she had thought with despair, she must get used to. She had wished the nurse would take the infant away. She had longed for a cup of tea, and to sleep.

She had become unwell, feverish with an infection, and it had been three weeks before Devlin had been able to drive her and her daughter home to Rosindell. Jessie had held Zoe in the car, whisking her away to the nursery as soon as they reached the house. By then, it had seemed to Esme that other people knew her baby far better than she did. Zoe had been a poor feeder, easily distracted, given to dozing off or choking, hard to comfort and difficult to settle. It had not been as though Esme had no experience of babies: there had been all those cousins' infants she had bounced on her knee. It was only Zoe she was unable to soothe, Zoe who seemed to have been born unhappy, able to express her discontent only in her thin, demanding wail.

The tiredness and low mood that had followed the birth had clung to her. At night she was kept awake by the shriek of a barn owl or the unearthly scream of a fox, and the house itself, with its chorus of rattles and creaks. During the first three months of her life, Zoe had seemed always to be crying, or touchily dropping off to sleep after crying, or stirring and about to cry. Pushing the pram, Esme had felt on edge, afraid that the bump of a wheel in a rut or the bark of the dog might wake her. Family and friends had called and said, 'Isn't she beautiful? You must be so proud of her,' and she had smiled and said yes, she was.

But it had been as if her first impression, that of the shocking weight of the infant, had never completely gone away. Whatever Esme had imagined motherhood to be, it had not been this, and her sense of failure persisted. After an hour's tussle with the feeding bottle had left both mother and daughter exhausted and weeping, Jessie would efficiently bring up the baby's wind, bundle her up in blankets, coat and bonnet in her pram and push her round the garden, and Esme would feel . . . what? A mixture of relief and shame and disappointment in herself.

Her shame was at its greatest when she observed Devlin's

powerful attachment to his daughter. Sometimes, when Zoe was inconsolable, he wrapped her up in a shawl and carried her round the grounds, propped against his shoulder. He could converse with Josiah or Mr Philips while Zoe was howling; her sobs did not seem to make him feel panicky or useless. His love for his daughter should have pleased her – it did please her – but the envy she sometimes felt, witnessing his easy tenderness with the baby and seeing Zoe's charmed response to her father, made her hate herself. How much lower could one stoop than to feel jealous of one's own kin – one's own child? She had not realised herself capable of such jealousy until she had come to Rosindell. This she had learned about herself: that she could resent anything that occupied her husband's love and attention – a woman, a baby, a memory, a house. These were thoughts she could never express to anyone, least of all to Devlin, and they shamed her.

Recently, Zoe had cried less and smiled more. As she suckled, the baby's eyes became dreamy and her lids drooped, and Esme ran through in her mind the arrangements for the evening. There were to be twelve dinner guests at this, the most important social function since Esme had come to live at Rosindell. A letter from Camilla telling her that she and Victor planned to tour the West Country in late May had prompted the occasion.

It would be the first visit that Camilla and Victor had made to the house. All Esme's previous invitations had been turned down. The de Greys had had prior engagements: a party, a picnic, a trip to Europe. That Conrad Ellison had also offered to come to Rosindell that weekend with the completed plans for the house had set the seal on Esme's decision. She had made her guest list and consulted Mrs Satterley about the menu, and Sarah had cleaned the most presentable bedrooms for the guests who were to stay overnight. Fishing rods and dog bowls had been hidden out of sight, and anything that might be considered a treasure — a snuffbox, a watercolour — had been put on display. Camilla would see Rosindell at its best.

Zoe had fallen asleep. Esme settled her in her cradle and went to check on the bedrooms. She had felt some compunction about putting Camilla and Victor's friends, Mr and Mrs Rackham, in the pink room, the room that had so frightened her on her first night at Rosindell, but the alternative had been damp and mould and peeling wallpaper. Besides, she felt a mild irritation with the Rackhams, even though she did not know them at all. It was as if Camilla had thought it necessary to bring her own friends with her in case of boredom, as one would bring a hot-water bottle in case of the cold.

Looking through the window, she saw Conrad Ellison heading back down the valley towards the house, a pail in one hand. There was the sound of a car engine; Esme hurried downstairs.

The front door was open, allowing her to see into the court-yard as the Hendricks' motor car rumbled down the drive. Devlin opened the passenger door and the Hendrickses climbed out: Robert tall, grey-haired and distinguished, Thea slim and elegant, with a mop of brown curls.

There was a flurry of greetings and kisses.

'Garden's looking splendid . . .'

'Philips does a grand job.'

'How is that dear little girl of yours? She almost makes me think of having another one.'

'Good Lord, Thea, we've only just got the boys off to school.'

The weather seemed to be improving, Esme thought, as she stepped outdoors. The wind had dropped, there was some warmth in the air, and where the sunlight fell between the clouds, islands of gold washed across the fields.

Camilla and Victor and the Rackhams were the last to arrive. Though a walk in the garden for a breath of fresh air was suggested, no one seemed keen and the idea was dropped. The

124

men had begun to look forward to a drink, the women worried about their silk stockings. So they gathered in the great hall, clustering on sofas and chairs or pacing about the room to stretch their legs after the long drive.

Apart from Camilla, everyone was downstairs, and everyone had a drink in their hand. Good.

Tom and Alice West and the Hendrickses: 'I've always thought the Western Isles so romantic.'

'Midges. Not romantic at all. Damned things get everywhere. We could only escape them on the yacht.'

The Rackhams, Conrad and Caroline, talking about motor cars. Denis Rackham owned a garage in Earls Court. He stood in front of the fireplace, a large, imposing man, florid and fleshy-faced, yellow-haired, his pose aggressive, feet set wide apart, mouth red and full-lipped, blue-green eyes flitting restlessly beneath heavy, slightly swollen lids. A handsome man, with a raw, animal energy, but he was of a type, Esme thought, that she did not much care for. His wife, Merline, was petite and pin-curled. Her small, neat, regular features were sprinkled with freckles and her primrose silk frock was sleeveless and fell to her calves. Perhaps Mrs Rackham had underestimated the chilliness of Devon in May. Perhaps that accounted for her sour expression.

'Can't beat a Peugeot.'

'Brilliant engine design. That's French engineering.'

Camilla came into the room. She had always had a way of making an entrance. That moment of pausing in the doorway so that heads turned to look at her, and then gliding through a room in a cloud of Mitsouko, her smile taking in the company in one sweeping movement before she chose the best seat.

'You don't mind, do you, Conrad?'

And they never minded. They squeezed up, they squashed against sofa arms for Camilla, in her pale pink chemise dress with its filmy overskirt, on which were sewn crystals like chips of ice. Sometime in the year since her wedding, Camilla's hair had been cropped in a smooth blond helmet close to her small head. Had she been wearing shirt and trousers, you might have mistaken her for a beautiful boy.

Settling herself between Conrad Ellison and Merline Rackham, Camilla looked up at Devlin. 'Such an extraordinary place.'

'Extraordinarily good or extraordinarily bad?'

'Neither.' A raise of plucked, arched eyebrows. 'Simply extraordinary.'

'Gin and it all right?'

'Clever Devlin. Chin-chin.'

Glasses chinked. Early evening sunshine burnished the polished floor, and the white lilac reflected in lucent polished wooden surfaces in a satisfactory manner. The Fawcetts, though, were sitting a little apart from the rest. Esme worried about them; they were less confident in company than the other guests. She tried to catch Devlin's eye. She had taken it on herself to talk to Victor, an effortful process interspersed with pauses, which she sought to fill, and in which she caught fragments of the other conversations in the room.

'Such a beautiful frock.'

'Chanel, you know.'

'You can't *teach* flair.'

'I'd spend all my time in Paris if it wasn't for the boys.'

'They know how to *live*, the French.'

'But the bathrooms.' A wrinkled nose, indicating disgust.

'But Merline, food and wine and gorgeous clever clothes.'

'Damnably cold in Paris sometimes.'

'I prefer to winter in the south of France.'

'Too enviable, escaping our English gloom.'

Denis Rackham spun his cigarette butt into the fireplace. 'Don't care to be chilly, do you, Camilla?'

'You know me, darling.' A complacent, feline smile. 'I like it hot.'

Rackham snorted.

'Where did you stay, Mrs de Grey?'

'The Côte d'Azur. I swam for miles every day.'

'You should come here again when the weather is better. The sea can be marvellously warm.'

'Perhaps I shall.'

'I'll come with you,' offered Rackham, and the sticky conversation that Esme was enduring with Victor de Grey, about the state of the roads in the south-west, limped to a halt again.

'Don't like the food, do you, de Grey?' drawled Rackham. 'All those damned frogs' legs.'

'My husband isn't an adventurous man when it comes to food.'

'No, you're wrong.' Victor's tone was cold. 'It's the company I don't care for.'

'The Parisians have a reputation for a certain froideur,' said Thea Hendricks, 'but Robert and I found the people in the countryside very friendly when we stayed in Arles before the war. We rented a villa there. Do you know Arles, Mrs de Grey?'

'We spent a few days there. Awfully sweet.'

'Robert wanted to sketch in the Camargue.'

'Did you ride, Mr Hendricks?'

Since Camilla had joined them, the focus of the room had altered. Radiant in her pink and pearls, she sucked the light in the room towards herself. The sailing conversation had broken up; the Fawcetts were still on their own.

'Best way to get about in the marshes,' said Robert Hendricks.

'I had a wonderful time in the Camargue.' Camilla bent closer to Hendricks so that he could light her pink cocktail cigarette. 'I had a little tent and I camped out at night under the stars. Too divine.'

'Still, there's no place like home, is there?'

'Do you think so? As soon as I'm back in England I can't wait to get away again.'

Esme said determinedly to Victor, 'Do you spend most of your time in Gloucestershire?' and his gaze, which was moving between his wife and Denis Rackham, trawled back to her.

'Fridays to Mondays.' The words snapped out.

'I suppose you must need to be in London during the week.'

'At the bank, yes.'

'It must be terribly interesting, working for a bank.' Dear me, she was getting desperate.

But Victor proceeded to explain to her about the gold standard, which was a result, of sorts, and she made suitable murmuring noises while worrying about the dinner – Dover sole for fourteen people, and Mrs Satterley was never at her best with fish – and continuing to eavesdrop on several conversations, a mild roar now.

'Absolutely necessary that we get the country back on the gold standard, or we'll end up in a mess, like Germany.'

'How many rooms are there?'

'I've never counted them.'

'Oh, come now.' This from Robert Hendricks. 'A man needs to know the extent of his estates.'

'It depends what you call a room. The attics and the cellars are a warren of alcoves and passageways.'

'Fix you up with a nice little runabout if you like, sweetheart.'

'Then I know better than you, Reddaway. I have a list. I've surveyed the entire building.'

'Just give me a bell next time you're in Town.'

'The problem is unionised labour. Wages need to be cut and the unions are digging their heels in.'

'A new house, Mr Ellison?'

'Not entirely new, Mrs de Grey. I've incorporated those parts of the old building worth saving into the new. The difficulty is creating a unity between the two halves. Devlin came up with the solution.'

'I recall it as being one of those happy occasions, Ellison, when the thought occurred to both of us at much the same time. Grace, you must tell me about that new spaniel of yours. Will you breed from her?' Devlin had crossed the room to talk to the Fawcetts, thank goodness, and was sitting with his back to the rest of the group.

'Rosindell's an isolated site,' explained Conrad. 'It would be ruinously expensive to bring in building materials from any distance, so for reasons of economy alone, it seemed sensible to re-use the Devon shale stone from the rooms that are to be demolished. And that will mean that the two parts of the house, the old and the new, will be in harmony.'

Rackham said, 'Wouldn't it be cheaper to knock the whole caboodle down and start again?'

'Cheaper, perhaps, if you consider it merely from a financial point of view. But think what you'd lose! History. A sympathy with the landscape.'

Rackham laughed. 'I wouldn't know, old boy. I have a mansion flat in Piccadilly. Suits me fine.'

'Do you remember, Devlin, that you once told me that you were going to rebuild Rosindell for *me*?' Camilla's voice, clear as a bell, broke through her husband's explanation of price inflation, crashingly dull. A beat, then she added, 'He thought he was in love with me at the time.'

What Esme first felt was, well, nothing. Blankness, as if thoughts could be wiped away, as one might wipe steam from a mirror. Then they appeared again, those thoughts. Funny how she could read Devlin's shock by the set of his shoulders. Funny how some strands of conversation went on, as if Camilla had unravelled a piece of fabric, leaving only part of the weft exposed.

'Ruinous consequences.'

'Lovely character, though she does *scratch*.'

Then, disbelief: such a thing could not be true, it was not

possible. Camilla must be making fun of Devlin. Devlin must tell everyone that she was fooling around. He must not remain so still and silent.

And yet he did. So it was left to Esme to say, 'You're joking, aren't you, Camilla?' Her words were thin and reedy, and accompanied, as soon as they left her mouth, by the realisation that she had only called attention to herself, and to Camilla.

'It was during the war.' Camilla gave a little shrug: *these things happen.*

Victor de Grey barked, 'What? What is it?'

Denis Rackham gave a snort of laughter. 'I have to hand it to you, Camilla.' He raised his glass in a mock toast. 'You really know how to make a party go with a swing.'

The door opened. The maid came in to announce dinner, saving them. Relief made the guests chatter again as they rose from their seats.

'Can't wait.'

'Ravenous appetite.'

'Looking forward to this for simply weeks, Esme.'

Devlin stepped forward to offer Esme his arm. Look for her mantilla, slung over the sofa, glance at the discarded glasses, scattered about, and the cigarette ends in the ashtrays. Anywhere but at him, as he escorted her out of the great hall.

The dinner had become something to be endured. She did not know how her food would not choke her. As she sat down at the end of the table, her gaze moved back to Camilla. A gloss seemed to have settled over her sister since her marriage to Victor de Grey, and her lovely face had the stillness and opacity of a mask. But then she had never understood Camilla; it was a failing of hers, Esme told herself, that what should have been one of her closest relationships had always been obscure to her. As she turned to her side and struck up a conversation with Conrad Ellison, she was aware of several

130

emotions: confusion and humiliation, yes, but also a sense of having been outplayed.

The evening seemed to retrieve itself, thought Devlin. The food was good and the conversation flowed along well-worn avenues: the servant problem, the inadequacies of the Lloyd George government, the return of the Diaghilev ballet to London. Victor de Grey was sitting on Devlin's right-hand side. De Grey's fury showed in his taciturnity and his drinking, which had brought a flush to his face. Thea Hendricks – seated, poor woman, between de Grey and Denis Rackham – made the conversational effort with de Grey that Devlin had quickly abandoned; he preferred to talk dogs and horses with Grace Fawcett, on his left.

Rackham, vulgar and coarse, ran his vulpine gaze over Mrs Hendricks and Alice West, who was sitting on his other side. Like de Grey, Rackham was drinking steadily, his intoxication showing in his slurred speech and unfocused eyes. Devlin wondered whether Camilla had brought Rackham to Rosindell to taunt him. Or to torment her husband. Both, perhaps.

Alice West, Tom Langdon's fiancée, was a dark, lively, attractive girl. Tom, on the opposite side of the table, was talking volubly and cheerfully. As the roast beef was brought in, Alice pressed her lips to her fingertips and blew him a small, discreet kiss.

To Miss West's other side sat John Fawcett, Devlin's estate manager; next to Fawcett was Mrs Rackham. Did one learn to put up with humiliation, to see it as the price to be paid for having married someone more sexually magnetic than oneself, or did Mrs Rackham give her husband hell in private? Perhaps the Rackhams had an understanding. Devlin's mouth tightened contemptuously.

And so then to Esme, at the opposite end of the table. She was wearing a new frock of a soft, deep greyish-blue and her hair was swept up in a complicated arrangement of plaits. Apart

131

from Grace Fawcett, who was in her forties, she was the only woman in the company not to have bobbed her hair. Modern fashions looked flimsy and insubstantial in the severe architecture of the medieval room. Camilla's pink was reduced to a dirty white and Merline Rackham's yellow frock became an unpleasant ochre. Their fairness was all that the two sisters shared, and even that was in each woman expressed differently, Esme rose-gold in the candlelight, Camilla's beauty cooler, silver-sharp. The candlelight lit up the beads on Camilla's gown with jewelled colours, and for a moment Devlin allowed himself to study the silky fall of her hair, the soft, exquisite sculpture of jaw and cheekbone and the full red curve of her lips. God forgive him, he still remembered the touch of those lips.

Do you remember, Devlin, that you once told me that you were going to rebuild Rosindell for me? He thought he was in love with me at the time.

Had she meant to spoil, to destroy? What had been her motive in speaking so publicly of a relationship long over? Or was it possible that she had intended to amuse, the remark ill-placed, one of those comments one instantly regrets making? It would not have been unreasonable for Camilla to have assumed he had told Esme about their engagement. Damn himself then, for not having done so. He should have told Esme about Camilla on the day he had proposed to her. *By the way, I was engaged to your sister but she broke it off. You don't mind, do you?*

No, not a conversation that would have gone well. After they had married, then. Casually flung into the over-dinner conversation. *Oh, I forgot to mention . . .*

No again. But sometime. Because his disinclination to open up old wounds, his sense of humiliation and his cowardice had resulted in this. Since Camilla had spoken, Esme had refused to meet his eyes, her glance veering away as soon as it threatened to collide with his. Although her guests probably noticed nothing, because she continued smoothly with her duties, overseeing the serving of dinner and the encouraging of quieter

132

souls into the conversation, Devlin knew what Camilla's words had done to her. Her smile never reached her eyes and there was a flatness to her voice. A different sort of woman might have taken her revenge on Camilla in all sorts of ways. *Oh that,* she might have said. *Goodness, I'd forgotten.* But not Esme, and particularly not now.

The first time Devlin had held his newborn daughter in his arms, he had rediscovered joy. The infant's red face had been pleated into lines like an old man's. Her eyes, as dark as sea anemones, had opened and closed, surveying her new world. An arm as fragile and slender as a frond of seaweed in a rock pool had moved languidly, and when Devlin had touched his daughter's palm her miniature, perfect fingers, each with their heartbreakingly tiny shell of a nail, had closed round his fingertip. Tears had sprung to his eyes and he had been overcome by a flood of emotion that had washed away some of the numbness.

From that moment in time, he had had something to lose. He had had purpose, and had thrown himself into his preoccupations with renewed vigour, working long hours at the boatyard and renewing his contact with the architect, Conrad Ellison. Whatever it cost, however long it took, he would rebuild Rosindell, for Zoe and for the future.

But Esme had seemed tired and nervous since the birth, and he bitterly regretted that this evening, in which she had invested so much, had been spoiled for her. He had hoped that as summer came her strength and spirits would return. Something was troubling her, but he did not know how to persuade her to confide in him. Or whether she would want to. So he had let her be, telling himself that he must give her time. Now he asked himself whether that too had been an evasion, like all his other evasions.

Their marriage had been hasty, the union of two dissimilar people who had scarcely known each other at all, his proposal born of guilt and of a need he had not understood at the time to go over the top once again, to throw himself into something, anything.

But Esme had married him for love. And perhaps love, in time, had disappointed. Since their marriage, she had changed. She had lost the schoolgirlish spontaneity that had both charmed and exasperated him. These things were inevitable. People grew up, they altered. But he disliked seeing her unhappy.

The conversation moved on. The Irish question, the rights and wrongs of the partitioning of the island, raged back and forth across the table. Devlin remained aware of Camilla, and of her incandescent beauty. And he remembered her ruthlessness. Chilled, he recalled the ease with which she had put him aside to marry Victor de Grey. He recalled sitting with her in the drawing room of Lady Clare's Belgrave mansion. *To me, a quarrel is a quarrel*, she had told him, *and neither time nor war nor anything else will heal it.*

Music, raucously, from the gramophone in the great hall. The rugs rolled back and the sofas and chairs pushed to the perimeter, and Merline Rackham dancing with Tom, Alice West with Conrad. The hems of the women's frocks flicking out with a kick of the heel or a pirouette, making bright swirls of colour, their long ropes of beads jumping and beating or grabbed by a hand and whirled like a Catherine wheel with a roar of laughter. Camilla's dress, with its miasma of crystal drops, had the curious effect, Esme thought, of dazzling the onlooker, so that it seemed possible to see her sister only as a series of glittering fragments: a white silk ankle beneath a sparkling hem, a shimmering overskirt blurring her slender figure, her peal of laughter echoing to the roof beams.

A change of partners: Tom led Grace Fawcett on to the dance floor. A small, full-busted woman, she shimmied with impressive agility.

My first dance at Rosindell, Esme thought, as Denis Rackham steered her round the room. My first summer dance.

Rackham's heavy-lidded eyes skated over her. 'Didn't know you could have so much fun in the country.'

'We try, you know.'

'You should come up to Town.'

'I'm not sure my galoshes would do for London.'

He gave her a look. *Very funny.* When the dance came to an end, he went outside to smoke and get some air. Rackham smoked Woodbines, Conrad Ellison little black Russian cigars. It was drizzling, and the twin ruby pinpoints showed through the dark and the wet.

Camilla was showing Devlin how to make a White Lady. 'No cocktail glasses, darling? Tumblers it must be, then.' A moan. 'No ice? You really must buy my poor sister a fridge, Devlin. I don't know how you manage without a fridge.'

The sickly sweetness of crème de menthe, the bitterness of Cointreau and the tart tang of lemon juice. 'How Ya Gonna Keep 'Em Down on the Farm' – someone had turned up the volume – and they were dancing again.

It really wasn't so hard to put on a party, Esme thought. You planned a menu, you bought a few ragtime records, and you put to the back of your mind the discovery that your husband had once been in love with your sister. Though the thoughts would keep creeping back. Had Camilla been lying? She liked to stir. But it had the ring of truth. The love affair, if that was what it had been, must have taken place in London during the war.

Suddenly the room was plunged into darkness. A curse, a shriek from one of the female guests, and then Devlin's voice.

'It's all right, it'll just be the damned generator. Esme, would you light the lamps while I go and have a look at it?'

He left the room. The gramophone still blared of Broadway and Paree while they stumbled about. The room came back into focus in stages as the lamps were lit. Victor, sitting stonily next to Mrs Rackham. Alice, wrapping an arm round Tom's waist. The white lilac on the table, the witch marks on the fireplace, the light now softly tawny, and the room, if one ignored the trappings of modern life – the cocktail shaker and gramophone – looking much as it must have done five hundred years ago.

Camilla adjusted the needle on the record and the song started up again. She slid into Denis Rackham's arms. Rackham, who was drunk, pawed her bottom. Camilla rested her chin on his shoulder, yet her eyes were open as they circled. There was a crash as Rackham stumbled against an oil lamp, which smashed to the floor. He seized a jug from the sideboard and flung water on the smouldering oil, then wove across the room and collapsed on to the sofa beside his wife. Conrad Ellison stamped out the flames. There was a scorch mark on the floorboards.

'Denis, you clumsy oaf,' said Camilla.

Later, someone suggested a game of hide and seek. The Fawcetts, pleading an early start the following morning, had left. After the first game, the Hendrickses, too, made leaving noises – the long drive, guests for Sunday lunch, such a super evening. Then they said their goodbyes.

Upstairs, rain beat against the window panes, distorting Esme's image as she looked into the glass. A vase of flowers on a side table appeared grey and crepuscular. The snap of a cigarette lighter somewhere ahead in the matt darkness of the corridors. The creak of a door, then a curse – 'Damn it, my *elbow*' – as Rosindell's hiding places were explored. Dozens of them, of course, cupboards and alcoves and attics and cellars.

Esme sensed, as the game went on, a certain weariness, participation becoming conscientious rather than pleasurable, as if they couldn't let the house get the better of them. Footsteps slowed, there wasn't much talk. Then it was Esme's turn to seek. An oil lamp in her hand, she lifted a curtain here, opened a door there. She had the sense of just missing someone; that someone – she could not tell who – was always a short distance in front of her, one step ahead, darting from room to room as she made her way through the upper storey of the house in a dogged fashion. A door closed, a curtain shivered in the wake of the unknown person's passing. Esme counted off those who were still playing. She had found Tom and Alice, hiding in a wardrobe, and Caroline, not making any effort really, reading a book in the library. Devlin was keeping Victor company in the great hall.

Four left: Conrad, Merline and Denis Rackham, and Camilla. In the kitchen, Mrs Satterley and Sarah were clearing up the last of the dinner things. The agency maid had long since cycled off to Kingswear.

There was a noise from the scullery. When she went into the small room, Esme found that it was empty. The door to the service rooms beyond was ajar. She thought she heard the patter of footsteps, leading her towards the medieval part of the house, but maybe it was the rain. Light footsteps, a woman's, soft, like the rain. She had always disliked these rooms, which were cold and comfortless and let in the weather. This part of the house was decaying, going rotten like a gangrenous limb. She would be glad when Conrad pulled it down.

Rain splashed into the puddles on the floor of the chapel. The stones from the ruined walls had been piled into heaps on the grass outside, like cairns. Devlin had built them. This was what he did when he wasn't working or running the estate: he took down the stones of the old chapel, one at a time, and put them aside to be used in the new house, sometimes working late into the night, through good weather and bad. He was taking apart the old house so that he could build the new Rosindell. Esme had believed that he was doing this for himself, to restore the patrimony of his forefathers, but now she wondered whether she had been wrong. Once, not so long ago, Devlin had intended to rebuild Rosindell for Camilla.

Which meant that he must have wanted to marry her. Esme

dug her fingernails into her palms as she stared out through the rain at the darkened lawn. The quarrel that had taken place at Camilla's engagement party — well, it wasn't too hard if you thought about it to fill in the gaps. Devlin had come back from the war expecting a marriage planned. Or they had fallen out, somehow, while he was away, and he had been trying to retrieve things. Something like that. *Did Camilla put you up to this?* he had asked her that afternoon she had turned up uninvited at Rosindell. And then he had kissed her, a kiss as bitter and malicious as a blow.

A flicker of movement in the shadows on the grass, as if a bird's dark wing was beating through the air, and she saw someone, *something*, running between the chapel and the back door to the lobby. She too ran across the lawn and back inside the house. Footsteps on the staircase above her. This unknown person was teasing her, taunting her. It must be Camilla — who else? — and it became imperative, because of the sickened, angry feeling inside her, that she catch her.

Upstairs, the vase of flowers that she had passed earlier in the game now lay on its side, water trickling to the floor. The window was open and the rain beat in.

She was tired; she wanted it to be over, the night to be over. She closed the window and mopped up the water with her handkerchief. Turning a corner, she saw someone step out of the darkness of an alcove. A sound escaped her throat.

'It's me,' said Conrad. 'Sorry, I didn't mean to scare you.' He came to join her. 'Have you found the others?'

'Tom and Alice and Caroline.' She looked at him; his hair was dry. 'It wasn't you in the chapel, then?'

'Me? No. By the way, Mrs Rackham is in the airing cupboard. Terrific party.'

'Do you think so, Con?'

'In a year or so's time, you'll be entertaining people in my new house.'

'Your house?' she teased him.

'I feel a certain attachment to it. And to the people who'll live in it.' The look he gave her offered a certain solace, because it told her that his loyalties were not only with Devlin.

She smiled. 'Mrs Esme Reddaway, gracious hostess of the summer dance at Rosindell. And a photo of me in my pearls in *Country Life*. Can't you just see it?'

'What is it?' he said gently.

Her smile fell away. 'I was thinking how hard it is to feel truly at home anywhere. Devlin only wants to be here. But I've never felt that I belonged to a place, never.'

'For some people place is unimportant. Perhaps you're happy wherever your friends and family are.'

She headed off in the direction of the airing cupboard. From one of the bedrooms she heard a muffled peal of laughter. The door was slightly ajar; she pushed it open an inch. Camilla and Denis Rackham were lying on the bed. Lamplight gleamed on their sweat-soaked naked bodies. Camilla's platinum-blond hair mingled with Rackham's straw-coloured locks.

Esme stepped back and quietly pulled the door to. She was trembling. Her room was a short distance away; she went inside.

She gasped. The contents of her dressing table had been thrown over the floor. Beads had looped themselves round a chair leg, her bangles had rolled across the rug, and a perfume flask lay on its side, liquid leaking from its open mouth.

Hurriedly, fingers fumbling, she gathered up her jewellery and hairbrushes and replaced bottles and jars on the dressing table. Something was missing: one of the three heavy silver bangles set with semi-precious stones that her father had given her on her last birthday. She knelt on the floorboards, to see whether it had rolled beneath the furniture.

But though she searched thoroughly, there was no sign of it. Leaving the room, she released Merline Rackham from the airing cupboard and accompanied her downstairs. Her voice, light and rushing, chattered of this and that. But she felt cold now, and spent, and as they talked, it came to her that Mrs Rackham *knew*. And it occurred to her that she herself had cause to be thankful that Camilla was wasting her time on a fool like Denis Rackham.

'Was it true?' she said. 'What Camilla said, was it true?'

They were in the bedroom. Their guests had retired for the night and Devlin had closed the door behind them.

'Yes.' He was unknotting his tie.

She sat down on the edge of the bed, dipping her head, exhausted by the evening and its consequences.

He said, 'I should have told you.'

'I suppose,' she said, studying him, 'it slipped your mind.'

'Esme, for God's sake. It was over, long over, and I saw little point in digging it up.'

'How long ago?' When he did not reply, she said angrily, 'Tell me, Devlin.'

She saw his mouth tighten, then he turned away, rolling his tie and putting it in a drawer. 'It was a wartime affair,' he said. 'Very short-lived, only a few days.'

'You wanted to marry Camilla.' Her tone clipped, cold.

'Yes.'

'Did she turn you down?'

He took out his cufflinks, sliding the gold studs through the slits in the cloth. 'No.'

This she tried to absorb, could not; said, 'What happened?'

'Must we—'

'What *happened*?' An upward slide in her voice.

She saw his flare of anger and his struggle to control it. 'I thought we had an understanding. It turned out that I was mistaken. I doubt if Camilla ever took it seriously.'

'But you did.'

Minutes seemed to pass. 'For a while,' he said.

'You were in love with her.' She whispered it. 'Was she in love with you, Devlin?'

A longer pause this time. 'I don't know. I thought so at the time. Looking back – I can't tell.'

Esme rose from the bed and went to the dressing table. Her fingers fumbled, taking out earrings, unclasping her necklace.

She said crisply, 'I think that when you came back to Devon after the war, you thought you were going to marry Camilla. I think that the day you came to our house was the first time you found out about Victor. I think that's what you were quarrelling about, that she had broken off the engagement.'

'It was never an engagement in Camilla's eyes.'

'Perhaps, but it was in yours. So.' She curled the necklace in its red velvet box. 'You asked me to marry you three weeks after that. I'm not sure – I'm not sure why you did that. I mean, I remember what you said to me at the time, that you needed a wife for Rosindell.'

'Esme, I wish you wouldn't do this.'

'But I can't help wondering now – and I've thought about this all evening – whether you married me out of *spite*.'

When he began to speak, she cut him off. 'Whatever you say, I won't know whether to believe you. I want you to tell me only one thing, Devlin. Are you still in love with Camilla?'

'No.' In a few strides he crossed the room to her. 'If I did love her once, then that has changed out of all recognition. Tonight I thought her vulgar and callous. She was trying to cause trouble. Surely you see that?'

Knotting his dressing gown, he left the room. She heard the tread of his feet along the corridor, and the bathroom door closing. She wondered whether she should have told him about Camilla and Denis Rackham, but that would have looked cheap, and she felt cheap enough tonight. Cheap and second-rate. *The second-best sister.*

141

Had he and Camilla been lovers? This she had not been able to bear to ask. They spoke little more before switching off the light. Intimacy – even this hurtful, angry intimacy – was alien to them.

She turned on her side, facing away from him. After a while, she heard the regular rise and fall of his breathing and knew that he slept. Her own mind reeled, revisiting events, making connections. Devlin was a reserved man, hard to reach. *I'm not sure I'm capable of falling in love with anyone any more*, he had said to her on the day he had proposed to her. Because of the war, she had assumed. But perhaps she had been wrong. Perhaps he had not been able to love her because he was still in love with Camilla.

Chapter Eight

June 1920

A mild, cloudy morning, and the water and mudflats of Galmpton Creek were the stern grey of battleships. The tide was out and a narrow stream ran in a sluggish channel through the creek to the river, between fishing smacks and rowboats, some of which had lain there so long they had rotted into the mud. One side of the creek was wooded, and a heron, ancient-eyed and motionless, perched on a branch from which trailed dried lichen-green ribbons of vegetation. Across the river the waterfront of Dittisham huddled in the murk.

The boatyard for sale was to one side of Galmpton Creek. Devlin had inspected the dilapidated sheds and offices and now he stood on the small concrete jetty, thinking. The yard was half a mile from Galmpton village, little more than two miles upriver from Langdon's boatyard at Kingswear. The buildings had a mournful air; the smell of stagnant water and decaying riverweed seemed to be accompanied by the stench of failure and broken dreams. Devlin saw possibilities, though, and a future, and was planning what to say to Charles as he put the car into gear and drove away.

'Never made a penny, Nicholson's,' said Charles, spooning sugar into his coffee. 'Bob Nicholson was a drinker, of course.'

The regular Tuesday morning meeting at the boatyard. Devlin, Charles and Tom, and Mrs Burnside taking the minutes. Mrs Burnside, a widow in her thirties, wore a crisp white blouse and horn-rimmed spectacles and took it upon herself to make fresh coffee and top up the plate of Nice biscuits. Charles put three spoonfuls of sugar into each cup and was looking red and hot.

Devlin said, 'It's a great opportunity. Because of the bankruptcy, we'll be able to get it at a knock-down price.'

Charles mopped his face. 'It's still money, money in a venture we don't need.'

'We do need it. The order books are full to capacity. Tom and I are having to tell prospective clients we can't make a start on their boat for six months minimum. Do that too often and people get impatient and start going somewhere else.'

He looked to Tom for support; Tom nodded and said, 'It's true. Jack Considine was thinking of placing an order with us, but when I told him how long he'd have to wait, he went with Stokes in Brixham.'

'It's a question of planning—'

Devlin interrupted Charles. 'However carefully you plan, there comes a point when you have to acknowledge that you've reached capacity. Langdon's has been at that point for months now.'

Charles snarled and reached for the last biscuit. Mrs Burnside took the plate and left the room. Tom eyed her neat black-stockinged legs.

Devlin said, 'You keep the fishing boats, coasters and some of the yachts here, and then the Galmpton yard will be able to specialise in luxury yachts and motorboats.'

'Luxury yachts?' repeated Charles. 'Motorboats? Who has the money for that sort of nonsense?'

'All the men who made money in the war. All the men who came back from fighting the war and want a bit of distraction. Young men with money to burn and a love of speed.'

144

'Luxury yachts,' muttered Charles. 'Rich men's toys.'

'Yes, if you like. Better they spend their money with us than with someone else. If we snap up this opportunity, we'll make the Galmpton yard known as the first port of call for fast sporting boats.'

Charles's mouth gave the sideways twist that told Devlin he was thinking. Mrs Burnside returned with the coffee pot and another plate of biscuits.

'It's risky,' said Charles eventually.

'It wouldn't be worth doing if it wasn't. But I know it'll work, Charles, and to prove it I'll offer to take my part in the risk. If the new yard loses money, then you can take the losses out of my share of the profits.'

'Rash of you,' Charles muttered, eyeing him craftily. 'I suppose you're assuming I'll give you the run of the new yard.'

The new yard. Devlin knew then that he had won. 'I'd like that,' he said, attempting to assume an expression of modesty.

Charles drained his sixth cup of coffee and rubbed his stomach with the palm of his hand. 'You'd best get me some figures, then, hadn't you?'

Quarter of an hour later, the meeting drew to a close. In the corridor, once his father was out of earshot, Tom muttered to Devlin, 'Thank God that's over. Drink?'

The two men left the boatyard together and walked to the Ship at Kingswear. The pub was full of fishermen and men from the chandlers and boatyards.

Over a pint and a plate of bread and cheese, Tom said bitterly, 'All that bloody performance you have to go through with him whenever you want to do anything. If he'd just once say, well, that's a good idea, instead of making us jump through hoops.'

'It's his money,' Devlin reminded him.

'Yours if you end up having to hand over your shares.'

'There's a chap I knew when I was in the army,' Devlin said. 'Allen's a Scot, an engineer, self-taught, and he knows every damn thing about boats. When things were quiet out there, we used to talk. He had plenty of good ideas for making craft that are sleeker and faster.'

Tom chinked his glass against Devlin's. 'Good luck to you then.'

Get the Galmpton boatyard going, Devlin thought as he drove home that night, make some money out of it, and Rosindell would rise from the ruins. Whenever he imagined the house translated from Conrad Ellison's drawings to reality, he always peopled it with his family. Esme whirling round the rooms, knowing how to put a vase of flowers here, a set of bookshelves there, to make a house look like a home. Zoe lying on a rug in the garden. She was learning to love Rosindell already: the shifting patterns of the clouds, the murmur of the leaves on the trees, the distant hush of the sea.

Camilla and Victor's flat was in Charles Street, in Mayfair. From the drawing room window you could see the tops of the trees in Green Park.

Camilla was wearing a white sailor blouse and a navy blue skirt; beneath the skirt her legs were bare and brown. Around her head was knotted a navy and scarlet silk bandanna. She said, as a red-headed maid let Esme into the flat, 'Frightful mess, you must forgive me. We had a party here last night.'

'I hope you don't mind me turning up.'

'It is rather a surprise. I'm afraid we shall have to keep it short and sweet, because I'm going away.'

'Where to?'

'Deauville. Jane, don't forget my pills, I have the most fearful headache.'

'Are you unwell?'

'No, not at all. I didn't think you came to Town.'

'Devlin has some business in London. And Zoe must have new clothes.'

'Would you like a drink?'

'Tea, please.'

Camilla gave a croak of laughter. 'Very proper. Tea it is. Excuse me a moment.'

There were four marble pillars in the drawing room, two standing to either side of the fireplace, which gave it a Grecian appearance, as though, Esme thought somewhat hysterically, one had accidentally turned up to have tea at the Acropolis. The walls were painted cream, bisected by a black stripe at waist height, and the chairs were also upholstered in cream and black. A Baedeker and a map, clumsily folded, lay on the sofa, along with a cigarette case, a lighter, and a jar of face cream, the lid missing. A dozen gramophone records, some out of their paper sleeves, had strewn a trail across the carpet. Someone – Camilla presumably – had tried several times to write a letter, because half a dozen crumpled paper balls spilled from the fireplace.

Above the mantelpiece and on the far wall of the room were two large, colourful abstract paintings, on which various elements – a horse, a wall, an arm, a tiled roof – floated about in a dreamlike fashion.

'Do you like my Kandinskys?' asked Camilla, returning.

'Wonderful.' Though they had a nightmarish cast, Esme thought, as if the artist knew what it was like to have his life unravel into its disconnected components.

'Victor loathes them,' said Camilla. 'So I'd keep them even if I hated them.'

The telephone rang. Camilla picked up the receiver. 'Mayfair 475.' A crackle. Then, 'Darling!' And, 'I'm afraid I can't. Frightfully sorry. So ridiculously busy.' As she was talking, she stuck a small black cigarette into her mouth and flicked a gold lighter. A woman wearing a white overall came in with a tray of tea things, which she placed on a low table, then left the room.

Camilla put the receiver back on the stand. 'Smoke?' She waved her cigarette case at Esme.

'No thanks.'

'Does Devlin know you're here?'

'No. He's meeting someone. I told him I was shopping.'

Camilla's eyes narrowed. 'Why have you come?'

'I wanted to ask you about Devlin. About your engagement.'

There, it was out, but before Camilla could say anything the red-haired maid came back into the room with two dresses draped over her forearm.

'The pink or the green, madam?'

While Camilla pursed her lips and made up her mind, Esme thought how thin and humiliating her last phrases had sounded. She should never have come here. She was abasing herself.

'The green,' said Camilla. When the maid had gone, she said, 'It was never much of an engagement.'

'A wartime fling, Devlin said.'

'Did he?' Camilla, pouring tea, studied Esme. 'Interesting.'

It was funny how one had to go on scratching at a sore point, digging deeper and deeper into the flesh. No, on second thoughts, not funny at all.

'Were you in love with him?'

Camilla passed Esme a cup of tea. 'I don't know.'

'You must do.'

Camilla's brow creased. 'I've often thought I was in love. But it always passes.'

'Does it? Not in my experience.' Esme regretted the words as soon as they left her mouth. Their ferocity gave her away.

But Camilla said lightly, 'I expect you think I'm cold and unfeeling. But I'm telling you the truth.'

The telephone rang again. This time it must be Camilla's dressmaker: a discussion about a shade of fabric no longer available, a touch of irritation about a blouse not yet finished.

When the call was done, Camilla said, 'I thought I was in love with him. But then I thought I was in love with Victor, God help me.'

A lowering of Esme's heart, like a lift plummeting too fast down a shaft. 'Devlin told me that it was you who finished it, not him.'

'Yes, that's true. Do you want one of these wretched cakes? I can't face them myself.'

'No thank you.'

'I don't suppose Devlin would have broken it off, no matter how much he hated me. He has his old-fashioned side, doesn't he? Too much the gentleman to jilt a woman.'

'There's nothing wrong with loyalty.'

Camilla sat back in the seat, frowning, her legs crossed. 'One chooses one's loyalties, doesn't one? Stick by one man and you end up fibbing to another.'

'You must have a very complicated life, Camilla.'

'I suppose I do. It stops me being bored. You see, the truth is I can stand anything but boredom.'

'Denis Rackham . . .'

'Is a fool. I shouldn't have brought him to Rosindell. I was angry with Victor, that's why I did it.'

'You're not in love with him?'

'No, of course not.' Camilla sounded scathing. 'Denis is fun, and he's good in bed, that's all.' Her gaze settled on Esme. 'If you've come here because you're thinking that I'm somehow hankering after Devlin, then you're absolutely wrong. Did he tell you that I asked him whether he loved me enough to give up his precious Rosindell? Did he tell you that?'

'No,' she whispered. 'What did he say?'

'Nothing.' Camilla laughed. 'He said nothing. Which told me everything.'

The doorbell rang. Esme swallowed a mouthful of tea as the maid answered it. There was a murmur of voices, then

149

the maid came into the drawing room carrying a large bouquet of roses.

'Good Lord,' drawled Camilla. 'Who are they from?'

The maid read the card. 'Lord Berners, madam. I'll put them in a vase.'

When they were alone again, Camilla, eyes narrowed, said, 'What is it?'

'You didn't love him. If you'd loved Devlin, truly loved him, you'd never have asked him to give up Rosindell.'

Camilla's mouth tightened. Slowly, deliberately, she lit another cigarette, inhaled, then let out a stream of smoke.

'When I love,' she said softly, as a small smile played round her lips, 'I want *everything*. I don't want half measures and I won't be second best. When I love, I want power and magnificence; I want – I want that *moment*, that moment of forgetting everything, of ecstasy. Of being *consumed*.'

Esme said, rather shakily, 'That isn't *love*. Is that what you think love is? How mistaken you are.' She stood up. 'I should go.'

The maid was summoned to help her into her linen coat. Camilla's voice followed her into the hallway.

'You should ask yourself why he married you. What he got out of it. And I don't mean this pallid, humdrum passion you seem willing to settle for. Go on, Esme. Ask him.'

Esme and Devlin had an early supper in a Lyons Corner House, then he saw her to Paddington station. 'You look pale,' he said, and she smiled and said that it was the heat.

'It'll be cooler once you're back by the coast.'

'Yes, of course.'

It was crowded at the station, men in striped trousers, black coats and bowler hats running purposefully for their trains. One knocked against Esme as he pushed through. 'Look out,' said Devlin sharply, and the man muttered a quick apology and

150

then ran on. Devlin put an arm round Esme's shoulders, steering her through the crowds to the first-class carriages. They found her seat; in the corridor he kissed her cheek and asked her to kiss Zoe from him, and then they said goodbye.

The carriage was empty except for an older, grey-haired woman who sat down in a corner seat as the train pulled out of the station, dabbing at her cheeks with a handkerchief. Esme wondered whether she should ask her whether she was all right, or offer her a piece of the chocolate bar Devlin had bought for her, or fetch a brandy from the buffet. But the woman turned so resolutely away, in such an obvious plea for privacy, that Esme said nothing and opened her book and pretended to read.

You should ask yourself why he married you. What he got out of it.

Camilla's words remained with her, corrosive and poisonous, as the train chugged through the London suburbs. She too could have cried, filled with a rising terror, because she understood what Camilla had meant. You married for love or you married for money. She had married for love, but Devlin had married for money. In marrying her, he had acquired enough money to secure Rosindell's future.

But he was a good man, she knew that, and a part of her rebelled at drawing this conclusion. He must have had other reasons.

And yet her own heart filled in the gaps. Devlin had married her because he had needed some woman, any woman, to replace the void left by Camilla. He had married her because he could not have Camilla, the only woman he had ever loved.

Covertly Esme's gaze returned to the passenger sitting in the corner seat. Did she weep, perhaps, because she was unhappily married? Because, years ago, she had settled for a pallid, humdrum passion? Or did she mourn a lost love, or someone soon to be lost, sick in hospital?

151

She felt unable to hold on to the disparate parts of her life – child, home and husband: all seemed about to fly out of her hands. The train whistle screamed. She would have liked to scream along with it, a howl of despair.

It was a dull, cool summer, a summer of rioting in Ulster, and in Kingswear the summer of the new boatyard. The sale went through at the beginning of August, and Devlin, Charles and Tom celebrated with a glass of whisky in Charles's office. The following Monday, labourers began to pull down the ramshackle sheds and to repair those parts of the yard worth preserving. There was to be a timber store, a machine room, a metal shop, a drawing office and a shed for commissioning the engines, as well as offices for Devlin, his marine engineer, bookkeeper and secretary. The slipway and dry dock were cleared of seaweed and broken branches and a new petrol generator was installed.

He had the yard up and running a fortnight later. They were still constructing the new sheds, so they all had to squeeze into one of the existing buildings, but he knew there was no time to waste. Meeting up with old army friends in London, he had secured orders for a luxury yacht and a speedboat. His chief draughtsman was a talented young fellow whom he had promoted from assistant draughtsman at the Kingswear yard and taken with him, along with the clerk, Alfred Petherick. The carpenters, machinist and bookkeeper had been recruited locally. His marine engineer, Murray Allen, had moved from Glasgow to a house on the outskirts of Kingswear, and was impatient to start work. Allen was an odd, taciturn man who appeared to need few friends, and who answered questions with a brusque economy that bordered on rudeness. But he was a brilliant engineer, with a sharp, creative mind, so Devlin didn't care if he ruffled a few feathers.

It was also the summer they began to build the new Rosindell. Devlin knew it was risky to make a start before the Galmpton yard was yet in profit. But he also knew that he needed to act, to demonstrate belief. Sometimes he woke during the night, oppressed by the thought that if the new yard did not succeed, he would have to forfeit to Charles his share in the profits of the company, at the same time as paying off the loans he had taken out for the rebuilding of the house.

They cleared the land, felling trees and digging trenches for the foundations. Devlin kept his nerve when the excavations brought to light the unexpected. A scattering of Roman potsherds. The fragile skeleton of a cat, wrapped in a disintegrating cloth shroud.

An underground stream filled the trenches with water overnight. A pump had to be brought in and an engineer consulted and the route of the stream diverted, adding to the cost of the project. A labourer slipped in the muddy morass and broke his leg and had to be taken off to the cottage hospital in Dartmouth.

He was doing it for Rosindell, and for the future. He was doing it for Zoe, because it was her inheritance.

This was the summer his daughter learned to crawl, her padded, frilly-knickered bottom bobbing in the air as she chased after a bee or a butterfly on the lawn. He took her down to the cove and sat her on the sand in the shade of the cliff, and together they watched the waves creep in and out. She had a round face and round eyes and fine black hair that curled in a question mark over her forehead and a way of looking seriously at the world that to him was surprising in a baby. So he explained things to her, and she looked at him solemnly, dissolving into chortles when he waved his head from side to side or pretended to nibble at the folds of fat beneath her chin.

The last day of August. The summer had grown tired and stale; they longed for the freshness of autumn.

They were at dinner. Esme had dismissed Sarah, telling her that they would take their coffee in the garden.

Devlin said, 'I'm going to tell the men to start taking down the chapel next week. I hope the work won't be too disruptive to you.'

Esme poured cream on her pudding. 'I'll be glad when those rooms have gone. I feel it most there.'

'Feel what?'

'A coldness.'

'If my father had acted when the structure first began to fail—'

She went on as if he had not spoken. 'An unfriendliness. Hostility – that's not too strong a word; yes, hostility.'

She lowered her head, dug her spoon into pastry. She had pinned her hair into a complicated knot at the back of her head, looping in buttery coils to either side of her face, shutting him off so that he could not see her expression.

'Hostility?' he repeated. 'In the chapel?'

She gave a little sigh. 'Yes, Devlin.'

'You feel the place is in some way hostile – to everyone . . . or to you in particular?'

'To me, certainly. To other people – I don't know, how could I?'

'Esme, that's ridiculous. You must know that.'

'I've often felt it,' she said obstinately. 'I can't believe you haven't.'

'I haven't, because it doesn't exist.' Devlin made an effort to take the heat out of his voice. 'Those rooms are cold and miserable, yes, it's true, but that's because of their ruinous state. Not because of' – he paused, not liking to express what she seemed to be hinting at – 'not because of anything supernatural.'

But he saw in her eyes a glitter, of triumph perhaps, and he regretted saying the word.

'You see,' she said, 'you *do* know. When I first came here, Josiah told me that Rosindell was an unlucky house.'

'Josiah talks a lot of nonsense. His purpose in life is to pass on as many dismal superstitions as possible. You shouldn't listen to him.'

154

'I listen to my heart,' she said softly.

'To assign emotion – feeling – to a house—'

'Have you never thought a place felt – oh, *sad*, or unhappy? Honestly, Devlin?'

He found himself recalling the battlefields of Flanders, the horror that even now on this mild summer's evening made his skin ice with cold sweat; trenches built from blood and bone and suffering.

He shut the thought away. 'If we know that terrible events have taken place, then it's natural to credit a place with some sort of – memory, I suppose.'

Esme leaned forward, eyes burning. 'Yes, that's what I meant – a memory. Perhaps something happened here, something bad.'

'Scratch away at the history of any house of Rosindell's age and you'll find tragedies and losses. They don't mean anything. If you searched through the records in the library you'd doubtless find a trail of accidents and illnesses and bankruptcies. The misfortune is to be found in the people, not the house.'

'So practical, Devlin.' There was mockery in her tone. She replaced her spoon in the bowl. There was a gleam of sweat on her upper lip.

'Rational, I would say.'

'Can't you see how a house might shape the lives of the people inside it?'

'Esme,' he said impatiently, 'what are you saying – that you dislike Rosindell?'

Her head bowed. 'Sometimes I love it,' she murmured. 'Sometimes I think it's the most magical place in the world. But at other times, when everything seems to go wrong for me, I wonder if it's like blotting a piece of writing. An impression is left on the blotting paper. Perhaps you can't read it, or even understand it, but it's there, ineradicable, poisonous.'

'That's ludicrous,' he said angrily. 'Unscientific. Juvenile.'

155

Her expression changed. 'Science can't explain everything.'

'Common sense should tell you that what you are describing is impossible.'

'Whose common sense, Devlin? Yours or mine? You don't see everything clearly, you know. You don't understand *everything*.'

When he had married her, he had thought her a gentle, biddable girl. But increasingly these past few months she had seemed to take pleasure in challenging him. More than that, he sensed that her words were underpinned by resentment, and that she was referring to something other than the phantoms she seemed to think stalked Rosindell.

'I've never claimed to,' he said coldly. 'But I refuse to give in to irrationality. You're tired, that's all. This weather.'

She stood up, folded her napkin, put it down on the table. Her eyes studied him, wounded and wondering.

'The trouble is,' she said, and now he found himself disliking the fact that her voice had taken on a hard, cynical tone, 'that I don't know what to believe. You say that you've never seen anything here, but how can I know whether you're telling me the truth? There's so much you don't say, Devlin. I try to work out what you want, what you think, but I expect I get it wrong most of the time. You know nothing of what lies in my heart and I know nothing of what lies in yours. But the difference between us is that I *want* to know.'

'No, you don't.' Now his anger returned, hot and unforgiving. 'You might think you do, but you don't. Shall I tell you what I see at night? Shall I tell you about *my* nightmares? Shall I tell you about the friend who took three days to die, impaled on barbed wire, weeping for his mother? Or the men blown to pieces, like joints in a butcher's shop?'

She gave a small gasp, then pressed her hands against her mouth. He said, 'Sorry. I'm so sorry,' and walked out of the room.

Chapter Nine

September 1920

Sunlight streaked the bay with silver and, as the tide pulled in and out, lit up the sugary pink stones. In the fields, the stubble gave way to the plough, brown ribbons of earth turning in the wake of the horses. They took the old chapel apart stone by stone, stacking the shales aside for use in the new building. Now, where high walls had once stood, you could see from the drive to the lawns and trees behind the house. As the room was dismantled, Esme felt as though something was being revealed, put up to the scrutiny of the light.

At the end of September, the fine weather broke. Outside, the rain, scarcely more than low cloud, hazed the garden in a watery grey film and blurred the outlines of the pines on the cliff.

Coming downstairs from the nursery in the early evening, Esme heard the rumble of a motor car. From the shelter of the entrance she saw Tom's Crossley heading towards the house. She came out into the rain as he parked in the courtyard.

'Tom! I wasn't expecting you. What a treat.'

Tom closed the car door behind him. 'Is Devlin home?'

'Not yet. Come in, out of the rain.'

He followed her into the house, slinging his mackintosh on to a chair. In the great hall she said, 'Would you like a drink?'

'Could do with one.' Grimly.

'Are you all right?'

'I'm fine. Tears and lamentations in the parental home, though.'

He had the privately gleeful look of someone who bore interesting bad news. Esme handed him a martini.

'What's happened?'

'Victor's thrown Camilla out.'

Big slug of gin, dash of martini, blob of tonic. Then she sat down.

'Thrown her out?'

'Yes.' Tom swallowed his drink, two mouthfuls, glass almost empty.

'A quarrel — they'll make it up.'

'Camilla doesn't think so.'

'Have you seen her?'

'She's at home. Only for tonight; she's heading off first thing tomorrow. Some place in Cornwall.'

'I'll get you another one.' Esme took his glass, went to the sideboard, said, 'Mummy . . .'

'Is hysterical. Weeping and wailing. Bit of a shock, her blue-eyed girl. Alice is with her. Couldn't bear it myself, so I had to get out. There were some papers to do with the Nicholson's sale, so I grabbed them and came over here.'

The shock of it seemed to pulse through her, hard and obdurate, as if she were swimming against a current. She said, 'Do you think I could have a cigarette?'

He held out his case to her, cocking an eyebrow. 'I didn't think you smoked. I've always assumed Devlin to be the sort of man who doesn't approve of women smoking.'

'Devlin isn't here.' A vision of Camilla sitting in this room smoking pink cigarettes came to her. 'Tell me everything she said.'

'That Victor wants a divorce.'

158

'A *divorce?*'

'Apparently he's spoken to his lawyers already. And get this, Esme, Camilla *wants* to divorce him.'

She stared at him. 'I don't understand. Why would she want that?'

'She says she wants to be free again.'

'Free?' A jangling of emotions, fear and jealousy uppermost. 'Why?'

Tom shrugged, turning down the corners of his mouth. 'God knows. Hey, cheer up, old thing, it'll all blow over eventually.'

'Is she upset?'

'Camilla? Angry, more like. She's furious with Victor because of the flat. As I understand it, he chucked her out *bodily*.'

'Where will she go?'

'A friend's house, she says.' Tom swallowed a mouthful of gin. 'You know Camilla, she won't do badly out of it, she never does.' He laughed. 'I always thought I'd be the one to bring disgrace to the Langdon name.' His smile faded and he puffed up his cheeks, blowing out air. 'But you remember how they were when they were here, Camilla and Rackham. Victor has grounds, you know.'

Tom left shortly afterwards. Esme put the dirty glasses on the tray and the bottles of gin and martini back in the sideboard. She went to the window and looked up the drive. Then she glanced at her watch. Half past six. She climbed the stairs to the bedroom to dress for dinner. Her reflection gazed back at her from the dressing table mirror, white and hollow-eyed. Her hair was a mess; she took it down, then put it up again, concentrating on pressing the pins in deep enough to hold it in place. One of them jabbed her scalp and she took an inward breath and closed her eyes. Camilla had left Victor. Camilla was free. Camilla wanted to be free.

Five minutes to seven. She looked out of the window again.

The drive and the courtyard were still empty. Might Devlin have gone to see Camilla? Invented some excuse, hopped on the ferry or taken the launch and gone to Dartmouth? She stared at the frocks in the wardrobe, took out a leaf-green silk and changed into it. Then she went to the nursery.

Zoe was asleep in her cot. Esme pressed a kiss on the child's pillowy cheek and thought how beautiful she was, so beautiful and so entirely unknowable to her, just like Devlin. What a fool she had been to think she might help Devlin, or look after him, or *heal* him. Such a fool.

She went downstairs. Sarah was clearing away the glasses from the great hall. Esme said, 'Mr Reddaway is going to be late. Would you please tell Mrs Satterley to keep his food warm.'

'Shall I serve your dinner now, madam?'

'No thank you.'

She felt as confused and displaced as she had the first time she had come to Rosindell, when, finding the house deserted, she had fallen asleep on the sofa. She murmured, 'I think I'll go out for a walk.'

She went outside. The fine drizzle beaded the oiled cloth of her raincoat. Mr Philips was working on the kitchen garden. She raised a hand to acknowledge him. The stream had thickened after a day of rain, and now, brown and knotty, rushed between the stones and clumps of iris leaves.

To one side of her lay the cleared land. Trees had been torn from the earth, their writhing roots exposed and clogged with mud. Devlin drove the restoration of Rosindell with such urgency. His love for Rosindell made him overlook the house's flaws and secrets; it occupied his waking hours and absorbed his energy. Such a strange, obsessive love, grown out of absence, neglect and war. And desire. Perhaps, whenever he looked at the house, he saw Camilla.

Down the combe and into the shrubbery of rhododendron, laurel and azalea. Raindrops gathered on the dark, leathery leaves, showering her as she brushed against the branches. Her evening pumps, soaked now, made impressions in the dark, fibrous soil. As she approached the gate, an owl loomed, its eyes jewelled circles, before it dipped its wings and flew away.

Now she was taking the path through the oaks and birches and the wet vegetation was brushing against the hem of her long skirt. Already she could smell the resinous scent of the pines and hear the hush and murmur of the sea. When she had come here earlier in the summer, the wild roses had been in bloom. Pines, salt water and roses: those were the perfumes of Rosindell.

She recalled the day after her wedding, the cliff edge so masked then by fog and vegetation that she had hardly known she had reached it until she was at the precipice. This was what she had always sensed at Rosindell, that behind the beauty lay precariousness and unpredictability. A feral cat, spitting in the dark. The play of shadows in the night.

Looking down, she saw that the tide was in and waves were slapping against the cliff, spraying arcs of white foam. The cliffs cast their deep shadow and the sea in its constant movement now and then revealed the sharply pointed rocks. She took a step forward, then another. One more step and her foot would teeter on the edge. Would the cliff hold her, or would it crumble and collapse? She pictured herself tumbling down to the cove, caught for a moment or two on the thorns of a gorse bush, but then slipping and sliding on the scree, her hands grabbing for something to hold on to but finding nothing. And then the cold, dark water closing over her head, numbing the pain, quietening her breath.

Her marriage had taught her that she did not love easily. Rosindell's isolation meant that she had often had to fall back on her own company, and really, she had not minded. She could not have said she loved her own sister – indeed, she felt for Camilla now only fear and dislike. She loved Tom, she loved her parents, and her few friends were much beloved and carefully chosen. But she would rather be alone than in the company of those she found grating or foolish.

But when she did love, it was with intensity and purpose and fire. Her love could not lightly be withdrawn or made to change direction. That Devlin did not love her she had thought she could live with. She had thought, even, that she had the better of the bargain, that it was preferable to know love than to feel nothing. Just as she had once believed that she could make do with what he offered her: a home, independence, a position in society. She had believed that to be with him would be enough for her.

Now she knew that she had deceived herself, and that what she had truly hoped was that he would change, and come to love her. Camilla had unearthed her self-deception, exposing it to the daylight. Liking was not enough, and that was all Devlin had to offer. It was impossible to live with such a pallid, humdrum passion. Her love degraded her; it made her abject, grateful for small kindnesses. It made her strip herself of expectation.

She walked back to the house. The sky had darkened, mutinous charcoal clouds rushing over the headland. As she made her way beneath the laurels, fragments of the house could be seen: a wall of grey slate, a clay chimney pot.

Devlin's motor car was in the courtyard. He called out to her.

'Esme, where were you?'

'I went to the cliff.'

'You're soaked.'

'Am I?' She looked down at herself. Her coat was darkened by the rain, her shoes wet and filthy.

'Come indoors.'

She said, 'Tom came.'

He looked at her, frowned, then said, 'Did he tell you about Camilla?'

'You knew?'

'I was at the Kingswear yard this afternoon. There was a telephone call – your father went home.'

She found herself lost in his eyes, dark and limitless and untranslatable. She said, 'Have you seen her?'

'Who? Camilla? No, of course not.'

'I should change my shoes.'

She went upstairs. In the bedroom, she stripped off her stockings, dried her feet and put on fresh stockings and a pair of sandals. She was unable to stop shivering. She slipped a cardigan over her dress and stood at the window for a while, watching the rain lash the glass. She wondered whether he was telling her the truth. Even if he was, he might lie to her in the future. And knowing that, she would feel whenever she looked at him, whenever he spoke to her, the same sick, angry dread.

In the morning, after Devlin had gone to work, Esme went to the nursery and told Miss Tapp to pack a case for herself and Zoe. There were questions in Jessie's eyes, but Esme did not answer them. In the bedroom, she packed her own case, the small leather suitcase she had taken to Rosindell on the day of her wedding. As she folded skirts and blouses, she felt as if she was putting away the flimsy remnants of her marriage.

She went outside to tell Josiah to ready the pony and trap. By the time she returned to the house, Jessie was waiting in the hall with Zoe. As Josiah clicked his tongue and the horse started up the drive, Esme found herself remembering the first time Devlin had driven her away from Rosindell, after the night of the storm. His strong brown hands controlling the reins, the breeze ruffling his black hair. The gentle blue of the sky, and the elation she had felt, sitting beside him as the trap rattled over the ruts.

Now, leaving all that behind her, she was raw with a sense of failure and hollowed out by despair. As they reached the curve in the drive, she looked back at the house. Rosindell shimmered in the rain, insubstantial and secretive. Esme shivered and then turned away, fixing her eyes on the road ahead.

Devlin had a long lunch with a man named Gillis Johnson, who owned a timber yard in Exmouth. Johnson was hoping to persuade Langdon's to buy their timber from him. On the drive home, Devlin ran through in his mind the pros and cons: Johnson's certainty that he could shave at least five per cent from their bills; the impossibility of persuading his father-in-law to cut loose from their present suppliers, Babbage's — Arnold Babbage was an old crony of Charles's; the likelihood or otherwise of Charles agreeing to him purchasing the Galmpton yard's timber independently.

The rainstorm intensified, and as he plunged deeper into the countryside, into narrow, high-banked lanes, he had to put aside his preoccupations and concentrate on the road. Water rushed down the gullies and deep puddles filled the potholes, and some of the time Devlin was driving blind.

It was a relief to find himself passing through Lethwiston and between the gates of Rosindell. As he parked the car in the courtyard, he scanned the garden out of habit — but of course, in this weather, Esme must be indoors. In the hall, he hung up his coat and hat. There was — he felt it straight away — a difference. Stillness and silence, reminding him uncomfortably of the months that had immediately followed the end of the war. He looked into the great hall, but Esme was not there. He went upstairs, but the bedroom, too, was empty. The nursery, then. Here, the silence felt ominous, and it occurred to him with terrifying clarity that Zoe might have been taken ill, that Esme and Jessie Tapp might be enduring some awful vigil in a hospital ward.

He went back to the bedroom. This time, he saw it straight away, the white envelope on the dressing table. He ripped it open, took out the single piece of paper and scanned Esme's handwriting.

She had left him. He sat down on the edge of the bed, winded, fighting for air. She had taken the baby and the nanny and had gone to her parents' house in Dartmouth.

No. He opened the wardrobe doors. Many of her clothes were gone, the hangers empty. The dressing table had been swept clean of her small collection of cosmetics.

Devlin left the room. In the hall, he had taken his coat and hat from the stand before he paused. He recalled their quarrels and her unhappiness these past months. Now he bitterly regretted his preoccupation with the boatyard and the house. He had driven her away, and if he tore over to Dartmouth now he was afraid that she would refuse to see him.

He poured himself a large measure of whisky. The house seemed deserted – where were the bloody servants? He remembered Esme mentioning something about Sarah taking a couple of days off to look after her mother, but this memory, of Esme sitting across the dining table from him, talking about ordinary things, seared him. What if she never came home? Sorrow washed over him and he knocked back his drink to deaden the pain.

The distant rumble of a car engine made him rise and go to the window and look out. She had changed her mind – Tom or Charles must have driven her home.

He did not recognise the vehicle that was coming to a halt in the courtyard: a small, sporty model, pale blue, something French and flashy. He muttered a curse under his breath, put down his glass and went outside.

He thought: a friend, a client, and had mentally composed the excuses he would make to put them off and send them on their way when he glimpsed, through the windscreen of the motor car, Camilla's pale blond head.

He crossed the courtyard, opened the driver's door. 'Esme isn't here,' he said curtly.

'I know,' said Camilla. 'The maid at home told me.'

'What are you doing here?'

'I came to see if you were all right. May I come in, Devlin?'

It was on the tip of his tongue to refuse her, but he saw how churlish that would be, so he said reluctantly, 'Yes, of course.'

Inside the great hall, her gaze fell on the glass on the table. 'May I have one of those?'

He poured her a whisky. She said, 'Thank you, darling. I could do with this.'

She was wearing a black dress of some fine, clingy fabric that moulded to her body. Her hair was combed smooth and tucked behind her ears and she didn't appear to be wearing any make-up. Her only jewellery was a brooch in the shape of a dragonfly, flashing with emeralds, pinned to the collar of her dress.

She took a mouthful of whisky and momentarily closed her eyes. 'What a ghastly couple of days!'

'She left a letter for me. A *letter.*'

'I'm so sorry, Devlin.' She touched his arm. 'You poor man. At least Victor and I talked face to face.' Her expression changed. 'Not talked. Yelled.'

'What a pair we are,' he said bitterly.

'Both of us, thrown aside. Only I deserve it, but I don't expect you do.'

'Will you go back to Victor?'

'I don't think he'd have me.' Camilla looked down, frowning. 'Have you a ciggie?'

'If you don't mind Navy Cut.'

Camilla let out a little puff of smoke. 'I suppose I married Victor because I was rather tired and fed up and couldn't think what to do with my life. That's not much of a reason, is it? And because he was there and you were not. I'd given up on you. I thought you'd be killed, like so many of my other friends. Of course, to my parents, he was a catch.' She tossed back her hair and smiled. 'Victor has a huge estate in Gloucestershire and a rather lovely flat in Mayfair.'

'You didn't have to go along with it.'

'My mother made it perfectly clear she'd be awfully cross with me if I didn't.' Camilla hunched her shoulders. 'I was a mess after the war, Devlin. I couldn't see straight. I thought I was in love with Victor – such a fool. I regretted my marriage before the honeymoon was even over.' She tapped the cigarette on the edge of an ashtray. 'There are other things I regret,' she added quietly. 'I came here because I wanted to tell you that I'm sorry for the way I behaved when I came here in the spring. I acted appallingly, I know that. My only excuse is that I was very unhappy at the time.'

He saw that her eyes were swimming with tears, which had an odd effect on him, reminding him of the Camilla he had known during the war, the vulnerability he had glimpsed beneath the lovely exterior.

'Water under the bridge,' he found himself saying. 'Forget it. It was a grim evening all round.'

'Then you forgive me?'

'There's nothing to forgive.'

'Thank you, Devlin. I should go. Though perhaps if I might just have one more drink . . .'

He topped up her glass, and Camilla gave a sigh and said, 'Such a wonderful house!'

'I thought you hated it.'

'I hated the idea of it, Devlin. I thought, oh, I don't know, drains and no hot baths.' She gave him a brilliant smile. 'As soon as I saw it, I could see why you loved it. And why it means so much to you.'

He went to the window. 'If you stand here, you should be able to see the site where the new wing will go.'

She stood in front of him, peered, and said, 'I can't see a damn thing, darling.'

'Down there.' He put a hand on her shoulder, guiding her, and she craned her head round. He could smell her scent, exotic and heady, and it instantly took him back to the night-club where they had danced during the war – her white satin dress, her little fur stole.

She said, 'I'd love to have a proper look at it.'

'It's pouring.'

'I'm sure it's easing off. Anyway, a little rain won't hurt us.'

They put on their mackintoshes, Devlin found an umbrella and they went outside. Camilla was right, the rain was easing off, though the ground was sodden. Beneath the umbrella, her hand curled round his arm. Through the scents of roses and greenery and wet earth there remained her perfume, underpinning the air like a bass line in music. Beads of water nestled like diamonds in the hollows of the leaves or refracted rainbow colours as a watery sun emerged from between the clouds. Rosindell had washed itself clean, bright and vivid and glorious, and as they walked side by side through the grounds, it came to Devlin that the house had never looked more beautiful.

At the site, sunlight gleamed on the water in the trenches. As he described the layout of the new building to Camilla, he could almost see it rising before him, Rosindell reborn.

'Greenwell was such a stuffy house,' she said. 'Like a mausoleum.'

They walked back through the garden. Rainwater ran off the slopes in a silvery course, and the pinks and blues of lupin and delphinium hazed like an impressionist painting. Camilla's hand rested on his arm as they set off down the grassy paths.

She peered into the decaying summer house. 'Too sweet . . . such a divine little place.'

Yet he sensed her words to be mechanical, said but not felt, and he knew that he too was giving their conversation only a fraction of his concentration, and that the pressure of her hand on his arm and a drop of rain sliding down the nape of her neck occupied him far more.

They reached the stables. 'Let's have a look,' said Camilla. 'I adore horses.'

Only one of the stalls was occupied, by the black stallion. Josiah must have driven Esme and Zoe from Rosindell in the pony and trap. Devlin's desolation returned, black and consuming.

Camilla said, 'What is it?'

'Nothing. Have you seen enough?'

'Don't rush me, Devlin. I adore the smell of stables, don't you? What's in here?'

'The tack room, that's all.'

But she had pushed open the door and gone inside. This was Josiah's sanctuary. An old chair stood on a rag rug, a jerrycan was beside a spirit burner. A tin of tobacco lay on the windowsill, a box of matches on top of it. It was warm in the room, which smelled of straw and leather and tobacco smoke.

'Camilla,' he said impatiently.

'I'm going to say it.'

'Say what?'

'That I regret not marrying you, Devlin.' She raised her chin defiantly. 'There, I shouldn't, but you should know, I regret it so much. I don't think you'd believe how absolutely awful my marriage has been! I know that everyone will blame me, because they all think Victor is such a kind, decent man, but he isn't at all like that in private, oh no!'

'Camilla, don't distress yourself. What are you saying?'

'No, I can't tell you!' She covered her face with her hands. 'I'm so ashamed! The things he made me do – dreadful things – I can never speak of them!' Her hands fell away; she looked up at him. 'I've never felt so lonely. Never, in all my life! Hold me, Devlin, please!'

He wrapped his arms round her, murmuring to her, despising

the brutish Victor de Grey. Tears glittered on her eyelids, and she rested her face on his shoulder.

She looked up. 'Oh Devlin . . .' she murmured. Her hands clasped round the back of his neck, locking them together, and then her mouth brushed against his. Her lips parted and her tongue flickered as she pressed herself against him. He felt the firm roundness of her breasts and the curve of her hipbones, and desire rose in him and he drew his hand down the small, knobbly bones of her spine and felt her hard muscles, that danced with her movements.

'Camilla,' he said, and took a step back.

She tugged her dress over her head; it fluttered, black and limp, to the floor. She was wearing silk underwear the colour of pearls, the colour of her skin. She began to undo the buttons of his shirt, forcing them through the cloth. He groaned and pulled her to him, reaching beneath the hem of her underskirt.

And then they were lying on the rug and she was naked, and he was tasting her cool, perfumed body. His hand ran up her inner thigh and she parted her legs for him. When he was inside her, they moved together, in rhythm with each other, until he heard her scream of pleasure.

They lay still. Skin clung to skin, hot with perspiration, and he felt the pounding of her heart.

'Yes,' she murmured. She let out a long breath. 'Oh yes, I needed that.'

'Camilla.' He heard himself whisper her name. In the dreamy pleasure of release, he closed his eyes. She made a small, satisfied noise and then wriggled from his grasp and knelt up.

He said, 'What are you doing?'

'Dressing.'

'Come back.' He held out his arms to her.

'I can't, I have to get on, I'm afraid, darling.' She was tidying her hair. 'I'm meeting someone. But you must give me a ring whenever you are in Town. I'm keeping the London flat. I'll

170

make Victor's life a misery if he tries to be difficult. I could tell you some things about the de Greys.' She smiled. 'All families have their secrets, don't they?'

'Don't go, Camilla.'

'I must, darling.' She dropped her petticoat over her head.

He felt ridiculous, half clothed on the tack room floor. He too began to dress. He said, 'We have to talk.'

She looked up. 'About what?'

'Us. This.'

'Us?' She laughed. 'Don't be silly, Devlin, there is no us.'

'I realise that in my position—'

'I meant, I shall have to go away, you must see that.' She gathered up a stocking, perched on Josiah's chair, and rolled it on.

'Go away?'

'Victor means to divorce me. I won't be humiliated. I won't endure public exposure.'

'I understand that. But—'

Her hand stilled, sliding on the other stocking. Her gaze settled on him and she frowned.

'Devlin, it was fun. Don't spoil it.'

As he stared at her, another emotion, far harder to bear than ridiculousness, began to encroach. He said slowly, 'Fun . . . And Esme? Was it fun for her?'

The frown sharpened. 'It will make no difference to her.'

'Really? What we've just done, you really think it will make no difference?'

'So long as you're sensible, she won't have a clue. Esme only ever sees what she wants to see.' Her tone was clipped and businesslike.

Esme only ever sees what she wants to see. With those words, desire was obliterated as quickly as it had burned into life. Following in its footsteps came remorse, along with a terrible awareness that what had happened was unalterable, that he could not go

171

back, and that what had just taken place had the capacity to haunt him for the rest of his life.

He said slowly, 'My God, you are a bitch.'

She gave him an angry look. 'Better a bitch than a fool.'

His fingers were clumsy, buttoning his shirt. 'Why did you come here, Camilla?'

'For heaven's sake, Devlin,' she said crisply, 'don't act as if this is the end of the world. We're two adults enjoying ourselves, that's all.' Her frown deepened. 'What? What is it?'

He picked up his jacket. 'You're right, I am a fool. I've been a fool not to see what you are. I was even more of a fool not to realise what a lucky escape I'd had.'

'Stop it.'

'I married a woman worth a hundred of you and I didn't see it. Well, God help me.'

'I said stop it.' Her expression was venomous; then she smiled. Moving nearer to him, she murmured, 'I could have you any time I wanted, Devlin. I'd click my fingers and you'd come running.'

'No. No, not any more. I may be the greatest fool in Christendom, Camilla, but you're hollow inside. Good for a quick fuck, but then you find there's nothing else.'

Her teeth bared. 'Damn you,' she whispered, then she grabbed her mackintosh and walked out of the stables.

Devlin knotted his shoelaces. He waited until he had heard Camilla's car drive out of the courtyard before leaving the stables and going to the house. In the great hall, the two whisky glasses were still on the table, the cigarette ends in the ashtray.

The door opened. Mrs Satterley said, 'There's a cold plate for you on the dining room table, sir.'

He thanked her. Then the doorbell rang. Good God, he thought, Camilla had come back. But he heard a male voice speaking to the cook – Mr Petherick, his clerk – followed by the door closing and footsteps on the gravel.

172

Mrs Satterley returned holding a manila envelope. 'This is for you, sir. Will there be anything else?'

'No thank you. You may retire for the night if you wish, Mrs Satterley.'

Alone in the room, Devlin stared at the envelope. Might Petherick have heard something, seen something? No, surely not.

He sat down on the sofa, closing his eyes. When he opened them, the room was just the same: the two glasses, the cigarette stubs and the ticking of the clock. Only an hour had passed since Camilla had arrived at Rosindell. He longed more than anything to wind time back to the moment when he had come downstairs after finding Esme's note. If only he had gone to Dartmouth. How could he have betrayed her? And with her *sister*? The contempt he felt for Camilla he now directed at himself with far greater force.

Shame washed through him and he groaned aloud. He examined what had taken place and found not a glint of light in it. He had broken his marriage vows – and for what? For a dream that had always been founded on sand. For nothing. He should have realised Camilla's true nature years ago, her capriciousness and her need for excitement. What slight bond there had been between them had been tempered by the drama and transience of wartime. Their relationship could not have – had not – survived exposure to everyday life.

His gaze ran round the room, coming to rest on the piano. He wished with all his heart that Esme were here now, playing a Chopin waltz or talking to him about Zoe, distracting him, erasing the bad thoughts from his head. He missed her. It shocked him how much he missed her. The room seemed filled by her absence, as though the lack of her was a physical thing – a cushion hollowed as if expecting her form, the knitting needles and a skein of pink wool poised for her to pick them up. He and the house had become accustomed to her, and without her Rosindell was an empty shell and all his labours to restore it meaningless. They both waited, he and the house, breathless, for the echo of her voice and her footsteps on the stairs, and it came to her then that he loved her, that he had loved her for months, but had been too blind to see it.

Too late. The bitterness of his discovery scorched him and he drained the glass in a mouthful. He stood up, knowing what he must do next. He must go to Esme and tell her what had happened. Though he dreaded it, he must make a clean breast of it. The alternative, to lie to her, and to go on lying for years and years, he must not even allow himself to consider.

He ripped open the envelope Petherick had delivered, took out the contracts inside it and put them on his desk in the library. Then he went upstairs to the bathroom, where he washed, scrubbing Camilla's scent from his skin. After he had dressed, he left the house, started up the car and headed at speed out of the drive.

She had pictured – oh, some sort of understanding, because, for goodness' sake, her mother had never liked Devlin. Instead, Annette had greeted her arrival at St Petrox Lodge with exasperation, and really, when she thought about it, Esme could not blame her – two daughters leaving their husbands within two days, more than any mother should have to bear.

As the day wore on, she knew it would not do any more, herself and her mother sharing the same house. Both women started whenever the doorbell rang, then slumped back into their seats, dismayed when it was only the grocer's boy or a Langdon aunt, visiting to share in the pleasure of their humiliation. Her mother talked endlessly about Camilla. Surely she would go back to Victor – Charles had driven to Greenwell; Esme should telephone Tom, to find out whether he had heard anything; Camilla could not possibly throw it all away – such a lovely girl; Victor could not mean it – the disgrace of a divorce in the family. And then

174

complaints about a headache, a sleepless night, and a misplaced order by Hawkes, the coal merchants.

What might she have to do to claim her mother's attention? Esme wondered as, that afternoon, while Annette was having a rest, she left the house. Dance naked on the wings of an aeroplane as it looped the loop over the Dart? This was not a homecoming; she had found no comfort here. So then, what now? Should she throw herself on a friend, Thea Hendricks for example, in Totnes? Or find a quiet cottage somewhere and work in a shop or an office to pay the rent? Or go back to Rosindell and tear up her note before Devlin had time to read it? As so often in the past, she had not thought things through.

Passing a hairdresser, she paused, then went inside. An hour later she emerged lighter, renewed. She headed back along South Town, past St Petrox Lodge, walking out of the town, parallel to the bank of the estuary. At Warfleet Creek she paused, leaning on the wall, looking down at the stream of brown water that ran out beneath the bridge. Rain dimpled the surface of the river.

She recalled the crunch of the hairdresser's scissors and felt the weightlessness of her bobbed head, but her fleeting elation had gone, brushed away like the locks that had fallen to the floor of the shop, and as she wept, the boats in the harbour blurred with her tears. Now, when she reflected, her behaviour seemed childish and self-indulgent, prompted by baseless assumptions and jealousy of her sister. Was she so spineless, so lacking in conviction, that she could throw away her marriage vows so easily?

A voice said, 'Are you all right, lovey?' and Esme turned to see an older woman standing behind her, a shopping bag in each hand.

'I'm fine,' she said, scrubbing her eyes with her sleeve. 'Really, I'm fine, thank you.'

She walked on through dripping woodland. Past the castle,

up the headland to where the cliffs faced the open sea. Then she sat down on a rock and watched the waves lash against the shore.

The raindrops cooled her face and staunched her tears, and she was able to reflect more soberly. She had only ever wanted Devlin Reddaway. Before her marriage, her days had often seemed long and futile. It had taken only a few hours of her mother's company for them to tire of each other. She had no particular talents, was a mediocre artist, a very amateur musician, had no interest in politics and had never wanted to change the world. She had approached motherhood with apprehension and still struggled with the reality of it.

So then, you reached a point in your life where you had to make the best of what you had. Devlin was neither cruel nor unfaithful and she had taken him on certain terms, so why protest against those terms now? Sooner or later you had to stick at something, or someone, even though sometimes – often – it hurt.

Looking at her watch, she saw that it was nearing six o'clock. She hurried back along the road to St Petrox Lodge. Annette was still in bed, so Esme dined alone. Over a dismal supper of oxtail soup and boiled white fish, it occurred to her that Devlin might have read her note and then gone on with his evening as if nothing had happened – drink, dinner, a walk to the site to see how the work on the house was progressing. This thought was lowering; her head throbbed, and she would rather have liked to retreat to bed herself.

The doorbell rang. The door opened; she heard his voice. She left the table and waited in the drawing room, running the palm of her hand over her shorn hair and chewing her lip nervously.

He said, 'Your hair. Your beautiful hair.'
She was standing beside the drawing room window. Beyond, the sails of the boats flecked the Dart. Devlin thought how pretty

she looked, with her blue cotton frock and her bell of honey-coloured hair. She was a little red around the eyes, perhaps.

'If you don't like it . . .' she said.

'I didn't say that.'

'It'll grow back. I wanted to have it bobbed.'

'Why?'

A sigh. 'I think,' she said, 'because I was tired of being me.'

'It suits you. You look different. Older, perhaps. A little daunting.'

'Daunting?'

'Just, as I said, a little. As if you've made up your mind about something.'

'I have, Devlin.' She stuck out her chin. 'I'm coming home.'

'Esme, I need to talk to you.'

'Don't you want me to?'

'Of course I want you to. Dear God, there's nothing I want more. But there's something I have to say to you, something I must tell you.'

'What is it?'

He opened his mouth to say, *Camilla came to the house today.* And all the rest that must follow. But then the door was flung open and Annette Langdon, knotted up in a shiny pink peignoir, stood on the threshold, bristling with outrage.

'Hetty told me you were here. The cheek of it!' She saw Esme and shrieked. 'Your hair! What have you done?'

'It'll grow back,' repeated Esme, rather irritably this time.

Mrs Langdon swung round to Devlin. 'It's your fault! You made her do it!'

Of this, at least, he was not guilty. 'Annette, I assure you I did not. Esme has a mind of her own. Besides, I've always loved her hair.'

'You drove her to it! I always knew you weren't good enough for her!'

'Mummy—'

'How you have the nerve to come here—'

'Mummy.'

'I was against the marriage from the start.' Annette Langdon's finger stabbed at his chest, pecking like a bird. 'I never liked the Reddaways, drinkers and ruffians the lot of them. I told Charles you wouldn't make her happy!'

'Mummy, please leave us.' Esme's voice, sharply authoritative, cut through Annette's words. 'You should go back to bed. Hetty will bring you some supper.'

Annette opened her mouth and made a strangled sound, then her soft, plump features seemed to deflate, and she allowed herself to be led away.

A few minutes later, Esme came back into the room. 'I'm so sorry. You must forgive my mother, she's had an awful couple of days.'

'There's nothing to forgive. And she was right, I haven't made you happy.'

'No, Devlin, that's not true.' She fiddled with one of the buttons on her dress, frowning. 'Did you mean that, about loving my hair?'

'Yes.'

'*Always* having loved it?'

'Yes.'

'Even when I was younger?'

He thought back. 'Yes, I think so. I always admired it.'

'But you were in love with Camilla.'

'Then I was a fool,' he said bleakly.

'I remember when you danced with me in this room. No one on earth could have been happier than I was then.'

He said gently, 'But you haven't been happy recently, have you, Esme?'

'No.' She hunched her shoulders. 'I was afraid that you loved the house more than me.'

Frowning, he studied her. 'Why would you think that?'

'I sometimes think it has a power over you. I've always had to compete with Rosindell. To be loved less than a house – that's hard to bear.'

'No,' he said forcefully. 'No, that's not true. The house is for you – for you and Zoe. I'm building it for you.'

'And then I was afraid that you were still in love with Camilla. Stupid of me, I know, but it crossed my mind.'

Into his memory came the image of Camilla, naked in the stables, her slim, pale limbs outspread on Josiah's rug. 'Actually,' he said, 'I despise her. I hope I never see her again.'

'I couldn't bear the thought that, now that Camilla's free, I'd always be waiting, always be afraid, wondering whether you'd go back to her. I know it's wrong of me even to think like that, but you see, Devlin, I love you so much. I always have done, from the first moment I saw you.'

Her voice was calm. If she had cried that day, there were no tears in her eyes now. What he had thought, seeing her for the first time that evening, remained. She had changed. She had acquired a sense of what was owed to her.

He said, 'I'm so sorry to have disappointed you.'

She frowned, standing by the window, one hand balled in the other. 'It isn't disappointment. And I don't think it's you, Devlin, who's at fault, but me. I shouldn't ask of you what you can't give.'

And he found himself saying, 'What? What is it you think I can't give you?'

She smiled, a small, warm smile. 'Love, of course.'

'You're wrong.'

'You don't have to say that. I can manage without.'

'I find it hard to see why you should. In fact, I find it hard to see why you would want to come back to a ramshackle house that you dislike and a husband whom you think doesn't care for you.'

'You've always been kind to me.'

'Have I? I'm not so sure. And is kindness enough? I don't think so. Certainly not for someone like you. I've always considered myself a passably intelligent man, but it has taken me a damnably long time to realise that I love you.'

'Devlin, please.' A small gasp, like a sigh.

Something had released inside his heart, and now he saw the truth at last. 'I'm no good without you, Esme,' he said. 'I lose my way. You brought me back to life, and without you I have no future. I love you. You must believe that. Whatever else you think of me.'

Her eyes were glassy with tears; she pressed the back of her fist against her mouth. 'What was it you wanted to say, Devlin?'

Should he tell her? He knew he should. But the moment had passed and time had moved on. The temptation to conceal the events of that day and to replace them with something of inestimable value was too much for him. Besides, he was only twenty-four years old, and in his short life, hadn't he suffered enough?

On the ferry across the Dart, he wondered whether it had been an act of cowardice or of kindness not to tell her the truth.

The steep cliff on which the houses of Kingswear perched precariously came closer. He had taken this journey so many times, through fair wind and foul, in anger and despair. But never, until now, with such resolution and hope in his heart.

What was done was done. He had made his choice. They stood side by side as the river slipped beneath them, rippled and opaque, lit by the evening sun. He felt the events of the day become ragged and then dissolve, like the last of the clouds from the sky, like a nightmare that he must put aside, telling himself, *That never happened.*

Love had come into his life, and he would never let it go. He would start again.

* * *

Always afterwards, Esme was sure that her son had been conceived that night. Matthew was born on 9 July 1921. It was an easy birth and Matthew was a contented and beautiful baby, eight and a half pounds in weight. He was born at Rosindell and was delivered by old Dr Spry, with the tap of hammers and the whine of saws from the building site muted for once.

This time her recovery was speedy. Within a week, she was sitting in a quiet corner of the garden, with Matthew swaddled up in the pram and Zoe, now nineteen months old, playing on the grass with Nanny. Now and then she rose to adjust the blankets and to check that the sun was not shining on the infant's face. Her gaze moved from one child to the other. Dark little Zoe was Devlin's, but golden-haired Matthew would be hers: she knew this already.

The tall blue spikes of delphiniums pushed high above poppies and pinks. A bee, powdered orange with pollen, burrowed into the trumpet of a lily, and a brimstone butterfly opened wings of yellow silk to dance on a current of air. Along the valley, walls made of green-grey Devon shale stone rose from the scarred earth. Rafters criss-crossed where the roof would be. The new house would be filled with light and the sound of her children's voices. *I can live here*, Esme thought. *I can be happy.*

On the train to London, Devlin tried to read through his accountant's summary of the last quarter's figures for the Galmpton boatyard. But his mind drifted, and he found himself looking out of the carriage window at the parched fields and dried-up streams, thinking about the news that Tom had passed on to him two days before.

Camilla, who had left England for Europe in the autumn of the previous year, had recently returned to London. And had brought back with her a baby daughter.

'A daughter,' he had said to Tom, blindsided. 'Whose?'

'I assumed that racing driver's.'

How old is the child? he had wanted to know. Had needed to know. Instead he had driven back from Kingswear to Galmpton, where he had stood on the jetty, watching the waders pad round the mudflats. The elation he had felt since the birth of his son had been punctured. He knew how much he had to lose.

Leaving the train at Paddington, he had a late lunch at a club in St James's with a man who wished to place an order at the yard. The meeting took a couple of hours, and afterwards Devlin walked to Piccadilly and booked into his hotel. From a booth in the lobby he placed the call. Waiting for the operator to put him through, he traced the toe of his shoe along the black and white floor tiles.

'Mrs de Grey's residence.'

He gave his name and asked to speak to Camilla. A long pause, during which he did not allow himself to think at all, and then he heard her voice.

'Devlin.' Her cool, ironic drawl. 'This is a surprise.'

'I'm sorry to trouble you, Camilla.'

'Are you in London?'

'Yes.' When the pause had gone on too long, he said baldly, 'Tom told me you'd had a daughter.'

'Yes. Are you astonished? I was. I've never seen myself as the motherly type.'

'How old is she?'

'Six weeks.'

In spite of the heat of the day, her sudden harsh laughter made a cold sweat ice his skin. 'Did you think she was yours?' she said. 'Is that why you're phoning me, Devlin? No, you shouldn't flatter yourself. The truth is that I was pregnant when we – well, you know. I'd rather hoped I might dislodge the thing, but no such luck. She's not Victor's either, by the way. I won't tell you whose she is, because it's none of your business.'

After he had put the phone down, he left the hotel and walked through Regent Street, towards St James's Park. Sunlight washed between the tall buildings and white clouds flecked a bland blue sky. The leaves on the London planes were limp in the heat.

The unpleasant taste in his mouth left by his conversation with Camilla was quickly washed away by relief. He knew that he had been given another chance, and after he had skirted round the lake in the park he headed for Westminster Abbey. An ex-serviceman was standing on the pavement in Parliament Square. Devlin bought a box of matches from him. Beside the match seller, a limbless veteran was propped against a wall, a cardboard placard – *Wounded at Mons* – on his lap. The unemployed servicemen, as well as the city itself, the buildings with their locked-in memories, produced in him a feeling of intense sadness. In spite of the summery weather, he still felt London to be enclosed within a veil of grief.

He went inside the Abbey. The tomb of the Unknown Warrior, which contained an unidentified corpse chosen at random from the hundreds of thousands of British soldiers who had died on the Western Front, was in the West Nave. As Devlin neared the simple rectangle of black marble, he noticed other men standing nearby, their heads bowed in respect.

They were the survivors, he and they and those others outside, begging for coins. They shared his memories, they limped through the streets, they hunched inside their greatcoats or jumped into their cars and dashed away to dance and drink themselves into oblivion. They carried walking sticks, or they sat in railway carriages and buses quivering like a kettle about to boil, or mumbling to themselves, until their wives pinched at their sleeves and they quietened. They, like he, were struck rigid and fearful by loud noises, by a child bursting a paper bag or the sound of an engine backfiring. A whistled phrase of a remembered song and they were unmanned by the tears that sprang to their eyes. The stench of blood from a butcher's shop and they were back in the mud of the Somme. They were caught up in the waves, sloshing back and forth, helpless in the knowledge that the sea might at any moment throw them against the rocks.

Devlin stood beside the tomb for a long time, remembering, and then he walked out into the sun.

Chapter Ten

1923–1932

June 1923: the first summer dance at the new Rosindell. Motor cars rolled along the drive, the low evening sun gleaming on paintwork and chrome.

The syncopated rhythms from the drawing room piano were punctuated by the pop of champagne corks and the loud hum of chatter and laughter. Roses tumbled from the vases on the mantelpiece, and more roses had been arranged in crystal bowls and placed on side tables. Their perfume filled the room. The women's dresses were lime green, chartreuse, rose pink and baby blue. They wore headbands studded with diamanté and plumed with feathers, and their bracelets, which clunked and jangled on their wrists, bore geometric designs in jet and diamond.

In the garden, glimpsed through the open French doors, a fat white moth flitted like a miniature Zeppelin from bloom to bloom. Devlin moved between the knots of people in the drawing room, exchanging a few words, answering a question.

'Simply gorgeous, Devlin.'

'You must be so thrilled.'

'What was the name of your architect?'

'I shall be inviting myself to stay for weeks and weeks.'

Excusing himself, he left the room. A long, high passageway, illuminated by square glass-panelled lights, took him through the main body of the new building. Opposite the sitting room, a tiled vestibule joined the new part of the house to the old rooms that Conrad Ellison had retained.

Three years, Devlin mused. Ellison's original estimate, that the new house would take a year or two to construct, had since lengthened to three. Even now there were parts of the house unfinished, servants' quarters that needed decoration, a bathroom that must be fitted out, pipes that leaked. The new build had disturbed the structure of the ancient house far more than either Conrad or his site manager had anticipated. Cracks had been discovered in the walls and the staircase had shifted. The old building had had to be underpinned, at considerable extra cost and the loss of months of progress. More bank loans had had to be taken out to cover the work.

Still, it had been worth it, even though there had been times when Devlin had felt finances, temper and sanity poised on a knife edge. The reward was driving home and glimpsing the new Rosindell from between the curtain of trees on the drive. The reward was Esme's happiness.

He went through the new dining room to the open loggia where they now ate throughout the summer months, and where in the warm evening air guests had gathered.

'What do you think of Baldwin?'

'The most divine little brooch in the shape of a scarab.'

'Coal prices up, thank God.'

'I'd support anyone who kept Lloyd George from power.'

Insects darted in the beams of light from the lamps. The flowers round the loggia were sweetly scented and luminous in the dusk. The sun was dying and the shapes of the pines stood like black cut-outs against a darkening sky. For a moment he imagined standing on the cliff and hearing the distant music of the dance mingle with the shush of the waves in the bay.

He went upstairs. Walking step by step away from the noise of the party, he felt a measure of relief, as if he was regaining his home, his sanctuary. The bedroom that he and Esme shared was above the drawing room and jutted out at an angle from the house so that it had a view over the garden. Esme had chosen soft furnishings of a pale peppermint green, edged in black. Curtains swayed at the open windows. A silk shawl had slid from the dressing table stool; he picked it up.

He heard a murmur of voices and turned to see Esme emerge from the nursery at the far end of the corridor.

'There you are,' he said, and smiled.

She was wearing a narrow dress of some filmy, transparent material, layered over a dense midnight blue. 'It was Matthew,' she whispered. 'He had a bad dream.'

'Is he all right now?'

'Sleeping soundly. I cuddled him till he dropped off.'

'How is Zoe?'

'Rather a fuss earlier, Nanny said, about having her hair brushed.'

'You look beautiful.'

They kissed. He ran his palms up her forearms, beneath the wide transparent sleeves of her gown.

'Do you think we could hide up here until it's all over?'

'Do you think anyone would notice?'

His hands followed the curve of her hips. Gently he brushed his chin along her bare shoulder.

She gave him a little push. 'Don't you want to show off your beautiful new house?'

'Not particularly.'

'I don't believe you.' She adjusted a hairclip and then threaded her hand through his. 'I think you've been waiting for this evening for *years*. Come on. Or they'll start the dancing without us.'

*   *   *

187

Esme had planned the interiors of the house herself. She had discovered that she had a gift for it, the matching of this paper with that fabric and the scouring of shops until she found the right lamps, an antique Persian bowl, overlooked in a corner of an auction house, or a lacquered Chinese cabinet. She chose colours that harmonised with the garden and the sea. Creams and golds and corals and soft blues and greens – a flash of kingfisher, a stormy grey.

The tiles in the nursery bathroom bore pictures of motor cars and boats to amuse the children. The dining table in the loggia had a blue marble top, chosen by herself and Conrad from a stack of marbles in a dusty stone yard in Whitechapel. The vases were by Poole Pottery and the lamps in the dining room were from Liberty – good God, a week's profit just so that I can see my dinner, Devlin had muttered. Conrad had sketched a cartoon of Devlin, standing on the loggia, looking out over the grounds. It hung in his study. The caption read, *Devlin Reddaway, surveying his demesne.*

But it was the garden that consumed Esme. She planned to create a series of terraces that would act as a bridge between the house and the less formal parts of the grounds. In them she would plant penstemons and ginger lilies, magnolias and buddleias. Against the walls of the house would grow jasmine, abutilon and wisteria, whose flowers in early summer would light up the grey shale with pale purple candles, and from the branches of the catalpa that Devlin's mother had planted twenty-five years ago, there now hung a statue of a girl on a swing. The light breeze made the bronze girl move back and forth, her long slate-coloured shadow shifting across the lawn.

There was the year all the guests at the summer dance moved down to the beach at midnight and carried on there, sixty of them descending the narrow steps to the cliff, the women clutching their skirts and shrieking, the men shining torches and showing off, leaping down the last twenty yards of tumbling rocks and then throwing off their shirts, bow ties and dinner jackets before running, luminous in the moonlight, into the sea. Someone had brought a portable gramophone and they danced barefoot on the hard, compacted sand.

There was the year Ivor Novello came to Rosindell. Devlin and Novello had a mutual friend, for whom the Galmpton yard was building a yacht. Sea trials coincided with the summer dance, and piano music drifted out of the French windows into the garden. Esme thought: you can't get much more perfect than this.

That was also the year Devlin bought her a car, a Baby Austin, and taught her to drive. She hated it; it terrified her, the noise and the speed and the thought that a child might run across her path or round a bend in the road might be a herd of cattle, blocking the way. But she saw that it would be useful to her and persevered, chewing her lip, white-knuckled as she drove along the high-banked Devon lanes.

There was no summer dance in 1926, because that was the year she lost a baby at five months. As she lay in bed, aching and bleeding, instructed to sleep, her gaze rested on the bedroom window. All seemed limp, exhausted and lifeless, the flowers of the wisteria already browning, the sky a tepid grey. She regretted that they had taken the stillborn girl away without her seeing her or holding her. She would have liked a sister for Zoe and Matthew: three was a good number. If you didn't get on with your sister there was always your brother.

Shifting on sheets that felt hot and crumpled, aware of the warm wetness between her legs, she thought that the house had demanded too much of their time, money and love. Rosindell was a house where you lost things – a hairbrush, a silver bangle, a child. She wondered whether in making the new house out of the stones of the old they had built in the bad luck, and if so whether they might never escape it.

As she looked out at the bleached sky, this thought clung to her, as flimsy and fragmented as the ragged cobwebs on the vaulted roof of the cellars.

There were no more pregnancies after that. Something had switched off inside her. One of each, Devlin said, trying to comfort her: perfect. She felt ashamed of her persisting grief, because her life was, as he had said, perfect. Her home was one of the most admired in Devon, her husband was handsome and adoring and the boatyard was going from strength to strength. She had two beautiful, healthy children, and she only had to think of poor Tom and Alice, trying for years for a baby and nothing happening, to know how fortunate she was.

From Country Life, June 1928:

Set in delightful grounds, which are enhanced by their proximity to the sea, all is peace and quiet at Rosindell. The architecture of the house teaches us that the old and the new can be brought together in a harmonious relationship. One of Conrad Ellison's earliest commissions, and showing the influence of his former apprenticeship with Lutyens, the architect set out to replace shoddy Victorian additions with a contemporary structure that would be equal to, and would not detract from, the existing fine early Tudor and medieval rooms. Rosindell's great hall is an acknowledged masterpiece, the beamed roof commonly considered one of the finest in south Devon. The Elizabethan staircase is notable for its barley-sugar balusters and carved finials. Ellison's additions to the house include a magnificent drawing room that exploits views over the garden to the sea, as well as a substantial roofed loggia, which makes the most of the aspect and favourable climate and is a striking addition to the building. Mrs Devlin Reddaway, who graciously gave permission for the photographs that accompany this article, tells us that although the recent additions can be considered modern in style, they are not flagrantly so, and that the architect's original remit has been achieved with simplicity and honesty. The house provides the perfect setting for Rosindell's annual summer dance, a delightful tradition revived by Mrs Reddaway.

When they disagreed, it was almost always about the children. Their worst quarrel took place when Matthew was seven. Devlin had assumed that the boy would go to boarding school at the age of eight, as he had done. Esme felt that eight was far too young. 'I know that you would miss him,' Devlin had said, 'and your feelings are perfectly understandable, but you need to put Matthew's future well-being first.' This had enraged her – the implication that she would not have given her life for Matthew, had that been required – and things had been said that they both later regretted: the inhumanity of the English boarding-school system and the sort of man it turned out, and that she favoured Matthew.

They had made up the quarrel and Matthew was not sent away to board for another two years, but Devlin's suggestion of favouritism had stung. Deep down, Esme knew that there was an element of truth in the accusation, and that made her uncomfortable. She had known from the day he was born what Matthew needed and what he felt and how to make him smile, but she was also familiar with the corrosive nature of favouritism, what it was to grow up in a household where one was overshadowed by a brother and sister. She tried to be even-handed but often failed. It was impossible to be cross for any length of time with Matthew. Bright, athletic and full of promise, he charmed her. He was the joy of her heart, the apple of her eye. He was her younger child, her last child, her baby. There would, after all, be no more.

Matthew was strong-willed and physically brave, even reckless. Once, he took the rowing boat out in bad weather and Devlin found him clinging to one of the rocks in the bay. He broke his collarbone falling out of a tree and knocked himself out sliding down the banisters in the old hall. But these were things that were excusable in a boy, Esme thought privately, even admirable. Better a daredevil streak than a boy who sat at home turning the pages of a book.

Devlin taught both children to ride and to sail and Esme taught them to swim. Devlin had a way of making excuses for Zoe, who was, some of the teachers at her school agreed, a difficult child. Not a disobedient one, nor by any means a stupid one – in fact quite the opposite – but not an easy one, either. Since she had been very young, Zoe had had one irksome habit after another. A refusal to go to sleep without the light on. An insistence that she dress on a particular day of the week in a particular colour. A need to cross her fingers or touch wood whenever someone said a certain word – not a bad word or a forbidden word, but a perfectly normal, everyday one. If one had to put up with these rituals day after day they became thoroughly tiresome.

Zoe was a fanciful, solitary child, not a joiner-in. Esme would sometimes find her sitting in a corner of the house or garden talking to herself. Dr Spry, when Esme consulted him, recommended cod-liver oil and company, but the little tea parties and outings that Esme arranged, to which she invited Zoe's schoolfriends, were endured rather than enjoyed by Zoe. That Esme herself had often found parties an ordeal when she was younger did not help. It dismayed her that she seemed to have passed on to her daughter all her most disagreeable characteristics. An attempt to share her love of exploring junk shops was quickly abandoned once she realised that Zoe, a very tidy child, found the chaotic messiness of the shops that she, Esme, adored, distressing. They limped along, she often thought, she and her daughter, managing to find some common interest in books and fashion, though even there their tastes were completely different.

*   *   *

In the summer of 1931, when Zoe was eleven and Matthew had just celebrated his tenth birthday, Camilla came to Rosindell.

It was more than ten years since Esme and her sister had met, on that memorably awful visit to Camilla's Mayfair flat. Camilla had spent much of the 1920s abroad. She was never spoken of at St Petrox Lodge, where her disgrace seemed to have aged Charles and Annette. Their golden girl, gone to the bad. You heard snippets, pleasurably shocked murmurs — a liaison with a writer who was rumoured to like the company of men, a journey through the north African desert with a French socialite.

It was a weekday afternoon and Devlin was at work. Camilla had a man in tow — a new husband — and she looked, well, *stunning*. White linen suit, white straw hat, hair shoulder-length and swept to one side, a slash of red lipstick. Esme, who had been gardening, was wearing an old cotton dress and plimsolls. Too much to hope, she thought irritably as she hastily tidied her hair, that Camilla might phone ahead.

Camilla's husband, who was called James Heron, was thirtyish, handsome, Oxford-educated and worked at the Foreign Office. He walked ahead as Esme showed them round the garden. 'So adorable,' murmured Camilla, blowing him a kiss. 'He's the love of my life.'

The third in the party was Camilla's daughter, Melissa. She was a pretty girl, slight and flaxen-haired, only a few weeks older than Matthew. As Sarah set out the tea things on the loggia, Esme remembered that Denis Rackham had been fair. You couldn't help wondering.

Mr Heron had brought a camera. The five of them — Esme, Camilla, Zoe, Matthew and Melissa — posed on the terrace in the sunlight. The two sisters stood at the back, Camilla smiling at the camera and Esme, putting up a hand to her hair, looking aside. The children were arranged in front. As the shutter closed, Matthew turned to call out to the dog, so that in the picture his image was blurred, as if he was running away.

After only an hour's visit, Camilla left. 'Do come again,' said Esme dutifully. Then they said their farewells and parted.

In October 1929, the economic boom had come to an end and the New York Stock Exchange had crashed. The repercussions of the economic collapse were felt throughout the world, causing widespread unemployment in both Britain and Europe. Now, when Devlin visited Glasgow and Newcastle to call on suppliers and customers, the desperation was tangible. Groups of men huddled on street corners, their clothing shabby and their faces gaunt. In the coal towns of Wales and northern England, unemployed miners picked over the slag heaps, searching for nuggets of fuel to warm their homes and cook their food.

Both Charles Langdon and Devlin lost money in the crash, investments that had seemed solid becoming, sometimes in a matter of days, worth little more than the paper they were written on. Money, which had seemed to flow so freely in the twenties, was now in much shorter supply. Fishermen in the West Country had been struggling for years, their catches unable to compete with those of the trawlermen of the Arctic and North Sea, and orders for fishing boats had dried up. The Galmpton boatyard, too, had been affected by the depression. Fewer people could afford luxury craft, and those men who had held on to their wealth knew that they could strike a harder bargain.

In 1932, Langdon's was compelled to lay off some of the workforce. It was a miserable business and wretchedly timed. Some months before, when the contraction had seemed likely, Devlin had broached to Esme the possibility of cancelling the summer dance that year. She had been unwilling to – it would cheer people up, she had pointed out, and besides, what message

194

would it send out if the Reddaways appeared to be cutting back? They always had a summer dance at Rosindell. And the evening provided temporary work for a substantial number of local people.

Devlin now regretted that he had allowed himself to be persuaded. It looked callous, wining and dancing only a few days after men had been sacked from jobs they had held, in some cases, for decades. It was with a heavy heart that he bathed and dressed on Saturday night.

Esme, too, knew that it had been a mistake. Sitting at her dressing table, searching through boxes and drawers for her pearl earrings, she sensed that Devlin blamed her. Her memory of having convinced him to go ahead with the dance despite his reservations had led her during the day to put on a breezy smile and adopt a false, efficient tone when discussing the arrangements. It must be done, she felt, so better to do it with grace and a smile.

It hadn't helped that they had had a call from Matthew's housemaster that morning. It was their policy to contact a boy's parents whenever there was a serious incidence of bad behaviour, Mr Osborne, a self-important man, had informed them. And then some story about Matthew going out of bounds the previous night – a dare – caught by the groundsman on his return to the school.

After Devlin had put the phone down, Esme said, 'The school should keep a better eye on him.'

'Don't make excuses for him, Esme.'

'I'm not making excuses. It's the sort of thing boys do. Think of you and Tom.'

'It was night-time. He had to cross a busy road. No doubt a thrashing will concentrate his mind.'

'A thrashing?'

'Yes, the unctuous Mr Osborne felt obliged to inform me of that, too. Don't look so horrified, his pride will suffer most.'

195

Esme found the idea of corporal punishment disgusting and said so. But Devlin's features had already taken on an expression that told her he had tired of the subject.

She said, 'Don't you mind?'

'No, I don't. I think he's got off lightly. It sounds as if he narrowly avoided expulsion.'

'Perhaps if I telephoned the school . . .'

'No.' Devlin's tone was sharp. 'Matthew needs to learn that his actions have consequences.'

'But he's a child!'

His dark eyes flickered. 'He's eleven. He's not an infant. If you go on spoiling him, then he'll still be pushing against the traces when he's eighteen.' He left the room.

Now, preparing for the party, Esme could have cried for Matthew. Underneath the bravado he was a sensitive boy. She knew that Devlin was probably right and that he would find the humiliation of a caning worse than the physical pain.

The wretched earrings were nowhere to be found. She could swear there was a poltergeist in the house, hiding her things. She gave an irritated tut and opened the small leather box containing the yellow diamond drops that Devlin had given her on their tenth wedding anniversary, and put them on instead.

She looked into the mirror. She was thirty-two years old. She felt suddenly weary and peered harder into the looking-glass, examining her reflection to reassure herself that there were no lines round her eyes or slackness about her neck. Her gown was of bias-cut black crêpe de Chine. She rarely wore black, but her dressmaker had suggested it – 'Wonderfully dramatic, Esme.' It had been horribly expensive, but now she was doubtful and wondered whether it suited her.

She could hear the distant discordant squeaks and hoots of the band tuning up. The weather was uncertain this year, watery sunshine interpersed with squally showers, so the musicians would have to play in the drawing room rather than on the terrace. Her apprehension, that this year the evening would not work, that it would be a flop, or that some disaster would occur, was, she sternly reminded herself, simply habit, the product of nerves. Everything had been organised. An army of local girls from Lethwiston and Kingswear, hired for the occasion, stood poised with trays of canapés. The cloakroom had been cleared of family clutter to accommodate the guests' coats.

Esme rose with resolution, applied a spray of Coty's Chypre, and left the room. She was in the kitchen, checking with Mrs Satterley, when the first motor car rolled into the courtyard. As she and Devlin went to the front door to greet their guests, he kissed her hand and said, 'You look beautiful, darling,' and the old feeling, that she always had on the brink of the summer dance at Rosindell, a mixture of excitement and nervousness and pleasure, flooded through her, and she smiled at him.

They were like owls' eyes, owls blinking, as the gleam of the headlamps was now and then masked by the trunks of the trees beside the drive. Zoe was kneeling on the window seat in her bedroom and counting the motor cars as they snaked down the slope to the courtyard. Their route was lit by torches whose proper name, Zoe knew, was *flambeaux*. They always lit the driveway with *flambeaux* at the summer dance, even when it was raining.

She recognised Uncle Tom's Alvis and Grandfather's Bentley. She willed Uncle Tom and Aunt Alice to look up to the bedroom and wave at her. Aunt Alice was wearing a pretty pinkish-purple gown, the colour of the inside of a foxglove. Just before she stepped into the house, she looked up and fluttered her fingers and Zoe waved back.

There was a long gap after the seventh car, which made Zoe feel anxious, but then a Baby Austin, like her mother's car, came bouncing down the drive. Her relief was momentary, because the Austin was joined by a large green vehicle. Zoe yawned: it was late and she was tired, but because that made nine, an odd number, she could not yet go to sleep. She tucked her nightie over her feet to keep them warm and fiddled with one of her curl papers, which was pulling at her scalp. It was rotten luck to have perfectly straight hair, so unfair that Matthew had the yellow curls, which, as her mother often said, ruffling them, was wasted on a boy.

A flurry of cars: she nearly lost count and had to kneel up and concentrate hard. Twenty. So many people. She almost went to bed, but she felt that prickling sensation on her back and knew that they were watching her.

Another half-dozen cars. Twenty-six, an even number: even numbers were all right. A party of eight from Lethwiston arrived on foot, Mr Fawcett and Miss Fawcett among them. Miss Fawcett, who was short and almost circular, was wrapped up in brown shiny stuff like a badly tied parcel, and she had brought one of her dogs. When Zoe was grown up, she would always invite dogs as well as people to her parties.

More headlamps coming down the drive. It was quite dark now and she could not tell the colours of the motor cars. She wondered whether her mother and father got fed up with greeting people and saying things like, 'Angela, Miles, so marvellous that you could come.' She suspected her father did. Daddy, when faced with some awful event like Granny coming to lunch, would grimace and say, 'Best foot forward, old thing.' Once, when she was little and they had been playing on the beach, Zoe had asked her father how he could tell which was his best foot, and they had both studied their feet for some time, trying to decide.

Twenty-nine. It was twenty-nine for a long time and Zoe felt uneasy. You had to make everything neat and orderly or they found a way of getting back at you. The feeling of being watched had grown stronger. Twenty-nine was an untidy sort of number, a prime, which meant that nothing divided into it except twenty-nine and one, neither of which counted. Miss Blake, at school, had taught her about primes.

Though her thoughts rattled on, agitation was creeping into the gaps between them, the same feeling she had when she hadn't dotted an 'i' properly or arranged the brushes on her dressing table correctly. Zoe squinted at her wristwatch. It was nearly ten o'clock. Perhaps no more guests would come. Along the corridor, a door closed and she stiffened. What if Nanny looked in on her? What if she made her go to bed? What retaliation would they take, what precious thing might they hide?

From outside, she heard the roar of car engines and a trio of latecomers sped into the courtyard.

'There,' said Zoe, out loud. 'An even number. So you have to go now.'

Then she jumped into bed.

Esme checked that the maids were serving the canapés, and that the band, who were taking a break, had refreshments. She looked for stray guests, sitting alone on sofas. Tom was part of a group of men standing in the centre of the room. His face was red and he was talking loudly as he clapped his neighbour on the back.

Heading back along the corridor, Esme noticed that the door from the vestibule to the older part of the house was ajar. Opening it, she found Alice sitting on the stairs, crying.

'My dear, what is it?' Esme sat down beside her and put an arm round her shoulders.

'So sorry — sorry, Esme.' Alice made a choking noise and began to cry again.

It was cold in this part of the house; poor Alice had goose pimples on her arms. Though Esme had had these rooms decorated in a more modern style and had bought what contemporary furnishings she had felt would suit them, they seemed to resist change and remained cold and dark. Shadows concentrated here, painting a black streak in the lee of the grandfather clock and a featureless triangle to one side of the stairs.

'I shouldn't have come,' said Alice. 'I'm afraid I'm not in a party mood.'

'What's wrong?'

'Oh, the usual. Tom and I quarrelled.'

'You too? Devlin and I had quite a set-to this morning. Between checking the prawns weren't off and doing the flowers.' Esme was aware as she spoke that she was trivialising it, that their disagreement about Matthew had nudged them a small but perceptible distance apart.

'I never imagine you and Devlin quarrelling.' Alice dabbed at her eyes with a handkerchief. 'You always seem so perfectly suited to each other.'

'Oh, we're like chalk and cheese. I flare up and Devlin sulks.' Now she was mouthing half-truths. Esme said gently, 'Was it a bad quarrel?'

'No worse than usual. But I'm tired of it.' Alice balled up her handkerchief in her palm. 'I asked him to stay in tomorrow, that was all. No.' Wearily she pushed her hair back from her face. 'That isn't true. I asked him where he was going.'

'What did he say?'

'That he was sailing. Then he accused me of not trusting him. And I said that it wasn't that, I'd just like some company.'

'You can always come here. We love to see you.'

'Actually, I don't trust him. There's always *someone* with Tom.'

Of some husbands, Esme discovered in that moment, one might have said, oh no, never, he adores you, but her brother, she realised discomfitingly, was not one of them.

She said, 'Have you talked to him?'

'No. What would be the point? He wouldn't tell me the truth. And if he did, and if I was right, what would I do then?'

'Would you like me to speak to him? Or perhaps Devlin . . .?'

'No. Thank you, Esme, you're very sweet, but no.' Alice took a breath. 'If I'd had a child, I might be able to bear it. But then everything would have been different. Sometimes I think he blames me for not being able to have a baby.'

Esme squeezed her hand. 'I'm sure that's not true.' Though she felt enormously sorry for Alice, she was aware of the party, a short distance away, needing her attention, and quickly added, 'He just feels sad, like you do. And anyway, there's plenty of time.'

'No, don't say that. It's better to stop hoping. Eleven years and nothing's happened at all. The awful thing is that a part of me thinks that if only I could stop hoping, really stop, then I might get pregnant. Aren't they silly, these self-deceptions we hang on to?'

'It's understandable. I've always had to make sure I have my own interests. Devlin's always so busy at work.' Although she had meant to express a common cause, she sounded smug, Esme thought.

'You have the children.'

'Yes, of course, I'm so lucky.' The sound of more guests arriving; she really should go and greet them. 'And you're a wonderful aunt to them, Alice, they adore you.'

Alice took a powder compact out of her evening bag and set to work on her face. 'I wish Tom wouldn't drink so much. It can't be good for him and it makes him . . . boorish. Do I look frightful?'

'Not at all, you look perfectly lovely. What you need is an enormous gin martini. I'll ask Devlin to make you one of his special ones.'

They went back together to the party. Devlin made Alice a drink and Esme sat with her mother and talked to her for a dutiful twenty minutes, with half an eye on the progress of the evening. The Scotts had driven down from London, arriving late and bringing a dozen of their good-looking, fashionable friends with them, and all the rooms now looked satisfyingly full. This dance was going to be as great a success as its predecessors. Esme felt a glow of pleasure that between them she and Devlin had managed to conjure up enchantment from such unpromising times.

Her parents left early; as they waved them away, Devlin kissed her.

'And now we must dance.'

The loggia was empty, the inclement weather having driven the guests indoors, but they danced there each year; it had become a custom of theirs, dancing beneath the glass roof to the music of Rosindell.

'Now this,' he murmured, 'is what I've been waiting for all evening.'

She couldn't resist saying, 'You don't mind, then?'

'Mind what?'

'That we went ahead.'

'I expect you were right, that to have cancelled would have given a bad impression.'

They were good together, she thought, as they circled the floor. She felt a rush of pity for poor Alice and Tom, with their fragile, unfruitful marriage. The rain had stopped, but its falling had brought out the scents of the garden, of jasmine and wet earth and grass. Some of the *flambeaux* beside the driveway had burned down, beads missing from the necklace of light, and above the trees on the cliff the golden sickle of a crescent moon showed itself between the scudding clouds. Esme forgot the bustle and chatter of the party as the moment distilled into the vastness of the night and the two of them, waltzing beneath the stars.

Looking up, she saw that one of the maids had come out of the dining room and was heading towards them.

'There's a gentleman to see you, Mr Reddaway,' the girl said.

'Can't it wait?' said Esme.

'He says he won't go away till he's spoken to you, sir.'

Devlin frowned. 'Who is it?'

'His name's Petherick, sir.'

'Damn it, this really isn't convenient.' Devlin took Esme's hands in hers and kissed them. He said to the maid, 'Send him to my study. Forgive me, darling, I'd better deal with this.'

Alfred Petherick had been one of the men whom Devlin had laid off earlier that week. You had to sympathise, yet he also had to suppress his annoyance as he made his way to his study. What the hell did Petherick think he was doing, coming to the house on the night of the summer dance?

Petherick was waiting, his cap in his hands. His demeanour, strained-looking and nervously fidgeting, made Devlin speak kindly to him.

'What is it, Petherick? Why are you here?'

'To ask you to give me another chance, sir.'

'Sit down, man.'

'I'd rather stand, Mr Reddaway.'

'As you wish. Drink?'

'No thank you, sir, I don't.'

Devlin poured himself a Scotch, using the time to gather his thoughts. 'It's not a question of second chances,' he said. 'I tried to make that clear when we spoke earlier in the week. It's nothing to do with your work. It's these difficult times we live in.'

But Devlin knew that this was not quite true. Alfred Petherick had worked for Langdon's since he was fifteen, and the truth was, it showed. He was set in his ways and found it hard to adapt to change, becoming flustered and irritable if asked to do anything out of the common run. And there was something in the man's attitude towards him that Devlin had always disliked, a surliness that was absent during Petherick's exchanges with Tom or Charles. Nothing approaching insolence, but Devlin had years ago classed Petherick as the type of old family retainer, loyal man and boy to the Langdon family, who viewed him as an interloper. His name had been top of the list when it had come to choosing who to lay off.

'None of us feels happy about this,' he said, 'but Mr Langdon and I felt there was no choice. It wasn't a decision that was taken lightly. We haven't the work coming in and the wages bill is too high.' He was aware, as he spoke, how thin this must sound to Petherick. He only had to look around this room to see the trappings of wealth.

'Then sack one of the others.'

These words, spat out, made Devlin realise that Petherick's restless agitation was the product of anger rather than nerves.

'Sack one of the younger ones. They'll find other work. I'm sixty-three. I won't get another job now. And there's my sister.'

There was a roar of laughter from outside the study door. Out of the corner of his eye, Devlin glanced at the clock. Ten to eleven. He was to make a speech at eleven, thanking his guests.

He said, 'I didn't know you had a sister.'

'She's not well. Dorothy's never been well. I've always looked after her.' The words were dragged out with obvious reluctance. 'You can hardly feed yourself on the dole, let alone another mouth, everyone knows that.'

'Surely some help could be found.'

'I won't have her put in an institution!' Petherick's face twisted with fury.

'No, of course not.' Devlin thought quickly. 'I'll have a word with someone, if you like. The church in Kingswear, perhaps.'

'I've never had to ask for charity and I won't be thrown on it now.' Petherick's fists were clenched. 'I've done everything that's been asked of me. I've always been loyal to Langdon's. All I want is my job back.'

If he weakened with Petherick, the other men who had been laid off would complain, and rightfully, and then the whole grim process must be gone through again. The violence of Petherick's anger, and the fact that he had chosen this night of all nights to plead his case, hardened Devlin's heart. No, he must stand by his original decision.

'You're not the only man with dependents, Petherick,' he pointed out. 'Thomas has five children, Abbott is engaged to be married. I'm sorry, but the decision has been made. I'll have a word with some people and see what can be done. I'm sure assistance can be found for your sister.'

Petherick whitened. His lips worked as if to speak, but no sound came out. Devlin opened the door. Catching sight of one of the maids, he signalled to her and asked her to show Petherick out.

It was eleven o'clock. Guests were pouring into the drawing room for the speech and the toast. As Esme returned from the kitchen after checking the champagne, she saw Alfred Petherick emerge from Devlin's study. His face was convulsed with emotion. She thought he was going to storm past her without speaking to her.

Catching sight of her, he stopped. He said, 'You should know what sort of man your husband is, Mrs Reddaway.'

Some of the guests gave Petherick and Esme a curious look. Esme murmured, 'You're not yourself, Mr Petherick,' and guided him into the privacy of the porch.

She closed the door behind them. The room was hexagonal in shape and an arched entranceway looked out to the courtyard.

Petherick said, 'I don't suppose you know.' His tone was venomous.

'About what?'

'I shouldn't think he's told you.'

'I don't know what you're talking about,' said Esme coldly. 'I'm afraid I must ask you to leave.'

'You've always been kind to me. Not like Miss Camilla. That day I saw them, she almost knocked me off my bicycle.'

What would have happened, she wondered afterwards, if she had done as she had intended and fetched Josiah and had him show Petherick off the premises? But she could not have done that. It was already too late. *That day I saw them*. The words would have always been there, the worm in the bud, eating away at her.

She heard herself murmur, 'Who? Who did you see?'

'Mr Reddaway and Miss Camilla.' Petherick's head jerked towards the garden. 'Here, in the stables. Mr Charles had sent me with some papers for Mr Devlin. I saw them together. They were embracing. Worse – I won't say it. It was vile. You don't forget something like that – no, never.'

Later, after he had gone, there was the remainder of the evening to be lived through. Some part of Esme marvelled that she was able to raise her glass in the toast, to make small talk and to move round the rooms as if her world had not ended, and some other part marvelled equally that her mind was clear enough to recognise this.

But strangely, that was what she had, an extraordinary and terrible clarity of thought. Her hope that Petherick had been lying to her had fallen away after his first few sentences. Nearly twelve years ago, Camilla had left Victor de Grey. Petherick had described the rain and the pale blue motor car hurtling past him as he had cycled from Kingswear to Rosindell. When he had arrived at the house, he had seen Camilla's Peugeot parked in the courtyard. Petherick had reached the shelter of the trees beside the drive as Camilla and Devlin had left the house for the garden. He had remained there until they had gone into the stables. Then he had crossed the courtyard and had looked through the stable window.

How could Devlin have betrayed her so profoundly, so completely? How had he been able to live a lie for so long? Because every day of their marriage had been a lie. Every kiss had been a lie. Every time he had made love to her he had lied. She had not known him at all.

Her hatred of Camilla dizzied her. Camilla must have returned to St Petrox Lodge while she herself had been out, walking to the castle. Someone – Hetty or her mother – must have told Camilla that she, Esme, had left Rosindell, and Devlin. And so she had seen her opportunity and had taken it.

The band started to play again and Esme was at last able to slip out of the drawing room. The house had become strange and unfamiliar to her, and as she made her way outside, she blundered against a chair, bruising herself, no longer sure of her way.

In the garden, crossing the stream as she stumbled towards the shelter and privacy of the catalpa tree, her gaze turned back to the house. The distant music seemed jarring now, the movements of the silhouetted dancers ugly and angular. But then she had always known that Rosindell was tainted, that the superficial beauty masked a rottenness underneath. An ashy smell beneath the scent of roses, the fruit on the trees pulpy under the skin, and a fat white grub glistening at the heart of each flower. The deep Devon countryside that surrounded the house went on as it always had, from century to century, oblivious to their passions and tragedies, indifferent to the dramas played out there.

Shame overwhelmed her and she covered her face with her hands. That that man had come here, on this night, and told her such a terrible thing – that he had known of her husband's adultery for years – she would have left Devlin for that

207

humiliation alone. She had believed he loved her, but now she questioned whether he was able to love anything, anyone, other than the house and his daughter. Had he even loved Camilla? But he had wanted her, with all the obsessive passion of which he was capable.

Could she stay with him? If only for the sake of the children, could she stay? No, she knew she could not. She would never be able to forget that he had made love to Camilla. Whenever she saw him with that faraway look in his eye, she would believe that he was thinking of Camilla, and whenever he touched her she would know that he longed to be touching Camilla. So she would take the children and leave him, and this time she would not come back.

Dry-eyed, she longed for the guests to go. A terrible weariness had come over her and she ached as if she had a fever. She dreaded the conversation that must take place once the last of their guests had left, not because she did not already know the outcome of it, but because what she had learned had extinguished some fire in her, something integral to her that she had assumed she would keep for ever. Now she wanted only to be alone, and for the night to be over.

No matter. He had betrayed her and that was an end to it. A part of her life had finished and eventually, she supposed, another one would begin, unimaginable though that now seemed. Midnight had come and gone and she must wait through the remaining hours until she could take her children and leave her home.

No, not her home, because Rosindell had never truly been hers. It had always resisted her, and she knew that when she left it in the morning, she would never return.

Part Two

Affinity

1939–1949

Chapter Eleven

July 1939

As the train drew into Warminster station, Matthew saw Zoe leaning out of the carriage window. She called out and waved and he loped along the platform and climbed into the compartment.

He put his bag in the luggage rack and sat down opposite her. 'Have you anything to eat?'

'Some sandwiches and a Kit Kat.' She handed him a paper bag.

'You look different. Something with your hair.'

'I had it cut in Paris. I shrieked when I saw how much he cut off.'

Matthew wolfed down a sandwich. 'How's Mum?'

'Fine.' Zoe's gaze flicked round the other passengers in the compartment. 'At least she didn't insist on driving us.'

Their mother's driving was an embarrassment to them both. She went at a top speed of thirty-five miles an hour, even on the main roads. Tails of other motorists formed behind her, hooting their horns and impatiently overtaking.

'I wish I could get out of this blasted party,' said Matthew. 'You know what it'll be like. Loads of people I haven't seen for years and I don't have anything in common with any more.'

In the summer term at Warminster, he had become part of

a small, exclusive clique who affected a louche, negligent manner that enraged some of the masters. In the evenings they liked to lounge on the dusky lawns, smoking cigarettes, talking about politics and philosophy. Because the others claimed to be communists, Matthew had done so too, though it didn't particularly appeal.

'How was Paris?' he asked.

'Wonderful. I'm thoroughly finished now.'

He wondered idly what girls did in finishing school, but the thought produced in him an uncomfortable mixture of sexual frustratration and boredom, and he balled up the empty paper bag, then stood up and stretched, his hands touching the ceiling of the carriage.

'I'm starving,' he said. 'Is there a buffet anywhere?'

They had the compartment to themselves between Totnes and Kingswear, so they sat in the window seats. Zoe peered out of the window, exclaiming at the familiar landmarks, while Matthew read *Sally Bowles*, which he had borrowed from his friend Fisher. He wished he was on a train heading towards some dingy, decadent European capital. It was ridiculous that at nearly eighteen he was still expected to spend the entire summer at Rosindell, as if he were a child. Outside the window, flashes of the river showed between the dark, heavy leaves of the trees. Matthew stifled a yawn.

The train pulled into Kingswear. Matthew hauled their cases down from the luggage rack and they left the carriage. Outside the station, they looked round and Zoe said, 'There's Josiah.'

Anger, that he sometimes forgot when he was away from Rosindell, flooded through Matthew. 'You'd think Dad could have made the effort,' he said.

'I expect he's at work.'

'He's always at work.' Matthew eyed the pony and trap. 'It'd be quicker running to Rosindell than going in that thing.'

'Go on, then,' said Zoe.

Last summer Matthew had run the three miles from Kingswear to Rosindell in half an hour, pretty bloody brilliant when you thought of all the ups and downs.

He said, 'I bet you half a crown I get to the beach before you do.'

'Okay.'

He slung his bag into the trap and threw his jacket after it. 'I'll wait for you there.' Flinging a grin over his shoulder to his sister, he broke into a jog as he headed up the steep roads that led through the village to the coastal path.

Neither the physical exertion nor the fine sunny weather erased his resentment, though. It was so typical of Dad, he thought, as he headed towards Kingswear Castle, not to even bother coming to meet them when he hadn't seen them for months. And if he really was working, then he could at least have sent the car, not that awful ancient trap. He swanned around in the Bentley while they had to put up with a Victorian leftover.

He headed down a steep incline. Far below him was a cove where waves smashed against the rocks. His plimsolls slapped against the narrow path and sweat glued his shirt to his back. He ran through a conversation he had had with a friend a couple of days ago. Like all of their set, Cavendish was expected to stay on next year in the third-year sixth to take the Oxbridge entrance exam. 'Can't see the point,' Cav had said while they were walking from the hall to their study rooms. 'Not when there's going to be a war. I'm going to join the RAF.'

Matthew had had vague thoughts about the RAF for a long time. He liked the idea of flying — like sailing, only better, because you'd be able to move in three dimensions, as free as a bird. It was one of those ideas which, though it had a strong appeal, he had not yet got round to putting into practice. When he had mentioned it to his mother the strength of her

213

disapproval had taken him by surprise. He had rather taken her support for granted. They liked the same things, found the same things ridiculous.

But the easy manner with which Cavendish had said, 'I'm going to join the RAF,' as if it was no less possible than posting a letter or writing an essay, had remained with him. They hadn't talked about it any more and Matthew hadn't raised the subject with Fisher or any of the others, because the accepted opinion among their set was that the war was a fiction encouraged by those in power to keep the workers in their place, producing armaments in the factories or cutting coal for a pittance in the mines, a theory that to Matthew had seemed increasingly unconvincing as the year of 1939, with its unending toll of bad news, had gone on.

But now, running along the clifftop, and with the hot afternoon sun burning his shoulders, he came to see that he could not go back to school next year, that there was no part of him that would be able to bear it, and that he wanted to join the RAF more than anything. The decision gave him some relief, and he felt a surge of exhilaration as he ran, faster than he had ever run before, the last half-mile of his route, sweat dripping from his face until he found himself in the shade of the pines above Rosindell Bay. He hurtled down the cliff steps two or three at a time, and, reaching the sand, threw off his shirt and trousers and launched himself into the sea.

Zoe had unpacked and given Sarah the bottle of scent she had bought for her in Paris (Les Cocquelicots Rouges), and then had reacquainted herself with her favourite places, noting any changes – though her father, almost as much a creature of habit as herself, never changed anything, and the house just looked a little more worn, the paintwork a little more scuffed, than when she had last seen it.

All this meant that Matthew won the bet and was at the

beach long before she was, and so she lost half a crown. But at least it had given him time to get out of his bad mood.

At six o'clock Zoe said, 'We should go back now. Dad might be home,' and pulled her cotton dress on over her swimsuit, which had dried in the sun, and began to climb back up the steps. Matthew sauntered behind her, a rolled-up towel over one shoulder.

The Bentley was parked in the courtyard when they emerged out of the woodland and headed up through the garden to the house. Her father was talking to Josiah; when Zoe called out to him, he turned and smiled and came to meet them.

She gave him a big hug. 'You look hot, Daddy.'

'And you're looking very French.' He took a step back. 'Very chic. Quite the Parisienne. It's good to see you again, darling girl.' He held out his hand to Matthew. 'Hello, Matt. How are you doing, old chap?'

'Fine,' said Matthew.

They went into the house. Sarah brought drinks to the loggia, lemonade for Zoe and Matthew, a gin and tonic for Devlin.

He said to Matthew, 'Looking forward to your birthday?'

'I suppose so.'

'How's school?'

'It's all right.'

'You've a good long break before next term. Six weeks. I envy you.'

'I might not stay here all summer. Some of the other fellows were talking about finding something to do in London.'

'London's pretty hot and unpleasant at this time of year. Why don't you invite your friends down here?'

'There's nothing to do here.'

'There's plenty to do. You can swim and take the boat out, or go hiking—'

'They don't really like that sort of thing.'

'What do they like, then?' Her father's voice had tensed.

215

Matthew shrugged. 'Talking about stuff.'

'You can "talk about stuff" anywhere.'

'You wouldn't understand, Dad.'

Conversations between their father and Matthew tended to go like this, Dad stilted, trying too hard, and Matthew either monosyllabic or condescending.

Devlin said, 'Have you spoken to your mother about this?'

'No.' Sulkily.

'We have an agreement, you know that, that you and Zoe spend the summer at Rosindell.' Zoe could hear the strain in her father's voice as he tried not to sound cross. 'It gives your mother the chance to get on with things and it means that I get to see you both properly.'

Before Matthew could respond, Zoe said, 'It's so lovely to be here, Dad. I've been longing for it.'

'You're not missing Paris, then?'

'Paris was wonderful, but I'd rather be here than anywhere else in the world.'

Matthew said, 'And anyway, I'm not going back to school next term.'

'Of course you are, old chap.'

'I'm going to join the RAF.'

Devlin frowned. 'Your mother wants you to take the Oxford entrance exam, Matthew. That's what we agreed.'

'That's what you and Mum agreed. I didn't. I'm joining the RAF.'

'No.' The word was low and quiet.

'Why not?' Matthew leaned forward in his wicker seat. 'Don't you think there's going to be a war?'

'Of course there's going to be a war!' Her father had whitened. Then he said, 'I'm sorry, Zoe. I shouldn't have alarmed you. But I'm afraid there is going to be a war, yes.'

Zoe felt sick inside, but Matthew said, 'Then I can't waste my time at school, doing nothing.'

'I'm asking you to wait, Matthew, that's all. Just for a while. Six months, if you're set on it. Will you do that?'

'If it's going to happen, what's the point of waiting?'

'You're only seventeen, that's the point.'

'Eighteen the day after tomorrow.'

'Yes. Eighteen.' Her father was silent for a moment, then he said, 'We shouldn't be talking about this now.'

'Christ.' Matthew's lip curled.

'*Matthew*. Look, just think about it, that's all I'm asking.' Devlin went to the tray with the drinks. 'I wanted to talk to you about your party. I thought you'd prefer it to be held in the evening this year, rather than at lunchtime, so you could have dancing, if you wish. I've asked Mrs Satterley to prepare a cold buffet.'

Her father's back was to them as he refilled his glass, so Zoe gave Matthew a sharp kick on the shin.

Matthew muttered, 'Yes. Thanks, Dad.'

'All your friends are coming. And Uncle Tom and Aunt Alice, of course, and your grandparents. They're bringing your cousin Melissa.'

Matthew said, 'Who?'

'Melissa. Your mother's sister Camilla's daughter.' Her father sat down again. Zoe saw how tired he looked, a small muscle jumping beside one eye. 'She's staying with your grandparents.'

'It'll be fun, Daddy,' said Zoe, who hated parties. 'I can't wait.'

'Good,' said her father, though he still looked tired and sad. 'Shall we eat out here tonight? I think it's warm enough, don't you?'

After dinner, Matthew went to his room and Zoe and her father walked round the garden. If, reading Milton, for instance, Zoe came across a mention of Paradise, she always imagined it much like the garden at Rosindell.

Her father said, 'I'm sorry I frightened you earlier, darling.'

'There won't really be a war, will there, Daddy?' She hoped he would say no, of course not, I just lost my temper.

'I'm rather afraid there will be.'

Zoe hated that her dread must come even here to Rosindell. 'But Mr Chamberlain *said* – last autumn, Daddy . . .'

'"Peace for our time". Yes, I know. He'll have that carved on his heart when he dies. I suppose he has bought us some time, at the expense of poor Czechoslovakia.'

'But now Hitler has *all* of Czechoslovakia.'

'Yes,' her father said heavily. 'I'm afraid that won't satisfy him. I'm afraid it will only encourage him to believe that bullying and lawbreaking gets him what he wants.'

'There *can't* be a war! It would be so – so *unspeakable!*'

'My feelings exactly, but it looks as if we're heading that way.' He hugged her, then smoothed back her hair from her face. 'Whatever happens, you and Matthew will be safe. Look, Zoe, I can't foresee the future, none of us can. Maybe Hitler will take a step back.'

She could tell he didn't believe that, though. 'What if he doesn't?' Her voice was small and tight. 'What if there are bombs?'

'Then you'll come here. Hitler will have no interest in Rosindell.' They sat down on a bench. 'Look, darling, let's not worry about it now. We'll get through it, one way or the other. And meanwhile, we should enjoy the summer. I wondered whether you'd like to do some work for me at the boatyard. Make use of that shorthand and typing course you did earlier in the year. You could earn some extra cash. Two or three days a week, so you've still time to have fun.'

'Oh *yes*, Daddy.'

'Good.' He looked pleased.

Not long afterwards, her father had to take a telephone call. Watching him walk away through the garden, Zoe thought of bombs falling on Oxford — and on Rosindell too, perhaps: her father could not, as he had said, foresee the future, and there were naval ships on the Dart. There was a tense, wormy feeling inside her as she headed back to the house.

Over the next two days, preparations were made for Matthew's party. It seemed extraordinary to Zoe that Mr Philips should be deadheading the roses when it would surely have been more sensible to dig trenches or build an air-raid shelter, and almost unbelievable that Sarah and Mrs Satterley were dusting and making little puff-pastry tarts when they should have been storing up food for when the war began. Zoe had brought her gas mask, a horrible thing, with her to Devon. She had practised wearing it, as she had been told to, and had managed, at best, ten minutes, and even then had felt sick and panicky. Sarah had told her that there weren't any gas masks for babies. Whenever Zoe thought of the poor babies and their mothers, who must be frantic with worry, tears sprang to her eyes. She wondered whether, if the Germans used gas, the wind would blow it away. And how long that might take. She could have asked her father but did not, knowing how much he hated to talk about the war, and anyway, he was busy most of the time, rarely coming home from work until after eight o'clock.

In her bedroom, she tried the gas mask on again to see whether she could bear it for any longer, if she could ignore the awful chemical and rubber smells. Outside the window, the garden and the cliffs were reduced to twin circles through which she could see Philips mowing the lawn for the party as if nothing terrible was ever going to happen.

Saturday evening. In the drawing room, the furniture had been cleared back against the walls. There would be dancing later, a prospect that appalled Matthew, who was leaning against the sun-warmed back wall of the loggia, one leg cocked, his foot flat against the rough stones. Now and then his eyes came to rest fleetingly on a girl, a Langdon cousin or the sister of a former classmate from his prep school.

He heard his grandmother's high, hectoring tones and he and Zoe exchanged muted grimaces. His grandfather came out on to the loggia and pumped Matthew's hand up and down and wished him a happy birthday while he stuffed a five-pound note into his pocket. Granny pecked him on the cheek and said surely they were not expected to eat outside: so chilly, and the flies, and perhaps Matthew could find her a comfortable chair, wicker creaked so. 'Let me, Annette,' said his father, and Granny sighed and put on her long-suffering look. It was then that Matthew caught sight of the girl who had arrived with his grandparents: Melissa, presumably.

She was stunning: small and slim, her golden hair falling in a smooth, wavy sheet to her shoulders. She was wearing a dark blue skirt and a dark blue and white striped jersey. All the other girls, in their floral frocks, suddenly looked lumpy or graceless. Melissa's skin was a sort of milky, creamy colour, her lips as soft and pinky-red as strawberries. The fact that he could only see her in terms of edible things disconcerted him.

'You must be Matthew,' she said. 'Happy birthday.' She handed him a parcel.

'It isn't my birthday till tomorrow.' *Gauche, witless*, he thought. 'I mean, shall I open it?'

'That's entirely up to you,' she said, with a small, patronising smile. 'You must decide.'

He unwrapped the parcel. Inside was a Penguin edition of André Maurois' *Ariel*.

'I wasn't sure whether you read French,' she said, 'so I thought it safer to buy it for you in English. Do you know it?'

'Yes,' he said.

'Oh.' She made to take the book back. 'I'll buy you something else, then.'

220

'There's no need. I haven't a copy, I borrowed it from a friend.' And he remembered to mutter, 'Thanks.'

The Fawcetts arrived with their dogs, creating a diversion, and Matthew, hot-faced with embarrassment and crossness, was able to slip away. He snaffled a glass of champagne from a tray, though he didn't particularly like it, too sweet and fizzy. The guests had spilled out from the loggia over the lawns and paths and terraces. There was something nightmarish, he thought, about being confronted with all these people from a past he now considered narrow-minded and embarrassing. He imagined describing his ordeal to Fisher, but then decided not to: frightful family parties were probably unimaginable to clever, cosmopolitan Fisher.

He was collared by his Great-Aunt Amy, who remarked on how much he had grown – highly original, he thought sarcastically – and then by a chap from prep school, a bore then and a bore now, boringly and predictably working for his family's legal practice. He saw out of the corner of his eye that Melissa de Grey was standing on the steps that ran down from the loggia.

Zoe murmured in his ear, 'She's wearing Chanel.'

'Who is?'

'Melissa.'

'She's the most frightful snob. Thinks we're country bumpkins.'

'I thought she was rather sweet.'

He scowled at her. 'I'm going for a walk,' he said.

'*Matthew*. It's your party. You can't.'

'Watch me,' he said, and strode off along the path that ran in parallel to the stream.

When he reached the cliff, he took a packet of cigarettes out of his pocket and lit one. His resentment simmered like the red, smouldering end of the Woodbine. He breathed in lungfuls of smoke as he looked down to the bay below.

A crackle from behind him, and he turned and saw Melissa de Grey coming towards him from between the trees.

221

She said, 'May I have one?'

Matthew gave her a cigarette. She cupped her hand expertly to shelter the flame of his lighter from the sea breeze.

'Why did you leave?' she asked.

'It's not really my sort of thing.'

'One has to endure a great deal, I find, that isn't one's sort of thing.'

'You wouldn't understand.'

Usually people said, 'Try me,' but Melissa just shrugged.

'Maybe not.' She took a few steps forward, peering through the brambles. 'Is that yours?'

'The cove? Yes.'

'May I see it?'

He wasn't sure why she was asking him. She seemed the sort of girl who did what she felt like.

'If you want,' he said.

He let her go down the steps first, but then, because she was stumbling in her little high-heeled sandals, he ducked ahead of her and led the way, offering her his hand now and then where the steps were steepest. Her fingers felt smooth and soft and cool.

At the foot of the path she took off her sandals and walked across the sand to the shore. She said, 'Why don't you like me?'

He blustered for a while, but she said, 'Matthew, I can tell that you don't. Is it because of my mother?'

'Your mother?' He stared at her, bewildered.

'Camilla. Our mothers don't speak, you must know that. I wondered whether your mother had said something about mine.'

'No.' He shook his head. 'She never talks about her.'

'Grandfather told me I should come tonight.' Melissa made that little dismissive shoulder movement again, like the lifting of a bird's wing. 'But I was afraid I might be *de trop*.'

'Do you think I care about their silly quarrels?' he said angrily. 'Do you have to be so condescending? Assuming I can't read French – assuming I don't even *read*.'

She looked troubled. 'I'm sorry, I didn't mean to be impolite.'

'It doesn't matter.'

'It does, and it's my fault. I suppose I thought you'd be like my grandparents.'

He scowled. 'You mean, staunch supporters of Chamberlain and never reading anything more demanding than Agatha Christie? *God*. No.'

She smiled. 'Silly of me, I can see that you're not. But they've been very welcoming, which is kind of them.'

He asked her where she lived, and she said, 'Well, with Granny and Grandfather at the moment.'

'I meant *live*. Not *stay*.'

'I've never lived in any one particular place. I was supposed to be staying with a friend for the summer but then her sister caught scarlet fever so that fell through, and I thought of my grandparents. It was either that or a hotel. And I don't much care for hotels, do you?'

'No,' he agreed, though he had no great experience of them.

'So I looked them up in the phone book and wrote to them.'

He felt confused. 'Don't you *know* them?'

'Granny and Grandfather? No, hardly at all, really.'

'But surely your mother . . .'

'I don't live with my mother.' The direction of Melissa's eyes, which were the crystalline greeny-blue of the sea in the bay, travelled from one outstretched arm of the cliffs to the other and then came to rest on him. 'I came here once ages and ages ago, when I was a little girl. There's a photograph somewhere. You're very lucky, Matthew.'

'It's pretty boring, actually,' he said, aiming for a world-weary manner. 'And most of the time I don't live here, I live in Oxford.'

But she gave him that look again, the one that had so riled him back on the loggia, a detached, frowning consideration, as if he was an insect pinned to a specimen board.

He said, 'My parents are divorced, you see.'

At school, only two other boys, brothers, had parents who were divorced. Over the years he had moved from shame to a sort of fragile pride in his louche status. Perhaps because he had expected shock or sympathy or even disapproval, and had not got it, he added, 'It was pretty miserable, actually.'

'What was?'

'The divorce.'

'Was it? Still, if your parents weren't happy . . .'

She began to walk along the sand towards the bathing pool. He noticed that she kept to the dry part of the sand, never straying on to the damp, shiny shoreline. In spite of the breeze that flicked at the waves, she still looked perfect. Even Zoe, who fussed about everything, ended up looking windswept on the beach.

'But you must have *somewhere*.' He could not stop the words bursting out. 'You must have a *home*.'

'No, not really. My mother has a flat in London. Sometimes I go there, but I wouldn't call it *home*.' Melissa turned to look at him. It was a somewhat kinder glance than her previous one. 'Listen, Matthew, my mother comes into my life now and then, when she feels like it. Sometimes she writes to me and then she doesn't turn up, and at other times she just appears. And maybe she stays for half an hour or maybe for a few days. Sometimes we go to Harrods or Chanel and she buys me clothes, and then she goes away and I don't see her again for years. But I don't mind. I like my boarding school and I have lots of friends. At Christmas I usually go to Provence. And there's Rémy, in Paris.'

'Rémy?'

'He was a racing driver until he had a bad accident. I often stay with him, he's fun. At Easter I went to James's parents, in Wiltshire. I think of them as my grandparents but they're not really.'

Matthew thought Melissa's life sounded rather enviable, excitingly cosmopolitan and free of the usual cloying smother of families. 'I didn't know,' he said.

'Why should you?'

He noticed that she hadn't mentioned her father. But he was afraid that any curiosity of his would be brushed off or met by one of her supercilious glares.

She said, 'I don't really know about families. I *observe* them, but I've never properly been part of one.'

'Lucky you.'

'Why do you say that?'

'Families fall out. Do you hate her?'

'Who?'

'Your mother.'

She raised her eyebrows. 'No. Why should I?'

'I hate my father.'

'Because of the divorce?'

'Yes.' And he began to tell her about his parents' rows and what an awful time his mother had had in the aftermath of the separation, and how unhappy she had been, and all because of his father's selfishness. But even as he spoke, he knew that Melissa's upbringing had been so much more extraordinary, rather unimaginable, in fact, and that he was boring her, and he found himself finishing up:

'When we got here, he didn't even bother to meet us.'

He saw how feeble he must sound to her, a girl who had had to look up her grandparents' address in the phone book. Annoyed with himself, he fell silent.

She peered inside the bathing pool. 'Do you swim in there?'

'I used to, when I was little. I prefer the bay now.' Suddenly wretched, aware that he had made a fool of himself, he said, 'I'm hungry. Let's go back. They should have put the food out by now.'

*　　*　　*

225

Devlin took Commodore Pritchard into his study and offered him a drink. Pritchard, whom Devlin had first met at the Admiralty several weeks previously, was tall and thin, with sparse greying fair hair and a sunburned face.

Pritchard said, 'You must forgive me, Reddaway, for interrupting your boy's birthday party, only I don't know when I'll be in your neck of the woods again.'

'I'm glad you were able to call in.' Devlin unlocked the safe and took out the plans for Murray Allen's new design of power motorboat. The two men talked about technical details, speed and manoeuvrability and weaponry, and then the naval officer put the papers in his briefcase.

'Give me a ring when you're next in town,' he said. 'Is the yard working to capacity?'

'Pretty much.'

'Manpower will be one of the chief difficulties over the next few months.'

Devlin recalled the earlier years of the decade, unemployed men dragging out their days on street corners or in public libraries.

'Training, too,' he said. 'There's labour out there but the men haven't the skills any more. We're modernising the Kingswear yard. When that's finished, some of the work can go there.'

'I shouldn't take too long about it. Can't think we'll have more than a few weeks before kick-off.' The lowering sun cast stripes from the window frame across Pritchard's face. 'Magnificent place,' he said.

'I'm rather fond of it myself.'

'My wife and I, we'd hoped to move to the countryside. Penny's never liked London. Can't see it happening now. How old did you say your lad was?'

'Matthew's eighteen.'

'I have three sons. The two eldest are in the navy, stationed

226

in Singapore. My youngest is the same age as your boy. I don't suppose it will be long before he's in uniform too.'

Shortly afterwards, they shook hands and Devlin showed the commodore out of the house. As he went back indoors, music seeped through the open window, along with the scent of jasmine. These things contained such powerful memories that for a moment he closed his eyes, almost obliterated by them.

He lit a cigarette and considered another whisky, then decided against it. He had put a great deal of time and effort into persuading the Admiralty to take an interest in fast boats, and if they were to put in a substantial order, his work would have paid off. The knowledge that war might keep both boatyards fully occupied for the foreseeable future was bittersweet. It would be good for Langdon's employees and a relief to him personally, because the difficult economic conditions of the decade had meant that he had been able merely to service his bank loans throughout the thirties, rather than pay them off. His expenses – school fees, and the cost of maintaining two establishments, the north Oxford house for Esme and the children, as well as Rosindell – were crippling. Sometimes, rattling round the rooms with only the servants for company, he found himself wondering what he had been thinking of, investing so much in the house.

But then, he thought, times had been different. When he had commissioned Conrad Ellison to restore Rosindell, he had had a wife and family.

An order from the Admiralty would be some comfort derived from an evening that was in so many ways a travesty of the past. Without Esme, he expected the gramophone to scratch, the food to be tasteless, and his own flatness and futility to infect his guests. Though he had hoped the party might distract Zoe from her fears, he doubted it had. As for Matthew, he hadn't wanted it in the first place, had made it clear that he considered it to be an imposition. He had a perfect knack, Devlin thought, of misjudging his son's moods and desires.

Now, when he recalled the arguments that he and Esme had once had over Matthew's upbringing, he regretted that he had been so harsh on the boy. The fact that his strictness had been born of fear for Matthew, a fear that his wildness — a wildness that he himself had once shared — would lead to disaster, was of little solace. Because they had always been at loggerheads, Matthew would not now listen to him. Because he had been too severe, Esme had spoiled the boy, and now she too lacked authority over him. The world was tipping into an abyss where it might soon become impossible for him to keep either of his children safe.

He went outside. The remains of the buffet littered the table. Standing in the open French doors to the drawing room, he saw to his surprise and pleasure that Matthew was among the half-dozen couples dancing to the gramophone music. He did not immediately recognise the pretty, golden-haired girl his son was holding in his arms, but then, with a feeling of disquiet, he realised that it was Melissa de Grey.

The dance came to an end. The two cousins separated and Melissa returned to her grandparents, who were sitting on a bench on the terrace. Shortly afterwards, to Devlin's relief, Melissa, Charles and Annette left for Dartmouth.

During the period after the separation, when she had needed some occupation to stop herself breaking down completely, Esme had taken to going round the junk shops of Oxford and the countryside that surrounded it. Driving, pottering from shop to shop, had occupied enough of her mind to give her a brief respite from the mental rerunning of the events that had led up to her leaving Devlin, like a spool of film showing the same sequence over and over. Her triumphs — a Regency card table and a tiny Corot, hidden beneath a dark accumulation of dirt — had given purpose to days in which she had gone through the motions of caring for the children and running a home while feeling inside as if she were breaking into fragments. She had furnished the small, pleasant detached house in a leafy north Oxford street with her finds, drawing on her experience with Rosindell. Since then, her pastime had grown into a part-time job. Her circle of friends — the wives of academics and professional women — now sometimes asked her to help with the decoration of their homes.

On the morning of Matthew's birthday, Esme rose early. After breakfast, she examined the set of bentwood chairs she had bought the previous day, checking for woodworm. At this time of day there was a pleasure in being alone in the house. The quietness of the morning seemed full of promise, when at night it oppressed.

At nine o'clock she phoned Matthew. 'Happy birthday, darling.'

'Thanks, Mum.'

'Did you like the shirt?'

'Yes, Mum, it's super. Snazzy colour.'

'How was your party?'

'It was good fun.'

This response surprised Esme. She said, 'Not too many old aunts?'

'No, it wasn't too bad.'

Esme felt rather deflated. Matthew's mimicry of his dottier Langdon relatives was a shared amusement and always made her laugh.

'I'm glad you had a good time,' she said. 'Now, I'm going to town on Monday and I was planning to call in at Peter Jones. You need a new cricket jersey, don't you, darling, though I suppose it would be better to wait till spring, in case you grow some more.'

'Don't buy me any more school stuff, Mum.'

'Shirts. I seem to remember they're looking worn at the collars.'

'Mum, I'm not going back to school next term.'

'Of course you are, Matthew.'

'I'm going to join the RAF.'

'Matthew—'

229

'Dad says I can.'

'It isn't up to your father. Darling, we talked about this.'

'I've already applied, Mum.' His voice had taken on a mulish tone.

'Is your father there? Let me speak to him.'

Rumblings and clunkings while Matthew put down the receiver. Esme scanned the sitting room. Every item of furniture, every book and ornament had been carefully chosen, but now they failed to give solace.

'Hello, Esme.' Devlin's voice.

'Matthew told me that you agreed to let him join the RAF.'

'That's not exactly true.'

'How could you? Surely you must know how I feel about it? Doesn't that matter to you at all?'

'Naturally it does, but—'

'He's only eighteen. Far too young.'

'Esme, there's a limit to what we can do to stop him, if he's made up his mind.'

'How can you be so complacent – and so uncaring?' Her voice rose. 'Doesn't it trouble you that he'll be risking his life?'

There was a silence, during which her words echoed, and she began to regret them. Into her head came a memory of the first time she had seen Devlin after the Great War had ended, limping along South Town.

He said, 'If you think that I feel *complacent* about the prospect of another war, about the prospect of my son having to fight . . .'

'I'm sorry.' She took a gulp from the teacup beside her, made an effort and said, 'This must be difficult for you too. It's just that I worry for him so.'

'I tried to get him to agree to wait, for six months at least. But I'm afraid he interpreted that as consent.'

'Of course he did!'

'If he's going to join up, it would be better for him to go with our blessing, wouldn't you agree?'

230

'But not yet! He's not even eligible for conscription!'

'If war breaks out, then boys of Matthew's age will be called up. They won't wait until we're on our knees this time.' She heard him sigh. 'I've been thinking. If Matthew doesn't want to stay on at school and he's not interested in university, then perhaps he could come and work for the firm. Maybe he'd agree to that, as a compromise, just for a few months.'

'Of course he wants to go to Oxford!' Esme cried indignantly. 'Hugo read one of his essays and said that he was most certainly Oxford material!'

'How is Hugo?' Devlin's tone was neutral.

'He's very well. Terribly busy, poor lamb.'

'Matthew's always been an active, practical boy. He likes *doing* things. I find it hard to imagine him shutting himself away in an ivory tower.'

Esme felt this to be a reflection on Hugo. 'You shouldn't assume all academics to be sluggish and idle,' she said huffily. 'Hugo was in a rowing eight when he was an undergraduate. And Matthew's not the least interested in *boatbuilding*.'

A silence, then Devlin said, 'Have you heard from your mother recently?'

'Not for a while, no.'

'Did you know that Camilla's daughter is staying at St Petrox Lodge?'

Esme stiffened. 'No.'

'I had no alternative but to invite her to Matthew's party. It would have looked very odd if I hadn't.'

'I don't want *my* son to have anything to do with *her* daughter!' She hated the thought of it, Matthew meeting Camilla's brat. 'You should have known that, Devlin.'

'There's no reason why they should run into each other again. Annette's hardly a frequent visitor to Rosindell.'

Shortly afterwards, Esme put down the phone. Though she had planned out her day, filling every moment of it, and though she

231

set to with a will, cleaning the set of bentwood chairs, then dead-heading the garden flowers and filling in the gaps in the borders with the pots she had nurtured in the little sunlit terrace at the back of the house, she found to her dismay that a shadow had fallen over everything she did.

In Dartmouth, Matthew looked at the naval ships on the river and bought a particularly filthy seaside postcard, on which he scribbled a couple of phrases summing up his boredom, before posting it to Fisher.

As he mooched around, he kept an eye out for her. Melissa would stand out, he thought, among the daytrippers and naval cadets. It was a hot afternoon, and the heat fed his frustration as he wandered away from the shops and harbour. From Above Town he could see St Petrox Lodge. He lit a cigarette and pretended to admire the view of the estuary. When a figure emerged from the house, his heart sped up, but it was only Hetty, the maid. He considered knocking on the door but was afraid that Melissa might not believe he had come to visit his grandmother, and might imagine him to be keen on her. He pictured her patronising little smile, threw the cigarette end into a plant pot and walked away.

Another week passed. He went back to Dartmouth and this time rang the doorbell of his grandparents' home. Melissa had a dental appointment in London and his aunts were visiting, and he had to endure an hour of brainless, nosy questions about school, his plans for the future and his mother's current arrangements before he was able to flee to the ferry.

Esme had met Hugo Godwin at a cocktail party the previous winter. She had liked the way he had waited until the evening was almost over before introducing himself, as if making sure the opposition was out of the way, and she had liked that he had walked her home through the starlit winter streets before heading off on foot back to his college. There had been something adventurous and romantic about his striding off through the dark. A few days later she had received a letter from him, telling her that he had tickets for a concert at the college, and would she like to come? She had thanked him by inviting him to supper. The following Sunday, they had walked on Port Meadow. And so the friendship had gone on.

Hugo was the only child of a clergyman and his wife, both of whom had been almost elderly when he had been born. His parents had died while he was studying for his first degree. He had had a lengthy love affair with a colleague's housekeeper throughout much of his thirties and forties, which had ended when the woman had died of tuberculosis.

Hugo preferred to dine at Esme's house, but as her cook-housekeeper was on holiday, they had arranged to meet at a restaurant in Turl Street. He was seated at the table when Esme arrived, a little late, at the restaurant. He was a tall, thin, distinguished-looking man with an English sort of handsomeness: a long, bony face and aquiline nose, grey eyes and hair the light golden-brown of fallen beech leaves. As he stood up to greet her, he automatically ducked his head to avoid the low ceiling.

'Hugo, darling,' she said. 'Sorry, I couldn't find anywhere to park.'

'They were going to put us in a corner but I asked them to change to a table by the window.'

'Clever of you.' They kissed and she sat down.

'I wasn't sure whether you would want wine.'

'Oh yes!' she cried. 'I think so, don't you? So much traffic, and I almost backed into a letter box.'

'I think you're very brave,' he said indulgently. Hugo didn't drive. He had a theory that motoring did not come easily to intellectuals.

They ordered food and wine, and Hugo described a

conversation he had had that afternoon with the Master's wife, a stupid, snobbish woman. They spoke about the book that Hugo was writing about the Civil War and Esme told him about the bentwood chairs. Then the conversation slid, as all conversations tended to do these days, to the possibility of war.

'Rumour is,' said Hugo, spearing his last morsel of lamb fricassee, 'that Chamberlain's finally thinking of negotiating with Stalin.'

'How personal these things have come to seem,' Esme said sadly. 'That it should matter to me what those two men have to say to each other.'

'Because of Matthew?'

'Yes, Hugo.' Appreciative of his understanding, she put her hand on his.

'Chamberlain loathes everything the Russians stand for. But only the Russians are strong enough to persuade Hitler to draw back. The Poles, of course, fear the Russians as much as the Nazis. And with good cause.'

The waitress cleared away their dinner plates. After she had gone, Hugo said, 'Fleming called me today.'

'Fleming?'

'My friend in the Home Office. He's coming down to Oxford tomorrow.'

'Is he? Why?'

Hugo lowered his voice, as if the waitress, now bearing purposefully towards them with the pudding menu, might be a German spy.

'It looks as if there'll be something for me when the balloon goes up.'

Esme hated the way men talked about war, in that trite, joking way, as if it was inevitable, even exciting. She said, disobligingly, 'I thought you hated London.'

'There are aspects of it that I dislike, yes. But one would want to be in the heart of things.'

234

'But your work . . .'

'Will become irrelevant.'

She looked down at her printed card, pretending to study the list of puddings. 'Don't you *mind*?'

'In a way, yes, of course. But I imagine that if one were to be employed by the government at such a time, one would have a sense of working towards the common good, of *purposefulness*. That might in some way make up for the loss of routine and congenial company. I don't want a pudding, do you?'

There was chocolate sponge on the menu, which she would have happily eaten for comfort, but then, her figure. She said, 'No thank you, Hugo.'

Esme felt gloomy. She suspected that her life was about to crumble away for a second time. It had been so painfully hard to create a new existence for herself after the divorce and she doubted she had the energy to do it again. But she was being selfish and egotistical; she could tell how flattered Hugo was to have been approached by this man, Fleming.

She said, 'Wonderful for you, darling, and I'm sure you deserve it. But I shall miss you terribly.'

The waitress returned and reclaimed the menus. Hugo waved away her suggestion of coffee. Then, after some throat-clearing, he said, 'Actually, I wondered whether you would think of coming to London with me, Esme.'

It took more than a moment for her to realise that this was, in fact, a proposal of marriage. She felt confused by such a turmoil of feelings that it was several more moments before she was able to say:

'That's very sweet of you, Hugo, and I'm awfully touched. But I'd never thought of' – he had not actually used the word, so she was cautious – '*committing* myself to anyone again. The divorce was so frightful, you see.'

'You never talk about it.'

'I try not to think about it. Such deceit, such betrayal.'

'"Passions spin the plot",' said Hugo, in a quoting voice. '"We are betrayed by what is false within." Meredith,' he added helpfully.

'People seemed to think I should forgive Devlin – even my mother thought I should forgive him – but it was impossible. I knew I'd never be able to think of him in the same way.'

He took her hand. 'Poor girl.'

'It was a long time ago. You do recover, to some extent, though at the time you think you never will.'

'Then will you consider what I've said to you? There's no need to rush. London may be months away.'

And she found herself responding, as much out of gratitude as anything else, 'Yes. Thank you, Hugo.'

The others had headed out to sea, and Matthew had begun to regret not having gone with them when, as he backstroked round the islet in the bay, he saw her, a flare of white at the top of the cliff.

By the time he had swum back to the shore Melissa was halfway down the steps. Matthew slung a towel round his shoulders and went to meet her.

'I tried the house,' she said, 'but there was no one there. I thought you might be here.'

'Did you come with my grandparents?'

'No, I cycled. You don't mind, do you?'

''Course not,' he muttered, though he was unsure whether that was true. He had quarrelled with his father that morning; his father wanted him to work at the boatyard, a dreadful and ludicrous idea, and he might rather have been alone, nurturing his ill-temper.

Melissa said, 'Where's your sister?'

'Some friends came round and they took the boat out.'

'Didn't you want to go with them?'

He shook his head.

236

'It's so hot, isn't it?' she said, crossing the sand to the place where Matthew had dumped his belongings. 'I couldn't think of anything nicer than going for a swim.'

And with that, she peeled off her white cotton frock, folded it and placed it neatly on top of her bag. Underneath the frock she was wearing a navy-blue bathing suit. She slid her feet out of her sandals, walked down the beach and waded into the sea, then struck off into the bay.

These actions, which took no more than a few moments, had such a profound effect on him that he stood staring at her golden head as it bobbed through the sea, jangling as if an electric current was running through him. Then he followed her into the water. But it was only after he had swum across the bay as fast as he could that he was able to put the image of Melissa pulling her frock over her head to the back of his mind, where it remained, powerful and disturbing.

She was a good swimmer and they fooled around for a while, racing each other to the islet and diving from one of the large rocks. Eventually, pleasantly tired out, they headed back to shore.

The sun dried them off as they moseyed around the rock pools. Melissa made a heap of flat stones and seaweed and rusty tin cans that the sea had washed up on the beach.

'What's that?' he said.

'It's my surrealist sculpture.'

'It's a shame there isn't a lobster.'

'A lobster wouldn't be *surreal*, Matthew,' Melissa said reprovingly, 'if it was on a beach. I once stayed in a house where they had a lobster telephone. It was terribly inconvenient.'

She mimed trying to talk through a lobster, which made them both snort with laughter, and it was only when he was able to stop that he said, 'God, you make me feel so *provincial*.'

She was lying on her back, squinting at the sunlight. 'You make me feel so *decadent*.'

'I'd like to be decadent.'

'No you wouldn't, Matthew. It's very grubby and uncomfortable and you never have enough to eat. Believe me, I know.'

They went back to their discarded clothes and Matthew shared out the sandwiches. Melissa wandered down to the shore and drank from the lemonade bottle. The brightness and the angle of the sun meant that he saw her only in silhouette, her features in shadow: the narrowness of her waist, that he imagined circling with his two hands, the swell of breast and hip black against the translucent green sparkle of the waves.

She handed him the lemonade bottle. Drinking from it, he thought about the warmth of her mouth and the taste of her lips. When they had finished eating they lay down on the sand, side by side. He liked that she didn't seem to want to talk much. The memory of his quarrel with his father was becoming distant and unimportant, as if the sun was melting it away.

He said, 'Do you know why our mothers don't speak to each other?'

Melissa rolled on to her side. 'Sooner or later my mother quarrels with everyone. Or she gets bored with them.'

He examined his own reflection in the black panes of her glasses. 'My father's such a hypocrite,' he said. 'All those years he was pretending to love my mother, and it was just a lie.'

'When did they split up?'

'Seven years ago. I was eleven. We have to come here every summer. Most of the time I try to keep out of his way.'

'You blame him.' This was stated as a fact, not a question.

'It was his fault. Mum told me.'

Melissa slid her dark glasses to the top of her head and propped herself up on her elbows. Close to her, he could see a tiny scar by her eyebrow and a fluttering of freckles across the bridge of her nose.

'We don't have to be like them,' she said. 'I'm only ever going to fall in love with one man and I shall stay with him for ever.'

Then she sat up and checked her wristwatch. 'I'd better go,' she said.

They dressed and walked up the cliff steps and through the woodland to the garden. Her bicycle was propped against the front porch. Matthew fetched his own bike and they rode side by side to Kingswear, where he waited with her in the queue for the ferry. People wheeled off bikes and the foot passengers ambled after them.

'Bye, Matthew. It's been fun.' Melissa stood on tiptoe and brushed her lips against his cheek. Then she wheeled her bicycle on to the ferry.

His school report cards often said things like, 'Matthew needs to apply himself more,' or, 'Matthew has a tendency to coast.' The truth was, he had never had to make much of an effort. He was good-looking and clever; what he wanted had come easily to him.

Instinctively, though, he knew that with Melissa he had to try. That he must give events a shove or risk something precious slipping away, something that might release him from frustration and futility.

As the ferry moved off, he called out to her, 'I swim every morning, nineish. Zoe doesn't usually come then because that's when she does her piano practice.'

Melissa waved to show him that she had heard. Matthew watched the craft recede until he could no longer distinguish her from the other passengers. But he still seemed to feel the patch of skin where her lips had touched him, a small, pleasurable sting.

Chapter Twelve

August 1939

S he runs a hand along the fire surround in the great hall, tracing with her fingertip the witches' marks incised in the stone. Josiah told her that the interlocking circles were put there to keep witches out, but if so, Zoe thinks, it hasn't worked, because whatever was inside Rosindell was already there, and is still there.

She looks up at the imps that squat at the ends of the roof beams. As a child, she imagined them coming down from their perches at night, their small brown faces gleeful as they capered round the house, stealing trinkets and hiding them in impossible places, leaving muddy footprints on the floors and startling you, sometimes, when you almost caught a glimpse of them.

You never saw them face to face. They existed in the corner of the eye, in the movement of a curtain, in the ripples on a bowl of water.

In Paris, she had been a different person. The old Zoe, the one with the rituals that often comforted but sometimes exhausted her, the rituals that exasperated her mother and worried her father, had vanished. She had been entranced by the city, its culture, language and people, and kept busy at Madame Félix's school, and the compulsion had disappeared.

And nothing dreadful had happened. This discovery had been a revelation. Some of Paris's style and zest for living had rubbed off on her during her six months there. She had learned how to make up her face properly, how to tie a silk scarf, how to make an hour's pleasure out of a *café crème* and a *tuile aux amandes* and a seat under an awning, watching the world go by. She had thought the changes permanent; it unsettled her that she was turning back into her old self.

Once, in the Rue de Rivoli, a very handsome man had seized her hand and kissed it. Then he had talked to her in extremely fast French until she had made an excuse and hurried into a shop. She wondered what might have happened if she had gone with him to a café or a bar. Might she now be an engaged woman, or even married, living in Paris in an elegant apartment in the sixteenth arrondissement? A part of her had wanted to see what might happen. But the larger part of her had been distrustful, and now she wondered whether, in her rush for safety, she had missed something.

Zoe and Matthew had always been close, but this summer he did not seem to need her. When she asked him what he was doing, he said, irritatingly, 'Just stuff.'

Suit yourself, she thought.

After an unpleasant dental appointment one morning, Zoe sat on the window seat in her bedroom, reading. Gingerly, she poked her jaw. The injection was wearing off and the tooth that old Mr Foster, squinting through his glasses, had filled was starting to feel sore.

A movement in the thick green fringe of trees on the cliff caught her eye. Matthew and a girl were walking out of the oaks and pines, through the laurels. Now and then they were masked by the trees and shrubs as they headed towards the garden.

The girl looked up and Zoe recognised Melissa de Grey. She

was wearing a pink frock and a wide-brimmed hat. Zoe knelt up on the seat, intending to tap on the window pane as soon as they were in earshot, but then she noticed that Matthew and Melissa were holding hands.

Oh, she thought. And *Well*. And *Matthew*.

She shuffled back on the seat and watched them go into the summer house and then walk up and down the long flower borders. Matthew pretended to give the bronze girl on the swing a push. Then he climbed up into the branches of the tree and leaped down on to the grass. *Show-off*, thought Zoe. Then, standing where the statue's shadow spilled over the lawn, he placed his hands on Melissa's hips and kissed her.

Zoe looked away. After a while, she heard them come into the house. She slid off the seat, wondering whether Matthew might call out to her, whether he would remember that she had had a horrible time at the dentist. But he did not; instead there was the creak and clunk of the door to the old part of the house opening and closing as they went through.

Silly, really, that she should feel deflated and left out. Or that she should mind that Matthew did not know Rosindell as she did. She imagined him blundering round, fooling about, forgetting to show Melissa the important places. But then, Zoe thought, no one, not even she, knew the contents of every drawer and cupboard or every meandering path of the attics and cellars. No one could completely know Rosindell, not really.

He said, 'Do you think it matters that we're cousins?'

'Kings and queens marry their cousins.'

'Hardly a recommendation. Think of the Habsburgs. Wasn't there a mad one?'

'They had funny chins.'

He kissed her chin, which was delightful and not funny at all. 'But there's no *law* against it, is there?'

They had cycled that morning to Brixham and were sitting

in a pub near the harbour. Fishermen and daytrippers sat at the tables; outside, in the drizzle, were marooned mothers and children, eating chips and wielding buckets and spades.

She said, 'We're kissing cousins.'

'What's that?'

'Just what it says. Cousins who kiss each other. If you know your cousin well enough, you kiss them.'

Their fingers threaded together like the cogs of a gear. 'Do you think,' he said, 'that if we'd always known each other – since we were children, I mean – we'd feel the same?'

'Yes,' she said.

'Do you think . . .' Beneath the table, he lowered their clasped hands until they rested on her thigh. 'Do you think we'd feel the same if we *weren't* cousins?'

This she considered carefully. Then she said, 'The first time I saw you, at the party, it was as though I knew you already. It was as if I recognised you. I'd only met you once, but I knew who you were before my grandmother told me. I saw you standing on the terrace, by the wall, and I thought, that's Matthew. Sometimes, when I look at you, it's like looking into a mirror. It's as if I've been waiting for you.'

'Kissing cousins,' he said.

'Yes.' She flashed a look round the pub to make sure that the fishermen were still busy with their beer, and then she pressed her lips against the corner of his mouth.

They talk about the Left Book Club, pacifism, swing music, the miserable conclusion of the war in Spain, awful English food compared to marvellous French food, the poems of Louis MacNeice, especially 'Bagpipe Music', sailing and horse-riding (Melissa prefers horse-riding, Matthew sailing), Charlie Chaplin, the uselessness and hypocrisy of the British and French governments, and surrealism, which Melissa dislikes and Matthew admires. They find their coincidences in taste extraordinary and their differences fascinating. They talk about their mothers, their fathers (Melissa doesn't know hers, wouldn't recognise him if she passed him in the street), their schools, and Melissa tries to list for him the many, many places in which she has lived.

He talks to her about the RAF, and the freedom he thinks he might find, up there, released from the ties of the earth. He imagines flying to be an ecstasy, rather like being in love.

Rosindell Bay was their special place. They liked the mornings best, the flood of blue-black shadow pulling back towards the cliffs as the sun rose higher in the sky. When the tide was in, there was a step halfway up the path where they could squeeze together, side by side, and watch the waves throw themselves against the rocks. Flecks of white foam reached them, high on their perch.

As soon as the sea receded, they walked down to the beach. The water drew back, tumbling tiny shells and pieces of grit and making the pink quartz glisten. The sea left behind gifts: a leathery brown length of bladderwrack, the tangled lattice of a fisherman's net, pieces of polished glass. They liked to dig their heels in and feel the wet sand sucked away beneath their bare soles, pulling them off balance so that they fell into each other's arms, laughing. Then, as the sun dried the beach, they chose a place for their encampment. A rock pool to cool the lemonade. Two towels slung side by side. She lay down beside him, her head in the hollow of his neck, his arm round her waist and her bare legs toppled against his.

His hands, scooping out the curves of her body in its damp swimsuit. Her hair, darkened by the water, falling in clammy ribbons against his face.

Talk a little, then kiss. Talk a little, then kiss. Kiss and kiss, until his only thoughts were of the meeting of his skin and hers, and the sea-scent of her, and the summer and the sun. Once, they lay there so long the incoming tide licked at their toes and they had to snatch up their belongings and run for the steps.

I love you. Sometimes he thought it, sometimes he said it. But every touch declared it. *I love you.*

The six chairs looked splendid, the beechwood having polished up to a warm light brown. She might see if Nita Watson wanted them for her dining room, thought Esme. She put her polishing cloth away and looked round for something else to do.

The phone rang. She picked up the receiver and said hello.

'Hello, Esme.'

'Devlin.'

He said, 'I thought you'd want to know that Melissa has gone back to London.'

'Good. Yes.' She let out a breath. 'Thank you.'

'Apparently her mother has asked for her.'

'I can't say I'm sorry she's on her way.'

'How are you?'

How was she? Like a coiled spring, Esme thought. 'Very well,' she said.

'Have you heard from Tom?'

'No, not recently. Has something happened?'

'Apparently he's going back into the navy.'

'Good God.' In the silence, she heard from the other end of the phone line the muffled cry of a seagull. Odd that the bird's raucous squawk, she thought distractedly, should make her feel homesick.

She said, 'But Devlin, he's older than *me*.'

'He had a word with someone in Portsmouth. Strings were pulled.'

'Alice . . .'

'I think she's part of the reason for going. I get the impression they may be about to call it a day.'

'Oh, poor Alice!'

'The navy might sort him out. Stop him drinking himself into an early grave.'

'I suppose so. But the boatyard . . .'

'It's damned ill-timed. We've just had a big order from the Admiralty. Your father's furious.'

'Yes,' she said, worrying for Tom, whom, whatever he did, she could always forgive. 'Oh dear. I shall write to him. How are the children?'

'Enjoying their summer. I don't see a lot of Matthew, he's out most of the time. But that's the other reason I wanted to speak to you. I'm a little concerned about Zoe.'

'She's not unwell, is she?'

'No, no, certainly not. But I think she's worrying about the political situation. I try to reassure her, but there's a limit to what one can do. She's an intelligent girl and she reads the newspapers.'

'Hugo thinks the Russians will give Hitler pause for thought.'

'I hope he's right. But if he isn't, if the Russians aren't cooperative or Hitler decides he'll have Poland anyway, I want you to know that the children will always be welcome here. If you don't feel they're safe in Oxford. And you too, Esme, the same goes for you.'

'I'm sure that won't be necessary, Devlin,' she said tartly, rather startled. 'And if I did feel the need to flee, there's always my parents. Though I might prefer to face the bombs.' Finding herself unexpectedly touched by his offer, she added, 'But thank you. It's a kind thought.'

After she had put the phone down, Esme lit a cigarette and went out into the garden. The sun filtered through the beech tree, dappling the lawn and terrace. She pulled a weed out of a crack in the brickwork, clipped a spent flower from a cosmos.

She had thought she would worry about Zoe or Tom, or even think about Devlin's surprising offer of sanctuary at Rosindell. But those things, important though they were, had been overshadowed. When she considered the future, it seemed to her that it was as if they were entering a tunnel, the sides of which narrowed, pushing them into darkness, compressing them, crushing them. And it frightened her to think that they might not all emerge undamaged.

She went upstairs and changed into a calf-length frock of dark green satin. She wondered whether it was too showy for a little college concert, but then decided she didn't care. How long might pass before she had the opportunity to wear such a frock again? She put on lipstick, then clasped her pearls round her neck. She supposed she should lock up and go and start the car, but she remained where she was, sitting at the dressing table.

Twenty years ago, she had married for love, but had in the end found it wanting. Love had been rash and misplaced and never, she had realised, fully reciprocated. Devlin had not loved her as she had loved him. It had torn her apart to discover this, and afterwards she had regretted the person she had been and had tried to change herself. She had tried to erase her impulsiveness, to harden her heart.

She was not blind to Hugo's faults, his self-congratulatory air, his lack of humility, his tendency to dominate a conversation. He was unadventurous with food and drink, preferring school dinner favourites to anything French or unusual. He dressed badly and had brought with him the same shabby raincoat to every one their dates. Esme put all this down to his great intelligence, his lack of worldliness and his absorption in his subject, history, which allowed no mental space for frivolities.

Sometimes she found these things endearing; tonight she did not. She found herself critically examining her own failings, and wondering whether in fleeing from the wild love she had once felt for Devlin, its opposite would disappoint, just as passion had.

*　　*　　*

Zoe was sitting on a bench outside the booking office, watching the passengers alight from the train. Catching sight of Matthew, she went to meet him.

'How was London?'

'Wizard,' he said.

'Dad thinks you've gone sailing.'

They came out of the station and collected their bikes. Zoe said, 'Have you told him about Melissa?'

'Of course not.'

'Have you told Mum?'

Matthew wheeled his bicycle on to the road. 'No.'

'Are you going to?'

He gave a careless shrug. 'Sometime, maybe. Not yet.'

'She might not like it. It might upset her. Mum doesn't like Aunt Camilla.'

'Then I won't say anything.' He gave her a pointed look. 'It's nothing to do with them. Actually, it's nothing to do with you either, Zoe.'

They cycled through the steep, narrow streets. Feeling a need to lower the tension, she said, 'How was Melissa?'

'Fine. Her mother had an operation a couple of weeks ago. Melissa's looking after her. We just sat in Hyde Park and talked about things.' Then he said, 'I've had a letter from the Air Ministry.'

'What did it say?'

'I'm to attend a selection board at the end of the month.'

The horrible, anxious feeling, which was never far away these days, made her stomach cramp, but she managed to say, 'Congratulations. That's terrific.'

'I haven't got through yet.'

'You will, though, Matt.'

'We talked about it,' he said. 'Melissa and I. You see, it doesn't matter what Mum and Dad think, because I'm not going to be at home any more. I can do what I want. Melissa and me, we can do what we want.' Then, putting on some speed, he cycled away, up the hill.

Matthew had to borrow some cash from Zoe to pay for his next train ticket to London, which was embarrassing after his declaration of independence. He would give her the money back as soon as he received his first pay packet from the RAF. On the train from Totnes, he revised his trigonometry. The selection board was in ten days' time and everyone said you had to know your trig. The importance of the board was weighing on him; a lot depended on it.

At Paddington station he made his way between the groups of uniformed men standing on the platform. Some stood beside heaps of kitbags; others were queuing to squeeze into carriages.

He went through the barrier and saw Melissa standing beside an advertisement hoarding pasted with notices about evacuation and air-raid protection. She was wearing a matching blue skirt and jacket, white gloves and hat. Her hair was scooped up off her shoulders and pinned in coils and shells beneath the hat. She looked grown-up and polished; if he hadn't known her, he might have thought her rather unapproachable.

They kissed and then walked arm in arm out of the station. Though sunlight fell between the tall buildings, heavy clouds were bubbling up in the distance. In Hyde Park, diggers had gouged out an ochre-coloured crater. The excavated sand was being used to fill the bags that were to protect London's buildings. Small boys ran to the edge of the crater and peered in. Some threw pebbles. The trenches that had been dug during the Munich crisis glistened with mud after the previous night's rain. Matthew saw that the city was ratcheting itself into a different form, getting ready for what was to come.

They sat down on a bench beneath a chestnut tree. He said, 'How's your mother?'

'Better today. One of her friends took her out to dine last night. She hates being stuck in the flat.'

'Will I meet her?'

'I don't want you to.' Melissa turned to look at him, her eyes shadowed by the brim of the hat. 'Bobby Lancaster is with her, so she doesn't need me today.'

He put his arms round her and they kissed again. He said, 'How much longer will you stay with her?'

'Not long, I shouldn't think. I can tell I'm beginning to get on her nerves.'

'Where will you go?'

'My mother suggested I go to a finishing school in Switzerland. But I can't see the point; my French and German are fluent already.' She threaded her gloved hand through his. 'I'd rather get a job. I thought I could learn to be a translator. Rémy knows someone who works in a publishing house in Paris. He's offered to put me in touch with him.'

The girl who had lain beside him on the beach, grains of sand glittering on her skin, had gone. The city, like the couture clothes she was wearing, had altered her. Matthew was afraid that she might drift away from him, back to her other life.

'I don't want you to go back to France,' he said.

Melissa was twisting the leather strap of her handbag. Her gaze settled on a point in the sky where an approaching rainstorm was making the buildings shimmer.

'One evening,' she said, 'when I was fourteen, my mother took me to the Café de Paris. She made a fuss of me; she let me have all my favourite things for supper and listened to me when I talked to her about school. She told me that she was going to take me on holiday to St Moritz so that I could learn to ski. I remember thinking how sparkling and beautiful the room was and how nice my mother was and how it was going to be different between us in the future. And then some of her friends turned up, and she didn't take any notice of me any more. I went to the bathroom, and when I came back to the table, everyone had gone. I waited and waited – I must have waited for an hour, Matthew, though I suppose that after ten minutes I knew they weren't going to come back. I remember that there was a nice waiter who offered to fetch me a taxi, but I said no thank you, someone was coming to meet me. I wasn't sure whether I had enough money for a cab, you see. So I walked back to the flat on my own. My mother didn't come home that night, or the next day, and in the end I had to call Rémy, in Paris, and he wired me some money. She'd forgotten about me, you see.'

The first drops of rain tumbled through the leaves of the trees. 'I'll never forget you,' he said. 'Wherever we are, even if we're far apart, you'll be first in my thoughts in the morning and last in them at night.'

'People say things and then they forget.'

'Not me.'

She gave him a clear-eyed look. 'You'll be busy, Matthew, you'll be learning to fly a plane. You'll be doing something that's difficult and important. It's not so easy for girls. If there's a war, I'll find something useful to do, but it might take me a while.' She rested her head against his shoulder. The straw brim of her hat tickled his chin. 'I shouldn't mind, not really,' she said softly. 'I've been so happy this summer.'

He sat up, facing her. 'There is a way we can stay together.'

Crackles of lightning illuminated the sky and there was a loud rumble of thunder, like someone moving furniture in an attic. The rain, a sudden heavy downpour, bounced off the path. Matthew threw his jacket over their heads as they ran with other refugees from the storm. And once they had found shelter in a pub and were dripping on to the wet lino, and he told her his idea, it seemed to both of them the obvious solution.

Eight o'clock, dinner time, and Matthew was not yet home. Devlin asked Zoe where he was.

They were having drinks in the drawing room, because throughout the afternoon and early evening, thunderstorms had been passing over the headland. Zoe was curled up on the sofa, the dog beside her. Through the window, Devlin could see the cliff, where the trees tossed their dark green heads in the same easterly wind that was driving the rain into the loggia, battering the plants in their pots and soaking the wicker chairs.

Devlin said, 'Zoe?'

'Not sure, Daddy.'

Looking out of the window, he was struck by a sudden anxiety. 'He hasn't taken the yacht out, has he?'

'No, Daddy.'

'If he has,' he said carefully, 'then you must tell me. I won't be angry, I promise, but I need to know.' Phone the coastguard, he thought. Round up some of the men from the yard, take out the motor launch and scour the sea. And hope to God he wasn't too late.

Zoe said, 'He's gone to London.'

'London? To see that friend of his?'

'No.'

'Where, then?'

The wind swung round and Devlin had to rise and close a window. He heard Zoe say, 'He's gone to see Melissa.'

'Your cousin Melissa?'

'Yes, Daddy.' She had dipped her head, burying her face in the spaniel's coat, and her next words came out muffled. 'He told me not to tell you.'

Neither of his children was up before Devlin left the house early the next morning. Clumsy with lack of sleep, he shaved and dressed and mentally refashioned his day. As he stepped out of the door, a break in the clouds made the ripples of sunlight on the swollen stream flash into his eyes. He could feel the headache gathering, waiting to pounce on him. The inevitability of it, and the inconvenience, infuriated him.

On the drive to Totnes, he stopped off briefly at the boat-yard, where he left instructions for the day's work. He parked the car at Totnes station and caught a fast through train to London. In the first-class compartment, he was surrounded by indications of the coming conflict. A headline in a news-paper; a woman with an ARP badge, joining the carriage at Exeter; a conversation in muted tones between the husband and wife sitting beside him, about their son, who had been called up. So wrong, he thought; this has happened before, why can't people see it?

And then his mind twisted back to his quarrel with Matthew the previous night. Zoe had gone to bed, but Devlin had waited up. It had been well after eleven o'clock before Matthew had returned to the house, and their confrontation had been awful, Matthew obdurate and insulting, refusing to listen, all the divisions between them stripped bare. He had handled it badly, he knew that. But then the shock, the shock of discovering not only that his son was infatuated with Melissa de Grey, but that he intended to marry her – this bombshell dropped by Matthew himself, some time around midnight – had stood in the way of rational thought, and he had found himself reaching for any weapon he might use, anything to make the boy see sense.

Now, in the morning's cooler light, he might have done things differently. But the impossibility of it – *marriage*, between his son and the daughter of the woman with whom he had betrayed Esme – remained. He blamed himself, of course. Preoccupied with his work, he had not kept an eye on Matthew. He could hardly criticise Annette for her lax chaperonage when it had been he who had invited the girl to Rosindell. He was responsible, and therefore he must put an end to it.

The remedy had occurred to him sometime in the early hours of the morning, and now, his copy of The Times folded unread in

253

front of him, the headache coming and going, Devlin found himself mentally urging the train on, impatient when it dawdled at a station or slowed for points. At last the wretched thing ground into Paddington. He caught an Underground train to Bond Street and walked from there to Camilla's flat.

The doorman let him into the block and showed him to the lift. Camilla lived on the third floor. Devlin pressed the doorbell and waited.

A maid opened the door. He said, 'Is Mrs de Grey in?'

'Mrs Heron's out, sir.'

'Forgive me, I meant Mrs Heron.' He had forgotten Camilla's second marriage. 'Do you know when she'll be back?'

'I couldn't say, sir.'

'Can you tell me where I can find her?'

'Mrs Heron is lunching at the Savoy.'

Devlin thanked the maid and went back downstairs. Leaving the building, he saw an empty cab and hailed it to the Savoy. At the restaurant, he asked the waiter for Camilla's table but was told that she had not yet arrived.

Damn, damn, damn. But it was early, only just gone twelve, and it occurred to him that she might be having a pre-dinner drink. He went upstairs to the American Bar.

Standing in the doorway, he scanned the glossy art deco interior, his gaze running over the couples and groups of men. And then he saw her, sitting alone at a corner table. Around the collar of her black jacket was draped a silvery fur stole, one end of which bore a sharp little nose and black glass eyes. Her pale hair was coiled at the nape of her neck beneath the dotted black veil of her hat.

He crossed the room to her. 'Hello, Camilla,' he said.

'Good God, Devlin.' Camilla put a hand to her chest. 'You gave me such a fright.'

'I'm sorry if I startled you. I went to your flat. Your maid told me where you were.'

'What is it?' She narrowed her eyes. 'Has someone died?'

'No, nothing like that.'

'Do sit down. You're making me feel nervous. Like some frightful consultant hovering at the end of one's hospital bed.' Camilla waved a hand to the barman. 'Harry, two more cocktails, please.'

She lit a pink and gold cigarette, making a waggling motion with her fingers to indicate that he should help himself.

'Thank you, but no.'

'Of course, you smoke Navy Cut, don't you, Devlin?'

She had not forgotten. The great hall at Rosindell: he had lit cigarettes for both of them. And then, that raw, disastrous physical encounter in the stables.

She said, 'You look just the same.'

'So do you.' Though this was not true. She was too thin, and her pale skin stretched over the sharp bones of her face. Her eyes, though, were unchanged, still that lucid sapphire blue.

A peal of laughter. 'Liar. I look frightful. I've been horribly ill.'

'I'm sorry to hear that. Are you feeling better now?'

'Oh yes, fighting fit.'

With a flourish, their drinks were served. When the waiter had gone, Camilla said, 'Why are you here, Devlin? Not that it isn't perfectly thrilling to see you. Shall we have lunch? I seem to have been stood up.'

'I'm afraid I'm rather short of time.'

'Don't be a bore, darling.' She touched his sleeve. 'For old times' sake.'

What possible old times, he wondered, could she believe worth celebrating? But he said, 'Your friend may turn up.'

'If he does, I shall tell him what I think of him.' Her mouth twisted. 'People today seem to have forgotten their manners. Even Victor, dull old Victor, was a gentleman.' She speared the olive in her martini. 'How is Esme?'

'She's very well, I believe.'

'Do you still see her?'

'Not often,' he said shortly. 'The children's birthdays, that sort of thing.'

'I thought you'd have her hanging round your neck for life. I never imagined she'd cut and run.'

'She had reason.' He longed to leave; there was a rottenness about her, he thought.

'Don't mind me,' said Camilla, with a shrug of her black-clad shoulders. 'I've had a lousy time and it makes me bad-tempered.' She gave him a close look. 'Do you have any regrets?'

'A great many.'

'When I was younger, I never regretted anything. Now, though . . . You and I, we didn't have much time together, did we? A week — it wasn't much.'

The air itself seemed clotted and hard to breathe. Her mood, fluctuating between sourness and flirtation, nauseated him.

He said bluntly, 'Did you know that your daughter is seeing my son?'

Her pale, pencilled brows drew together. Letting out a puff of smoke, she said, 'No. No, I didn't.'

'They met while Melissa was staying with your parents in Dartmouth.'

'Now, this is all rather a surprise. Melissa always seems such a goody-goody.' Tipping back her head, Camilla tightened her lips. 'When you say *seeing* each other . . .'

'There is — an attachment. They appear to be infatuated with each other.'

'Good Lord.'

'Matthew has told me he wants to marry her.'

Camilla scrubbed her cigarette end into an ashtray. 'Well, that's impossible, of course,' she said sharply.

'I'm glad you agree. I came here to ask you if you would speak to Melissa. End this thing. Take her away somewhere, perhaps. I've tried to talk to Matthew, but I'm afraid he refuses to give her up.' Devlin could feel a muscle beside his eye ticking away. The pain in his head was intensifying and he took a mouthful of martini to steady himself. 'We need to put a stop to it, that's the point.'

'The devious little creature. Well, well.'

'They're far too young, for one thing. Without our permission, they can't marry till they're twenty-one, and by then, I feel sure, the whole wretched infatuation will have fizzled out. I wanted to know that you were in agreement.'

'You mean, present a united front. A common cause.' She leaned forward to him, smiling.

'Yes.'

'How funny that you and I should be on the same side at last, Devlin, after all these years.'

Finish saying his piece, he thought, make sure she was going to get her daughter out of the way, and then push off. His head was aching badly now. The metallic gleam of the room, the heavy richness of Camilla's perfume: they sickened him.

'They're cousins,' he said. 'First cousins. It's in every way unsuitable. I'm sure that when Matthew has time to reflect . . .'

'Does Esme know?'

'No. And I'd rather keep it from her, if possible.'

'Why? Don't you think she'd approve?'

He felt a rush of loathing for her. How had he once desired her, ached for her?

'It would hurt her badly,' he said. 'You must know that.'

'I wouldn't have thought you'd care.'

He pulled at his shirt collar. 'I've done enough harm. I've no wish to add to it. So long as I have your agreement.'

She sat back in her seat, frowning, her eyes narrowed. 'Good God,' she said. 'You're still in love with her, aren't you?'

Movement behind him as the occupants of the next table rose to leave, jostling against him, sending shockwaves of pain through his head. 'My feelings for Esme have never changed,' he

257

said, his voice low. 'But that's no business of yours. I came here to speak to you about Matthew and Melissa. Only that.'

Camilla put her fingers to her mouth, pressing them against her upper lip. Devlin noticed the slackness of the skin around her eyes, the web of fine lines, the pallor beneath her suntan.

He said, 'I'll be on my way. I'm relieved that you feel the same way as I do about this business.'

'Oh, I do. Though perhaps not for the same reason.'

'What do you mean?'

'Melissa can't possibly marry Matthew. But you're wrong, Devlin, they're not cousins.'

Weary and longing only to be on the train, heading back to Devon, he said, 'Of course they are.'

'No, they're not. I'm afraid I lied to you the last time. Matthew and Melissa are brother and sister.'

'No.'

'You're her father, Devlin.'

Nausea scorched his throat as he stared at her. 'I don't believe you.'

'You should do. After all, I should know.'

'You're lying.'

'No. Not now.' A flicker of a smile, a baring of teeth. She sat back in the chair, tilting up her chin. 'I know that I told you I was pregnant when we made love at Rosindell, but I'm afraid that wasn't true. Melissa is your daughter.'

'God help you, Camilla, if you're lying to me.'

A sharp cutting motion with her hand. 'I was angry with you. I didn't want you to think you had any part in anything of mine. But now you need to know the truth. It would be awful to think that the two of them might . . . Well, young people get carried away, we both know that, whether they're married or not, and we wouldn't want that, would we? For their sakes, you needed to know. And so do they.'

'No,' he whispered. Crackles of pain shot down the side of his face.

'Yes.' Camilla adjusted the silver fox stole, then slid her cigarettes and lighter into her bag. 'Think about it, Devlin,' she said crisply. 'We can refuse them permission to marry. But will that be enough? Mightn't they disobey us? Rush off to Gretna Green? I wouldn't want to be responsible for the consequences, would you? Incest is a pretty nasty thing. No, they must be told. I'm afraid I can see no alternative.'

He watched her walk out of the restaurant. He was trembling, and black blots were flowering over one side of his vision. It was all he could do to throw some money on the table for the drinks before rushing to the gentlemen's cloakroom, where he was violently sick.

Not long till our wedding day, she was murmuring. *Not long, Matthew.* She was lying on the sand beside him, wearing a long white dress and a veil. When he moved the veil aside to kiss her, he saw that her features were disintegrating, like a piece of cloth fraying. Holes formed in her cheeks, and her eyes were dull and black and empty. Though she was unravelling before his gaze, her lips still moved.

Not long till our wedding day . . .

Matthew woke, gasping for breath. He flung open his bedroom window and took in deep breaths of cool air, trying to exhale the shreds of nightmare. Then he washed and dressed and went downstairs.

He had thought he might go to London to see Melissa, but he was short of cash and in the end he hung around Rosindell. He felt tired and headachy after a rotten night's sleep. Even a run along the coastal path and a swim in the bay could not shift the miserable, ominous feeling that was the legacy of the previous night's scene with his father.

In the afternoon, he cadged a couple of aspirin from Zoe,

charmed Mrs Satterley into making him a very strong cup of coffee, and then went to his room and tried to plan. His entire wealth, if he included the contents of a post office savings book, amounted to £4.7s.6d, which was pathetic. He put some things in his rucksack and thought of phoning his mother, but then decided not to. He had an inkling that his mother might, like his father, disapprove of his engagement to Melissa. Instead, he phoned the de Greys' London flat, but the maid answered and told him that Melissa was out. He lay down on the bed, his head cradled in his hands, thinking.

He must have dozed off, because he was woken by the sound of his father entering the house. A door closed; Sarah was saying something. Then, footsteps on the stairs and along the corridor.

A rap on the door. 'Matthew?' His father's voice. 'May I come in?'

Blurred by sleep, Matthew opened the door. 'Dad.'

His father looked awful, white-faced and ill. *Can't we leave it for tonight?* Matthew wanted to say, but then his father spoke.

'Have you thought any more about what I said?'

'I don't need to. I'm not going to change my mind.'

'Matthew, you must.'

'No, Dad.' An intense weariness came over him, along with unhappiness that they must always be like this, he and his father. 'We'll wait three years if we have to. I'd rather not, because if there's a war I'd prefer us to be married, but if you won't give us your permission, then that's how it will have to be.'

'You can't marry Melissa. You just can't.'

'Dad,' he said softly. 'Don't you see, it doesn't matter what you think. It's my life, not yours. I know you think we're too young, but we're not. I know you think I don't know my own mind, but I do. I've never felt so sure about anything.'

His father was still standing in the doorway, one hand on the surround, as if for support. He said, 'Your relationship—'

'It doesn't matter,' Matthew interrupted. 'Lots of cousins

260

marry. We've talked about it. We're not even sure we want children.'

'Matthew,' his father said softly, 'please reconsider, I beg you.' And he moved forward, as if to touch him.

Matthew lurched back. 'Why do you always have to spoil everything? Don't waste your breath, Dad.' He began to stuff things into the rucksack. A rugby shirt, the copy of *Ariel* that Melissa had given him.

'Melissa is your sister.'

Matthew froze. Slowly he turned and looked at his father. 'What?'

'Melissa is your sister. Your half-sister.'

He jabbed the book into a side pocket with an angry shove. 'What are you talking about, Dad?'

'I'm Melissa's father. I'm so sorry, but you have to know, you have to know that any marriage, any *liaison* between you, is impossible.'

'Why are you saying this?' he shouted. 'Her father's called de Grey! Stop trying to control me, Dad, I'm not a child any more.'

'Melissa's mother was married to Victor de Grey at the time, but he is not her father.' Devlin sounded hoarse and tired. 'I had a very brief affair with Camilla many years ago. I regretted it then and I regret it even more deeply now. But Melissa is my daughter.'

Matthew shook his head. 'You're lying.'

'I wish I was.'

It was impossible. Surely it was impossible. Matthew swallowed. 'I don't believe you.'

'Someone told your mother about the affair on the night of the summer dance. That was why she left me.'

Matthew remembered that night. He had fallen asleep lulled by the sound of dance music. By the time he had woken in the morning, their suitcases had been packed into the car. His mother had driven them out of Rosindell with the tears streaming down her face.

He whispered, 'No . . .'

'I'm so sorry, Matthew, but it's true.'

'No.' He shook his head.

'I went to London today, to see Camilla. She's going to speak to Melissa. Matthew, I'm so sorry.'

Matthew hissed, 'You're disgusting. *Disgusting*,' and pushed past his father. Then he was running downstairs, through the drawing room, out of the French windows and across the garden, tripping over plant pots, crushing flowers beneath his feet, sloshing through the stream.

In the shrubbery, blots of rain tumbled from branches that smashed against him, leaving weals across his face. He fumbled with the gate to the woods, hurled himself through it and then ran on, beneath the trees, through the wet fronds of ferns, only stopping when he reached the cliff's edge, where he threw himself on to his knees in the bright, thorny gorse, and wept.

The following day, news broke of the German and Russian non-aggression pact. The two foreign ministers, von Ribbentrop and Molotov, had signed an agreement that in the event that either country went to war against a foreign power, the other would remain neutral. In doing so, they crushed any hope that Russia would side with Britain and France. The treaty paved the way for Germany's invasion of Poland.

Parliament was recalled, and the government granted emergency powers for the defence of the realm. Military reservists were called up and ARP personnel were warned to stand ready. The atmosphere was one of nervous anxiety and weary repetition, as well as a little of something that felt almost like indifference, or resignation, as the country went through the same preparations for war it had made less than a year ago, at the time of the Munich crisis.

*   *   *

Esme had phoned the porters' lodge, putting Hugo off, but he couldn't have received her message, because she looked out of the window and saw him coming up the front path.

She opened the door. He held out a bunch of chrysanthemums, rather knocked about. 'I thought you might need cheering up.'

Because she was in the frame of mind where any thoughtfulness was intolerably touching, she said, 'Oh Hugo,' and dabbed at her eyes.

'They were for sale outside a house up the road,' he said, sounding bewildered. 'They weren't expensive.'

He followed her into the kitchen, where she had gone to find a vase and the opportunity to sort out her face.

'I suppose it's inevitable now,' she said. 'All that toing and froing of Mr Chamberlain's was completely pointless.'

'We're better prepared than we would have been a year ago. At least now we all know where we stand. But I don't suppose you feel like that. Not with your son.'

And with that she began to cry, the flowers tumbling into the sink as she pressed her hands over her face. Hugo put his arms round her and patted her back, and said things like, 'You poor girl,' and, 'You must try not to worry.'

When she was able to speak, the words tore out of her. 'Oh Hugo, I'm afraid he'll never forgive me!'

And then she was sitting at the kitchen table and Hugo was trying to make tea, in the manner of a man unaccustomed to doing domestic tasks, and she was telling him the whole terrible story.

Devlin and Camilla. Matthew and Melissa.

The tea arrived, an odd colour. Hugo said, 'His half-sister?' and she nodded at him, grateful that he had caught on and was not yet expressing disgust.

'Yes,' she said dully, having cried herself out. 'Devlin is Melissa's father. I didn't know till yesterday.' She wrung her handkerchief. 'Should I have told Matthew about the affair? But I couldn't, I just couldn't.'

'I don't know,' he said. 'I have no children.'

She was grateful for his honesty, though it gave no comfort. 'Matthew blames me,' she said. 'Naturally, he blames Devlin more, but he's lumping us both together now, I could tell that when he phoned. He asked me whether Devlin was telling the truth. He wanted me to say that he was lying. But the timings work, and Camilla says that he's the girl's father.'

'Perhaps after Matthew has had time to think . . .'

'Perhaps,' she said, though the memory of her son's hostility and intransigence chilled her. She would telephone him in a day or two, she thought unhappily, assuming she could track him down, but she felt it possible that Matthew might refuse to speak to her or that any conversation would simply repeat the icy judgement of the morning's phone call.

'I am afraid for him.' She spoke more quietly now. 'He loves her, Hugo. Thank God, it seems to have gone no further than a few kisses, but what have we done to him, to make him endure such pain?' Slowly she shook her head. 'It's a strange thing. I feel that I have every right to hold Devlin wholly responsible for this. Quite apart from what he did in the past, he should never have introduced them. He can be careless – yes, that's his greatest fault, his carelessness; that, and a weakness for a pretty face – and I hate him for that. But I can't help feeling that I'm somehow to blame as well, though I can't quite see where. I have not protected Matthew. And this has hurt him so deeply.'

'Did your ex-husband know that this girl was his daughter?'

'No, I don't think so. He said not and I think I believe him. What you must think of us all. Poor Hugo, your life always sounds so soothing, so lacking in tumult.'

'Oh no!' he cried. 'Not at all. The college is a hotbed of rivalries and feuds. Love affairs too.'

264

'You must tell me some day.' She stirred her tea in an attempt to make it palatable, then sighed.

Hugo said, 'Fleming called today.'

'Your Home Office friend?'

'He'd like me to start work as soon as possible.'

'Oh Hugo.'

Her life was fragmenting again. Matthew would join the RAF; both the personal and the political meant that was now inevitable. She did not know when Zoe would return to Oxford. They must all have an occupation now, she saw that, just as they had had in the first war, and they might no longer have much choice in where they lived. And now Hugo was to go to London. She had not until this moment realised how much she had come to rely on him. Loneliness, she had learned, had a shape, a density. It spread itself over everything you did, seeping into the minutest crevices of your life, infecting it with its cold futility, muffling hope and happiness.

She began to clear away the tea things and for a second time to arrange the flowers in a vase. She heard him say:

'Come to London with me, Esme.'

He had risen from his seat and was standing next to the Baby Belling cooker. His tie was askew and a seam on one of his jacket pockets was unravelling, and she felt a pang of affection for him.

'Dear Hugo.'

He swept up her hair to kiss the back of her neck. It was this gesture as much as anything, and the desire she read into it, that made her twist in his arms and return his kisses. He kissed her clumsily but enthusiastically, kisses different in quality from their previous ones, that easily awoke a fire in her that she had tried for a long time to disregard. He was a little rough, perhaps, but she put that down to their mutual rustiness. When, her blouse unbuttoned and untucked, he said, 'Should we go upstairs?' she said, 'Yes, Hugo,' and led the way.

* * *

Sarah was putting up the blackout at Rosindell. She had started before dusk, before they had to put on the electric lights, but the drawing of curtains and the putting-up of blinds, the pinning of blankets over small peepholes and skylights that she had forgotten about took so long that she had not completed the task before the sky began to darken. It was hard to see in the gloom, but she knew the house so well she could have navigated it with her eyes closed. She made sure she was quiet, because Mr Reddaway was ill in bed with one of his headaches and was trying to sleep.

Miss Zoe had offered to check the outbuildings. Because of the blackout, and because Mr Reddaway was unwell, Zoe had suggested she dine in the kitchen with the servants. Mrs Satterley hadn't been keen, Sarah had seen that – Mrs Satterley believed in people knowing their place – but Sarah had intervened, agreeing, suspecting that the girl didn't fancy eating on her own, not with everything that was going on.

The last curtain was hauled into place and now the drawing room was in darkness. Sarah opened the door to the old part of the house.

She went from room to room, checking that no one had left a light on. Miss Zoe sometimes came in here, and Mr Reddaway occasionally got a book from the library. Sarah had a torch in her pocket, in case she took fright, but as she climbed the stairs and looked about, she felt only the house's emptiness. She seemed to hear the intense quiet, which tonight was full of echoes. She smelled the dust and damp of rooms that, no matter how conscientiously she cleaned them, had not been lived in for too long.

She went up the stairs to the attics. Forty years ago, all these rooms would have been occupied by servants. She opened the door to the bedroom in which, before the Great War, she and Jane had slept.

Jane was on her mind today. The small room had a sloping

ceiling, which had meant that even then, though they were only young girls and neither of them tall, they had had to stoop when they had washed at the stand. The room had been very cold in winter, and in the summer, heat had gathered in the shallow space. Once, in a fierce heatwave, they had opened the skylight and crept out on to the roof tiles. Sarah remembered how they had sat there, she and Jane, in their nightdresses, feeling the cooler air against their limbs. Or rather, she had worn her nightdress. After a while, Jane had taken hers off and danced on the tiles naked, laughing up at the stars. At twelve years old, Jane had had the beginnings of a woman's body, and Sarah hadn't known where to look.

The servants' quarters in the new part of the house were much nicer, and Sarah, who was tired now, looked forward to being in her own room and reading again the letters that had arrived for her that morning. One had been from her boyfriend, William, and the other from Jane. William would be all right, Sarah told herself. At forty-one, even if he were to be called up, they wouldn't send him overseas, would they? But Jane had written to tell her that she was to return to France with Mrs Heron, which worried Sarah. If your country was at war, you ought to be at home. Their dad had died three years ago, so there was no reason now for Jane not to come back to Devon.

Once more she found herself remembering Jane dancing on the roof, the moonlight painting her skinny limbs silver, a wildness on her face as she leaped and twirled. Then she left the attic and went downstairs, locking the door to the old house behind her.

Chapter Thirteen

September 1939

The first change comes with the arrival of a boys' school, evacuated from Enfield in north London, two days after the outbreak of war. The boys, aged between seven and thirteen, sleep in attic rooms that were once used by servants. The staff are housed in the Tudor bedrooms, two or three to a room. The great hall and library and the modern drawing and sitting rooms are used as classrooms.

Boys slide down the banisters and run through the attics, their footsteps thudding on the wooden floors. They play games on the lawn and, while the weather holds, swim in the bathing pool on the beach. The younger ones are taken for nature rambles and the older boys are sent on cross-country runs, skirting ploughed fields and flocks of sheep. Farmers shout at them when they forget to close gates. The less fit puff and pant up the narrow stony footpaths.

There is a lull: the bombs do not yet fall on London and the headmaster of the school wonders whether he should shepherd his charges back to the city, back to civilisation. Parents complain about the disruption and the long journey to the Kingswear headland. But then the Enfield school buildings are requisitioned, so there's no going back; they are there for the duration. Sarah puts up the blackout each evening and two of the older boys are charged with the task of patrolling the house, checking for chinks of light. Mrs Satterley, permanently at war with the cook who has been evacuated with the pupils, serves up vast trays of macaroni cheese and shepherd's pie.

April 1940: the war, which has been smouldering in eastern Europe, catches fire. Norway is invaded, Denmark occupied. In May, almost a thousand people are killed in an air raid on Rotterdam, and the following morning poor overrun Holland capitulates. The German armies blitzkrieg their way south through Belgium and into France, trapping the French army and the British Expeditionary Force in the north-west of the country. The exhausted and half-drowned remnants of the Allied armies queue in the sea for transport out of Dunkirk. Boats from Dartmouth are among the flotilla of naval ships, ferries and pleasure vessels that transport the men across the Channel to England.

Devlin takes his army pistol out of the safe, in case of invasion. He and Philips search through sheds, cellars and attics, looking for weaponry. The Home Guard parades on Rosindell's lawns, armed with shotguns, pitchforks and an ancient duelling sword.

After two months of fierce aerial combat, the Battle of Britain is won and the prospect of invasion is averted, at least for now. The Blitz rains down bombs on London, and half a dozen mothers and babies, refugees from the East End, are squeezed into the new part of the house. The mothers complain about the dullness of the countryside, the lack of shops and picture houses. The days, dreary with greenery and dripping nature, stretch out before them, and they wheel their charges through the high-banked roads to Kingswear, looking for a bit of life.

Roses and delphiniums are wrenched out of the soil and the garden is cleared for the growing of vegetables. Metal railings, spare saucepans and some of the uglier candelabra are sent off to be melted down and made into aeroplanes. Sarah leaves

Devon for Walton-on-Thames to work at the Vickers-Armstrong factory, making aircraft parts.

Inside the house, there are muddy footprints on the Marion Dorn carpet and one of the deco lights in the corridor is broken after a boy aims a cricket ball at it. There are scuff marks on the walls and someone has scribbled on the bathroom tiles, with their sketches of cars and trains. Someone else, one of the bored mothers perhaps, has stubbed out a cigarette on Esme's blue marble table, leaving a round black mark like a bullet hole.

In May 1941, a nine-year-old boy slides down the banister of the old staircase, misjudges his speed and lands awkwardly on the flagged hall floor. Dr Spry, come out of retirement because of the war, drives him, white and shivering, to the cottage hospital in Dartmouth, where it is found that the child has fractured his spine. He never returns to school.

Afterwards, the pupils are forbidden to play on the stairs. Philips hammers chunks of wood into the banisters so that they are no longer a temptation. It crosses the mind of one of the masters, a man who has noticed how his charges turn restlessly in their beds at night, as if twisting out of the grip of nightmares, something he'd like to put down to homesickness or the dislocations of war, that the house, in a fit of spite, has caused the accident. After all, they are invaders, they don't belong here. Then, carefully, he puts the thought away.

Matthew was late, over half an hour. Zoe, who was, as always, exactly ten minutes early, tried not to check her watch too often, fended off offers of drinks, and wondered whether he was going to turn up.

The pub was on the Strand, not far from Shell Mex House, where Zoe worked as a secretary in the Ministry of Supply. When she had first come to London, she had worked at the Ministry of Information, in Bloomsbury. Hugo, who was something secret and important at the MoI, had found her the job. In the spring of 1940, her boss, Rupert Shelbrooke, had taken her aside. 'We're on our second director in six months,' he said to her, 'and rumour is that Reith won't last long. We're directionless and leaderless and the press is making us look a laughing stock. I've been offered a transfer to Supply and I'm thinking of taking it. I wondered whether you'd like to come with me, Miss Reddaway, as my assistant. You take half the time anyone else does to do what I ask of you.'

Zoe had accepted. She liked Mr Shelbrooke, who had been a publisher in peacetime and was the father of two school-age children. He was tall and thin, with almond-shaped hazel eyes that had a way of crinkling up at the corners whenever something amused him. His desk, which Zoe tidied every morning before he arrived at work, always looked by the end of the day as if he had taken a wooden spoon and stirred round all the papers and pens and pamphlets.

In the worst of the Blitz, she had picked round bomb craters and through rubble to get to work. She always took the same route from the Holborn lodgings she shared with a schoolfriend, Davina Mason: along Kingsway and round Aldwych to Shell Mex House. Rationally, she knew that deviating from her course would make no difference to the progress of the war or her chances of surviving the air raids, but why take the risk?

She had on the whole found London a relief. Davina was tidy, so they had had none of those fallings-out girls had about stockings dripping in the bath or washing-up left in the sink. Zoe sensed a certain spirit in the city, not the fictional cockney jollity of the MoI's early information films, but a dogged determination to put up with things.

Now it was June, and a month since the last heavy raid. Looking up, Zoe saw Matthew winding through the huddle of uniformed men around the bar.

'Hello, Matt.'

271

They hugged. She offered to buy him a beer, but Matthew said no, he would get the drinks, and slotted himself into the queue. Zoe tried to make out how he was from the angle of his fair head and his air-force-blue back.

He returned to the table with two glasses of beer, peeled off a Woodbine and offered her the packet.

'No thanks. You look tired.'

'Busy, busy, busy.' He drew on the cigarette. 'How is Mr . . .' He waggled his fingers to indicate that he had forgotten Zoe's boss's name.

'Mr Shelbrooke. We've just come back from York.' She thought of telling Matthew about York – the lengthy train journeys, the grimness of the hotel, even Rupert's confiding in her about his concerns for his elder daughter, Margaret, who was homesick at her boarding school, which had been evacuated to Wales – but then, seeing how her brother's gaze flicked round the pub, resting on nothing for more than a second or two, she decided not to.

Instead she said, 'I might have to move in with Mum.'

'You're kidding, surely.' He blew out smoke, looking at her. 'What about the awful Godtwit?' This was their name for Hugo Godwin.

'Davina's younger sister's coming to London. So, obviously, Davina needs the bed.'

'Can't you find anywhere else?'

'Well, no. Lots of people have nowhere to live at the moment. I've asked around but I haven't found anything yet. Hopefully it won't be for too long. Anyway, Mum wants me to come and live with them.'

'But do you want to live with her?'

You often thought, talking to Matthew, that he wasn't concentrating at all, and then he said something that got to the heart of the problem.

'Well, there's Hugo, of course,' she said.

He smirked. 'Imagine, Hugo at breakfast.'

'Awful if they're lovey-dovey with each other. And Mum and I . . .'

'What?'

Zoe shuffled her seat so that some soldiers could squeeze on to the table beside them. 'We get on better when we don't see each other very often. Always have. Coffees and lunches at the Corner House, that's all right. Actually, I will have that cigarette.'

He passed her one. She said, 'The trouble is, if Mum's in a mood, everyone knows it.'

Matthew grimaced. 'Not Hugo.'

'Yes, it must be nice to be so . . . so impervious to atmosphere. But when I get home after work, all I want is to be quiet and peaceful.'

'How is she?'

She gave him a look. 'Why don't you go and find out?'

His eyes, heavy blue slits in a suntanned face, moved to where a group of WAAFs were standing by the bar. 'I will do,' he said. 'But not today.'

'And Dad . . .'

'No,' he said softly.

'He's coming to London in a couple of weeks' time. I'm going to meet him for dinner. Please come, Matt. Just for a drink.'

His gaze swung to her. 'Why?'

Because it's breaking my heart. But she said, 'Because he misses you.'

'I don't think Dad cares one way or the other. I think you have this little fantasy about getting us all back together again, a nice happy family.'

Zoe dug her teeth into her lower lip and looked away. A Polish airman, sitting on the other side of the room and dashing in his uniform, raised his glass to her.

She heard Matthew say, 'Sorry. Sorry, I didn't mean it. It's just' − he let out a breath − 'what he did was so disgusting.'

Zoe worried that the person who most disgusted Matthew was himself. 'I wish you'd—' She broke off, tightening her mouth.

'What?'

'Nothing.'

'Forgive him? Was that what you were going to say? I won't ever forgive him.'

She said nothing, and after a while he sighed. 'I'll do it, though, if I have leave, if it's what you want. But not for him.' He looked at his watch. 'I'd better head off.'

'So soon?'

'I've a date.'

'Nicola?'

'No, she was ages ago.'

'So. Go on. Tell me.'

'She's . . .' He spread out his hands. 'Pretty, I suppose. She's called Ivy.'

Her mother would have said that Ivy was a housemaid's name. But Zoe said lightly, 'Be good, then.'

He grinned. 'Oh, I will.'

They left the pub. Parting at Charing Cross Underground station, she hugged him. 'You will be careful, won't you, Matt?'

'I'm always bloody careful.' He ruffled her hair. 'I never thought you'd stay in London. I thought once they started dropping bombs you'd run a mile.'

'I've often wished I had. But, you know, where would I go?' And she headed down the steps into the station.

Matthew walked to Charles Street, in Mayfair. The knot inside him, which was there almost all the time now, except when he was tight or with a girl, tensed as he neared the de Greys' flat. It might have been bombed to smithereens, or there might be a hole in the ground where the building had once stood.

But though the house looked a bit battered, cracks in the

window panes and a chunk out of the front doorstep, it was no worse than its neighbours. Matthew took out his cigarettes, turned his lighter a few times in his hand, then put both back in his pocket and went inside.

No one was in the porter's cubbyhole, and the lift wasn't working, so he walked upstairs. The flat was on the third floor. Two men, talking in French, passed him in the corridor. This time he didn't allow himself second thoughts, and pressed the doorbell.

The door opened. A young, dark-haired man in khaki looked at him.

Matthew said, 'Is this the de Greys' flat?'

As soon as he spoke, he knew it was hopeless. The soldier was wearing French insignia. Matthew could see through an open doorway to a sitting room where half a dozen men were lounging in armchairs and a radio was playing.

The Free French soldier was calling back to his comrades. Matthew said, 'It's okay, it doesn't matter,' and headed quickly back down the stairs. In the vestibule, the porter had returned to his post; he looked up as Matthew appeared. Matthew gave him a cheery wave and headed outside.

In the street, he had to stop and take a gulp of air, almost as if he had been holding his breath underwater. A woman pushing a pram gave him a curious look as he walked towards Piccadilly. Inside a pub, he got himself another beer and drank it quickly, standing at the bar, then ordered a second.

During the Battle of Britain, when he had been flying Spitfires, he had been able to forget both Melissa and his father. You flew, you fought, you ate, you slept, you tried to stay alive. You didn't think about anything else, because if you did you would lose concentration, and you simply wouldn't survive, up there in the sky, if you were to lose concentration.

Now his day-to-day work involved escorting bomber crews to drop their payload of bombs on France. 'Taking the war to the enemy', they called it. There may have been a time, when he was younger, when he might have felt sorry for the poor bastards on the ground, bombs landing on them from a great height, but not any more. He did the job to the best of his ability and breathed a sigh of relief as soon as the white cliffs, and England, were in sight again. He didn't feel sorry for the French, nor angry – much – with the Germans, except when one of them was trying to kill him. Or, indeed, furious with his father any more. He felt nothing towards his father, nothing at all, and so he would, if he had leave, go along with Zoe's scheme, because she had asked him, and because he remembered that in the aftermath of the break-up with Melissa, Zoe had been very decent to him. She had listened to him; she had, one particularly awful evening that he tried not to think about, hugged him as he wept. It wouldn't make any difference, but for Zoe's sake he'd put up with his father for an hour.

He bought another drink and, glancing at his watch, downed it quickly. As, a little tight, he left the pub for the restaurant where he was to meet Ivy, he wondered where Melissa had gone. In their last conversation she had told him she was thinking of going back to Paris. If she had, she had probably been interned.

He and Ivy had supper, and Ivy, whose curling blond hair surrounded a sweet pink and white face, chattered and laughed at his jokes. After the restaurant, they went to the theatre, to see a musical. He must have drifted off, because, surfacing at the interval, he felt a moment's confusion, seeing all the other people and seeing Ivy.

He apologised and hoped he hadn't been snoring or sleeping with his mouth open.

'Oh no,' said Ivy. 'You look very handsome when you sleep. *Noble.*'

This remark, in all its stupidity, broke through his brittle cheerfulness. He stayed awake throughout the shenanigans on stage during the second half. He knew that girls thought him handsome, and he didn't object, knowing that he had a better time than the jug-eared and buck-toothed. *Noble*, though. There was a type of girl who assumed you were heroic just because you were in RAF uniform. Though he might have started out with heroic ideas about King and country, these days he just tried to stay alive.

Noble. He wondered what Ivy would say if he were to murmur into her ear that he had fallen in love with his sister. First she wouldn't believe him, and then, when eventually she did, she would run a mile. What sort of man fell in love with his own sister? Not a noble one, that was for sure.

He regretted going to the de Greys' flat. It showed that he wasn't entirely free of her; that, more than a year and a half since he had last seen her, she was still there, lodged in his brain. Sometimes he hated her, but sometimes still he dreamed of her, tormenting, desire-ridden dreams in which her pale body twisted and turned through the blue-green sea of Rosindell Bay, just out of reach.

As the curtain went up and the cast took their bows, Ivy reached for his hand. Matthew let their fingers interlink as they shuffled out of the row of seats.

In the street, he said, 'A chap has lent me his place in Covent Garden. Would you like to come back for a drink?'

A silence; he knew she was weighing it up. He coaxed, 'I have to head back to base early tomorrow morning. Could be a while before I'm in London again.'

She looked up at him. 'All right.'

The flat belonged to Flying Officer Tommy Hesketh. At RAF Manston, it was known as the Love Nest. If you had leave and were going to London, you asked Tommy if you could borrow it in case you got lucky.

Inside the flat, Matthew poured them both a whisky. Ivy prattled, fast and nervously, about her job at the BBC. The sound of

277

her voice began to irritate, and he took her glass out of her hand and put it on the sideboard. As he kissed her, he reached round and unzipped her dress. Her body was narrow and childish apart from her full breasts, and her skin was fine-grained and silky. Thought dropped away and he peeled off her clothes. He noticed that she was trembling and asked her whether she was cold. She shook her head. Then whether she wanted him to stop. Again a shake of the head.

He made love to her swiftly and efficiently, and afterwards he lay back on the sofa, his arm round her, her head on his chest. The knot in his stomach had unravelled and he felt himself drifting off to sleep, the deep, empty sleep he needed, where he wouldn't dream at all.

Then she said, 'I love you so much, Matthew. You do love me, don't you?'

He murmured, 'You're very sweet,' and gave her a squeeze, hoping she'd get the message and shut up.

'But you do love me, don't you?'

'I adore you.'

She shuffled upright. 'I want you to say it.'

He couldn't, though. You'd think it would be easy, but he couldn't get the words out. All he could think of was sitting beside Melissa on their perch on the cliff, watching the waves. *I love you, I love you, I love you.*

His *sister*.

He stood up. 'What are you doing?' she said.

'Getting dressed.' He glanced back at her. 'You can have the bathroom first.'

'*Matthew.*'

'What?'

She was kneeling on the sofa, naked except for her stockings. She seemed about to speak, but then she gathered up her clothes, clutching them against her, and went to the bathroom.

Five minutes later, she emerged dressed and with her hair combed. It was obvious that she had been crying. She said, 'You'll phone, won't you?' and he said, ''Course I will.' He offered to walk her down to the street and hail her a taxi, but she said no, she would take the Underground.

After she had gone, he felt relieved. It was nice being in the flat on his own, pottering around, scratching together something to eat out of the sparse contents of the larder. When he had finished his supper, he lay on the bed, his head cushioned in his hands, staring at the ceiling. What would he have done if Melissa had answered the doorbell to the Mayfair flat? If she'd said, hello, Matthew, do come in? What had he imagined? That they would talk and laugh and that everything would somehow, miraculously, be all right?

Her mother said, 'Are these pots and pans yours?'

'No, Mum, they're Davina's.'

Her mother had offered to help her with the move. Zoe would rather have done it by herself but had been touched by the offer.

Esme looked at the suitcase and the two shopping bags. 'There doesn't seem very much.'

'Makes life easier, doesn't it?' Zoe hoped that her mother was not going to say, *At your age I was married with a baby.*

Instead Esme said, 'Have you heard from Matthew?'

'I saw him last week.'

'Here? In London?'

'Yes. He didn't have long, Mum,' she added, catching a glimpse of her mother's expression. 'Only a very short leave.'

'Was he all right?'

'Yes, I think so.' Not true at all, that. If she'd touched Matthew, he would have jangled. She added, 'He looked tired.'

'I worry about him all the time.' Her mother folded a blanket and put it in the large shopping bag.

Zoe opened drawers and cupboards, checking that she had forgotten nothing. Then they left the room, Zoe carrying the suitcase, her mother the shopping bags. Going downstairs, Zoe felt a pang of loss. In that room, she and Davina had given supper parties, sheltered under the table from the bombs, and talked about everything, long into the night. One evening, after several drinks and in the aftermath of one of Davina's periodic stormy quarrels with her naval officer boyfriend, Zoe had told Davina why she had felt it imperative to leave both Oxford and Rosindell. 'Golly,' Davina had said, her eyes wide, after Zoe had explained about her father's affair with Aunt Camilla. And then, 'Honestly. *Parents.*'

'And your father,' said Esme suddenly, as they reached the bottom of two flights of stairs and put down the bags to get their breath back.

'What, Mum?'

'Does Matthew write to him?'

'I don't think so.'

Zoe felt despondency sink through her as they started up the road. Twenty-one years old, and here she was, going back to live with her mother and stepfather. She should have joined one of the women's services. Or become a Land Girl, up to her knees in mud. The evening sunlight caught the silver bubbles of the barrage balloons, bobbing in the sky.

She said, 'How's the WVS, Mum?'

Her mother explained that she was currently engaged in calling from door to door collecting clothing and blankets for families who had been bombed out of their homes.

'We launder them at the church hall,' she said. 'I'd do them at home, but Hugo worries about the hot water. Some of the things they give us are in the most awful condition, fit for rags, really. Not just from the poorer households. You'd be surprised.'

This conversation, along with her mother's description of her WVS friends and the hauling of bags and suitcase up and down stairs and escalators, occupied them for the remainder of the journey.

From South Kensington Underground station it was only a short walk to Esme and Hugo's mews house. The building had once been a carriage stables and was now part of a row of houses that faced directly on to the street. Her mother unlocked the front door and they went inside. On the ground floor there was a narrow hallway, a large sitting room and a small kitchen. The bedrooms and bathroom were on the upper floors.

There was a man's hat and jacket on the coat stand. Esme made a little twitching movement of her mouth. They left the luggage in the hall and went into the sitting room.

A large window looked out on to a small brick courtyard. Hugo was seated in an armchair beside it. Shadows from the latticework of sticky tape on the glass, to prevent blast damage, criss-crossed his face.

He sprang to his feet. 'Are you here? I would have thought it would have taken you longer.'

'Zoe hasn't brought much luggage. Isn't it lovely to have her staying with us, Hugo? We've been so looking forward to it, darling.'

'Yes, Mum.'

'Still, the walk,' said Hugo doggedly. 'Two, two and a half miles? Did you come by Eaton Square?'

'We took the Underground,' said Zoe.

'Zoe bought the tickets,' said Esme.

'Oh, I see. You're welcome, Zoe, to our humble abode.'

'Thank you, Hugo. I really appreciate you letting me come and stay here.'

'I'm not sure the stew will go round,' said Esme. 'I thought you were having supper with Monty.'

'No, that's tomorrow evening.'

'Silly me. Have you had tea?'

'Not yet.'

'I'll take Zoe upstairs and show her her room, and then I'll make us all some.'

The spare bedroom was on the top floor of the house, under the eaves. Zoe recognised some of the pieces of furniture from the Oxford house. Her mother had not sold her house on her marriage, a fact that Zoe found comforting, but had let it out to war workers.

Zoe unpacked, putting her clothes inside the chest of drawers and arranging her books on top of it. There was no wardrobe, a sloping ceiling preventing one, but hooks and hangers had been provided on the back of the door. From below, she could hear her mother and Hugo's voices, the rise and fall of them, but not the words. She wondered why her mother had lied to Hugo about the Underground tickets, which Esme had insisted on buying. Or perhaps it had been a mistake and she had forgotten buying them. But what an odd thing for Hugo to think, that they would haul the heavy bags all the way from Holborn.

She went to the window and looked out at the roofs and chimneys and the bobbling barrage balloons. She knew already that this would not work, felt instantly ill at ease with her mother's enthusiasm and Hugo's false bonhomie, and made up her mind, in that moment, to find herself a room elsewhere, shared if necessary, as soon as was decently possible. She felt a longing so powerful it almost hurt for Rosindell, the one place she loved without reservation. Now her reasons for refusing the offer of work at the boatyard that her father had made to her at the outbreak of war seemed capricious and incomprehensible. Closing her eyes, she concentrated until she could visualise the garden as it ran in its shallow valley down to the cliff edge, until she could almost smell the earth, the salt spray, the roses.

Her mother called up that tea was ready, and Zoe went downstairs. She and Hugo had a conversation about her job, though she could tell he wasn't listening to what she said. He had a way of turning any remark to himself. Mention any colleague, and if Hugo hadn't direct experience of him, hadn't clashed swords with or triumphed over him, he would produce a similar experience or an acquaintance with comparable characteristics. It was a different sort of not listening to Matthew's and Zoe found it far more tiresome. Or perhaps it was that she loved Matthew but merely put up with Hugo.

Her mother was in the kitchen while they talked, doing something to make the stew go further. Now she came into the sitting room and peered into the teapot.

'I should be able to squeeze another cup out of this.'

'Plenty more in there,' said Hugo heartily. 'Dry out the tea leaves and they'll do for after dinner.'

'Yes, Hugo.'

Zoe thought her mother seemed subdued. She put it down to the long day trawling round the streets, collecting second-hand clothes, and the tiring journey with the bags and suitcase. She said, 'Can I help you in the kitchen, Mum?' and Esme gave her a warm smile and said no thank you, darling, but it was lovely to be asked.

Zoe never chose as her friends people who wore their hearts on their sleeves. She found those types tiring and demanding. She preferred the rational, the measured, the bright, knowing herself well enough to be aware that she had a tendency to gloominess. She disliked overt displays of anger or even of affection, finding the one frightening and suspecting the sincerity of the other.

You didn't have to be a Freudian therapist to work out the root of it, of course. She had grown up among temperamental people, her mother's emotionalism and her father's periodic retreats into depression. If Mum's in a mood, she had said to Matthew, everyone knows it. Since infancy, Zoe had witnessed her

283

mother's ability to infect an entire household with her state of mind.

So, her mother and Hugo exchanging sweet nothings over the morning toast and marmalade would have been hard to bear. To her initial relief, this did not materialise. Her mother's quietness, which Zoe had observed on her first evening, persisted. It didn't take long for her to notice that it was in Hugo's company that Esme seemed reduced, the colour rubbed out of her.

A fortnight after Zoe came to live at the mews house, there was an unpleasant little incident at the breakfast table. It was a Sunday, so neither Hugo nor Zoe was at work. During the week, leaving the house at different times, they ate breakfast in shifts, but Sunday morning meant a family breakfast.

They were sitting at the dining table and the wireless was rumbling of the German invasion of Russia and the obstacles the Wehrmacht was meeting: the dusty plains, swamps and forests.

Hugo said, 'Jam, Esme.'

'Oh!' Esme leapt up. 'Sorry.'

She took a jar out of the back of a cupboard, unscrewed the lid and peered inside. 'Oh dear, I'm afraid it's gone mouldy.'

'Give it to me.' Hugo gazed into the jar. 'It's fine.'

'Hugo, there are hairs. And it's only a scrape.'

'I'm afraid your mother is sometimes rather wasteful, Zoe,' said Hugo. 'It's perfectly nutritious.' And he spread a thin layer of jam, along with its coating of bristling white hairs, on his slice of toast. Then he held out the jar to Esme.

'I don't think . . .' said Esme faintly.

'Zoe, then.'

'Perhaps I do fancy it after all,' her mother said. She took the jar from Hugo and scooped out the remainder of the jam.

Zoe, who had lost her appetite, excused herself shortly

afterwards and went back to her room. Ten minutes later, she had come downstairs to ask her mother if there were any soap flakes, so that she could wash her stockings, when she heard, from the kitchen, Hugo's voice.

'After all,' he was saying, 'it's more than two years since you've lived in it. I can't think why you want to hang on to it.'

'My lodgers are so settled there.' Her mother. Zoe assumed that they were talking about the Oxford house.

'They'll move out as soon as the war ends, if not before. You may not be able to find anyone else to take their place.'

'There's no harm in waiting.'

'I'm only thinking of you, Esme. Of what's best for you.'

From the sitting room doorway Zoe caught a glimpse of Hugo in the kitchen, flapping a tea towel ineffectually. His expression, something eager and manipulative in it, chilled her.

'I can't think why you're being so stubborn about this,' he said. 'It's almost as if you don't trust me.'

'Hugo, that's not true.'

'It's an unattractive characteristic, distrustfulness. Especially between a man and wife.'

'Mum?' said Zoe, and Hugo, turning, produced a closed-lipped, mollifying smile. 'Are there any soap flakes?'

'I'm afraid not, darling. None to be had for love nor money.'

'Shall I dry the dishes?'

'I'll do them for you,' said Hugo, but Esme wrenched the tea towel out of his hands.

'Sweet of you, Hugo, but you must be tired. You sit down and I'll bring you a cup of tea.'

When he had gone, Esme lowered her voice to Zoe.

'He always leaves smears. I'd only have to wash them all over again.'

September 1941: a pub in Manston, Kent, on the part of the Isle of Thanet that jutted out, facing France.

There were two new WAAFs, a redhead and a brunette, among the crowd helping Tommy Hesketh celebrate his twenty-fifth birthday. The redhead was toothy and angular, a jolly, talkative girl with an infectious laugh, and the brunette was tall and slim. Her mouth and eyes turned up at the corners, as if she found everything amusing.

The redhead was taking a cigarette out of a packet. As Matthew wormed through the knots of men standing at the bar, one of his friends said, 'Angels one five, watch out for Reddaway, coming in at six o'clock.' Matthew told him to shut up.

He flicked his lighter. The redhead turned and dipped her cigarette into the flame.

'Hello,' he said. 'I'm Matthew Reddaway.'

'Val Williams.' She indicated the brunette. 'And this is Georgie Sinclair.'

'Georgie and Val, what charming names,' said Matthew. 'Welcome to Manston.'

Tommy Hesketh said, 'Val's from Ramsgate, so it's almost like coming home, isn't it, Val?'

'Georgie and I popped back to my parents' for Sunday lunch the other day. It was fun, wasn't it?'

Georgie smiled.

'The weather was nice so we had a flask of tea on the beach,' said Val. 'Such a hoot to be sitting there with all the barbed wire.'

Matthew said, 'So it's no good me offering to show you girls round the area?'

Georgie spoke for the first time. 'No, I shouldn't bother.'

The put-down startled him, but he covered it by buying a round of drinks. They got in a couple more rounds before closing time and then they all began to straggle back to the base.

Matthew thought it worth another try and offered to walk Georgie home.

She was tucking her dark curls under her cap. 'No thanks,' she said. 'And don't think of trying your luck with Val. We've both been warned off and we'd rather take our chance in the blackout.'

Speechless for once, Matthew watched the two women leave the pub. Well, damn and blast you, he thought, then hooked up with his friends and headed outside.

Over the following two weeks Matthew flew patrols over the Channel, escorting Blenheims so that they could drop their bombs on the French mainland. On the last patrol of the fortnight, two Spitfires from Manston were shot down. One of them was Tommy Hesketh's.

After landing and handing his plane over to the ground crew, Matthew discovered that he couldn't face the officers' mess. Instead, after he had washed and forced down a sandwich and a cup of tea, he cycled to Ramsgate. He walked along the harbour and then went into a small hotel where he and his friends sometimes had a drink. Passing the lounge, he saw through the doorway that a girl in WAAF uniform was sitting beside the fireplace reading a book. He recognised Georgie Sinclair.

He went into the lounge. 'Hello,' he said.

She looked up. 'Hello.'

'Do you mind if I join you?'

She glanced round the room, which was empty apart from a table at the far end, where two elderly men were playing dominoes.

'It's a free country.'

He sat down. 'What did you mean, you'd been warned off?'

'You have a reputation. A love-you-and-leave you merchant.'

'That's unfair.'

'Is it? That's not what I've heard. I can look after myself, but Val's a sweet girl and you should leave her alone.'

'I've no intention of—'

'But you're not fussy, are you? Anything in a skirt, that's what one of the other girls said.'

He felt furious. 'That's not true.'

She shrugged. 'Have it your own way.'

'I'll leave you in peace then.' He stood up.

Surprising him, she closed the book with an audible snap. 'It's a load of old rubbish. I shan't waste my time.' Then she yawned, stretching out her arms. 'Still, there isn't a lot of other company and I'm awfully bored. Shall we go for a walk?'

'What, us?' he said, startled.

She glanced at the dominoes players. 'I could ask them, I suppose.'

'I'm surprised you trust yourself with me.'

Georgie smiled. 'I know the enemy, I've learned to recognise him.' She rose, buttoning up her jacket. 'Are you coming? You may as well. Clear your head, and there's nothing much going on here.'

Matthew followed her out of the hotel. They walked through the town to a beach. Georgie turned up the collar of her jacket as they crunched along the sand and pebbles. He was glad that they hardly spoke; his tiredness, which he could not imagine ever going away, seemed that evening to be a solid, tangible thing, and their short conversation in the hotel had taken it out of him.

They stood on the shore, watching gunmetal-grey waves heave and crash against the beach. She said, 'I'm sorry about Tommy.'

'You heard.'

'Yes. Is there any chance . . .?'

'Not much. He was a decent bloke.'

'How long have you been on active service?'

'A year.' Matthew rubbed a hand through his hair. 'Feels longer. How long have you been in the WAAF?'

'Only a few months. I used to work on a newspaper. I used to write the headlines. "Tot dies in horror fall", "Tragic bride in death crash", that sort of thing. But then, after my husband died, I needed to do something different.'

'You were married?'

'Yes, to one of your lot. Tony was stationed at Tangmere. I don't wear my wedding ring. People ask questions and it gets tedious.'

'I'm sorry.'

'For Tony or the questions? Don't be. We were only married for six weeks. And we only knew each other for six weeks before that.'

'But you loved him.'

'Did I? I suppose I must have. Silly me. I don't know what I thought I was doing, actually, because I'm not the marrying type.'

'Is there a type?'

'Don't you think so? The sort of woman who wants a house and babies?'

'And you don't?'

'No, I don't.' Georgie wrapped her arms round herself. 'God, it's freezing. Awful to think that it's autumn already. I assume you're not the marrying type either.'

He took a second before answering. 'No, probably not.'

'Oh,' she said, with a smile. 'Don't tell me you've loved and lost? Don't tell me that Matthew Reddaway, Manston's Don Juan, is covering up a broken heart?'

Her cynicism stung; he said, 'Put a sock in it, won't you?'

'Did she die tragically, or were you dumped?'

'Actually,' he said furiously, 'I found out that she was my half-sister.'

She blinked, then stared at him. 'Jesus. That's a new one.'

As soon as he had said it he regretted it. It wasn't something he spoke about generally. Only when he was very, very drunk.

'God, Reddaway,' she said, clearly amused. 'Your sister.'

'Obviously I didn't know that.'

289

'Obviously.' She took out a packet of cigarettes and offered them to him. 'Were you separated at birth or something?'

'Something like that.'

'So you don't trust yourself to form relationships – there's always the fear that you might find out—'

'I told you, stop it,' he said angrily.

She nodded. 'Okay. I've never cared much for being psycho-analysed either. I prefer to keep my neuroses to myself.'

She struck a match, sheltering it from the wind with her hand, and they lit their cigarettes and then walked on.

'I've come to the conclusion that love is overrated,' she said. 'Nice while it lasts but something always goes wrong. Best avoided, in fact. My father ran off with the nanny when I was five. That didn't do a lot for my faith in men as a species. But even if you aren't parted by death or desertion – or in your case by finding out that your beloved is a blood relation – it always goes kaput. I mean, what if you discover they're a dyed-in-the-wool Tory? Or they drag you off to some dreary marsh for a day's birdwatching? Or, simply, boredom sets in? If you think about it that way, the whole wretched business of will-they-won't-they and weeping into your pillow is so pointless.'

'You're very hard.'

'I told you, I used to work for a paper. It made me hard.' She examined his face. 'But you're the same, aren't you? Underneath the charm.'

This disconcerted him. *Hard.* He hadn't thought of himself like that. They walked on. Debris had been flung on to the beach and had caught in the coils of barbed wire. Struts from packing cases – or maybe aeroplanes – a blue glass bottle, the black curve of a sea-smoothed tyre.

'I mean,' she said, picking up the conversation as if five minutes of silence had not lain between them, 'I don't suppose either of us is looking for love.'

He gave her a swift glance. He liked the impishness of her face, the tip-tiltedness of her features and the athletic leanness of her body. She had a pale, opaque skin; he imagined that when she was not suntanned, and if she was tired, she might look haggard.

'Sex, though,' she added.

'Well, that's always nice,' he said easily. 'Takes your mind off things.'

'Exactly.' Raising herself on her toes, she brushed her mouth against his, then gave his lower lip a little nibble.

'Have you eaten?' she said.

His heart was beating hard, echoing the waves thumping the shore. 'Not really.'

'I'm starving. Shall we find somewhere?'

In December, shortly after the Japanese bombed Pearl Harbor, bringing America into the war, Matthew was taken off ops and posted as an instructor to an operational training unit in Cambridgeshire. Although he tried to persuade his commanding officer to let him stay at Manston, a part of him knew that the posting had come just in time, because he had begun not to care particularly whether he lived or died. Up there in the sky, he had too often recently had to fight the temptation to lift his hands off the controls, to close his eyes and let the wind and the sky take him where they would.

Every few weeks, he took the train to London, where he met Georgie in a nightclub or restaurant. Though everyone assumed they were lovers, they did not become so until several months after they had first met. And even when it happened, in a dingy hotel near King's Cross station, he though that *lovers* was the wrong word. They were good friends, he and Georgie, and they enjoyed each other's bodies, lying under the frayed sheets, sharing a cigarette as they looked out at slate roofs that glistened in the rain. But there was a space where her heart was, and he knew that he was the same.

And yet he liked it when she rested her head, with its springy black curls, on his chest and nuzzled the crook of his neck, and he loved it when he moved inside her. And when, in the bleak autumn of 1942, just before the news of the Allied victory at El Alamein, he heard that she'd been killed in a car crash – some drunken idiot with a few drops of petrol left in the tank of his sports car – he felt a piercing pain. Needing to be by himself, he tramped round the flat brown Cambridgeshire fields, and as he waited for the ache to subside it came to him that he had a heart after all, and that Georgie had found her way into it.

Chapter Fourteen

February 1943

After Zoe moved out, Esme and Hugo had two Irish nurses billeted in the mews house. Though Hugo resented the chatter and disruption and Eileen and Clodagh's consumption of food and coal, Esme enjoyed the girls' company, and was thankful that they acted as a cheerful barricade between the two of them.

She had cleaned out Eileen and Clodagh's bedroom one morning, and was hauling wet sheets out of the copper when the postman knocked. Among the day's delivery was a letter for Hugo. The postman apologised for its battered condition, the result of an air raid.

The heading of the letter peeked out through the torn envelope. Esme hung the washed sheets outside in the small courtyard, where they hung limply in the grey February gloom. Then she went back inside the house.

She looked at the envelope again. Through the aperture made by the tear, she was able to read the name of a firm of solicitors in Oxford. She put the letter aside and returned to the kitchen, where she took out the ingredients to make the half-dozen meat and vegetable pies that she cooked each day for a foreign servicemen's friendship club. She measured out flour, and sifted it. Then, wiping her floury hands on a tea towel, she went back into the sitting room, eased the letter out through the hole in the envelope and read it.

Hugo's solicitor described at some length a problem with the drains in a house in Leafield, a village in Oxfordshire. The tenants were disputing who was to pay for the repairs. Esme had to read through the letter several times before she was able to accept that the house, without question, belonged to Hugo. A house she had never heard of, and that he had never mentioned to her.

She folded the letter, worked it back into the envelope, and smoothed everything down with a fingernail. Then she put it in the middle of the pile of Hugo's mail.

Hugo was away from home over the next few days. At midday on Friday he returned from his trip, red-nosed and complaining of a cold. Esme made him a cup of tea and found him aspirins and watched while he went through his mail. She noticed that he glanced briefly at the solicitor's letter and then stuffed it in his pocket. She thought this furtive, but then everything he did or said now seemed furtive.

Then he said, 'A colleague of mine, Armstrong, is looking for a house in Oxford. He'd be prepared to give you four hundred pounds.'

'What?' she said. She was trimming scrag end. There was, she thought, a lot more scrag than end.

'The house,' said Hugo. 'Armstrong's made you a good offer.'

'My house?' Esme came into the sitting room, a kitchen knife in her hand.

'I'll get the papers drawn up.'

'Hugo, I haven't agreed to sell. In fact, I have no intention of selling.'

He blew his nose loudly. 'I can't think why you are being so obstinate,' he said peevishly. 'Armstrong won't wait for ever.'

'Then why don't you sell this *Armstrong* your own house?'

She dipped back into the kitchen, where she hurled chunks

of meat and bone into a pan. When she looked up, he was standing in the doorway.

He said, 'You read my letter?'

'Yes.' She stirred the pan. 'The envelope had torn.'

'How dare you?'

She saw that he was furious. Hugo was rarely angry, preferring to sulk when he didn't get his own way, and the malice in his eyes momentarily alarmed her.

But her own fury won out, and she said, 'How could you keep such a thing from me? A *house*, Hugo? To own a *house* and not to tell me?'

'It was no business of yours. I saw no reason to mention it. You shouldn't have read my letter. It's despicable behaviour.'

'No more despicable than keeping such a thing from me,' she said scornfully.

'I owned the Leafield house long before I met you.'

'As I owned mine long before I met you. Yet you're always trying to persuade me to sell it. Why is that?'

He snuffled wetly. 'You're not good with money, I've noticed that. You're wasteful. A house is an investment. I'm merely offering to look after it for you.'

'An investment? It was my *home*! It was where, for at least some of the time, I was happy! Unlike this place!' Esme was still clutching the knife. She imagined plunging it into Hugo's bony breast. The urge was so powerful, she had to put the knife down on the worktop.

'I blame myself, of course,' she said contemptuously. 'How could I have been so stupid not to have realised your meanness, and your secretiveness! What a fool I was. To think that I thought it romantic that you offered to walk me home on that freezing cold night we met. When it was because you didn't want to pay for a taxi!'

'Your first husband spoiled you,' said Hugo. 'That was obvious to me when we first met. I've always disliked overindulged women.'

'Then why did you marry me? Oh,' she said, with an exaggerated air of discovery, 'I know. Because you needed a housekeeper. You knew you would have to leave Oxford because of the war and you needed someone to look after you. Someone you didn't have to pay for.'

'Esme, you're making an exhibition of yourself.' The look in Hugo's eyes was cold and supercilious. 'You're becoming hysterical. Perhaps your charity work is too much for you.'

'My charity work, as you call it, is at least useful. It at least gives me some sort of dignity – and independence.'

'I should have a word with Mrs Maddox.' Mrs Maddox ran Esme's branch of the WVS.

'Don't you dare!'

'Or Dr Haslam.' Hugo bared his teeth. 'I can't have you making yourself ill.'

She wanted to scream at him, but she could see that he knew he had frightened her, and the realisation humiliated her. She turned away, stabbing at the stewed meat with a wooden spoon.

Hugo spoke again. 'You need to learn more self-control, Esme. Reading other people's letters, losing your temper – it's hardly normal behaviour.' He glanced at his watch. 'I shall be lunching at my club. You'd better prepare dinner early; six will do. I've to work this evening.'

He walked away. Esme heard a rustle as he took his raincoat from the coat peg, and then the front door slammed.

Throughout the preparation of vegetables, the shredding of meat from bone and the encasing of the filling in pastry, her rage smouldered. Would Hugo carry out his threats? Mrs Maddox was a sensible woman and would support her, she was sure, but she was less certain of Dr Haslam. She had changed doctor when she had moved to London, and Haslam, a college friend of Hugo's, was of the old-fashioned, patronising type. She felt isolated, and a long way from home.

She was tired, it was true, but then they were all tired. The war had gone on too long, and though one learned to live with fear and deprivation, there was no doubt that they depleted. Esme pinpointed her fear: that Hugo and Dr Haslam between them might wear her down. That she might give in to them, sell her house, and in doing so lose her possibility of escape.

The pies were a little tough, a little burned: not made with love, Esme reflected. The phone rang as she placed them on the windowsill to cool.

'Kensington 355. Mrs Godwin speaking.'

'Esme, it's Devlin. I'm sorry to disturb you, but I'm trying to find Zoe. I phoned her office but they weren't very helpful. I wondered whether you knew where she was.'

The line was crackly; wartime lines had a habit of cutting off, so she said quickly, 'She mentioned that she was to travel somewhere. To the north, I think.'

'Ah.' She heard his disappointment. 'No matter. I had the opportunity and I thought, an early supper.'

The house, and the chill, grey weather that surrounded it, oppressed her. And she dreaded Hugo's return home.

'You may take me out for supper if you wish, Devlin. If,' she added quickly, 'you have nothing better to do.'

'No, I don't think I do. Can you make it here for half past six?'

Esme glanced at the clock. It was after four. She said, 'Where are you staying?'

While she wrapped up the pies in tea towels and placed them in a basket, and during her own rapid self-transformation from pinafored housewife to the sort of woman a man might enjoy having supper with, Esme's fury with Hugo remained undiminished. After she had delivered her pies to the servicemen's club, she made her way to the Underground, where she propped herself against a metal pole in a crowded carriage as the train rattled on to Paddington.

At Notting Hill Gate, she slid gratefully into a vacated seat and prised fragments of pastry out from beneath her fingernails. It was possible, she now saw, that Hugo had inherited the Leafield house from his mistress, the housekeeper who had died from tuberculosis. The woman had lived in a village in Oxfordshire. Perhaps Hugo had nagged her to leave the house to him. It was also possible that he was the sort of man who set out to pursue well-off women. Perhaps that was why he had put up with a spoiled, indulged woman like her; maybe that was all he had ever seen in her. Had there been any love between them? No, she did not now think so. Sex with Hugo tended to be quick and functional, except when he'd had a few drinks, when it took longer. Then, Esme ran through shopping lists in her head while Hugo pounded drearily on top of her. No, he had never loved her, and she knew that whatever she had once felt for him, whatever unfortunate impulse had prompted her to agree to marry him, had been cheap and shallow compared to what she had once, a long time ago, felt for Devlin.

As she made her way out of Paddington station and into the murk that wetted the roads and pavements, she longed to feel something other than the anger, anxiety and exhaustion that had been her predominant emotions for a long time. She longed to feel passion again. She had once loved Devlin so much, and she knew that she had come here this evening, aware of the utter failure of her marriage to Hugo, to find out whether she was still capable of passion.

The blacked-out headlamps of vehicles, with their narrowed slit eyes like cats', came and went. Her shoes click-clacked on the damp pavement. The fog and the blackout seemed to sweep the city back through the years, as if another, more ancient London was pushing its way back into place, toppling the shattered roads and ruined buildings, sucking them back into the earth.

She ran a hand over her hair, checking that it was tidy. Through the sooty haze she caught sight of a painted sign and a run of steps.

Devlin was waiting for her in the foyer of the hotel. He rose as she came through the door.

'Esme. You look well.'

'Thank you.' She kissed his cheek. He would always be a handsome man, she thought, but he looked older now; the years had not been generous to him.

They left the hotel, walking a couple of streets to a small restaurant behind the station. The eight tables were served by one waiter, an elderly man with a limp. Grubby yellow lampshades bestowed on the room a sulphurous light. A wireless rattled away, the dance music interspersed by a compère with a phoney American accent.

She said, 'Tell me what's happening in Devon.'

Devlin talked about the business. The two boatyards were full to capacity. They worked twelve-hour days, six days a week – seven sometimes.

'I sleep at the yard some nights,' he told her. 'Easier, you see, without the car. Anyway, the house has become intolerable.'

'Your evacuees?'

'I shall throttle the next small boy I find catapulting stones at the gargoyles.'

'Poor Devlin.'

He gave a wry smile. 'Rosindell seems to be retreating to its former state. Heading rapidly back to the swamps.'

The waiter came and took their order. When he had gone, Devlin said, 'What's wrong?'

'Wrong?'

'I know you well enough, Esme. Is it something I've done?'

299

'You? No, not this time. I actually wanted to kill Hugo today. I had a kitchen knife and I actually wanted to kill him.'

'But you didn't.'

'No.'

'Esme, we're all under a lot of strain.'

'Hugo's not a likeable man. Actually, he's a bully. I felt frightened of him. It was a horrible feeling.'

He said sharply, 'Has he hurt you?'

'No, and I don't think he ever would. He isn't a physical man. But he's good with words and he has a way of making me feel foolish and worthless. And I'm afraid that if I stay with him then I might start to believe him and end up feeling like that all the time.' She took a sip of wine. 'I should never have married him, Devlin. I will leave him, it's just a question of when. I'd rather do it without a lot of fuss, so I shall wait until he has to go away because of his work, and then the whole thing will be done and dusted long before he returns.'

'If you leave him, where will you go?'

'Back to Oxford. I shall cook and clean for my lodgers. I don't want to be dependent on anyone any more. That has been my great mistake, I see it now: that it took me so long to learn the importance of independence, of financial independence in particular. Zoe seems to have realised it far quicker than I. I daresay she's learned from my faults.'

Their soup arrived. The salt cellar was empty; Devlin made to ask the waiter for another one, but Esme touched his sleeve.

'No, it doesn't matter, let's not make a fuss.' She took a bread roll. 'Perhaps you and I would have managed differently if I'd had something to occupy myself with.'

'We managed well enough. And you were hardly short of things to do. The children, a large house – and the garden.'

'And a nanny, cook, housemaid and gardener. To think that I once thought Rosindell short of servants. When I married Hugo, I had to buy a book and teach myself to cook. I'm not too bad at it now, when I put my mind to it. I dislike the floor-scrubbing and the laundry, but needs must.'

These days, she looked back critically on her younger self, appalled by her ignorance and the narrowness of her experience. As for Rosindell itself, it seemed remote, temporally as well as geographically, something that had absorbed her for a while, in a different life.

'You and I were always too unequal,' she said. 'When I married you, I was such a child. I knew nothing.'

'And I too much.'

'Yes. But there were good times, weren't there? Do you remember the night we all danced on the beach?'

'I remember our first summer dance,' he said. 'We had to close the doors and hide the unfinished parts of the house away.'

'I don't think I've ever wished I hadn't married you, Devlin, even at the worst times.'

He said bluntly, 'I hate what I've done to the children.'

'Both of us.'

'No. No, I am solely responsible. I did such harm.'

She felt that this was not completely true; she had a vivid memory of the way in which she had confided in Matthew in the bitter aftermath of the break-up, had leaned on him, had spoken too freely of her hurt and anger. If Matthew's natural inclination had been, because of their closeness, to take her side, then she had reinforced that.

'We hurt what we love most in the world,' she said sadly. 'How did that happen?'

'All I know is that it took me far too long to realise the value of what I had.'

'I never thought I'd be the sort of woman to have two failed marriages. Sometimes I don't think I'm any better than Camilla.'

'Your father told me that she's married again.'

'An American film star. He's called Todd Hadley.' Esme said

the name with a Texan twang. 'I expect he's a scoundrel. I don't think the girl, Melissa, lives with them.'

'I suppose all I can do is to keep trying. At least Matthew no longer returns my birthday gifts.'

He looked so wretched that she said, 'He'll come round, Devlin.'

'I'm not so sure. It appals me to think of what I exposed him to. First love has such impact, such power, and for them to be torn apart in such a way . . .'

She saw that he was not to be comforted, and said, 'I sometimes think that if we'd lived somewhere more ordinary, we might have had a better chance. If we'd lived in a nice little house in Kingswear, for instance.' She took a sip of the rather sour wine the restaurant served. 'My upbringing was very dull. I remember always being bored. From around the age of twelve until I married you, I was almost always bored. I think that for me Rosindell was the wild, romantic antidote to everything that had gone before. I imbued it with glamour even before I saw it. And it didn't disappoint.'

They had finished their soup some time ago, but Devlin did not yet call for the waiter. She suspected that he was reluctant to interrupt their first honest and amiable conversation in years.

She said, 'Are you seeing anyone, Devlin?'

'Not at the moment. There was a friend I used to go to the theatre with, when I was in Town, but she married someone else.' His eyes slid over her. 'I think she became tired of waiting.'

'You didn't love her, then.'

'No, I didn't love her.'

'What a pair we are.'

'I'm sorry about Hugo.'

'Are you? I'm not.'

'I meant, that I would want you to be happy.'

She said carefully, 'I am not unhappy. Not now that I've made up my mind. And there are consolations, aren't there? I've discovered that I like to be busy. And I've learned so many new things and have met so many different people.'

The waiter arrived at last and served their main course. They talked of the children and of the progress of the war, and then made the mutual decision to skip pudding. He had a bottle of brandy in his room, Devlin told her. Emergency rations.

They walked back to the hotel. The lounge was raucous with American airmen, so they went upstairs. Devlin's room, which must once have been elegant, contained a bed with a patched olive-coloured eiderdown, a chest of drawers missing some handles, and an armchair. Cracks ran round the ceiling, and the blackout curtains had been drawn.

He took her coat and hat and opened the brandy bottle. 'I think my father brought this back from France at around the turn of the century,' he said. 'Of course, the vultures who've flocked to Rosindell have had most of the contents of the cellars, but there are a few hiding places they haven't yet managed to find.'

He handed her a glass. Esme took a sip and sighed. 'Oh God, Devlin, how blissful.'

'When I look back,' he said, 'I have these memories of you – playing with the children in the garden and swimming at the cove . . . and the summer dances. And they are quite perfect.'

She watched him replace the brandy bottle on the chest of drawers and loosen his tie, then she put down her glass and, reaching behind her, pulled down the zip at the back of her dress. As she stepped out of it, he crossed the room, took her in his arms and kissed her.

'For old times' sake,' he said.

'*Good* old times.'

She put her face up to be kissed again. And then, because it was cold in the room, he peeled back the blankets and they slid between the sheets.

*   *   *

303

There was a time in the night when she dreamed that they had returned to Rosindell. She saw it all with such clarity: the train journey and the bright flickers of river between the dark green trees, and Josiah meeting them at Kingswear with the pony and trap, and then the ride across the headland, the walls of the hedgerows falling away once they reached the bare, high land. Then on through the half-dozen houses of Lethwiston until she saw Rosindell: the gate, the grey slate of the roof, and the house itself, cradled in the valley. In her dream, it was summer, and the roses and delphiniums were in bloom; and as they wound down the drive she breathed in the scents of Rosindell: roses and the sea. She heard all around her, like a murmuring from the house itself, the sound of the waves, and she felt a longing so intense, so painful, that it woke her. As she stared into the darkness, tears were poised cold and wet on her eyelids.

When she woke in the morning, Devlin was dressing. 'I have a meeting,' he said. 'But you must stay here as long as you like.'

She uncurled her arms, yawning. '*Heavenly* sleep.'

He bent and kissed her. 'Last night was beautiful,' she said. And it had been. She had forgotten that sex could be so transformative, so comforting.

Stroking her hair, he said, 'Come back with me, Esme.'

She sat up. 'Devlin, I can't.'

He turned up his collar, picked up his tie. 'Then after you've spoken to Hugo.'

'No.'

He swung round to her, frowning. 'I've always believed that one day you would come back to me. I've always told myself that if I only waited long enough, eventually you would return. If you won't come back to me because of Rosindell, then be damned to the place. I'll sell it, and we'll live somewhere else.'

If he left Rosindell, she thought, he would always long for it. 'I wouldn't ask that of you,' she said.

304

Knotting the tie, he studied her. 'I told myself that one day you'd forgive me. It was just once. And you knew what Camilla was.'

She said softly, 'Devlin, she was my *sister*.'

'And because of her, we stay apart. Tell me, if it hadn't been her, if it had been anyone else, would you have forgiven me?'

When she did not reply, he said, 'You don't hate me any more.'

'No. I did for a long time, but not now.'

'But you don't love me either.'

She looked away, unable to bear the anguish in his gaze. 'I'm sorry.'

He nodded, then took his jacket off its hanger. 'And do you think,' he said, 'that you'll always feel like this?'

'I think I may.'

'Esme, I beg of you . . .'

'Everything has its time, doesn't it?'

He went to the window and drew back the curtains. Then, placing his hand on the window, he brought it down the glass, leaving a stripe in the condensation.

'I love you,' he said. 'I've never stopped loving you. Well, so be it, if this is what you want. But be very sure it is, Esme, because if you don't come back with me now, then I shall do my damnedest to forget you.'

He checked his watch. 'I have to go. They serve breakfast, but I wouldn't recommend it.'

He left the room. Esme climbed out of bed, wrapping the eiderdown around herself. At the window, she placed her palm on the clear patch his hand had made, and watched him walk down the street. There was a moment in which she wanted to claw her fingers through the glass, to reach out and call him back. But then she turned away, and drawing the curtains, began to dress.

*　　*　　*

In January 1944, the bombers came back to London. Caught in an unfamiliar part of the city, Zoe spent the night sheltering in an Underground station, rolled up in her coat. In the morning, she emerged from the tunnels into a changed landscape. You couldn't at first tell where the roads were supposed to be. As she walked to the Strand, it seemed to her that every building she passed had something wrong with it. There were black holes where there had once been windows, and slates slid from the roofs, and a powdering of brick dust covered sills and dormers and porches.

She finished work at seven that evening and walked to the house in Bloomsbury in which she rented a room. A secretary from Supply, a girl called Brenda, had persuaded her to go on a double date that evening, a promise that Zoe had felt hesitant about at the time and now regretted. In her room, she took off the clothes in which she had slept the previous night and put them into a laundry bag. It was very cold, so she pulled on a pair of slacks and a jersey and two pairs of socks.

After she had written a letter to her mother, who, having left Hugo Godwin, had returned to the house in Oxford, Zoe cleaned her room. She swept beneath the bed-settee and inside the cupboard in which she kept her food and under the chest of drawers. She washed over the walls and ceilings, careful of the water, because the previous year had been dry and there were shortages. Then she washed up her plates, bowls, cups and cutlery and her saucepan and teapot, and dried them, making sure there were no smears. When it was done, she put everything back in its right place, lining up her books in order of size and placing her pen parallel to her notebook.

While she worked, she thought about Rupert Shelbrooke, her boss, with whom she had fallen in love. She knew that it was wrong, because Rupert was married, and she had accepted, or thought she had accepted, that there was no chance of her love ever being reciprocated. There were days when she enjoyed being in love with him, but today was not one of those days. She was cold and lonely, and London's return, the previous night, to the chaos and fear of the Blitz had shocked her. She ached with tiredness but could not rest. Now and then, throughout the day, she had forgotten where she was and what she was supposed to be doing. She could not think of anything that might stop her feeling tired.

She took her towel and dressing gown and went to the bathroom that she shared with the other residents of the house. She was careful not to let herself or her belongings brush against anything dirty or unpleasant. Then she went back to her room and put on a frock and arranged her hair.

She met Brenda at the bar of the Berkeley Hotel. Brenda introduced her to their dates, two soldiers from the Royal Engineers. One of the soldiers was called Michael, the other Gerald. Brenda, pouting and flicking her hair, made a beeline for Michael, and they went off to dance, leaving Zoe with Gerald. He had a thin, sharp face and straight, slicked-back dark hair. His narrow brown eyes darted round the room. Zoe had the idea that he was a little drunk.

He said, 'Fast mover, your friend.'

'Brenda's all right.'

'Surprised she isn't after one of the Yanks.'

There were a number of American soldiers in the room. Zoe said, 'She seems to like Michael.'

'Most girls *seem* to *like* silk stockings and chocolate better. Want a smoke?'

'No thanks.'

'The good old British Tommy hardly gets a look-in these days. I suppose time will tell whether these airy-fairy types shape up on the battlefield. Chloe, did you say your name was?'

'Zoe.'

'Zoe . . . Not many Zoes where I come from.'

'Where's that?'

'Leeds. Can't you tell?'

'I'm not very good at accents.'

He flicked cigarette ash on the floor. 'I've tried to chip a bit off mine. Doesn't get you far in the army, letting them know that you're as common as muck. Do you want to dance?'

'Not particularly.'

'Me neither.' He tipped back his head, studying her. 'Let me guess. Daddy works in a bank or owns a factory. You went to some posh school. And now you're doing a bit of typing because you think it helps the war effort.'

She said, 'Actually, my father makes motor torpedo boats.'

'*Actually* makes them or gets someone else to make them for him? My dad started down the mine when he was twelve.'

She looked away. Searching through the crowds, the uniformed men and women and the girls in evening frocks, she could not see Brenda.

'I'm going to get a drink,' said Gerald. 'Do you want one?'

'No thanks.'

'"No thanks",' he mimicked. 'You like having your own way, don't you, Zoe?' He leaned close to her, so that his lips were only a few inches from her ear. 'Think I'll head off, then,' he murmured. 'Can't see any point in wasting my evening on a stuck-up little bitch like you.'

Zoe remained on the sofa, rigid with shock, as he made his way out of the bar. Some girl threw herself into the seat that he had vacated, laughing with her boyfriend as she prised off her shoe and poked at a blister. Zoe tried to catch her breath, couldn't, and felt as if she was about to choke. She wanted to run out of the room but was unable to move.

A voice said, 'Here, have this.'

She looked up. A short, stocky man with wavy light brown hair and wire-rimmed glasses was holding out a glass.

'It's an Old-Fashioned,' he said. 'Whisky, bitters, a little sugar, a little lemon rind. Though I wouldn't guarantee the sugar or lemon these days. Go on, knock it back, it'll make you feel better.'

She noticed that he spoke with an American accent. She took a large gulp of the cocktail; the spirits scorched her throat. *You like having your own way, don't you, Zoe?* She looked up, afraid that Gerald might have come back.

The American said, 'It's all right, he's gone.' Because there were no spare seats, he was perched on the sofa arm. 'How d'you get landed with a creep like that?'

'It was a double date.'

'Ah.' He smiled. 'Always a lousy idea, double dates. The girl who's arranged it gets off with the decent guy and her friend gets dumped with his sidekick.'

'I don't know why I *mind*!' The words burst out of her; she pressed her hand over her mouth.

'He was uncivil to you. Why shouldn't you mind?'

'I didn't even like him!'

'Only his mother would like him. And even she might struggle.' He handed her a handkerchief and Zoe blew her nose. She was making an enormous effort not to cry, and she was thankful when he began to talk about other things – the crowds, the music.

He said, 'Hey, have you eaten? Would you like to go get some supper somewhere?'

'My friend . . .'

'I think she's looking after herself, don't you?'

They went to an Italian restaurant in Soho. As they waited for the food to arrive, he told her that his name was Reuben Ames and that he was a major in the infantry. He came from New York and was thirty-two years old.

He took a photograph out of his wallet and passed it to her across the table. 'That's my wife, Norah, and my little boy, Lester. Isn't he just the cutest thing you ever saw?'

He was a sweet little boy, it was true, but Zoe understood

that Reuben Ames was also making certain things clear. Terms of engagement, you might say.

By the time the food arrived, her appetite had returned. Reuben asked her about her job and Zoe told him about recruiting women into war work, and the committees that she helped Rupert set up with the trades unions and employers. And then she talked about her family, the whole complicated, divided lot of them, and about Rosindell.

'My father's been living in two rooms for ages,' she said, 'but now the army's requisitioned our house. The school had to leave as well. Daddy's living with my old nanny in Kingswear. It's hard to imagine Rosindell without him. When I saw him at Christmas, he told me he was all right, but I know that he hates it.'

Reuben Ames said, 'When I came to London, it was a big shock. I mean, you see the newsreels and the photos in the papers, but you can't get the scale of it. Loathed it to begin with, if I'm honest. Cold and wet all the time and everything in pieces and so *grey*. But you've got to admire people's spirit. All those women standing in line for food. Girls like you, making an effort to look nice when you go out at night.'

Zoe could see by then that there might come a time when she would be able to pretend to laugh at what had happened that night, even if the memory of Gerald's words – *You like having your own way, don't you, Zoe?* – had left a scar, because they seemed to her to contain a truth.

'I'm not sure I should have bothered,' she said. 'I might have done better to stay at home with my knitting.'

'But then we'd never have met. And that would have been a shame, don't you think?'

She had a good look at him then, at his kind, intelligent grey eyes, and she decided that she liked what she saw.

After the restaurant, he took her to a jazz club in Soho. He was an excellent dancer. He talked to her about jazz and swing and the blues, which he loved most of all. A small, hollow-faced black woman hunched herself over the microphone, her long, thin hands making shapes in the darkness. Zoe and Reuben danced as she sang about desire and betrayal. As the song finished and a ripple of applause ran round the dance floor, he kissed her, a light, questioning kiss on the mouth.

'My hotel's not far away,' he said. 'I should apologise for it in advance. It's a brown sort of room. Hellishly brown.'

The room had a brown carpet, a brown eiderdown, and brown curtains and wainscoting. Zoe sat on the bed and he wrapped the eiderdown round her, then took a bottle out of a drawer and poured them both bourbons. While they drank, sitting side by side, he told her about New York, and how he had met Norah at high school when he was just fifteen years old, and how the two of them had saved for a trip to Europe after they were married.

'We lived in Paris for six months.' He grinned. 'We thought we were Hemingway and what's-her-name, that girl he fell in love with. Or Scott Fitzgerald and Zelda.'

When her glass was empty, he took it out of her hand and placed it on the bedside table. He said, 'I'd like to make love to you now, but I'm not going to, because I think that what you'd really like is a good night's sleep.'

He helped her off with her shoes and stockings and frock, and she curled up under the eiderdown, wearing only her slip, his arm around her, his warmth keeping her warm, and fell asleep straight away.

He made love to her in the morning, though. Her first time: she never forgot it. She never forgot that he made her want him, and he made her feel beautiful, and always afterwards she was grateful to him for that.

June 1944. In their encampments from Devon to Dorset, troops wait for the order to be given for the invasion of France.

On 5 June, in spite of stormy weather, Eisenhower issues the command.

The soldiers move out of Rosindell in the early hours of the following morning. A door left open at the back of the house slams in the wind. The drive and lawns, scarred and rutted by military vehicles, are silent now. Men no longer lounge on the terraces or stick their gum beneath the windowsills or use the plaster cherubs beside the hall clock for target practice.

Most of the barley-sugar banisters on the Tudor staircase have been broken into pieces and used as firewood. Someone has taken a ladder to the roof of the great hall and hacked away the faces of the wooden gargoyles. The oak panelling in the library has been carved with the initials of the departing men, and someone – homesick, no doubt – has attempted a miniature of the Stars and Stripes.

Later that day, a dozen boys from Lethwiston and Kingswear swarm round the house and gardens. They discover a crate of mortar shells, overlooked by the departing troops. Two boys carry the crate to the cliff, where they take turns throwing the shells on to the beach below and watching them explode. They grapple with each other, trying to push one another down the rocks and scree, excited by the noise and destruction. One boy has the idea of breaking the dam around the bathing pool. Quieter now, their expressions intent and gleeful, they hurl the shells until the wall breaks and the sea rushes in.

Chapter Fifteen

April 1948

He said, 'Look, you'd better come back with me to my house. I've a jerrycan of petrol there. You can warm up while I get your car going.'

'I don't want to cause you any trouble,' she said.

'It's only half a mile or so. And you look frozen.'

She shivered. 'This winter seems to have gone on for ages, doesn't it?'

He held out his hand to her. 'My name's Devlin Reddaway.'

'Bonnie Gresham,' she said. 'Thank you. This is so awfully kind of you.'

He had found her lost on the Lethwiston road. She had been trying to drive to Brixham and had run out of petrol. 'I'd thought I'd enough in the tank to make it,' she told him. Her clothes looked old, just as everyone else's did, but she wore them well. As he started up the Bentley and they headed towards the village, he shot her a glance. He estimated her age to be thirty, maybe thirty-five. He admired the thick dark hair that spilled over her shoulders beneath her green felt hat.

He said, 'Have you been living in Brixham long?'

'Only a few months. It's hard to find a decent place. What about you?'

'Oh.' He threw her a smile. 'The Reddaways have lived at Rosindell for centuries.'

He drove through the gates and beneath the canopy of trees. It was twilight; the hour had changed only the previous Sunday, lengthening the evenings.

He heard her small inward breath. 'Is that your house?'

'Yes, that's Rosindell.'

'Crikey.'

He laughed. 'It may look grand, but it isn't, I'm afraid.'

He parked the car in front of the house and opened the passenger door for her. She was slender and petite, a head shorter than him, even though she was wearing heels. He said, to put her at ease, 'My housekeeper will have lit the fire in the sitting room. I'll let her know you're here and then I'll sort out your car.'

He led her into the house. In the better light, he saw that her eyes, which he had taken to be brown, were in fact a dark, olivine green.

When he showed her into the sitting room, she went straight away to the fire, holding out her hands. 'Goodness,' she murmured. 'Goodness.'

'How long were you marooned there?'

'Ages.' She gave him a narrow, curving smile. 'It felt like ages but it was probably only half an hour. I'm so hopeless with motor cars. I used to leave all that to Colin.'

'Colin?'

'My husband. He was killed at the D-Day landings.'

'I'm sorry.'

'It's all right, I've got used to it now. It's funny how you can get used to almost anything, isn't it?'

He offered her tea, which she accepted appreciatively. After he had spoken to Mrs Forbes, his daily, he went back outside. There was a jerrycan of petrol in the stables, kept there rather than in the house because of the risk of fire. Josiah had died the year after the war had ended and the horses had gone before that, sold to one of the estate's tenant farmers. Fetching down the can from its hiding place behind a row of dusty bottles – petrol was still severely rationed and there had been instances of theft – he thought that the building had outlived its usefulness. The stables seemed cold and lifeless, a leftover from a forgotten era. And always, for him, a scene of regret and betrayal.

He buttoned his overcoat up to his chin as he set off back along the drive and then along the Lethwiston road. It took him fifteen minutes to reach Mrs Gresham's Morris Eight. He noticed that he could see the lights of Lethwiston from where the vehicle had come to a halt. He supposed she had felt afraid to leave it, poor little thing.

He transferred the fuel, then started up the car and drove it to Rosindell. He went into the house. In the sitting room, Mrs Gresham was standing in front of an oil painting.

'All done,' he said. 'You should have enough in the tank to get you back to Brixham.'

'I can't thank you enough, Mr Reddaway. It's so kind of you.' She nodded to the painting. 'I have to ask you. Who is he?'

'A rather disreputable old scoundrel, I'm afraid. My great-grandfather. I keep him in here because this is my private room and I don't wish to inflict him on anyone else.'

'Then I shall leave you to your privacy.'

'Unless you'd like to stay for supper?' The invitation came out spontaneously, surprising him.

But she said, 'No, so good of you, but I wouldn't presume. I should drive back to my lodging house. My landlady will be thinking I've come to a sticky end.'

She picked up her handbag and gloves. In the lobby, he helped her on with her coat. They shook hands and then he stood at the door and waved her away. When the Morris was out of sight, he closed the door, shutting out the cold.

*   *   *

Two days later, he received a letter inviting him to lunch with her in her lodging house in Brixham. 'You must allow me to thank you for your great kindness,' she had written.

Suspecting that the food in the lodging house would be dire, Devlin offered to take her to the Royal Dart Hotel instead. That day, she wore a grey skirt and jacket with a cream blouse. This sober clothing seemed only to highlight her prettiness and vivacity. Her features were neat and regular, her face heart-shaped, with high cheekbones and a small, retroussé nose. Her green eyes were long-lashed, alert and full of expression.

They talked about the weather and the locality, with which she seemed unfamiliar. He told her a little about the boatyard. After the waiter had presented them with their bill, she fumbled in her handbag for her purse.

'You must let me pay for this. I owe you for the petrol.'

'Not at all, I won't hear of it.' Devlin put a note and some coins on the plate.

Mrs Gresham looked flustered as she pulled on her gloves. 'I feel indebted to you.'

'Nonsense.'

'This is what I detest about my present position!' The words burst out of her. 'I feel I've nothing to offer.' She sounded upset.

'Listen,' he said gently. 'I often bring people here. They know me, and I know they'll serve us a decent lunch. My usual dining companions are businessmen and government officials. Very dull, most of the time, and their company doesn't give me a fraction of the pleasure yours has.'

'It's good of you to say so.'

'Have you time to come back to Rosindell, for a sherry, perhaps?'

'If you're sure I won't be a nuisance. Thank you, Mr Reddaway.'

'Devlin. Please call me Devlin.'

'I've never heard that name before.'

'It's an old family name. You remember the ugly old goat in the portrait in my sitting room? He was a Devlin.'

'I like those old English names. My mother was a Scot. She called me Bonnie because she thought I was such a pretty baby. Well, that's what my dad always told me. She died when I was little.'

'Mine too,' he said.

'So we've that in common.' Her eyes found his. 'I wondered, when I met you. I thought I saw some sadness in you. I don't think other people quite understand that you never completely get over it, a loss like that.'

He helped her on with her coat and they left the restaurant. On the drive to Rosindell, he told her about the places they passed through. After he had parked the car, she stood for a moment in the courtyard, looking round.

'It's so beautiful,' she said softly. 'Simply heavenly. How lucky you are!'

'My mother planted the trees and shrubs and laid out the parterres fifty years ago. It was my wife who created the terraces. I wish you could have seen them at their best. In the war, of course, many of the ornamental plants had to go.'

'Your wife?' She turned to look at him.

'My ex-wife, I should have said. Esme and I were divorced a long time ago.'

Inside, she begged him to show her round the house. He found himself seeing it through her eyes, the shabbiness that he had become accustomed to and now hardly noticed.

'Such an elegant room!' she said as he opened the door to the drawing room.

'It's a summer room, my daughter always says. She likes to open all the doors and windows.'

'Is this your daughter?' Bonnie picked up a photograph from a side table.

'Yes, that's Zoe.'

'She looks like you.'

'She has my colouring, but she's a great deal prettier. I've a son as well, Matthew. He and Zoe both live in London. Do you have any children, Bonnie?'

'I'm afraid not. Colin and I, we planned . . . after the war, but then . . . It's one of my great sadnesses, that we never had a child. Children bring such joy to people's lives, don't they?'

And sorrow, and regret, he thought, but said, 'Yes, they do.'

'Is this your ex-wife?' She was looking at another photograph.

'It was taken at one of our dances,' he explained. 'In 1928, I think. It was one of our traditions, to give a dance here in the summer. It was always quite an event. When it was fine, the band would play outside on the terrace and couples would dance on the loggia.'

'It sounds so romantic.'

'I suppose it was. I keep the photograph out for my daughter's sake. When you have children, you can't sweep away the past, however much you might like to.'

Bonnie's gaze moved slowly round the room. 'I love this style, so fresh and bright.'

'My architect, Conrad Ellison, always saw his new additions to Rosindell as a link with the Arts and Crafts tradition. With an art deco influence, of course. The earlier parts of the house are very different in style. They're much older, pretty much lost in the mists of time, you might say.'

'I should love to see them.'

'If you're sure it won't bore you.'

She pursed her lips. 'Everything's so dreary now, isn't it? So grey and cold and drab. It cheers me up, coming to a place like this.'

Inside the great hall it was noticeably colder than the newer part of the house. Devlin had given up even attempting to heat

318

it, and the damp and cold of years of neglect had seeped into the fabric. Dust veiled the surfaces and the fireplace gave off the rank, organic smells of wet ash and soot.

Devlin heard Bonnie's intake of breath as she looked up at the beamed ceiling. Her gaze darted to him and then back round the room. 'Oh Devlin,' she said. Then she closed her eyes.

'What are you doing?' he asked her.

She opened her eyes. 'Imagining.'

Watching her, he felt as if he was coming alive again. It was as if he had been living in the twilight for years, convinced that the best part of his life was over. And now a crack seemed to have opened in his heart and the sun was pouring through it, much as it now poured through the high, dusty windows of the great hall.

Zoe and Cleeve Connolly worked in different parts of the city, Zoe in the office of a department store in Oxford Street, Cleeve for a firm of solictors in Blackfriars. They had met eight months earlier, when Zoe had briefly worked at the same offices as Cleeve, as a temporary typist.

The first time she had seen Cleeve, he had been leaning against the doorway of her office, trying to cadge some paper clips. He was tall, his light brown hair curled and his features were regular and beautifully shaped, like those of a Renaissance princeling. He was twenty-nine, much the same age as Zoe, and had sailed on the North Atlantic convoys during the war. The hesitancy that she noticed during their first conversation was completely erased when, a few days later, encountering each other as they left the office at the end of the day, Cleeve began to talk to her about his passion, politics. His socialist principles, which had been instilled in him since childhood by his father, who had worked at the London docks, had been reinforced by the war and its aftermath. The country, Cleeve said to her, must not go back to its bad old ways. They had all shared the deprivations and terror of wartime; they must all share equally in a better future, free from war and economic depression. Over a beer in the pub, they had discussed the aims and achievements of the Attlee government. Later, before they had parted at the bus stop, he had wrapped the halves of his navy duffel coat round her and they had kissed.

A parliamentary seat in north London had become vacant following the death of the incumbent and Cleeve had been put forward as a potential candidate at the by-election. One Friday evening in May, Zoe hurried straight from finishing work at the department store to Ye Olde Cheshire Cheese, a pub in Fleet Street, where she and Cleeve had arranged to meet. Cleeve had hoped to hear back from the parliamentary selection committee earlier that day. Zoe imagined the two of them celebrating his success, going on to dinner, and perhaps later to dance.

In the small, gloomy interior, she caught sight of Cleeve at the bar and waved to him.

'I got it!' he called out to her. 'They want me!'

Threading through the crowds, she kissed him. He gave a huge smile and hugged her, lifting her off her feet. It was one of the things she loved about him, how pleased he always was to see her.

'I couldn't help hoping,' he said. 'I thought the selection committees had gone well, but when Abbott told me, it still took a moment to sink in.'

'That's wonderful. You're wonderful. Congratulations.' Zoe kissed him again.

Then she noticed that he was scooping up in his large, strong hands four glasses of beer.

Four?

He said, 'Come and sit down with the others while I get you a drink.'

Others. Some of her good spirits evaporated. She spied them

sitting in a snug, Cleeve's friends, one of them a man called Slattery, whom she found particularly trying.

'Cleeve,' she said, but he was pushing through the crowd, glasses in hand. She thought of making a fuss, pointing out that this was supposed to be a date, not a get-together for his friends, but then, she told herself, with luck they would move on after one drink. And anyway, it would be unkind to puncture his good mood.

She said hello to Slattery, and to Mack, who was a clerk at the same firm of solicitors as Cleeve. Cleeve introduced Zoe to the third man, Jeff Donaldson, a fellow Labour Party member. Then he went back to the bar to buy her a shandy.

When he returned to the table, Zoe raised her drink. 'To Cleeve's parliamentary career.' Glasses chinked.

'He's not there yet,' said Slattery importantly. Slattery was in his late thirties. He had a round, shiny face and his Brylcreemed brown hair was receding at the temples. He said, 'There's an election to be won first. A lot of work to do.'

'I'll help.'

Cleeve smiled. 'Thanks, Zoe.'

'You must concentrate on the National Health Service, Connolly, when you're on the doorsteps.' This from Slattery, running a hand over his jowly features.

'They must be counting off the days in that part of London,' said Mack.

'Don't bother with numbers and statistics.' Slattery tapped his pipe on the table for emphasis. The sight of the pipe, with its encrusted bowl, always made Zoe feel ill. 'Remind them how their nan couldn't get her thyroid treated or how their mum went without food to pay the doctor.'

'Mine did, often enough,' said Donaldson.

Slattery proceeded to monopolise Cleeve, talking about the finance for the campaign, the opposition and tactics. Jeff Donaldson offered to buy another round of drinks.

321

When he came back to the table, Donaldson said to Zoe, 'Cleeve'll do a great job. He'll put his back into it.'

He had a soft Northumberland accent. Zoe found herself wondering as he struck up a conversation with her whether he felt sorry for her. Or was it possible that he did not realise that she was Cleeve's girlfriend and was chatting her up?

Taking Cleeve's hand and interrupting Slattery in mid drone, Zoe said, 'We should head off if we want to find somewhere to eat.'

'Ten minutes,' promised Cleeve.

Slattery was leafing through a diary and noting down with a chewed stub of pencil the evenings and weekends Cleeve must be available for visiting his prospective constituency. Ten minutes passed, and they were still roughing out on a scrap of paper his first speech. Twenty minutes, half an hour; the table was littered with glasses and crumpled crisp packets, and the white worms of cigarette stubs were writhing in the ashtray.

Zoe glanced at her watch. Rising, she said to Cleeve, 'I'd better go.'

He blinked at her. 'I thought we were having supper.'

'It's getting late. I have to be up early tomorrow to catch the train. I told you I was going home for the weekend.'

Cleeve smacked his forehead. 'I'm an idiot. I forgot.'

'It doesn't matter. You've had other things to think about.'

They walked to the door of the pub. He said, 'Are you sure you don't want to get some fish and chips or something?'

'No thanks, I'd better get home, I need to pack. I'll be back in London on Tuesday. When will I see you?'

'Tuesday evening? No, I think I've a meeting. I'd better check with Slattery.'

Zoe hated that her social life was dependent on Slattery. She said, 'I don't think I'm going to see much of you until the election's over, am I?'

Cleeve frowned. 'You are happy for me, aren't you?'

'Of course I am,' she murmured.

They kissed, and she almost changed her mind, but then the thought came to her of Slattery inviting himself along for fish and chips and Cleeve being too kind to say no to him, and she headed for the bus stop.

For the past year, Zoe had been living in a room at the Earls Court end of the Cromwell Road. She found a window seat on the top deck of the bus, and as the vehicle heaved along streets still pitted and scarred by the Blitz, she admired the blossom on the ornamental cherries, a clean, pale pink against the soot-stained buildings. Winter's grip had relaxed at last and wild flowers were springing up on the bomb sites, around the jagged ruins of church, house and office block.

Zoe admired Cleeve's idealism and energy, and loved him for wanting to change the world. Cleeve believed the world was willing to be changed. When she was with him, Zoe believed it too.

When she had first gone to bed with him in the attic room Cleeve rented near King's Cross, she had been blissfully happy. She had existed on the memory of that evening's perfect happiness for a long time, but recently doubts had begun to creep in. The trouble was, everyone loved Cleeve. He was as generous in his friendships as he was in his desire to make a difference to the lives of the poor and the needy. Increasingly she found that she disliked having to share him; increasingly she disliked herself for her resentment of the time and energy that other people sapped from him. She disliked that his absences, both physical and mental, seemed to force her into the unappealing position of choosing between being demanding or a doormat. Tonight, when she looked back, the recollection of the whine in her voice as she had said, *I don't think I'm going to see much of you until the election's over, am I?* made her cringe.

There were a dozen other tenants in the boarding house in which she lived. The house, like its neighbours, looked dilapidated. Zoe liked to imagine filling in the cracks and shrapnel holes in the brickwork, giving the peeling black paint on the front door a coat of glossy blue and scrubbing the brown and cream lobby tiles until they shone.

Collecting her mail, she went upstairs. On the first-floor landing, she almost collided with a man who was manoeuvring himself through the doorway of one of the other rooms, his arms full of cardboard boxes. He was tall and rangy, his untidy hair somewhere between blond and brown, and when he turned and smiled at her, she saw that his eyes were a washed-out blue.

'Hello,' he said. 'I'm Ben Thackeray.'

'Zoe Reddaway.'

'Pleased to meet you, Zoe. Are you one of my neighbours?'

Australian, she thought, from his accent. She hoped he wouldn't have a crowd of noisy friends who would disrupt the peace of the house.

'I've a room on the second floor,' she said.

He dropped the boxes on a sofa in the room. One of them – which, oddly, she saw, contained stones – slipped off and landed on his foot. He took an indrawn breath and hopped around for a while.

Zoe said, 'Are you all right?'

'Never better.' He had an open, friendly smile. 'Could you let me have a cup of milk? I forgot to buy any and the shops are shut.'

'Of course.'

He began to burrow in a box. 'There's a cup in here somewhere, I know there is.'

'It's okay, I'll lend you one of mine.'

In her room, Zoe poured some milk in a cup, then took it downstairs. Ben Thackeray's room was smaller than her own and dizzyingly full of his belongings.

'Thanks,' he said. 'You'll have a coffee, won't you?'

324

'No thanks, I have to get on. Just drop the cup back when you've finished with it.'

Climbing the stairs, Zoe added the fault of unfriendliness to those of resentment and jealousy, and, with a feeling of relief, shut the door to her own room behind her.

The following morning, she caught the eight o'clock train from Paddington. A few hours later, as the train headed alongside the Dart to Kingswear, she thought, as she always did, *Over there, only a few miles away, is Rosindell.* Her spirits rose. She tried to go home once a month. Though she needed the anonymity and busyness of London, she also needed Rosindell. It seemed to her that she was only truly herself when she was there.

Her father was waiting for her outside Kingswear station. On the drive, looking out of the Bentley's window and pleasurably taking in all the old, familiar landmarks, Zoe talked about her job, to stave off the moment when her father might ask her about Cleeve. She had introduced them one evening a couple of months ago, when her father had been in London on business. The meeting had not been a success. Cleeve had been perfectly charming, but her father had been imperious and fault-finding. It had been one of the few times in her life when she had felt annoyed with him. It was easier, she felt now, to avoid the subject.

The sky, decorated with small, scudding white clouds, was the perfect blue of hyacinths. Everything was just as it always had been, and she felt a rush of delight as her gaze ran over the sage-green rise and fall of the hills. The hedgerows that they raced past were bursting into leaf. Primroses and violets clustered on the verges.

Scabbacombe Lane, and then the turn-off to Lethwiston, with its clutter of small cottages, pub and shippon. And there were Rosindell's gates, and there were the heavy green heads of the trees by the drive, rustling their greeting.

Her father parked the car in the courtyard and took her overnight bag out of the boot. They went indoors.

In the lobby, Zoe said, 'Dad, where's the bench?'

A small wooden bench had stood beneath one of the windows in the hexagonal lobby for as long as Zoe could remember. When she and Matt had been little, they had liked to stand on it, watching for their father's car coming down the drive on his way home from work in the evenings.

Her father said, 'Mrs Gresham thought it looked shabby.'

'Who's Mrs Gresham? Has Mrs Forbes left?'

A voice said, 'Devlin, is that you?' and a woman appeared in the corridor ahead.

Her father said, 'Zoe, let me introduce you to Mrs Gresham. Bonnie, this is my daughter, Zoe.'

Zoe offered her hand. Bonnie Gresham's dark brown hair was swept up into curls on the back of her head. Her slanted green eyes were framed by high arched brows. Her mouth was a narrow curve, like a crescent moon, and her nose was short and tilted. For a daily woman, she was quite smartly dressed. What a nerve, though, to make her father change the furniture round.

Then her father put his arm around Mrs Gresham's shoulders, drawing her to him. 'I'm so pleased you two have had the chance to meet.'

'It's a pleasure,' Mrs Gresham murmured. 'But I'm afraid I'm going to have to dash.'

'I thought you were going to stay for tea?'

'Darling, you two will have so much to talk about. I wouldn't want to be in the way.'

'You wouldn't be.'

'Sweet of you to say so. I've been longing to meet you, Zoe. Devlin's told me so much about you.'

Her father said, 'Let me run you back to Brixham, Bonnie.'

Bonnie, thought Zoe. Her father had a friendship − or something − with a woman called *Bonnie*.

'I wouldn't dream of it,' said Bonnie. 'I have my bicycle.'

'She's a brave little thing,' said Devlin as he watched Mrs Gresham head up the drive, 'cycling all that way on her own. I wanted her to come with me to meet you at the ferry, but she wouldn't; she thought she'd be in the way. But you wouldn't have minded, would you, Zoe?'

Devlin took Bonnie Gresham to Totnes, to see a play, an amateur production of *The Barretts of Wimpole Street*, in which Thea Hendricks had a small role. Afterwards, the four of them had supper together in a restaurant in the high street. Traces of stage make-up lingered on Thea's face, making her eyebrows a sooty black and her mouth scarlet. The food was indifferent, the decor drab, but at least the modest restoration of the petrol ration had permitted this small outing.

On the drive home, a full moon flickered in and out of the clouds, helping to light their way. Devlin was aware of Bonnie in the passenger seat beside him, of the pillowy curve of her cheek and the soft, pale dewy flush of her skin. She was wearing her hair down that night and it tumbled to her shoulders in rich curls. Everything about her had a sort of sheen, he thought, a patina. Since he had found her stranded at the roadside, he had not felt lonely.

After he had walked away from the Paddington hotel where he and Esme had made love, Devlin had done his damnedest to put her out of his mind. The despoiled Rosindell that the soldiers had left behind had occupied what spare time he had had. Sometimes it had seemed that the years he and Esme had lived there had been nothing more than a dream, one of light and colour and music, long since dissolved by the grey dawn.

But then, unexpectedly, miraculously, Bonnie.

He heard her say, 'What are you thinking?'

'Of how used and worn you must think me. How imperfect.'

327

'No one's perfect.'

The headlamps traced out the road ahead. 'You are,' he said.

'You're very kind, Devlin.'

'I'm very old. Too old for you.'

She laughed. 'Such nonsense.'

'I'm fifty-two,' he said bluntly. 'I'm divorced and I have two grown-up children.'

'I thought Zoe was delightful.'

'She is. I'm very proud of her.' He saw a field entrance ahead and drew into it, flicking on the light inside the car. Bonnie gave a little frown.

'It's all right,' he said. 'I'm not going to pounce on you. But we need to have this conversation and I might lose courage if I don't broach it now. Bonnie, I seem to be becoming rather fond of you. And for both our sakes, I think it would be better to put a stop to it now if you have any reservations.'

Her eyelids lowered. 'Reservations?'

'Because of my age, for instance.'

'I've always preferred older men. They're more civil and they know more about the world. Young men can be so clumsy and awkward and pushy. They don't always give a girl time.'

'I'll give you all the time you want. But . . .'

'But?'

'As I said, I'm falling in rather deep.' He gave a short laugh. 'It's quite a shock to the system.'

She put her hand over his. 'And you're afraid of getting hurt.'

'Something like that.' He let out a breath. Her gloved hand rested on his. 'What I'm trying to say is that if you're not interested in me in that way, then we should call it a day. No hard feelings, of course.'

She did not reply. Instead, twisting in the seat, she touched her lips against his. Her hands threaded round the back of his neck and then he scooped her into his lap. They kissed like teenagers, with no great finesse, just kissing, nothing more, he delighting in the taste and smell of her, the taste and smell of youth, which seemed to restore him to vigour and energy and optimism. Perhaps he was not so old. The age difference must be less than twenty years – and as she had said, what did that matter?

The chill of the June night seeped into the car; she wriggled back into the passenger seat and Devlin started up the engine.

He said, 'I should like you to meet my son, Matthew.'

'I'd love to. But I wouldn't want your children to think that I'm – well, trying to take over.'

'I'm sure they won't think that.'

'Children find these things difficult. Your daughter, particularly. A girl can feel quite put out if her father shows interest in another woman.'

'They're hardly children.' The road narrowed, the high hedgerow walling off the moon as the car took a tight corner. 'My relationship with Matthew has been very difficult for many years. He took the divorce hard.'

'You mustn't blame yourself.'

The lights of Brixham lay beneath them. 'It was my fault entirely,' he said. 'I was unfaithful to my wife.'

'You don't have to tell me, Devlin.'

'You need to know the truth. By way of mitigation, I'd want you to know that it was once, and that I was very young.'

And then he told her, quickly and dispassionately, about Camilla, and about Matthew and Melissa and Camilla's eventual devastating revelation that Melissa was his daughter.

Bonnie said, 'She sounds a bitch.'

'Yes, I suppose she was.' He remembered Camilla in black, the last time they had met, at the Savoy. She had taken pleasure, he thought, in her destruction of him.

'She was manipulative and cruel,' he said. 'But nevertheless, I did what I did.'

'You have a soft heart, Devlin. That's nothing to be ashamed of.' Bonnie glanced out of the window. 'Just drop me here, would you?'

'I don't like to think of you walking these streets on your own. Let me take you to your lodgings.'

'Darling, you must see that would put me in an impossible position. As a widow, I have to be so careful. People gossip. At my last lodgings, I had a gentleman friend. We used to play cards once a week. One day I overheard one of the other lodgers call me "the merry widow". It was so hurtful.'

'Forgive me, I hadn't thought.' The car drew to a halt by the kerb. 'I won't nag you any more, then.'

He opened the passenger door and Bonnie climbed out and they kissed again, a short, chaste touching of lips. Then he stood at the corner of the street and watched her until she was swallowed up by the darkness.

Matthew had been working at a garage in Hammersmith for the last six months. He turned his hand to whatever was necessary, helping the mechanics when they were busy or closing the sale of a second-hand car. He liked the job but suspected he wouldn't have it much longer, partly because trade was poor, and partly because he had drunk too much one lunchtime and had got into a stupid argument that he now regretted with the owner of the garage, Patrick O'Connor. O'Connor was a decent chap – Matthew knew him from the RAF – but it wasn't the first time he had picked a quarrel. He never meant to let rip, but sometimes, after a drink, anger boiled up inside him.

His lodgings were in Hammersmith too, in a dismal boarding house. There was a concrete yard behind the house where he kept his car, a pre-war Morris. The Morris was a hefty creature and Matthew had previously only been able to drive it after purchasing some black-market petrol from a chap at the pub. But he was fond of it and spent the evenings and weekends tinkering with the engine. O'Connor let him borrow tools from the garage and had sold him spares at cost price. Matthew had kept away from the pub since the argument with O'Connor, and so the Morris had for some time lain idle.

When he got home from the garage one evening, the landlord handed him a postcard from Zoe. It said, simply, *Matt, you must phone me.* Matthew stuffed it in his pocket and forgot about it. A few days later, another postcard arrived. *If you don't phone me, I shall come round.* Zoe's coming round would entail criticism of the way he lived, exhortations to tidy his room, write to his mother and generally sort himself out, so Matthew trudged off to the telephone box and dialled his sister's lodgings.

Zoe answered. After greeting him, she said, 'Dad's met this woman.'

The receiver clamped between his shoulder and jaw, Matthew nudged a cigarette out of a packet. 'So?'

'She's called Bonnie Gresham. She's about half his age.'

He stuck the cigarette between his lips and lit it. 'Zoe, I don't care, I'm not interested.'

'She made him move the bench we used to stand on.'

'Bench?'

'You know, in the lobby.'

'I don't remember.'

'You must. We used to watch out for Dad's car, coming down the drive.'

He really didn't remember. Zoe claimed to recall all sorts of things about their childhood that he had completely forgotten. He sometimes wondered whether she made them up. Or whether he had brushed the memories away, like a duster sweeping a blackboard clean.

'Okay,' he said. 'He's met a woman, she's made some changes.'

'She made him get rid of the dining room rug. The one Mum chose. She said it was old-fashioned.'

Matthew couldn't have cared less, not the tiniest fraction of an iota less, but he knew Zoe, knew how once she got her teeth into something, she wouldn't let it go, and so he scratched round for something soothing to say.

'I suppose if it makes him happy . . .'

Zoe shrieked. So plainly, then, not the right thing.

'You wouldn't say that if you saw her!'

'What's she like?'

'Pretty,' Zoe conceded. 'Small and dark and pretty.'

Matthew's patience was running out. 'Look,' he said, 'so Dad's seeing this woman. So what?'

'They're coming to London in a couple of weeks' time. Dad wants you to meet her.'

Matthew saw where the conversation was heading. 'No.'

'Matt, you have to.'

'I don't, you know.'

'You owe me.'

This was quite literally true. Zoe had lent him money when he had been short and he had not yet paid her back. Matthew felt the mixture of boredom, resentment and fury that was his common reaction to anything to do with his family.

'You have to help me,' Zoe added.

'Help you to do what?'

'Get rid of her, of course.'

Her father had booked a table at a French restaurant in Soho. Zoe had arranged to meet Matthew at Tottenham Court Road Underground station. It was drizzling and Matthew was late, so she sheltered in the station entrance, peering out into the street. After twenty minutes, she caught sight of him, threading through the traffic. Zoe tried to hurry him along Charing Cross Road.

In the restaurant, she found her father and Mrs Gresham waiting for them, her father looking impatient over the starched napery. His hair was cut differently, parted to one side, and he was wearing a tie Zoe hadn't seen before, of a bright colour.

To defuse things, Zoe murmured something about her bus being late.

'No it wasn't,' said Matthew. 'You don't have to fib, Zoe. I'd forgotten the time, that's all.' He announced this, hands in pockets, a superior smirk on his face, as if he found the whole thing — restaurants, punctuality, good manners — beneath him.

Zoe reddened with embarrassment. Her father said, 'Never mind about that, you're here now. Bonnie, I'd like you to meet my son, Matthew. Matthew, this is my friend Mrs Gresham.'

'Pleased to meet you,' said Matthew, shaking Mrs Gresham's hand. Then, 'Nice frock,' he said.

It was then that it dawned on Zoe that Matthew was drunk. Of *course* he was drunk. Of *course* Matthew would have taken the very step guaranteed to make an already potentially sticky evening worse.

Zoe said quickly, 'It *is* a lovely frock, Mrs Gresham.'

'Bonnie. You must call me Bonnie. I want us to be friends.'

Zoe wanted to be sick, but went on fawningly, 'That colour suits you. I'm never sure whether I can wear green.'

'It is a difficult colour,' Bonnie conceded.

'Did you buy it in London?'

'No, no, at a little dressmaker's in Bristol. I rarely come to London.'

The waiter arrived to take their orders. Matthew picked up his glass as soon as the waiter had filled it. The best tactic, Zoe decided, was to try to keep him out of the conversation. You could sometimes do that with Matthew, talk about something else and he seemed to switch off, hardly noticing what was going on around him.

She told her father and Mrs Gresham about the by-election, Cleeve's chances, and the speech he had made at Conway Hall the previous weekend. By the time the first course arrived, the three of them had settled down to a mild disagreement about the government's economic policy.

Then Bonnie said, 'Your father tells me you work in a garage, Matthew.'

Matthew looked up. '*Used* to work in a garage.'

'Matthew?' said Devlin sharply.

'I got the sack this afternoon.'

'Why? What happened?'

Matthew shrugged. 'This and that. I was getting bored with it anyway.'

'You have to settle to something. This won't do. You're not a child, Matthew. You have to make your own way in the world.'

Derision flowed into Matthew's eyes. 'Spare me the lecture, Dad,' he drawled. 'After all, you're hardly a shining example, are you?'

'Matthew,' said his father, but Bonnie put her hand on his arm, saying gently:

'It's all right, darling. I think Matthew has had a little too much to drink, perhaps.'

'Too right.' Matthew sniffed. 'Sorry.'

He applied himself to his toast and paté with great gusto, as if he was starving. And it occurred to Zoe — a miserable, miserable thought — that Matthew might indeed be hungry; that so often these days he had a thin, grubby look, as if he didn't look after himself properly. She wondered whether rent, car, drink and cigarettes swallowed up his wages and allowance. She wondered whether he neglected to buy food. She must have him round to supper more often, however annoying he was.

The meal ground on, the conversation never really getting going. As soon as he had finished his pudding, Matthew lurched to his feet, toppling over a glass and dragging at the tablecloth.

'Have to go. Bye, Dad. Bye, Bonnie. Be good.'

'Matthew,' snapped Devlin.

'Darling, just leave him to it.' Bonnie's eyes flickered from Matthew to Devlin. 'I don't think one should indulge childish behaviour, do you?'

As Matthew stumbled out of the restaurant, Zoe caught sight of the satisfied, calculating smile that sprang to Bonnie's face. She could almost have imagined it, it came and went so quickly. Almost.

At the end of the evening, the taxi dropped Zoe off in Earls Court, and then her father and Bonnie drove away to their hotel. In the lobby, she dialled Cleeve's number. The phone rang out for a couple of minutes before she put the receiver down.

The front door opened and Ben Thackeray came in, the shoulders of his mackintosh darkened by the rain.

'I've just had a memorably awful evening scouring Peckham to find a friend's cat,' he said.

'Did you find it?'

'Eventually, in a coal hole. And then the ungrateful beast scratched me.' He held up a hand with a deep diagonal scratch across the palm.

'You should put some antiseptic on that.'

'No need, it's fine. Would you like a coffee?'

'No thanks.'

He fixed her with his light eyes. 'I've some real, proper coffee. *Ground* coffee. French.'

Zoe's mind was in its jangling, uneasy state, which invariably meant that it would take her hours to get to sleep. Perhaps being kept awake by a cup of real coffee would be preferable to a night of tossing and turning, thinking about that awful dinner.

'Okay,' she said. 'A quick one. Thanks.'

In his room, Ben wrapped a none-too-clean handkerchief around his grazed hand, and then measured coffee into a jug.

'Sit down,' he said.

Sit down *where*? There were two chairs beside the small gate-leg table where he was making the coffee. One had a pile of books on it and the other a pair of shoes. On the sofa were more books, a heap of unironed shirts, and copies of journals and newspapers.

'Just dump them on the floor,' said Ben.

There was no space on the floor either. Zoe began to fold the shirts. Ben looked around vaguely. 'Cups, cups . . .'

'Here.' Zoe handed him a mug from beneath the sofa. A dark circle had solidified in the bottom of it.

'I'll give it a wash,' he said.

She put the folded shirts on top of a chest of drawers. By the time Ben came back from the kitchen, the kettle was boiling. He poured the water into the coffee jug and gave a sigh of pleasure.

'Takes me back to Paris.'

'You know Paris?'

'I lived there before the war.'

'Me too. What were you doing there?'

'Taking part in an archaeological dig in Clichy. And working in a bar in the evenings, to pay my way.'

Zoe remembered the cardboard box full of stones. 'You're an archaeologist?'

'Trying to be one. I studied history at university and I did a year of my PhD before the war. Now I'm writing up my wretched thesis, if I don't shoot myself first. And then I shall go off somewhere and unearth something amazing. What about you?'

'I work in a department store.'

He grinned. 'I imagine you selling dresses, looking glacial.'

She said stiffly, 'I work in the office, actually.'

'Do you always do that?'

'Do what?'

'Tidy up people's rooms.'

He was staring at the newspaper she was smoothing into shape. Zoe gave it a final twitch and put it on top of its fellows.

'Only *messy* people's rooms,' she said pointedly.

336

'Milk and sugar?'

'Just milk, please. My boyfriend won't let me tidy his room. He says he can't find anything.'

Ben was looking distractedly round the room. 'I was sure I had some biscuits. Perhaps you're attracted to untidy people.'

'No, I don't think so,' she said indignantly.

'Perhaps you like sorting their lives out.'

She made a scathing noise. 'If I do, then I'm wasting my time.'

He plonked the heap of newspapers on the floor and sat down beside her. 'What's up?'

She shrugged. 'You're not the only one who's had a memorably awful evening.'

'Not looking for a cat, I take it?'

'No. Dinner with my family.'

He took an exaggerated inward breath. 'Ah.'

'They are beyond tidying up.' Ben had given her the mug she had found beneath the sofa. Zoe had to steel herself to drink out of it.

'Your family can't possibly be any worse than mine,' he said. 'I travelled ten thousand miles to get away from them. Beat that.'

'You're Australian?'

'Through and through. Irish roots. We like to nose in everyone else's business. You?'

Zoe told him about Devon, and Rosindell.

'If you love it so much,' he said, 'why do you live in London?'

'It's an adventure. I needed to do something new.' Though she was not sure whether that was still true. Or indeed, whether it ever had been true. She had left Rosindell, she sometimes thought, to get away from the messiness and disorder of family life.

'Some day I'll go back,' she said. 'What about you?'

His coffee cup was balanced precariously on the arm of the sofa. He hooked up a long, corduroy-clad leg, narrowly avoiding it.

337

'I miss home sometimes. I miss the sun. No wonder you lot are all so miserable. But it would mean having to put up with my brothers again.'

'How many do you have?'

'Four. I'm the youngest of five. Imagine.'

'No sisters?'

'Not one. You?'

'Just a brother. Matthew's younger than me.'

'Do you get on?'

'Oh, we get on, we always have. But Matthew seems to have become one of those people who enjoys getting people's backs up.'

Zoe suspected the mug hadn't been washed properly and that a mark to one side, like a dark teardrop, had been there when she had unearthed it from the sofa. She turned it round so that she could drink from the other side.

'My parents are divorced,' she explained. 'My father brought his new girlfriend along tonight. She's utterly frightful.'

'What's so frightful about her?'

On the surface, Bonnie was pleasant and polite. But Zoe saw through her, even if her father did not. Tonight she had noted the carefully enunciated vowels and the way Bonnie watched and copied Reddaway manners. The woman was vigilant. Yes, that was it. She watched and listened, trying to make a certain impression.

'She's pretending,' she said. 'Pretending to like him.'

'Why would she do that?'

'My father's rather well off. To someone like her, he'd be a catch.'

'"Someone like her"?'

'Someone common.'

He whistled. 'You English.'

'I'm not a snob.'

'You can find yourself frozen out, you know. All those little

338

ways the English middle class have of letting you know you're not one of them.'

'I don't think she really cares about my father. If she was nice, if I thought she'd make him happy, I wouldn't mind. He's been unhappy for such a long time.' She glared at him. 'I know what you're thinking. You're thinking I'm jealous.'

'Are you?'

'Maybe.' Zoe took another careful mouthful of coffee.

'Maybe you should have an open mind. Give her a chance.'

Every instinct rebelled – and yet, she asked herself uncomfortably, was she being fair? After all, she had seen Bonnie on only two occasions, the first for no more than ten minutes, the second tonight's dinner – which must have been as much of an ordeal for Bonnie as for the rest of them.

'Okay,' she said, with a sigh. 'I'll try.'

Esme was in the kitchen of the Oxford house, making a pie for her lodgers' supper using gooseberries she had bottled the year before. Her friend Kate was talking about her lover, Nathan.

'And now our weekend's gone! She says they have to go and see Petra next weekend, even though it was always going to be the weekend after because of Nathan's concert.'

'She' was Nathan's wife Carlotta, a demanding woman, and Petra was his daughter, who was at boarding school. Kate, a small, plump, vivid woman in her late forties, was a teacher at a girls' private school in north Oxford. She and Nathan, a violinist, had been having an affair for six years.

Esme knew her role in the conversation. She tutted sympathetically. 'What a shame. Couldn't you and Nathan go away the weekend after?'

'I promised I'd go and see Dad.' Kate's elderly father was in a nursing home. 'I'm sure she does it on purpose. Would you like me to make some little tarts out of this?' She was balling up the offcuts of pastry.

'Please.'

The phone rang. As Esme went to answer it, Kate called out, 'What shall I put in them?'

'Anything you can find that's remotely edible. Not the jam, it's for the sponge tomorrow.'

Esme picked up the receiver and said her name. It was her mother. She steeled herself and sat down on the stairs.

'Hello, Mummy.'

Five minutes later, Kate looked up as Esme came back into the kitchen. 'Problems?'

'My father's ulcer again. They've taken him to hospital. Poor old Dad. I said I'd go to Dartmouth tomorrow. Poor Mummy, she finds it hard to cope.' Esme caught sight of the half-dozen golden syrup tarts and the completed gooseberry pie. 'Kate, you're an angel.'

'Is there anything else I can do?'

'No, you've been wonderful. I could do with another cup of tea, couldn't you?'

The first of the lodgers returned to the house shortly after Kate left. There were three in all, old faithfuls, old friends almost: two women, one a nurse and the other a secretary, and a gentleman, Ronnie, who was a travelling salesman in the garment trade. Ronnie, who claimed to have gypsy blood, sometimes after supper swirled the leaves around their teacups and told their fortunes.

Esme dried the last saucepan and put it away. There was a great deal to do – menus must be organised for the days of her absence, she must phone her daily woman and ask her to drop in over the weekend to clean and do the washing-up, and she must contact Zoe and Matthew. But all that could wait ten minutes. She poured herself a small glass of sherry, lit a cigarette and went outside.

It was just about warm enough to sit in the most sheltered part of the garden. Though much of the back garden was still given over to vegetables and soft fruit, Esme had begun this spring to plant flowers again. She felt this to be an expression of confidence in the future. The newpapers might be giving awful warnings about Soviet might and ambition and fingers hovering over nuclear buttons, but Esme preferred to hope that they were heading to a time when a garden could once more be planted with roses and lavender. Just as she longed for the day when food rationing ended and she would no longer have to create dishes from scraps and scrapings.

As her father's health had worsened over the past year, Esme's relationship with her parents had altered. It was painful to see her once strong father becoming frail. Unexpectedly, she had become her mother's confidante and support, a position that still felt strange to her. She had become the favourite daughter by default, she thought. Her parents heard only rarely from Camilla, whose marriage to the American film actor had, surprising no one, fallen apart.

Invalided out of the navy in 1943 after a lengthy bout of bronchitis, Tom had returned to Dartmouth, and Alice. In September 1939, Alice had taken in three brothers who'd been evacuated from the East End. After the children's parents were killed by a V-1 rocket, the boys had remained in Dartmouth with Tom and Alice, who had formally adopted them shortly after the war had ended. Tom and Alice's lives were now happily taken up by parents' evenings, rugby matches and fishing trips.

Esme stubbed out her cigarette. She had another role in the family. She knew that Tom had had love affairs and that Alice had almost left him because of it. She knew, of course, that Devlin was Melissa de Grey's father. She also knew through her mother, who occasionally received letters from Melissa, that Melissa was now living in Paris. Before that, she had worked for UNRRA in Germany, in a camp for displaced people.

No one else in the family knew all these things. She had become the keeper of secrets. She hadn't chosen this role either; again, it had attached itself to her.

Chapter Sixteen

June 1948

Devlin was parked outside the Royal Dart Hotel. Bonnie was sitting in the passenger seat beside him. The ferry was coming in, sliding across the green water.

'There she is,' he said.

Zoe and Esme were staying at St Petrox Lodge. Zoe was coming to dinner at Rosindell, and then afterwards Devlin would take her back to Kingswear.

Devlin got out of the car and waited for the ferry to dock and Zoe to disembark. After he had hugged her, he said, 'How was Charles?'

'Awfully yellow. He hates being in hospital, Dad.'

'He was never one for sitting still.'

'Granny fusses and he gets cross with her.'

They walked together to the car. 'How's your mother?' asked Devlin.

'She's worried about Grandfather. And she hates hospitals too.'

'She always did. I remember when you were born, she couldn't wait to get out.'

He opened the door for her and she climbed into the back of the Bentley. They headed out of Kingswear and up into the peninsula. It was late June, and the hedgerows frothed with wild flowers. Zoe wound down the window and stuck her head out. Honey-scented air washed into the car.

Bonnie put her hand to her head. 'My hat . . .'

'Zoe,' said her father, and Zoe put the window back up.

Devlin said, 'The best time of year, I think.'

'So glorious,' said Bonnie. 'Look at those pretty pink daisies.'

'They're red campions,' said Zoe.

Devlin drove through Lethwiston, towards the gates.

'Those trees look rather overgrown,' said Bonnie.

He changed down a gear as they turned into the drive. 'I've often wondered whether one day I'll come home and find that the wilderness has taken over.'

'It's a question of keeping on top of things,' said Bonnie.

'Of course, my dear, you're right.' He smiled at her.

They ate supper in the dining room. Mrs Forbes had prepared the meal earlier in the day and Bonnie had volunteered to heat it up and serve it. She was wearing a striped apron over her flowery summer frock.

Devlin opened a Fleurie to go with the lamb navarin. Bonnie was talking about her shopping expedition that afternoon. She had taken it on herself to go round the shops to find material to make new curtains for the drawing room. It touched him that she took such an interest in the house. He had been afraid that she might find it off-puttingly old and shabby, but her pleasure in it, which he had noticed that first time he had shown her round Rosindell, had not diminished. It was, he thought, rather miraculous that he had stumbled by chance upon a woman who appeared to feel about Rosindell as he did.

'I found a nice stripe in that little draper's near the harbour,' said Bonnie. 'Do help yourself to more potatoes, Zoe, they mustn't go to waste. Yellow stripes with dear little pink flowers. It would brighten up the room.'

'It's a bright room anyway,' said Zoe. 'Conrad designed it to be bright.'

'I like a little colour.'

Devlin's gaze moved from one woman to the other. Both were beautiful, he thought, though in different ways. Zoe was cool and elegant, and though her hair and eyes were even darker than Bonnie's, her complexion was paler. Bonnie's golden skin was flushed tawny from the heat of the kitchen. She had put her hair up for the evening. Devlin longed to take out the pins one by one, to see the curls spring and tumble against her slender neck.

Zoe said, 'Do you have a garden, Mrs Gresham?'

'Bonnie.' She turned to Zoe and smiled. 'Do you remember, when we met in London, I asked you to call me Bonnie?'

'Sorry. Bonnie.'

'The boarding house has only a rather drab little garden, I'm afraid. And one doesn't always like to sit in it; sometimes the other lodgers try to strike up a conversation. They seem to assume an intimacy, which is rather unpleasant.'

'You know you can always come here, Bonnie,' said Devlin. 'Whenever you need some peace and quiet. You must treat Rosindell as your own.'

'Thank you, darling. I do adore gardens. I was brought up in the countryside. If you've lived in the countryside as a child, it's always in your heart.'

Zoe said, 'Where? Where were you brought up?'

'Shropshire.'

'Shrewsbury? I know Shrewsbury quite well. I worked there for several months during the war.'

'No, not Shrewsbury.'

'Ludlow, perhaps.'

'No. It was a tiny little village in the middle of nowhere. You wouldn't have heard of it.'

'I might. Rupert and I used to have to travel round a lot. What was it called?'

'Dear me, what a grilling!' They had finished their first course. Bonnie stood up and began to collect plates.

'I just wondered—'

'That's enough, Zoe,' said Devlin. 'We've all had a long day.'

'Yes, Dad.'

While Bonnie took the dirty plates out to the kitchen, Devlin asked Zoe about her job. If Zoe took after him in her need for independence and autonomy, a need that sometimes bordered on aloofness, he thought that she also shared traits with her grandfather. She had Charles's tenacity and drive; she just needed to find some cause to apply them to. He hoped that she wouldn't throw herself away on Cleeve Connolly. Devlin had met him once and had known that Connolly would not do for her. A pleasant enough fellow, but he had too many other passions. Zoe's powerful imagination, her great loyalty, even the anxieties that haunted her, required, Devlin felt, a far more devoted man than Cleeve Connolly. Devotion tempered by humour. Zoe needed – deserved – someone who would put her first.

Bonnie brought in the pudding, apple pie and custard. Zoe asked after the Fawcetts, at the tenant farm. He was thinking of buying a puppy from Grace, Devlin told her. Grace's Tessie had just had four puppies, dark chocolate brown every one of them.

Someone had taken the umbrella stand out of the lobby, the stand that Zoe and Matthew used to call the goblin vase because of the faces carved on it. That same someone had put away the Burleigh Ware dragon jugs and the lovely old Belleek pottery that Zoe's Reddaway grandmother had collected, and had taken down the crackled silver Venetian mirror from the hall. Tasteless knick-knacks had been scattered round in their place. These things had survived the war, hidden in the cellars, but they had not survived Bonnie.

And where was the photograph that had always stood on a side table in the drawing room, the photograph taken at the summer dance, of her mother wearing an embroidered evening gown with a huge bow at the hip, a gown that Zoe still remembered, though it must be twenty years since she had seen it?

Her father was talking about Grace Fawcett's spaniels. Zoe ate her apple pie. The sight of Bonnie Gresham sitting in the passenger seat of the Bentley when she had disembarked from the ferry at Kingwear had jolted her. And then the banality of the conversation, Bonnie muddling up campions and daisies – this from a woman who claimed to have been brought up in the countryside!

After they had finished their pudding, Devlin offered to help Bonnie clear up and make coffee.

'No, you go and sit down, darling.' Bonnie was busily and proprietorially stacking bowls. 'Zoe will help me, won't you, Zoe?'

'Yes, Bonnie.'

Calling her Bonnie, rather than Mrs Gresham, was an effort, a bit like coughing up a boiled sweet that had lodged in your throat. As she collected up the wine glasses, Zoe permitted herself to think of Cleeve, in London. A few days ago, she had delivered election leaflets with him. They had walked down long rows of terraced houses and she had stood at his side as he had knocked on doors and earnestly tried to persuade his prospective constituents of the benefits of voting Labour in the by-election. Zoe wondered whether Cleeve would miss her today. Or whether Slattery, tapping the matted tobacco from his pipe, might not do just as well.

She took the glasses into the kitchen. Bonnie was at the sink. The kitchen was a mess, dirty dishes everywhere. Bonnie obviously wasn't a person who tidied up as she went along.

'I'll wash up, if you like,' said Zoe.

Bonnie turned round and smoothed her hands down her apron. 'I think you and I need to have a little chat, Zoe.'

Startled, Zoe said, 'What do you mean?'

'You know perfectly well what I mean. Don't try to make trouble. If you attempt to come between us, you'll regret it.'

'I don't want—'

'All those silly questions at dinner time. Don't try to make me look a fool. You see, I mean to have Rosindell. And if you get in my way, then I'll destroy you and your family.'

A short silence, during which Zoe tried, and failed, to absorb the shock of Bonnie's words.

Bonnie smiled. 'And don't think of running to Daddy telling tales. If you do, I'll say that you're making it up.'

Zoe found her voice at last. 'He wouldn't believe you.'

'Wouldn't he? Are you quite sure about that? Now why don't you make the coffee?'

Bonnie turned back to the sink. Zoe spooned coffee into a jug. Her hands trembled, the teaspoon making little tap-tap-tap sounds against the side of the jug.

On the drive back to Kingswear, Zoe wondered why she hadn't said anything. Why she hadn't said, for instance, after Bonnie had made her threat, *Go away, we don't want you here.* Or why she wasn't now telling her father what Bonnie had said, but was leaning against the car window, her eyes closed, pretending to doze.

'Are you sure you won't stay the night?' her father said as they rattled into town. 'We can turn back.'

'No, it's all right, Dad, I promised Mum I'd go back to Granny's.'

'You look tired.'

'I'm fine, honestly.'

'You're worried about your grandfather, aren't you?'

'Yes, Dad.'

'Try not to worry too much. Charles is a tough old bird. I'm sure he's being well looked after. And thanks for coming

347

this evening, old thing. I enjoyed having the chance to talk to my two favourite girls.' He glanced at her. 'You do like Bonnie, don't you? She's very fond of you, you know.'

Now the words burst out of her – 'Did *she* move Mum's photo?' – and she saw his expression alter.

'Zoe, I'd rather you didn't talk about Bonnie like that. And no, I put the photograph safely away because I could see that it upset her. You mustn't think my friendship with Bonnie will make any difference to us. Rosindell is your home, just as it has always been.'

Parting from her father at the ferry, Zoe sensed that he was still annoyed with her. On the boat, heading for the other side of the river, she realised that before tonight she had thought of Bonnie as another Hugo, a tedious interloper, covetous and selfish. But she now saw that she was far more dangerous. *I mean to have Rosindell.* This stated in the tone of voice in which one might have said, 'I mean to have a weekend in Bournemouth.'

And if you get in my way, then I'll destroy you and your family. The most chilling thing was that Zoe believed her.

A Sunday: they had lunched together, and now the newspapers were spread out on the loggia table and tea was cooling in the cups.

Bonnie said, 'Look at this.' She handed him a photograph. 'I found it in one of those funny old bedrooms. You've all sorts of stuff in there. They could do with a good clear-out.'

A flicker of something – disquiet? – at the thought of her opening drawers and cupboards. But that was wrong of him, when it was he who had told her to treat Rosindell as her own.

He looked at the photograph. A couple in late Victorian evening dress were standing in front of one of the *trompe l'oeil* pillars in the old ballroom. 'It must have been taken years ago,' he said. 'At one of the old summer dances.'

'Why don't *we* give a summer dance, you and I, Devlin?' Bonnie's face was flushed, her eyes shining with excitement.

The idea revolted him. 'That won't be possible, I'm afraid,' he said.

'You told me that it was one of Rosindell's traditions. We could start it up again. We could invite everyone, all your old friends.'

'No. I'm sorry, but no.' Devlin flicked his newspaper, hoping she would let the conversation drop.

'Why not?'

'It would be too expensive, for one thing. What liquid funds I have need to be spent on getting the estate back up to scratch. And the house is hardly in a suitable state to show publicly.'

'But I've tried so hard to help you!'

He saw that she was hurt. 'Of course you have, darling. You've been wonderful.'

'All those little things I've found in the shops for you — it's taken me *hours* . . .'

Tactless idiot, he thought. 'Forgive me,' he said. 'I hugely appreciate what you've done.'

Bonnie was frowning. 'I thought you'd be *pleased*. Is it because of *her*?'

'Who?'

'Esme. Your wife.'

And it was, of course. A summer dance at Rosindell — a summer dance without Esme — could only be a travesty. He said, 'It might rake up unhappy memories, yes.'

'I see.'

'I'm glad you understand.'

'What I understand,' she said coldly, 'is that you don't want to take the opportunity to make our friendship public.'

'No, that's not true.'

'You don't think I can be as good a hostess as her. You don't think I'm good enough for Rosindell.'

'Bonnie, it isn't that at all.'

'I've tried to be patient, but I'm not sure what you want of me.'

'What do you mean?'

'What exactly are you after, Devlin? What is it you think you're going to get from me?'

Her words, coarse in their implication, jarred. He said, equally coldly, 'I thought we enjoyed each other's company.'

'It all seems so hole-in-the-corner. I do wonder what Mrs Forbes thinks.'

'Mrs Forbes?' he repeated irritably. 'I doubt if Mrs Forbes has any opinion of us at all. She has enough to think of with four children and a husband still sick from years in a Japanese prison camp.'

'I've asked so little of you – I've been so patient . . .'

There was a loss of control to her voice that startled him, and the thought flashed through his mind that he hardly knew her at all. He found himself saying, 'If that's how you feel, then perhaps we should call it a day.'

She stared at him, then took a shallow, shuddering breath. 'I didn't know you could be like this. So, so *cruel*!' And she ran inside the house.

Devlin followed her. She was weeping; guilt rushed through him.

'Please let's not quarrel,' he implored her. 'That's the last thing I want.'

'No, it's my fault,' she murmured. 'I expect too much of you. It's just that I'm never sure what you truly feel for me, and that breaks my heart. Please forgive me.'

His anger vanished. 'There's nothing to forgive.'

'Hold me,' she whispered. 'Then I'll know you're not cross with me any more.'

He took her in his arms. They kissed, and as her soft, pliant frame pressed against him, her perfume mingled with the scent

350

of the roses that wafted through the open doors and windows. He felt the jut of her hip, the narrowness of her waist, the swell of her breasts. When he made to undo the pearl buttons down the front of her frock, she did not push him away. Instead, her small hands went to his tie, loosening it and dropping it to the floor.

He carried her upstairs to the bedroom he had once shared with Esme and made love to her there. Afterwards, she lay cradled in his arms, her dark curls spilling over his chest.

She said, 'About the dance . . .'

'Whatever you want,' he murmured. 'Anything. And I do know what I want of you. I know exactly what I want. I've just been afraid to say it. I've been a fool, Bonnie. But not any more.'

After leaving work, Zoe travelled to Ye Olde Cheshire Cheese, where she spun out a gin and tonic for half an hour. Cleeve was often late. If she herself had arrived ten minutes late, like any normal person, the wait would not have seemed so long.

She looked at her watch again. Quarter to seven. A voice said, 'Let me get you another of those,' and Zoe looked up.

Forty or so, sheepskin coat, once handsome, gone to seed. 'No thanks,' she said.

'Boyfriend stood you up, has he?'

The sheepskin coat sat down on the other side of the room. Zoe pretended to look through her handbag. She wished she had brought a book or a crossword.

Twelve days had passed since she had last seen Cleeve. During that time she had neither written nor phoned. The problem with playing hard to get was that it only worked if the person you loved noticed. In the end, it had been she who had crumbled, she who had picked up the phone.

She'd give it till half past seven. During the final few minutes, she tried not to think about anything at all. The minute hand touched the six but she waited a little longer, in case her watch was fast. Then she left the pub.

When she returned to her lodgings, she found a letter from her father on the hall table. Inside her room, she read it. Then she opened a bottle of wine given to her on a previous visit to Rosindell and poured herself a glass. She drained it quickly and filled it again. She was starting to feel better; after a third glass she felt rather marvellous. She didn't need Cleeve. She would forget him.

She put Glenn Miller on the record player. Perhaps Cleeve had been delayed somehow. Perhaps he had been tearing through the traffic and had reached the pub just minutes after she had left. She danced round the room to 'Moonlight Serenade', singing along with the lyrics. She remembered dancing with Reuben in a club in Piccadilly to the same song. *I'll sing you a song in the moonlight, a love song, my darling.* Songs in moonlight, partings, absences. Tears sprang to her eyes and she drank some more wine in an attempt to recapture the careless elation she had felt earlier. But instead she just felt more miserable. How could Cleeve have forgotten her? Whatever he felt for her, it did not compare to what she felt for him. She could not have forgotten him, any more than she could have forgotten one of her own limbs.

Later, as she curled up under the eiderdown, she wondered what it was about her that made her so easy to abandon or ignore. Rupert, Reuben, and now Cleeve. And her father.

Loneliness and fear washed over her. What might Bonnie do? And how would she get through the days, the weeks and the months if she did not have Cleeve?

In the middle of the night, she got up to go to the bathroom and was horribly, disgustingly, sick. Back in her room, she lay down, shivering, wrapped up in her dressing gown. Her head ached badly; she supposed she should take an aspirin but was afraid to move. She was turning, she thought, as she lay awake in the spinning darkness, into one of those girls who were perpetually disappointed in love. She shut her eyes, but the spinning persisted.

Waking with a pounding headache a few hours later, she stared at the clock and realised that she had slept through the alarm. She had never been late for work in her life, not even during the Blitz, but she would be today. She hurried to wash and dress and get out of the house. The smells of sweat and stale clothing in the Underground, and the hot airlessness of the tunnels, made her stomach churn, and she had to concentrate hard to avoid being ill again.

After a long, unendurable day, told off by her supervisor, her muddy brain struggling with the simplest calculations, she went home. She counted off the stations on the Piccadilly Line: Knightsbridge, South Ken, Gloucester Road. Then a walk, and then the utter relief of reaching the house.

She had taken off her coat and hung it up when there was a knock on the door. Ben was standing on the landing. He looked even scruffier than usual, a button dangling from a shirt cuff, a smear of something – ink? – on his jacket pocket.

'Look,' she said. 'I've rather a headache.'

'I've been stuck in *all day*,' he moaned, 'and I've written two blasted pages.'

The evening yawned emptily. No letter, no phone call from Cleeve. 'All right,' she said. And then, peevishly, as he came into the room, 'Don't walk so loudly.'

'Lord have mercy, Zoe Reddaway's got a hangover.' Ben had seen the empty bottle on the windowsill.

'Don't gloat,' she muttered.

'What you need is a strong coffee and a couple of aspirins.'

'I've run out of aspirins. And tea, not coffee.'

'I'll make it,' he offered.

'No thanks.' Ben making tea would involve splashes over the tabletop and a trail of sugar.

353

He went downstairs to fetch aspirins while Zoe put the kettle on. When he came back, she poured out the tea and swallowed the aspirins and said, 'Tell me about your thesis.'

'Okay. My subject's Anglo-Saxon burial mounds in Suffolk.'

'Sutton Hoo.'

'Among others. There's a whole lot more that no one's had a look at yet.'

'But you'd like to.'

'Very much. But you have to have money to finance a dig, and you have to have the permission of the landowner. I'm hoping that my thesis will stimulate some interest. I need my own Lord Carnavon. You couldn't mention me to a wealthy benefactor, could you, Zoe?'

'Sorry. Is that what you want to do, travel round the world digging for buried treasure?'

'A few interesting pots would do. But yes, that's my plan, more or less. What about you?'

'I don't really have any plans.'

'I can't believe that. People like you always have plans.'

'What do you mean, people like me?'

'Organised people.'

Was that how he saw her? Controlled, dull, restrained? The words burst out without her being able to stop them. 'I thought we'd get married! I thought we'd have *children*!'

He frowned. 'You and Cleeve?'

'That's what I *thought*!'

'Was that why you hit the bottle last night?'

'We're finished!' she said, with a gasp. 'We were finished ages ago but I was too stupid to realise!'

He took a step towards her – oh God, he was intending to put a comforting, brotherly arm round her shoulders. She waved him off: she was not – *not* – going to weep in front of Ben Thackeray. She had made enough of a fool of herself, one way and another, over the last few months.

354

'I'm okay.' She picked up her cup, then put it down again. 'I waited for him for an hour and a half yesterday evening, Ben. And he hasn't even remembered that he forgot!'

'If it's any comfort, when I was seventeen I once hitchhiked from Melbourne to Perth – heck of a distance – to see a girl. Waited for her *two days* and she never showed up. In fact' – he dropped on to the sofa beside her, sprawling messily – 'my love life has been a bit of a disaster all round. There was Pippa, who went off with my best friend. And Christine, who went into a nunnery.'

In spite of herself, Zoe giggled.

'I don't think it was my fault, the nunnery,' he said.

Zoe counted them off on her fingers. 'Rupert, my boss at the Ministry of Supply. Married. He never knew I was in love with him. I don't think. Then there were some disasters, and then there was Reuben. American, utterly sweet, but he was married as well. He went off to France at D-Day and I never saw or heard from him again.'

'Did he survive?'

'I don't know. I don't want to know. I like to think he just thought, him and me, it wouldn't do, and so he went back to New York and his wife and child. Then, after Reuben, a few more disasters, and then there was Cleeve. And I love him *so much.*'

'But he's not making you happy.'

She looked away. She heard Ben say, 'Get away somewhere for a few days. Go and see your dad.'

'I can't.'

'Why not?'

'Because of *Bonnie.*'

'The fortune-hunter?'

'The bitch, you mean.' She found herself telling him. 'She *threatened* me. She said that if I tried to get in her way, she'd destroy my family. She meant, if I tried to stop her getting her claws into my father.'

355

'Jesus.' He studied her, frowning. 'Seriously?'

'There's no point me saying anything to Dad, because he refuses to believe anything bad about her. He's completely under her thumb. And she was so *calm*. It frightened me, Ben.'

He said, 'Don't,' and put his hand over hers. She looked down, startled. Without noticing, she had lined up the pens and pad of paper on the table in parallel, a careful inch between them.

'You do that when you're upset,' he said.

She snatched her hand back into her lap, mortified that he had noticed. 'I had a letter from Dad yesterday. He and Bonnie are planning to give a summer dance. At *Rosindell*.'

'Maybe that'll keep her happy. Maybe she's one of those women who needs to be the centre of attention.'

'No.' Zoe shook her head violently. 'You don't understand. When my parents were married, they used to give a dance there each summer. And now Bonnie wants the same thing. I know what she's trying to do. She's trying to take over. She wants my father and she wants the house. Or maybe she wants the house and she's using my father to get it. Yes, I'm sure it's that. And to get her hands on Rosindell, she needs to take my mother's place. It's as if she's trying to *erase* my mother. I hate it, Ben.'

'What will you do?'

Zoe shook her head. 'I don't know. Dad wants me to come to the dance.'

'Will you go?'

'I can't leave him to face it on his own.'

'If you like, I'll come with you. Only if you like,' he added quickly. 'Moral support. Two heads are better than one, all that. And it would give me an excuse not to write my thesis.'

She was torn – he was irritating, accident-prone, and she was unsure whether she could endure an entire weekend in his company. On the other hand, she could see that it might be useful to have someone there to help her.

In the end, she said grudgingly, 'Thank you.'

'How much do you know about Bonnie?'

'Not much. She says she was brought up in the countryside – in Shropshire – but I don't believe her.'

'Perhaps you should try and find out a little more.'

She frowned. 'Perhaps I should.'

Rosindell had never looked more beautiful. Some of the old flowers that his mother and Esme had planted, the seeds of which must have lain dormant for years, had bloomed again. The heavy heads of the roses drooped in the early morning sunlight, pearled with raindrops. A gust of wind, and petals tumbled like snowflakes from the jasmine. When Devlin brushed his hand against the sky-blue spire of a delphinium, it came away wet with dew.

Why, then, did he feel uneasy? Why had he woken at five, a tightness in the pit of his stomach, a sensation that had swept him back through the years to the trenches of northern France, the blood-red dawn light, the waiting for something to happen?

Walking through the garden, he spied a coil of black zigzags on the sun-warmed dry-stone wall of a terrace. The adder's beady eyes seemed to look around, surveying Rosindell's grounds. This was not, of course, an omen. He should be happy today. He would be happy today.

Hours stuck in a train with Ben, telling her about Anglo-Saxon ship burials, Australia, and his friend Griffiths, shot in the head at Monte Cassino and never the same since, the one with the cat that liked to go roaming. They had brought bikes, Ben's idea; Zoe had seen the sense of it, though the hauling of them from one guard's van to another when they changed trains jostled her overstrained nerves.

Totnes, Kingswear, then the cycle ride to Rosindell. The house polished and shining; Mrs Forbes and a girl from the village, a Fox, a niece of Sarah's, rushing about. Flowers in vases, cooking smells from the kitchen.

Just like old times, she thought sourly.

Her father, hair cut too short, a new jacket, shaking Ben's hand. Zoe could tell, just by looking at him, that he was dreading it.

When Bonnie turns up an hour before the summer dance is due to begin, Zoe slips away to show Ben the old part of the house.

She likes the fact that he's *knowledgeable*, that he understands the function of a great hall, that he's been to Penshurst Place and can compare that great hall with Rosindell's, and that he knows, without her telling him, what the witches' marks are.

They go to every room in the house. The library, the dining room, the bedrooms and attics. Zoe opens every cupboard, peers into every alcove.

He says, 'What are you doing?'

'I'm looking for the things she's taken away.'

But she doesn't find any of them. Funny, that. You'd think they'd be there, somewhere, the Belleek china and the Marion Dorn rugs and the lovely old looking-glasses. She wonders where they are.

As she goes down the steps to the cellar and unlocks the door, she finds herself telling Ben about Rosindell's ghosts. She has never told anyone else, not Reuben, not even Cleeve. She tells him how, on the night of the summer dance, they'd be there, waiting, trying to cause trouble. How they disliked interlopers. And how, if you annoyed them, they took your things and hid them − a christening bangle, a favourite doll, a diary.

Sometimes they took things just for spite.

Ben shines the torch over the rooms and passageways of the cellars. 'Jeez,' he says, 'I wouldn't want to be down here on my own on a dark night.'

They walk along vaulted stone passages. The circle of light sweeps over racks of dusty bottles and there is a smell of damp, as if the sea is seeping up through the earth. Objects, shrouded beneath dust sheets, put there for safe keeping during the war and never retrieved, loom through the darkness.

'What's along here?' says Ben, at the opening of another passage.

'A couple of creepy little rooms.'

'Let's have a look.'

A few minutes later, Ben straightens, fails to notice a low doorway, and whacks his head. He staggers, dazed, and they abandon the cellars as Zoe takes his hand and leads him outside. Blood marks the stone flags. Outside, she mops up the cut on his forehead with her handkerchief and makes him sit down for a while in the shade.

A summer dance at Rosindell. Devlin had drawn the line at a band, but the piano had been tuned and someone engaged to play it. It was a fine night and the guests spilled out of the house, over the loggia and terraces and through the garden.

The Hendrickses were there, along with a decent number of the great and the good from Dartmouth, Kingswear and Totnes. No one from London – Devlin felt a wave of nostalgia, recalling the parties of a dozen or more who had once driven down from the capital. Shame about Conrad, too, sick with some vile disease, poor devil, and fading away like a ghost. Grace Fawcett had come on her own, which was good of her, her brother having died the previous year. Also Tom and Alice, Zoe and her chap, and, at his own insistence, some of the men who worked for him at the boatyard.

There were absences. He minded that Matthew had not come. Charles and Annette had made Charles's recent bout of ill-health their excuse, though Devlin saw how it might seem to them, another woman taking Esme's place. Of course, no one could ever take Esme's place. But he had wrapped up his memories of those years and set them aside. He was good at that; he'd had practice, with the war. You couldn't go on mourning someone, missing them. You had to live again.

His gaze moved to where Bonnie stood on the loggia, talking to Robert Hendricks. Her dark red evening gown clung to her figure, wrapping closely to her hips, spilling off her shoulders and showing off her creamy skin. Watching her, he felt the ache of desire, and the reservations he had recently begun to feel, when she was not with him, seemed unimportant. Who among them did not have their rough edges? She'd had a tough time of it, poor little thing. And he needed her, needed her youth and vitality and beauty to keep his demons at bay.

How much do you know about Bonnie? Ben had asked her. Her father had invited all his friends, but Bonnie did not seem to have asked any of hers. No one else at the party appeared to know anything about her. She was wearing a new frock – crimson satin, Hardy Amies, recognised Zoe, who liked to wander round the fashion floor of the department store during her lunch break. How was Bonnie, the war widow, able to afford a Hardy Amies evening gown? And why had she no family, no sister or mother or cousin – had they all so conveniently perished?

She watched Bonnie and Bonnie watched her. Bonnie went around the house with a self-satisfied smile, as if she owned it already. She adjusted a bunch of flowers in a vase and instructed Mrs Forbes to take away the empty plates from the dining table. She ran a hand to smooth a tablecloth and bent to murmur to the pianist, her red-lipsticked mouth an inch from his ear. When Zoe tried to talk to Doreen Fox – the Foxes knew everything – Bonnie intervened. 'You must let the servants get on with their work, Zoe.' A warning flash in the green eyes. Zoe talked to this person and that, trying to find the crack in Bonnie's armour.

At ten o'clock, all the guests were invited into the drawing room. Her father was standing by the grand piano, Bonnie at his side. Doreen Fox moved among the guests with a tray of drinks. Zoe looked for Ben in the crowd, found him. There was a large piece of sticking plaster on his forehead. She caught his eye, then slipped out of the room. Furtive as a thief, she headed upstairs to her father's bedroom, where Bonnie had left her things.

First she went through the pockets of Bonnie's coat, but found nothing but a bus ticket and a handkerchief. Then her handbag. Cheap, scuffed brown leather with a brass clasp, which made an audible click as Zoe opened it. Methodically she examined its contents, opening the pocket sewn into the lining and leafing through the contents of the purse.

Tucked inside a zipped compartment, between a chemist's receipt and a shopping list, she found a photograph, an inch square, of a child. A blond boy, dressed in striped buttoned rompers, sitting on a chair.

A sound, from somewhere below in the house. Zoe put the photograph back in the purse and the purse in the handbag. The coat and handbag were replaced on the bed exactly where she had found them. Leaving the bedroom, she went downstairs.

And slipped into the drawing room just in time to hear her father announce that he and Bonnie were engaged to be married.

There was a flurry of applause. Devlin took the emerald ring out of his pocket and slipped it on her finger. 'Oh darling,' said Bonnie, looking down at it. And then he kissed her.

More applause. Someone proposed a toast, and the pianist struck up 'For He's a Jolly Good Fellow'. Devlin looked for Zoe in the crowd and found her standing by the door. He should have told her first. Perhaps he had been clumsy. *What are you suggesting, Devlin?* Bonnie had asked him when he had earlier broached the idea to her. *That we ask her permission?*

Bonnie's arm was linked through his. A surge of happiness: he was unable to believe his luck. At an age when he had thought the best of his life over, to find such a woman. Zoe had threaded her way through the crowds to stand at his side. She hugged him.

The pianist struck up a dance number. Devlin and Bonnie danced alone in the centre of the room, the scents of the summer night drifting through the open windows. But a stale weariness had fallen over the party, and shortly afterwards the guests began to drift away. As he stood in the courtyard, waving to the cars' shrinking headlamps, Devlin felt the beginnings of a headache tightening the bones of his skull.

Bonnie turned back into the house. 'Why didn't your London friends come?'

'I suppose the long journey.'

'Next year they must come. Next year we'll have a band and a sit-down dinner.'

'You're very ambitious,' he said, amused.

'I don't care for half-measures.' She plumped up a sofa cushion and glanced at the clock. 'I should go home.'

He ran his palms over the slippery fabric of her frock, tracing the contours of waist and hip. 'I thought you might stay the night.' His mouth nuzzled her neck.

'I don't think so, Devlin, with Zoe here.' She pulled away. 'I should feel rather cheap. Besides, I'm tired.'

He stifled his disappointment. 'I'll drive you back. But you enjoyed yourself?'

'Yes, very much.' She ran her gaze round the room. 'I think we need to make some changes. These furnishings – so old-fashioned.'

He drove her to Brixham. Past midnight, heading back to Rosindell, the darkness seemed to play tricks on him, the narrow lanes and high hedgerows walling the car in so that it seemed as if he was travelling through a long trench cut into the earth, with no end in sight. Light flashed in the perimeter of his vision and the Bentley jolted as the near wheel bumped against the verge. Devlin braked, wound down the window to let in the cool air, and drove the remainder of the journey at a snail's pace.

Heavy grey skies and a chill in the wind, which had changed direction during the night. Zoe and Ben were on Brixham's breakwater, eating party leftovers.

Ben said, 'How many more guest houses are there?'

'Only a couple.' The clogged, disjointed feeling, the consequence of a sleepness night, was being blown away by the wind, leaving her with only dread. Unless she found a way of stopping it, her father would marry Bonnie Gresham.

'Don't go so near the edge,' she said. She imagined him losing his footing, tumbling into the waves.

'Maybe it's interesting that we haven't found out where she lives. Maybe she's been lying about living in Brixham.'

Zoe looked at her watch. It was just after two. 'We'll give it another hour, then we'll have to go for the train.'

Waves slapped against the concrete wall of the breakwater. A few hardy souls braved the wind, walking along the beach. In the harbour, trawlers bobbed up and down on a choppy sea.

He said, 'Say you found out something. Say the kid was hers and Bonnie's been hiding it because she thought your father might not want to take on another man's child. And say you told him. Are you sure he'd thank you for it?'

'Of course he would. She's a phoney.'

'Your father's in love with her. People forgive anything when they're in love with someone.'

Zoe knew that she was afraid of telling Cleeve what she needed because she was afraid that he would be unable to give it to her. Sometimes you wanted someone at any price. She looked back to the road that ran by the harbour, where the daytrippers were ambling and the townspeople walking off their Sunday dinners.

She said obstinately, 'Dad needs to know the truth.'

'He may not want it shoved in his face. He may have some idea that Bonnie's not all she makes herself out to be, but—' He broke off. 'What is it?'

Zoe was heading smartly towards the harbour road, her eyes on a woman and a child, a little boy of three or four. The child was fussing and pulling at the woman's hand. A sharp slap on the back of the legs and he howled.

'It's him,' Zoe said. 'It's the boy in the photo.'

Matthew's life, which was often complicated, had recently become a great deal more so. He had for some time been having an intermittent affair with a woman called Avril Kilmartin. Mrs Kilmartin was bored, thirtyish and blonde, and married to a surgeon at the Royal Brompton Hospital. Matthew had met her at the garage, when Mrs Kilmartin had brought in her motor car because it was coughing out black smoke. The mechanic being busy and Mrs Kilmartin notably attractive, Matthew had crawled about and found the hole in the exhaust. When he had booked the car in for repair, Mrs Kilmartin had offered him her phone number. 'Do ring,' she had said, and so he had. Their meetings took place in cheap hotels on the Fulham Road, though once, in the early stages of the affair, she had come to the garage after hours for a quick, breathtaking coupling on Patrick O'Connor's desk.

'I'm rather afraid Jonno might have some idea,' she had told him the last time they had met. She had drawn the outline of her mouth in red lipstick, then blotted her lips together. 'He's being rather funny with me.'

'Jonno' was Jonathan Kilmartin, Avril's beefy, rugby-playing husband. A few days before O'Connor gave him the sack, Matthew had spotted Jonno lurking outside the garage and had had to slip out the back. When he phoned the Kilmartins, Avril cut him off. He imagined her telling her husband it was a wrong number.

Several weeks passed without him seeing Jonathan Kilmartin and Matthew began to relax. He spent a pleasant evening with some former RAF friends. At closing time, leaving the pub, they slapped each other on the back, called out cheerios, and went their separate ways. He was rather tight, Matthew realised, and there was nearly a nasty incident with a newspaper van as he crossed the road. Brakes screeched and the driver leaned out of the cab and yelled at him. Matthew waved an apologetic hand.

He was a couple of hundred yards away from the house when he recognised the hulking shape of Jonno Kilmartin beneath a lamp post. Suddenly stone-cold sober, he turned and rapidly retraced his footsteps. There was a narrow alley that ran parallel to the lodging house, towards the disused factory frontage where he kept the Morris, and from where he would be able to use the house's back door. He headed down the alleyway, glancing over his shoulder once or twice.

He heard a car engine start up and spotted the black Jaguar belonging to Ronnie James, seller of black-market petrol. Matthew owed Ronnie money. Ronnie wasn't the sort of bloke to let a debt go unpaid. Matthew began to run away from the lodging house. The Jaguar swooped straight at him, grazing his arm, and Matthew hurled himself at a picket fence and landed with a thump in someone's back garden. Running up the grassy top of an Anderson shelter allowed him to jump over the next fence. A shoulder into a rotten piece of planking in the fencing on the far side of the garden, and then he was hurtling down a cinder path too narrow for the Jaguar to follow.

Ten minutes later, walking along Hammersmith Road, he thought of going to Zoe's flat, but then he remembered that Zoe was at Rosindell, visiting Dad and his tart – because she was a tart, Bonnie Gresham; Matthew knew the type, and it had cheered him to see his father making a fool of himself.

No one else seemed to be around and the moon was a hazy disc, high in the sky. He had the clothes on his back and one and six in his pocket and no idea where he was going, but it felt surprisingly peaceful to be ploughing along by himself, unencumbered by anything, weightless and free, almost as if he was flying.

The unpleasant thing was that Ben had been right. Zoe had known it, in a way, before she had picked up the phone and dialled the number for Rosindell; her hand had hovered over the receiver, suddenly reluctant.

But she had done it anyway. She had told her father what she had discovered that afternoon in Brixham, and what Ben Thackeray had since found out for her at Somerset House. That Bonnie Gresham had never been married, and that she had an illegitimate son whom she boarded out with a woman in Brixham. 'You're sure about this?' her father had said. 'Yes, Dad,' she had replied. Then, 'I'm sorry.'

They had exchanged a few more sentences, but she had heard the diminishment and shock in his voice. Then he had ended the call. A week had passed and she had received a letter from her father telling her that he had broken off the engagement. It seemed to her that there must be something she could say to him, something that would make it better, but if there had been, it had not occurred to her.

Now she was in Ye Olde Cheshire Cheese once more, waiting for Cleeve. She had applied a ruthless honesty to her father's affairs, and it would be hypocritical, she saw clearly, not to do the same to her own, not to end with equal clarity what had once been between them. And yet she shrank from it. The lies you told yourself, she reflected, her gaze resting on her glass of soda water, the excuses you made when a love affair had gone sour. Tonight she found that she wanted him to be late. Or to forget, or not to come at all.

The door opened; she looked up and saw Cleeve. She half rose, and then sank back into her seat.

*   *   *

There's no fool like an old fool. The phrase rattled through his head as he went about his daily business at the boatyard, at Rosindell.

His folly had been limitless. The signs had been there, plain to see: her reluctance to allow him to drop her at her lodgings in Brixham — she had not lived in Brixham, but further along the coast, in Paignton; the feathering of little pearly marks around her belly that he had noticed when he had made love to her, where her skin had stretched to accommodate her pregnancy. Esme's body had been similarly marked, after Zoe. All this, and so much else — her manipulativeness, and a certain coarseness — he had disregarded. It chilled him to think that she had even tried to turn him against his children.

And her temper. A flare of it when he had tried to refuse her the summer dance. There had been a part of him, as he had confronted her with the information that Zoe had unearthed, that had hoped for an explanation, something that would allow him to forgive her, but she had turned on him like a cornered animal, screaming her contempt for him, for his children and his way of life. He would never be able to forget the things she had said to him. Or how she had lashed out at him, her nails clawing at his eyes.

He supposed that he had saved Rosindell from her, at least. Remembering her fury, he locked doors, was vigilant. Because Rosindell was what she had wanted, what she had thought herself due; she had left him in no doubt of that. They had shared the same obsession, he and Bonnie. And though he loved the house, as he always had, it was imbued now with melancholy and a sense of failure.

Chapter Seventeen

January 1949

Two weeks after the turn of the year, Charles Langdon died. The phone rang at nine o'clock in the evening, as Esme was clearing up the kitchen. After she had put the receiver down, she stood still, struggling to absorb the shock. But it was not possible; the loss of a parent was too momentous.

She picked up the phone again and dialled Matthew's lodging house. When she could not get through, she contacted the operator, who told her that the number had been cut off.

Then she called Zoe. Zoe had always been fond of her grandfather, and Esme heard the break in her daughter's voice at the other end of the line. She tried to offer comfort: he had been a good age, none of them would have wanted him to suffer.

'I'll go to Dartmouth first thing tomorrow,' she said.

'I'll come down as soon as I've arranged some leave. Take the train, Mum. Buy yourself a first-class ticket.'

'Darling, I can't find Matthew. Do you know where he is?'

'He's got a room in Battersea. I'll tell him, if you like.'

Esme made more phone calls, to her daily, and to the station, to check train times. She spoke to her lodgers, and then she packed.

A taxi picked her up the following morning and took her to Oxford station. She bought a first-class ticket, as instructed, though the habit of parsimony, ingrained by the war and wretched Hugo, made her conscience prick. But she had hardly slept the previous night, and she was grateful for the window seat and the rush of the bare winter countryside outside.

Alighting at Kingswear, hauling her case down from the luggage rack, she felt tired and crumpled from the long journey. As she walked out of the station she found herself thinking, *Back there, only a couple of miles away, is Rosindell.* She remembered the first time she had walked there, nineteen years old, through the storm, not knowing what she might find, and driven by – what? Optimism and youth and an instinct that she had never in her life since replicated, for what was valuable and out of the ordinary. The Langdons were not ordinary after all; they were vain, egotistical adventurers, who expected the exceptional and who demanded from those closest to them admiration and absorption. But she had loved Devlin with a sureness of touch that had since been denied to her, and it occurred to her, as she headed through the town, that she had been mistaken, and that she loved him still.

Too late. Far, far too late. Tears poured down her face and she walked blindly on, in search of some privacy. She was not even sure what she was crying for – her father, of course, but also for the mess they had all made of their lives, and because in the clarity of grief she had had a glimpse of what might have been, had she been able to forgive. She needed Devlin now, she needed his strength and his kindness, and just then the memory of love hurt almost more than she could bear, and so, coming across an empty bus shelter, she went inside and sat down on the wooden bench, trembling and sickened.

But the storm blew over, as storms always do, and eventually she was able to wipe her eyes and search in her bag for her cigarettes and lighter. Then she picked up her case and walked to the ferry.

*   *   *

Matthew arrived in Kingswear on the morning of his grandfather's funeral, having stayed overnight with a friend in Warminster. The steamer that had met the train docked on the Dartmouth side of the river, and once he had disembarked, he headed through town to St Saviour's church.

Among the crowds in the streets, he caught sight of a face that he recognised. It took him a moment to place her, and then he remembered: Billie, Betty, *Bonnie*, that was it, Bonnie, his father's floozy. She was wearing a blue coat, frayed round the cuffs, and scuffed lace-up shoes. As Matthew watched her make towards Bayard's Cove and the ferry, he smiled to himself. He hoped she was planning to stir up trouble for his father. The old bastard deserved it.

A church bell tolled. Hell, it was eleven o'clock, and the service was due to start. Matthew sprinted for the church, darting between cars and pedestrians. The undertakers' cars were parked outside. He ran a hand over his hair and slipped through the entrance. The church was crowded; spying an empty seat in a pew halfway back, he sat down. From the front of the building his mother gave him a frantic wave, beckoning him to join them, but Matthew shook his head. He didn't care for a ringside seat.

As the service began, his mind wandered. His eyes drifted round the congregation, picking out Langdon cousins, grown fat and self-important, and old aunts, frail in their black. His father, sitting across the aisle from Uncle Tom and Aunt Alice. Zoe and his mother, to either side of his grandmother. Men from the boatyard, men Matthew had known all his life, who, when he had been a small child, had produced sweets from their pockets or sat him on their knees and taken him for a run round the bay in the Langdon launch, and whose voices, true and strong, now joined forces to sing the first verse of 'Jerusalem'. Moved, Matthew took a deep breath and looked round the church again.

A fall of fair hair beneath a black hat. Golden hair, the colour of the sand at Rosindell Cove. *Melissa.*

She turned her head a little, and Matthew saw her milky skin, flushed with the same pale pink of the quartz pebbles that gleamed on the shoreline.

Bring me my spear: O clouds unfold, bring me my chariot of fire. Matthew, his heart swelling, sang too.

Mourners filled the rooms of St Petrox Lodge. Charles Langdon had been well liked. A glass of wine in one hand and a plate of sandwiches in the other, Matthew talked to his mother and his grandmother and to the bevy of Langdon aunts who insisted on making a fuss of him. He kept glimpsing Melissa out of the corner of his eye. He was afraid that she would leave while he was failing to extricate himself from his relatives, that he'd look for her and she'd have disappeared again.

'Matthew.'

His father was standing beside him. Jesus, he looked old.

'Dad.'

'How are you?'

'Fine.' Matthew began, 'I've found a job. Assistant bursar at a boys' school—' but his father interrupted.

'I didn't mean that. I meant, are you all right? It's hard, losing a grandparent.'

'I'm okay,' he said. And then, surprising himself, 'What about you, Dad? What about the boatyard?'

'Charles left his shares to Tom. It's up to Tom now to decide what he wants to do with it.'

Matthew saw her again, then, and, excusing himself to his father, slipped out the doorway after her. Melissa was standing at the end of the corridor, looking at a print of a tea clipper.

'Hello, Matthew,' she said. 'I wondered whether you'd be here.'

'I'd no idea you'd come.'

'Would you have come if you'd known?'

'Yes,' he said simply. 'Always.'

'I was in London, visiting an author, when Granny wrote. My grandfather was always kind to me.'

'Where are you living now?'

'In Paris. My mother sold the flat in Charles Street after the war.' She gestured to a door. 'Shall we go in here?'

Large windows looked out over the river and light flooded in from the estuary. Melissa was the same age as him, give or take a few weeks; thinner than he remembered. The passing of ten years had fined down her features, making her, if anything, more beautiful. His *sister*. He searched for evidence of kinship in her face, but apart from their fairness could find little.

He said, 'I came to look for you once.'

'When?'

'In the war. Middle of 'forty-one. There were Free French soldiers staying in the flat. Where were you?'

'In the south of France by then. I was with Rémy, but he was Jewish, so after Paris was occupied we knew we had to leave. We were lucky; we managed to make our way south.'

'Were you interned?'

She shook her head. 'I can pass for French easily enough. My friends found someone who could make me false papers. Did you join the RAF?'

Matthew nodded.

'I met quite a few British airmen,' she said. 'They'd had to bail out of their planes over France and we used to help them over the border to Spain. Whenever I got a message telling me there was another one, I always used to wonder whether it would be you.'

'Where was your mother?'

'In America. She sailed from North Africa quite early on.'

'Didn't you want to go with her?'

'She asked me, but I said no.'

'Because of what happened?'

'Between you and me?' Melissa pleated the black fabric of her skirt between finger and thumb. 'No, not because of that. No one was to blame for that. No, because of France. Because I realised that it was my home.'

No one was to blame for that. He marvelled that she could say it so easily. '*They* were to blame,' he said, but out of habit, he discovered, unsure whether he now believed it. 'Your mother. My father.'

'Do you think so?'

Her tone, the look in her eye, reminded him of why she had so riled him when they had first met, all those years ago. A barely disguised surprise that he could read a situation so mistakenly.

'They could have told us,' he said.

'They wanted to spare us. At least' – she gave a little Gallic shrug – 'I'm sure your father did. My mother . . . who can tell?'

He went to the window, staring out at the boats. 'They shouldn't have done *that* in the first place.'

'Have you never done anything you regretted?'

So many times, he thought. She came to stand beside him. 'You are, at least, my brother,' she said tenderly. 'So wonderful to have a brother. When I'm feeling blue, I remind myself of that.'

He hadn't thought of it that way before. Tears prickled his eyes and he had to concentrate hard on the sparkle of the river to send them back.

'I suppose,' he said, 'that I could come and visit you, in a brotherly way.'

'I suppose you could.' She smiled at him.

'Is there anyone?' He glanced at her hand and saw that it was ringless. 'A boyfriend, anyone?'

'Yes, he's called Philippe. I might marry him.'

'You love him?'

'No, I don't. But I'd like a child, you see.'

Matthew found himself a little shocked. Melissa said, 'Philippe is a practical person, like me. I won't lie to him. He loves me and I like him a lot and we get on well. I think that counts for a great deal, don't you? What about you?'

'No one. Well, lots of someones, but none have lasted.'

'You should settle down.'

'I'm not sure I'm the type.'

'You are, Matthew.'

He heard sounds from the corridor: the funeral party taking their leave, the door opening and closing, and his mother's voice, calling out thanks and goodbyes.

Melissa rested her head on his shoulder. She said, 'What I came to realise was that I could choose whether I wanted to be happy.'

'Is it a choice?'

'I think so.'

They stood for a while in silence, looking out at the river. Eventually she said, 'Rémy died.'

'In the war?'

'Yes. Someone gave him away and he was sent to Drancy, and then to a concentration camp. After the war, I tried to find him. I was working in a camp for displaced persons, for UNRRA, as a translator. I found out that he had died a few days after Auschwitz was liberated. I've lost so many people, Matthew, and I've seen some terrible things. I'm sure you have too. But I thought I would try to be happy. And you can't be happy if you're holding resentment in your heart.'

Then she turned to him, smiling brilliantly. 'I should go. A friend of mine is giving me a lift to Amesbury.'

'To the Herons' house?'

'Yes. We keep in touch.'

They embraced, and as he closed his eyes, he seemed to feel, for the first time in a decade, the weight slip away from him.

At the door, a kiss on the cheek, and then he watched her walk down the road.

He went back inside the house. Most of the guests had gone. He sensed his grandfather's absence fully for the first time. The house and the people inside it seemed greyed by Charles Langdon's passing.

In the drawing room, Zoe was sitting with their grandmother, who was complaining about the buffet. 'Ham, when I particularly asked for beef. Charles would have been so disappointed.'

'Where's Dad?' asked Matthew.

'He went home a while ago.' Zoe made frantic *help me* signals with her eyebrows, which Matthew ignored.

His mother was in the kitchen, making tea. Matthew could not pinpoint why he felt uneasy, when just a few minutes ago he had seemed, at last, to cut himself free of the past. Then he found himself remembering the face in the crowd, the frayed blue coat. Bonnie. Bonnie heading for the ferry to Kingswear. And after that, *where?*

'Just nipping out for a breath of fresh air, Mum!' he called, then grabbed his coat off the stand and slipped out of the front door.

As he approached Bayard's Cove, he saw that the ferry was at the far Kingswear bank. There was a phone box nearby; inside it, he dialled Rosindell's number. No reply. Dad's in the garden, he's gone for a walk, he told himself. Why should Bonnie go back to Rosindell? What business could she now have with his father?

But, seeing the ferry pull into the slipway, he ran back to the cove and climbed on to it. Insufferably slowly, it chugged over the river. He could have swum quicker. Gulls wheeled in a cement-grey sky. He should have said something. He should have warned his father.

At Kingswear, he pushed to the front of the queue and was off the boat before anyone else. No taxis in sight; he spotted

375

a bike propped outside the post office. A quick look up and down the road, and then he was cycling uphill.

As he sped up to the high ground, some of the optimism he had rediscovered that day returned. It would be fine. His father would be fine. He'd check on him and he'd make a start at bridging the gulf that yawned between them. But he stood on the pedals, pushing the machine harder and faster.

Scabbacombe Road and then the right turn to Lethwiston. Higher and higher, the grassy fields scattered with a few stunted trees. He reached the crest of the rise and looked down to Lethwiston, and Rosindell.

And saw the column of smoke rising from behind the trees. A chill caught at his heart; he hurried on, afraid now, and caught the scent of ash in the air.

Part Three

Division

1960–1962

Chapter Eighteen

June 1960

'Zoe works too hard, of course,' said Esme. 'And poor little Stephen, at that dreadful school.'

'Is it a dreadful school?'

Esme was helping Devlin make a place where he would be able to sit outside in fine weather. There was a sheltered site to one side of the valley where you could be out of the wind and yet glimpse a piece of the sea between a gap in the pines where a tree had blown down in a storm. When Devlin sat there, he would face away from the house and would not see the rough, smoke-blackened wall at the southerly end of the building, nor the wasteland that still lay to one side of it. Esme suspected that whenever Devlin looked at Rosindell he remembered what it once had been.

She recalled the arguments they had had about schools, she and him, when Matthew was little. 'Zoe feels Stephen needs the company of other boys,' she said. 'But he seems so *young*. Not much more than a baby.'

He did not, as she had half expected him to, point out that Stephen was ten years old, but instead said, 'He's a quiet little chap, isn't he? You can't help feeling protective towards him.'

'And I'm afraid Zoe will be lonely. *Lonelier*. Oh Devlin, I do wish she would find someone else!' Esme gave a stone a vicious poke with the hoe. 'You know how much I loved Russ, but I do believe it's the only thing that would make her happy again!'

'If she isn't ready . . .'

'Almost six years since poor Russ died, and she won't even try. I asked her and she bit my head off.' Esme sighed. 'She's like you, that's the trouble. Unsociable by nature.'

'Independent,' he said.

'Unsociable,' she said firmly. 'You're on your own too much, Devlin.'

'On the contrary, my last week has been a flurry of social events. I had lunch with the Hendrickses in Totnes, and I ran into Grace Fawcett when I was walking back from Kingswear.'

'How are they all?'

'Robert has retired. Grace is looking frail, but she's a game old bird and still walks the dogs every day.'

'Have you found another daily woman yet?'

'I don't need another one. I have Mrs Adams.'

'Mrs Adams just moves the dust around. Can't any of the Fox girls come and work for you?'

'Esme, I'm fine,' he said firmly. 'Shall we have a break? I'll make some tea.'

As she watched him walk towards the house, she felt a tug of pity for him. His limp from his wartime leg injury seemed more pronounced recently. He denied that it troubled him, but she did not believe him. His left arm, which had been badly burned in the fire, hung loosely by his side. His hair was now a great deal more silver than black, and though the right side of his face was, in Esme's eyes, as handsome as ever, on the left, a strip of skin from hairline to jaw was reddened and distorted.

She fetched two canvas deckchairs from the shed and put them up on the section of ground they had levelled. The laurels would act as a windbreak.

Devlin came back with the tea. He said, 'You were always right about Matthew. I was too hard on him.'

They had talked of this often; she knew that it haunted him.

'You did your best, Devlin. We both did our best.'

The dog, which had been rooting around in the earth, put her head in Esme's lap, and Esme scratched her long, silky ears. 'My mother had a letter from Melissa,' she said.

'How is she?'

'Well, I believe. And so is her daughter.' She shot him a glance. 'Do you ever think . . .'

'What?'

'She's your child, Devlin.'

'I'm nothing to her. I've given nothing to her. Worse than nothing.'

His voice, the sadness in it, made her say, 'I don't think it was only because of Melissa with Matthew. I think it was the war, too. He lived too close to death for too long.' Brushing a cobweb from the wooden strut of a deckchair, she sat down. 'He may be dead. I know he may be dead.' Her fingers fluttered. 'It's all right, I can bear it now.'

'You don't know.'

'No,' she conceded. 'But I do know how unhappy he was. He may have had an accident. He may . . .' But she could not say: I'm afraid he was capable of taking his own life. So she said instead, 'He was always rash. He'd stopped taking care of himself.'

Old griefs and well-worn conversations, gone over so many times. Esme was grateful when Devlin changed the subject and enquired after the plumbing of the cottage she had recently moved into. It was in Little Coxwell, in the Vale of the White Horse in Berkshire. The re-plumbing was a lengthy and expensive business, involving the replacement of a well in the back garden.

At three o'clock, preferring to drive home in the light, she walked back to her car. 'I'll see you next month,' she said, and kissed him on the cheek. 'I'll bring some plants.'

As she drove away from Rosindell, the thoughts tumbled

through her head. *Did I spoil Matthew? Did I? But I thought we were so close — how could he just go away?* Rounding a corner and finding herself in the path of a van, which hooted at her, she lurched towards the verge. Her heart pounded. 'Pull yourself together, Esme,' she said to herself sternly, and drove on.

A decade had passed since the fire that had almost destroyed Rosindell. Bonnie had set alight the new part of the house, Conrad Ellison's glorious light-filled rooms. The blaze had been out of control by the time Devlin had returned to Rosindell after the funeral. In the course of trying to stop it spreading to the old rooms, he had been badly burned; it had been Matthew who had dragged his father out of the building. By then the fire engine had arrived and so the older part of the house had been saved.

Matthew had been a witness at the trial, five months later. Shortly after Bonnie Gresham had been imprisoned for six years for arson, he had left the country, working his passage on a ship of the Blue Funnel line, the *Aurora*, bound for India. When the *Aurora* returned to Southampton, Matthew was no longer on board.

After that, the trail had run cold. No letters, no phone calls, no clue at all to where he might have gone. Esme knew that Matthew held himself responsible for what had happened to Devlin and to Rosindell. He had seen Bonnie Gresham in Dartmouth on the morning of Charles Langdon's funeral and he blamed himself for not warning his father.

It had been thought at first that Devlin might not survive. Esme and Zoe had taken turns sitting at his hospital bedside. During his slow recovery, Esme had continued to visit him, at the nursing home where he went to convalesce, and eventually at Rosindell, where, against all advice, he returned when he was well enough. She listened when one evening Devlin spoke to her of his shame and his awareness of his own folly. He had fallen so easily for Bonnie Gresham's deceptions. Vanity, he said bitterly. I suppose she appealed to my wretched vanity.

Born and brought up in London, the daughter of a neglectful mother and an absent father, Bonnie had left school at fourteen to be apprenticed to a dressmaker, quitting after only three months. A series of short-lived jobs and several convictions for shoplifting had followed. Her son, Trevor, the product of a brief liaison with an American soldier during the war, had been boarded out with a woman in Brixham. Most humiliating of all, Devlin had discovered at the trial that he had not been the first well-off older man that Bonnie Gresham had pursued. There had been others before him.

Why, Esme had sometimes asked herself, had she continued to visit Devlin even after the doctors had signed him off, pronouncing him as fit as he would ever be? Out of pity, of course, because she knew what the wounds to his body and his pride had done to him. And because she was afraid that he would not take care of himself, and who else would keep an eye on him? She knew him well enough to fear that his reaction to injury would be to shut himself away, to cut himself off from other people, to retreat into solitariness and black despair.

But also because, during her long vigil at the hospital, love had begun to creep in. She had thought at first that it had a different timbre to what she had once felt for him, that it lacked passion, was the ashy remains of what had once existed between them, just as the smoke-blackened rooms were all that was left of the wonderful house on the headland. A skeleton of love, a grey, wispy ghost of it. But it came to her after a while that the embers had never been completely extinguished, and that his need for her had rekindled the flames.

In hospital, they gave him morphine for the pain while he was recovering from the burns. The drug killed memory; he would surface and say, *Esme, is that you*, and reach out his good hand to her. Then he'd drift off again only to flicker awake an hour or two later.

Esme, is that you?

The joy in his voice, and the gratitude. That was why she stayed.

After Charles Langdon's death, Tom had considered selling the boatyards, but his eldest adoptive son, Christopher, had shown an interest in the firm, so in the end Tom had held on to the business. Since the fire, Devlin had cut down his hours of work. Though he still nominally managed the Galmpton yard, he knew himself to have been sidelined. Christopher Langdon and his brother, William, drove the business, and not always in the direction that Devlin would have chosen. But he held his tongue. He was sixty-four years old, and on the way out. He would not invite the derision of the young by harping on about how things had been done in his day.

Every afternoon, Devlin walked along the cliff path as far as the old gun battery at Froward Point and then back along the narrow tarmacked road, past the daymark tower, breaking off to turn across the fields through Lethwiston and then to Rosindell. He never missed a day. The years had not been kind to him, and the injuries heaped on him by the past – by the war and the fire – hurt and slowed him. He walked because he was afraid that if he did not do so, his damaged body would fail him and he would end his days a dribbling fool in a wheelchair, deprived of the sea and sky he had always loved.

In Lethwiston, he passed the pub and the row of thatched cottages. He had sold the end cottage to Sarah Fox – Sarah Trent, since her marriage – after the Fox girls' father had died. Sarah and her husband, William, had remained in Walton-on-Thames after the war, but Sarah's widowed mother preferred to stay in the house in which she had brought up her family. A porch had been added to the front of the building and was now wreathed in roses. Sarah's chap, William, had come over not so long ago to give the door and windows a coat of paint.

The changing moods and wild beauty of the coastline were a part of him. As a boy, he had run these paths with a gang of urchins from Lethwiston. As a youth, he had ridden his father's horses, hooves drumming on the baked earth in the summer months. After he had returned from the war, he had made himself limp along this same route, angry and frustrated as his injured leg had dragged like a dead thing. He had walked here with Esme and later with the children, holding tightly to their hands as they headed along the clifftop. Sometimes now, walking through fair weather and foul, it came to him that he was back where he had been in 1918, living alone on a derelict estate full of memories. He missed his family. He even missed Josiah.

These days he often felt reluctant to return to the house. The house that his father had neglected, that Esme had loved and feared, and that Bonnie had wanted beyond reason, now repelled him. He saw it as the implacable embodiment of his own obsessions: with Camilla, and with Rosindell itself. He remembered how, crippled and feverish on his first night home after the war, he had hauled the stones of the derelict chapel through the wind and rain to mark out the walls of the new house he would build for Camilla.

I'll make Rosindell glorious again for you, he had promised her. *Whatever it takes, even if it destroys me.* And so he had built his love for her, his unreasoning, destructive love, into the fabric of the house, where it stained the lives of those inside it. There had always been a darkness at Rosindell: look too closely at its history and you found madness, sickness and cruelty. These days, Devlin preferred the deep silence of the combe and the bright changing vista of the sea.

A tall, fair-haired man with a rucksack slung over one shoulder was walking along the pavement. Zoe, who was mentally going over an argument she had had with her manageress that afternoon, drove past him. Something in the set of the man's shoulders made her glance in her rear-view mirror. She frowned, braked, and flung open the passenger door.

'Ben?' she called.

Ben Thackeray ran to catch up with her. 'Zoe!' He peered at her. 'I thought I'd drop in.'

Drop in, she thought. Typical. After – how long? Three years? Yes, getting on for three years. And there was no food in the house and she had work to do that evening.

She said, 'Get in,' and Ben unhooked the rucksack and slid into the passenger seat.

He was deeply suntanned. His hair had bleached to the colour of straw and his faded linen shirt was much the same washed-out blue as his eyes.

'You're very brown,' she said.

'Mediterranean sun. You look thin.'

'I'm always thin, it's how I am. Were you digging things?'

He grinned. 'Yeah, that's right, digging things.'

Zoe, too, smiled. 'Did you find any treasure?'

'This and that. I'll tell you about it.'

'Where are you staying?'

'With Griffiths, in Peckham.'

'How is he?'

'Just the same. His memory's still shot. Sad thing is, he remembers the war but he'd forgotten I was turning up yesterday. How are the shops?'

'Doing rather well, actually. I'm changing the stock in the smaller Richmond shop, buying in clothes aimed at younger women.' Zoe had sensed with the turn of the decade that change was coming. You heard it in the music, sexy and insistent, that blared from the coffee bars.

'Moving with the times,' Ben said.

'That's the idea.'

They had reached the house. Zoe parked in the driveway. Indoors, Ben said, 'Where's Stephen?'

'At school. He's been boarding since the beginning of the year.' She scowled as she hung her jacket on the coat peg. 'Don't you start.'

'What?'

'My mother doesn't try to hide the fact that she thinks I'm the worst mother in the world for sending him away. Even though Matthew and I both boarded.'

'I'm sure you had good reason. And if he's happy, what's the problem?'

'He is,' she said quickly. 'He's very happy.' Though she wasn't completely sure that that was true. He *said* he was happy, but that wasn't necessarily the same thing. 'I want the best for him,' she said. 'He hasn't a father, so I need to make it up to him. And anyway, I can't be with him all of the time, because of the shops.'

'Zoe, I thought he was a great kid last time I saw him, and I'm sure he's still a great kid now.'

'He is.'

She felt an awkwardness in the silence that ensued. She noticed that Ben had shed some of the scruffiness that had once both irritated and endeared him to her. The blue shirt had seen an iron. She felt a momentary regret for the carefree boy he had once been, along with a fleeting sadness for a friendship that seemed to her just then to have burnt out.

Ben had gone abroad shortly after her wedding, but had returned to England six months after Russ had died. He had, in his way, been helpful, giving her a hand when things had gone wrong with the car or the washing machine, taking Stephen to the Science Museum or to kick a ball in the park. And then, three years ago, he had had the opportunity to take part in an archaeological dig on Crete. Zoe had been surprised to find that she had missed him, though she had not missed his habit of turning up at inconvenient times, or his untidiness, or his fondness for disagreeing with her, or the general disruption he seemed to bring to her life.

He padded into the kitchen after her. Zoe said, 'Black? Two sugars?'

'I've given up sugar.'

'How commendable.' She glanced at the larder. 'I'm afraid I've nothing much to offer you to eat.'

'No worries. Let me take you out to dinner.'

'Thanks, but I've work to do.'

'You need to eat.'

'I had an enormous lunch.'

They took the coffee into the sitting room. Zoe said, 'How long are you back for?'

'Not sure. I'm working on a site in East Smithfield.'

'Not as exotic as your usual places.'

'It's a mass grave. We think it's plague victims.'

'Horrible.'

'Interesting.' Ben folded his long limbs into an armchair. 'The burials were unmarked, but laid out in rows. So they were buried with care – with reverence, I'd say – even if the interment was hasty.'

'Don't you ever think that—' She broke off.

'What?'

'That you're meddling with something best left alone.'

'The bacterium can't survive any length of time outside the human body. You're talking about deaths that took place six centuries ago.'

'I meant' – she handed him a cup – 'all that misery, all that suffering.'

'The way I see it, we're paying tribute to them. We're making sure their suffering isn't forgotten.' He looked at her closely. 'Or did you mean that we might bring it back to life somehow?'

'Don't be ridiculous. That's not possible.'

'I'm never quite sure what I think about ghosts. The belief in them is so widespread. Every culture has its spirits of ancestors and places. Modern scientific thought tells us that all that's, as you say, ridiculous, but how many of us are completely immune to it? On a dark night, say – or when we're on our own in some old building?'

She thought, or if we're grieving for someone. For many months after Russ had died, Zoe had sensed his presence, urging her to keep going, not to falter. A soft breath on her cheek at night when she wept. A dream of his arms around her; when she had woken, she had still felt his heart beating against hers.

Ben was looking at her. 'How are you, Zoe?'

'I'm okay, honestly, I'm doing fine.' She smiled. 'Stephen and I, we're both doing fine.'

She told him about the shops, whose running she had taken over after Russ had died. She had recently redesigned the frontage and shortened the name, changing *I. Russell Ladies' Outfitters* to the more modern *Irwin Russell*, lettered in plum and burnt orange. She had an eye for what would sell and a nose for the next fashionable colour or hemline. She employed six full-time staff, two part-time and three Saturday girls, had savings in the bank and a cleaning lady, and was able to send Stephen to a good school.

She said, 'Stephen's missed you.'

'I've missed him too.'

Another silence. She glanced at the clock.

'Ben, I've work to do, I'm afraid. It's lovely to see you, but I really must get on.'

She had met Russ in a pub in Fitzrovia, six weeks after the fire, February 1949. She had felt obliged to put in an appearance because her colleague Gail, whose birthday it was, had covered for her at work when her father's life had been in the balance.

She caught sight of him sitting at a corner table. Something in his broad, handsome face made her want to look at him again. Light reddish-brown hair, parted to one side, brown eyes like a bird's, quick and bright. Crisp white shirt, dark red tie, navy blazer. Russ was always a sharp dresser.

He had a pad of paper in front of him, on which he was drawing. People came and chatted to him. A curly-haired girl slipped an arm round his shoulders; a man in a striped jacket sat down opposite him, and the two of them had a short, intense discussion, fingers stabbing at the paper.

Eventually he rose, slipping the sketchpad into his jacket pocket. He walked to the bar and Zoe heard him order two drinks. She wondered whether the second drink was for the curly-haired girl. She glanced at her watch, trying to decide whether she could decently slip away yet.

Then a voice said, 'I've guessed a gin and tonic. Or something else? Or we could go and get something to eat, if you'd prefer.'

And he was standing in front of her, a glass in each hand.

His name was Irwin Russell, but everyone called him Russ. He lived in Kingston upon Thames, in a detached Victorian villa he had bought before the war. He was thirty-nine when they had met, almost ten years older than Zoe, and owned three dress shops in Kingston and Richmond, the third very recently acquired. He took the pad of paper out of his pocket and showed her his design for the new shop front. *I. Russell Ladies' Outfitters*, pencilled lightly above two large windows, each of which contained a roughly sketched mannequin. Her customary wariness – that he might be a philanderer, a mad axe-murderer, or simply a bore – never materialised. There was that cliché about feeling that you were the only two people in a crowded room. She had felt that with Russ. They had felt that about each other.

After they finished their drinks, they had gone not to a restaurant, but to Richmond, to see the new shop. She remembered Russ striding about the premises. 'The counter here – no, *here* – keep the window displays simple: I hate clutter, don't you?' By the time they left the shop, the restaurants had closed, so they bought sausage rolls from a van in a side street and ate them sitting in the dark on a bench by the river. Afterwards, they kissed, the pads of his fingers drifting lightly on the back of her neck, the rough brush of his chin against her cheek.

She had loved him because he was warm, kind, talented, generous and funny. She had loved him because of his many friends – he had been the sort of man who fell into conversation with a stranger at a bus stop and invited him home for supper. Or to a party. Russ had loved a party. He'd come home from the shop on Saturday evening and half an hour later he'd be phoning round his friends and sending out for food. An hour after that, the house would be full of people, the gramophone playing Rosemary Clooney or Hank Williams, Russ uncorking bottles of wine in the kitchen. He loved a drink, a cigarette, and a spur-of-the-moment trip to Paris or Edinburgh, Zoe and Stephen wrapped up in the passenger seat of his sports car, the baby paraphernalia stuffed in the boot.

Russ hadn't been the sort of man she had thought she would marry. He had shown her that she could be a different sort of person. Zoe chewed this thought over as she sat on the sofa, checking her order book for the autumn and winter collections, listening to the silence and emptiness of the house.

She wanted the phone to ring or to hear a friendly footstep on the stairs. She regretted shoving Ben so promptly out of the house. She poured herself a large glass of wine, then went back to the sitting room and switched on the television. Voices filled the room; she drank the wine and felt better.

A couple of weeks later, she met Ben for dinner. He was waiting for her in the street when she came out of the Richmond shop.

'You look stunning,' he said.

'Thank you.' She kissed his cheek. 'I have to, I have to be a sort of walking advertisement.'

In an Italian restaurant in Kew Road, she asked him about his work, the burial site.

'We've uncovered twelve skeletons,' he said. 'It's touching to see them emerging from the earth.'

'Touching? Not creepy?'

'I don't find it so. All those loves and lives. I wonder if they kept on hoping, right up to the end. Or whether they knew they were going to lose everything. Maybe the younger ones fought it.'

'Why only the younger ones?'

'You can't kid yourself so easily as you get older, can you?'

'I suppose not. How's Griffiths?'

'Much the same. His sister's visiting at the weekend, the sister from Wales, so I'm having to move out for a couple of days.'

Ben's friend Griffiths lived in a small one-bedroomed flat. Zoe said, 'Where will you stay?'

'Oh, I'll pitch the tent somewhere.'

She stared at him. 'Ben, you can't.'

'Why not?'

'This is London, not Crete. And you're forty, not some boy scout.'

'Forty-three.'

'You have a job. You can't just — camp out.' And she found herself saying, though a part of her suspected she would regret it, 'You can have the spare room for the weekend, if you like.'

He twizzled a strand of spaghetti round his fork. 'Won't I be in the way?'

'Of course not.'

'Then if you're sure . . .'

Zoe shrugged.

'I won't make a mess, I promise.'

She read in his gaze that he knew her too well, that he understood the mental gymnastics she was putting herself through.

She sighed and said, 'My mother keeps telling me I should get out more, make more friends.'

'And do you?'

'Not really. I'm too tired with the shops.' But she knew that was not quite the truth, and found herself admitting, 'I get so I won't make the effort. I *can't* make the effort. I know it's wrong, but it just seems easier to be by myself, not to have to try to please people. Not to get *involved*, I suppose.'

'After Russ?'

'After Russ. It's just . . .' She clicked her fingers. '*That*, and he was gone.'

He offered her his handkerchief; she checked that it was reasonably clean, and blew her nose. Then she slid her glass towards him and he refilled it.

'Gets me through the evenings,' she said.

He topped up his own glass. 'I've sat through some bloody long evenings myself.' He looked at her plate. 'Eat up.'

'I'm not hungry.'

'One more meatball.'

'You sound like me with Stephen,' she said crossly, but speared a meatball to keep him quiet. 'Tell me about the Mediterranean.'

'I spent the last eight months on Malta and Gozo, looking around the Neolithic sites. Some of those places are pretty remote; you don't talk to anyone for days.'

'I never think of you as being lonely.'

He said lightly, 'I've never been convinced that you think of me at all.'

'Oh, sometimes I think, where's that wretched Ben? Why hasn't he sent me a postcard?'

'I decided to leave you in peace.'

'I missed your postcards. They're funny. I've always imagined lots of tents, the stars, you and your friends talking about whatever it was you dug up that day.'

'No, that's not so; recently I've been on my own most of

the time.' He paused, then said, 'There was a girl from Australia, not far from where I was born, but she couldn't put up with it. We went round a few of the islands together, but after a while she pushed off.'

'Perhaps she wanted hot running water and a comfortable bed.'

'Rather than a sleeping bag and a pan of water from the nearest stream? You're probably right.'

'Were you in love with her?'

'No.' He gave a wry, lopsided smile. 'She probably caught on to that as well.'

'Have you ever been in love with anyone?'

'Oh yes.'

'Who?'

'Maybe I'll tell you one day.'

'Ben.' But he shook his head.

She had a thought. 'If you like, you could come with me to Stephen's cricket match on Saturday.'

'I'd love to.'

'Good. You can explain to me what's going on. Stephen always asks me questions and I haven't a clue.'

'Another meatball.'

'Don't fuss,' she said. But fondly, because, unexpectedly, it touched her that he cared.

Ben bawled from the sidelines during the cricket match, and in the duller moments, of which there were many, Zoe checked over the latest invoice from her Paris supplier. When the match was over, they met Stephen for a tea of sandwiches, scones and cake.

Later, after Zoe had said goodbye to Stephen and they were walking back to the car, Ben said, 'I'll drive, if you like.'

'I'm fine.'

'It's okay to howl.'

'No it isn't, and I'm not going to.' She sniffed and stalked off. It was almost the end of term, she reminded herself. A few more weeks and Stephen would be home for the school holidays.

Back home, she hung her coat on a hanger in the hall and went into the kitchen. 'Supper'll be whatever's in the larder.'

'Terrific.'

What was in the larder was eggs and baked beans. Zoe beat up eggs for an omelette and handed Ben the tin-opener.

She heard him mutter, 'Hell,' and turned to see him clutching his hand. Blood welled between his fingers and trickled down his wrist to the cuff of his shirt.

'Cut my hand on the lid,' he said.

'Let me have a look.'

He showed her the diagonal slice across his palm. 'A plaster,' he said.

'Don't be silly, that needs stitches.'

'If you just stuck it together—'

'Ben, shut up and sit down. You're as white as a sheet.'

She gave him a light shove and he sat on the kitchen stool. Then she fetched a clean tea towel and bound it tightly round his hand. She dialled the doctor's surgery, but the doctor's wife told her that Dr Penrose was out delivering a baby, so she bundled Ben into the car and drove him to Kingston hospital.

Saturday evening in Casualty and the drunks were already lining up in the rows of seats, while a road traffic accident sent doctors and nurses hurrying towards the ambulance bay. Zoe tried to keep Ben's spirits up, making light conversation, though goodness knows it was hard enough in such a miserable place, surrounded by people coughing tubercularly and scratching at rashes.

Eventually a nurse came and led Ben away. Zoe deeply regretted giving him the tin-opener. She blamed herself. She should have known. He couldn't take a walk without tripping over his own feet and injuring himself.

He seemed to be gone an awfully long time, during which

the familiar nagging ache of anxiety asserted itself and she began to wonder whether he had passed out, or whether it was more than a simple cut – he had damaged a tendon, perhaps. She hated hospitals. She hated this hospital in particular, because it was where the ambulance had taken Russ when he had fallen ill. They had been to a party that evening, and when they had come home, Russ had told her he had a headache and had gone to bed. They had both put it down to the rough red wine at the party. She had been clearing up the kitchen when she had heard the thump of him collapsing to the bedroom floor. The ambulance had taken him to Kingston General, and then she had sat in this awful place, waiting, waiting and imagining – but somehow not imagining that. She who had always imagined the worst had not on that occasion done so, had not anticipated that her beloved husband would die of an aneurysm at the age of forty-five. So she had been unprepared. Not, she saw now, that preparation would have made any difference at all.

She looked up and saw Ben coming out of a blue-curtained cubicle. Breathless with relief, she went to meet him.

'How is it?'

'A few stitches, that's all.' He held up his hand, wrapped in a white bandage.

Back at the house, Zoe mopped up the blood, dried now to brown blots, found aspirins for Ben and opened a bottle of wine. They both needed it – she felt jittery and he looked fed up.

She said, 'Do you want the omelette?'

'Not really.'

She dug around the larder until she found several Penguins and a tube of Smarties, treats for Stephen. They took the wine and chocolate into the sitting room.

He said angrily, 'I can't believe I've made a fool of myself in front of you again.'

'I wouldn't worry about that. Though it sometimes amazes

me that you've survived this long. I mean, the army, all your trips abroad.'

She knew immediately, looking at him, that her attempt to lighten the mood had been misjudged.

'Funnily enough,' he said, 'I got through the whole of the Italian campaign with hardly a scratch.'

'It's me, then?' When he did not reply, she said, 'Oh,' and looked away.

She knew she made people nervous. She had seen for a long time how, when she went into the shops, the assistants straightened, quickly tidying their hair, their carefree chatter coming abruptly to a halt. She tried to put the girls at their ease but knew she wasn't much good at it, that she hadn't the knack. Russ had, and her father also had that happy ability of being able to talk to anyone of any class. She often imagined the shop assistants letting out a sigh of relief after she had gone, or even a ripple of laughter. It irked her, because she had had no choice but to become efficient and decisive when she had found herself forced to take over Russ's business – how else could she have survived? But she suspected that her employees translated efficiency as coldness, and what she thought of as decisiveness they labelled bossiness. Well, too bad, she had often thought. I have to get on.

But she found that she minded that Ben appeared to have the same opinion of her, and she said miserably, 'I'm sorry if I make you feel on edge. I wasn't aware that I did.'

'Zoe, it's not your fault. It's me, I'm an idiot.'

'I have to get things done, you see.'

''Course you do.'

'It's been tough.'

'Zoe, I know.'

'Do you think I'm hard?'

'Hard? No, of course not.'

She looked down at her glass. 'I once overheard one of the

397

wholesalers call me a hard bitch. He thought I was out of earshot, you see, but I heard him.'

'What I see is someone who's been through a hell of a lot.'

'I know I'm fussy about details, but you have to be if you're in fashion; it's the details that make the difference. A white collar, a row of nice buttons – that's what makes a frock sell.' She was smoothing out her Penguin wrapper with her forefinger, making it square and flat and neat. 'It's what I'm good at, making sure everything's just right. But people don't like you for it.'

'Don't they?'

She shook her head. 'No. The people in the shops, they don't love me like they used to love Russ.'

'How can you know that?'

'I can tell, that's all.'

'Good at telling who loves you, are you, Zoe?'

'Yes,' she said, a little startled. 'I think so.'

His expression was unreadable, but after a moment he held out his arm to her and said, 'Come here.'

She sat down beside him. He put his arm round her, and at that moment it seemed entirely natural to lay her head on his shoulder and close her eyes.

'Oh dear,' she murmured. 'What a pair we are. At least I never feel I have to try too hard with you, Ben. I suppose that's why I like you.' She opened her eyes, looked up at him. 'That sounded awfully rude. You see what I mean. Even my mother finds me hard to put up with.'

'I don't.'

'Ben, that's not true. You're always disagreeing with me.'

'I only bother to disagree with the people I'm fondest of.'

'Are you fond of me?'

He looked down at her. 'Of course I bloody am.' Then he kissed her, a long, lingering kiss on the mouth that took her breath away and robbed her of speech. When he drew back, he said, 'Actually, I'm in love with you. Always have been, and I'm afraid always will be.' And he kissed her again.

Why did she not pull away? Because, she told herself, it would have looked awkward, as if she cared too little for him, or too much.

But she wasn't being honest with herself. A hard-faced bitch she might be, but she was good at being honest with herself. She had kissed him because she had wanted to. For once, she didn't pause to examine her motives, this sudden compulsion. Instead, she knelt up and kissed him again. And then again.

When she opened her eyes, dawn was delineating the dark squares of fireplace, armchair and sideboard. The clock on the sideboard told her that it had just gone four.

She was lying on the sitting room sofa, naked, covered only by the tartan blanket she kept there for chilly evenings. Beside her, Ben slept, snoring lightly, also naked. His skin clung to hers, his hand rested on her thigh. The heaviness of her sleep – she hadn't slept so deeply for ages – meant she had to make an effort to remember. When she did, a wave of heat ran over her along with a lowering of her spirits, a mixture of shame and regret and disappointment in herself.

They had pulled off each other's clothes, tugging at sleeves and dragging buttons from threads, fumbling with belt buckles, wrestling with stockings and suspenders. She had tried to say something and he had said roughly, 'Don't talk. You and I, we say the wrong things when we talk.' Their lovemaking had been rushed, sweaty, urgent.

Three times. He had made love to her three times.

Very carefully, she slid out of his embrace and off the sofa. She gathered up her clothes from the floor, then tiptoed out of the room and up the stairs. In her bedroom, she put on her nightie, folded her clothes and put them on a chair. Then she lay on the bed. Daylight filtered into the room. As the objects inside it gained clarity, so her guilt expanded and grew to fill the space.

How could she have made love to another man in this house, Russ's house? Her home would always be imbued with Russ's presence. The furnishings had been bought by him before they had met, his books were on the shelves, his records stacked beside the record player, and there were those other traces: spirit, memory, and the tie of blood that ran through Stephen. Yet this evening she had forgotten Russ. Looking back, it seemed to her that she had behaved like an animal, that her desire had been frenzied and degrading. Had she been drunk? Or had she torn Ben's clothes off simply because she was now free, attached to no one else? *Free* – the word disgusted her. Was she free of Russ – could he be slotted neatly away into the past, no longer able to hurt her, no longer mourned, *forgotten*?

Zoe lay awake as sunlight filled the room, the start of another fine day. She heard movement in the sitting room below. There were the sounds of Ben rising and dressing and she wondered what he would think, finding himself alone.

She knew what he would think, and for a long, aching moment she wanted to run downstairs to him.

But she remained where she was until she heard the front door open and close and his footsteps on the path. She had done the right thing, she told herself. And if it surprised her that she felt confusion, or something worse, then she put that aside.

Chapter Nineteen

July 1960

It happened on Matthew's birthday, driving to Zoe's house in Kingston upon Thames. Esme was heading along a straight stretch of road near the border with Buckinghamshire, towards an area of heavily wooded land. Something about the trees disturbed her, the blocks of darkness between the silvery trunks and the way the shadows moved on the tarmac. Her heart thudded and she found herself gasping for breath as she pulled into the side of the road.

The panic attack ebbed, but when she took her hands off the steering wheel, they left slick marks of sweat. She unclasped her handbag to find a handkerchief, cranked down the window, and heard the whirr and whizz of other cars passing by.

Birthdays and Christmasses, those family occasions, brought with them such deep despair, such particular pain. The fear that she might never see her son again, that she had lost him for ever, had a way of overwhelming her without warning.

She climbed out of the car and walked around the verge, beside the elders and hazels. She found herself remembering the day Matthew had been born, the infant's cry interrupting the quiet that had fallen over the house after Devlin had asked the workmen to down tools. And another birthday – Matthew would have been five or six – when he had sneaked into the kitchen and eaten the icing from the cake Mrs Satterley had made for him and had afterwards been horribly sick.

More cars hurtled by. You only have to follow them, Esme told herself. You've driven this road a hundred times before.

But she couldn't. The darkness, the fear that it would happen again. Instead, she took out the map and worked out a different route. Then she waited until the road was empty before making a three-point turn and heading back the way she had come.

That night, staying at Zoe's house, she dreamed of her son. She was walking along a narrow isthmus that ran between two seas. To either side of her waves reared up, vast and glassy and threatening. She was carrying Matthew in her arms, but he was a small child again, two or three years old, flaxen-haired, light, fragile. She must bear his weight, and yet the waves to either side of her were surging higher and higher and the water was slopping over the narrow walkway, and though she tried to hold on to him, his clothes had become sodden and slippery and he slid out of her arms into the sea.

Matthew left the site earlier than usual, at seven, before the light had gone, and drove out of the city across the Golden Gate Bridge. Reaching Marin County, he headed up through the hilly scrub towards the small town of Sausalito. He parked his car on the strip of land between the road and the harbour, gathered up the bouquet of flowers from the passenger seat, and made his way along the track to the boat on which he lived.

Susan was in the galley. When she saw the bunch of lilies and orchids, she said, 'Matt, you shouldn't have, it's your birthday.' Then she stood on tiptoes and kissed him.

His wife was black-haired, brown-eyed and beautiful. She was also tiny, five foot three in heels. Her real name was Xiu Mei, but she preferred to be called Susan. 'Easier for people to say. Susan is a regular American name.' Matthew preferred Xiu

Mei, which meant beautiful plum. She taught English at an elementary school in Mission, and they had met four years before when his construction business had been in its infancy and he had had to turn his hand to anything. Susan had called out a builder to repair the leaking faucet in her tiny apartment; Matthew had fixed the faucet and then had asked her out for dinner. It still made him go cold, to think that her small, tapered finger might have skimmed past 'Reddaway' in the phone book and come to rest on Richardson, perhaps, or Rutkowski.

She said, 'They're so beautiful. Thank you, Matt. How was your day?'

'The plastering's done, we're waiting for the window frames. I'll have to give Gertler a nudge. That smells wonderful.' Peering into a pan, he picked out a shrimp and ate it.

'I've cooked all your favourite things.'

'Clams with black bean sauce?'

'Naturally. And roast squab.'

'I love you for ever.'

'Cupboard love,' she said, and laughed.

They dined on the top deck. Before he had met Susan, Matthew had sometimes, on humid nights, slung a hammock on the upper deck of the old vessel so that he could sleep outside. It had been Susan who had thought of putting a table and wicker chairs up there so that they could eat in the open air. She had decorated the area with pot plants and tonight had lit candles.

After dinner, she gave him his birthday present, a checked shirt and a sweater from Macy's, and some thick socks, because they liked to hike the trails through Muir Woods. It was a warm night, so they remained outside, cuddling up together on the wicker seat. Her hair was perfumed by the lily she had tucked behind one ear.

'Matt,' she said. 'I've another birthday present for you.' She had swivelled round to face him.

'What's that?'

'Well . . . I went to the doctor this morning, and he told me I'm going to have a baby.'

'Sweetheart . . .' He straightened. 'You're sure?'

'Completely.' Her eyes were shining. 'Isn't it wonderful? Are you pleased?'

'Pleased?' he said. '*Pleased?*' He swung her into his lap, and then worried that he was hugging her too tight. But she only laughed, and they kissed and talked about due dates – mid January – and whether it would be a boy or a girl.

Susan said, 'I'd like to tell my mother tomorrow.'

Susan's father, who had died fifteen years before, when she had been twenty, had been of Scottish origin. Her mother was Chinese and lived in the city, in Chinatown. The remainder of Susan's large family was scattered throughout San Francisco.

Matthew said, 'I'll drive us over there.'

'Thank you, darling.' She kissed him.

His gaze scanned the boat. 'We'll have to move into a proper house.'

'I like it here.'

'If he's anything like I was, we'd be constantly fishing him out of the ocean.'

'Were you an adventurous little boy?'

'I was a daredevil; I was always in trouble. Yes, I shall build us a house.'

'I'd like that, Matt.' She snuggled back in his arms.

'Most of my childhood, my parents were building our house.' He laughed. 'I was a damn nuisance, I expect, poking my nose into everything, running across the concrete before it was dry, getting in the way. But I was fascinated by it.'

'That's why you work in construction. You've never forgotten. Was it a beautiful house?'

'Very.'

'Was this the house that burned down?'

'Yes.'

Early on in their relationship, Matthew had told Susan everything. About his discovery that Melissa was his sister, not his cousin, and the disastrous consequences of his subsequent resentment and anger towards his father on that January morning when he had seen Bonnie Gresham in Dartmouth. And of his shame and guilt about what had happened to his father and to Rosindell, and his need to leave England, to make a permanent break.

He heard Susan say, 'When our baby is born, will you tell your parents?'

It was the closest she had ever come to questioning his decision. He knew that it troubled her that he had cut himself off from his family, and he had always been grateful to her for not pushing him to make contact.

'Beautiful plum,' he said softly. 'I can't.'

'Sometimes you seem unrooted, Matt. It worries me.'

'We're married. That's pretty rooted.'

'I want our child to have grandparents. Grandparents are important.'

'They wouldn't want to hear from me. Not after all this time.'

Susan frowned. 'Is that what you believe? If it was our child' – and she placed a hand on her flat belly – 'I'm sure that would be the worst thing in the world, to lose him like that. I'm sure that whatever he had done, no matter how we'd fought or how much distance lay between us, we would want to know that he was alive and well. It would break our hearts if he turned away from us.'

When Matthew woke, it was still dark. Through the porthole he could see the lights of the ships that dotted the bay. In his arms, Susan slept soundly. Knowing that he would not go back to sleep, Matthew gently disentangled himself from her, pulled on trousers and a shirt and left the room.

Contentment and hard physical labour in the open air had cured him of the habit of waking in the small hours, and it only happened occasionally now, when he had things on his mind. He made himself coffee and found a notepad and pencil, then took them to the top deck. The air was warm and silky and perfumed by the lilies and hoya that Susan had planted in pots. Opening the notebook, he began to sketch out ideas for the house he would build. For some time he had had his eye on a piece of land up in the hills above Sausalito, with a view of the bay.

But he couldn't concentrate, and after a while he put down the pencil. He was gripped by an odd mixture of elation and unease. The elation was because of the baby, of course; he and Susan had talked of having children, and it was wonderful to know that the first was on the way. The unease came from a nagging sense of having left something important undone. He ran through in his head the progress of the house his construction company was building in West Portal. The work was a couple of weeks behind schedule, but that was nothing to worry about. All the paperwork had been cleared, the appropriate forms sent to the appropriate city departments, and he was having no problems with the unions.

Matthew had been at his lowest ebb when he had first arrived in San Francisco seven years ago. After leaving England in the early summer of 1949 he had spent a couple of years as a deckhand on merchant ships. He had travelled in the Far East and to Australia and through the Pacific. The life had suited him. You worked when you were on board ship, you drank and whored when you put into port.

He had jumped ship one day after his cargo boat had docked in Newfoundland. After a few months in Canada, he had stowed away on a truck across the American border, emerging in the hills and forests of Montana. During the following three years, some of which he could not remember, some of which he wished he could not remember, he had been rootless. His existence had been hand to mouth and he had kept himself fed by labouring on farms and building sites or waiting in diners. There were ways of cutting yourself off from your thoughts, and he had tried most of them. Falling in with a hip young crowd in New York, he had dabbled in drugs. He had lived off a well-connected older woman in Chicago for six months, had flown stunt planes for a little travelling fair until he was fired for drunkenness, and had hitched through the dusty plains of the Midwest, sleeping rough. He had pumped gas, picked oranges, mopped floors, and served beers in redneck bars off state highways.

He had got into fights and cooled off in police cells. He had, when he was very hungry, stolen food.

He had fallen ill, a niggling pain in the guts that he had put down to too much booze and not enough to eat. Suffocated by the huge land mass of the Midwest, he had travelled through the baking ochre heat of the desert to the Pacific Coast. He had felt relieved to reach the sea and had walked across the white sand at Santa Barbara and waded in the surf. He had travelled north, to San Francisco. He drank to stifle the pain in his belly, which was starting to frighten him. He had no money, and his clothes were filthy. At night he bedded down on the sidewalk near the docks with half a dozen other hobos – black, white, old, young, several of them ex-servicemen and all in their different ways lost. Some made fortresses of cardboard boxes; others squabbled over the ownership of a stinking blanket or a lice-ridden coat. Matthew dreamed of Rosindell. When he woke in the morning and smelled the sea and opened his eyes to the shimmering purity of the light, he thought for a moment that he was at home. He thought of plunging into the ocean, such a short distance away, falling down, down, his mind first clearing, then becoming numb.

There was a day when he couldn't get up. The others moved

on, but Matthew had remained on the sidewalk, doubled up, his arms clutching his belly. A cop, Irish and kindly, asked him what was wrong. An ambulance was sent for and he was transported to a public hospital, where he was operated on later that day. His appendix had burst and he was dangerously ill for three weeks. Once he began to recover, his only visitor was the Irish policeman, who gave him a bunch of grapes and a piece of paper on which was printed the name of his brother, who owned a construction company in the city. Matthew's well-connected Chicagoan lover had, during their early, amorous days, managed to obtain for him a green card, so six weeks later Matthew started work for Kevin O'Sullivan. He stopped drinking and smoking and hard physical labour brought him back to health. He learned every aspect of the building trade during his three years with O'Sullivan, and was often invited to Sunday lunch by Kevin or his brother Michael. The decision to start up on his own had been taken with Kevin's blessing; the Irishman still sometimes sent work his way.

And then, Susan. Matthew had known from the beginning that Susan was his miracle, his second chance. He loved her for her gentleness, grace and beauty. She had made him a better person. He felt privileged that her family had accepted him without question and had made him one of them.

When our baby is born, will you tell your parents?

Leaning his forearms on the handrail and looking out to the bay as the coming of dawn brightened the sky, Matthew knew what was troubling him. He would have done anything for Susan. Anything except this one impossible thing.

A fortnight later, they were ready to fit the window frames in the house in West Portal. Traffic was slow that morning over the Golden Gate Bridge, but Matthew reached the site before eight o'clock. Gertler was already parked on Taraval Street. Matthew helped him unload the truck and they spent the day fitting the frames. The house was Spanish in style, with a high-ceilinged front room with large picture windows looking out over the road. By late afternoon, with the windows in place, it was looking, from the outside at least, as if you could live in it.

On his way home, Matthew took a detour and drove up to the half-acre of land for sale, high up on the hill above Sausalito. From that vantage point you could see the boats, some of them relics from the wartime dockyards, clustered like insects on the water's edge.

A tall Monterey pine stood beside the entrance to the plot, its bright green needles whispering in the evening breeze. The site had once been part of the neighbouring garden. A tumbledown shed was festooned with nasturtiums and magenta-coloured bougainvillea and, in a dark gully, Matthew spied the paper-white cones of calla lilies. He felt this to be a good omen. Callas were Susan's favourite flowers.

He paced the boundaries, taking measurements and making notes. The site sloped steeply and there was the gully, through which in wet weather water would run. But there was room enough for a good-sized house and the view was breathtaking. If he purchased the land, it would take every spare penny he owned, and then some. But he could already see in his mind's eye the house he would build there – raised up on stilts so that it almost seemed to float in the air, with two or three terraces looking out over the bay. The back of his neck prickled with excitement.

Since his birthday, Susan had not referred to their conversation about his family, but it had remained at the back of his mind, to be chewed over in quiet moments. Matthew wondered whether his parents had felt as he did when they had begun to rebuild Rosindell, whether they too had experienced that rush of anticipation at the thought of creating something new and wonderful. A house could shape your life. It could allow you to have a better life.

He understood why, after so long, Susan had asked him to contact his parents. It was because his refusal to do so would affect not just him, but also their child. *Grandparents are important.* As a boy, he had sometimes felt short-changed by having only two grandparents rather than the standard four. His child would have only one grandmother. Would he, too, feel a little isolated, a little unlucky? Would he feel *unrooted*?

And what, in time, would he tell his son or daughter? Would he lie to him – would he fabricate a past for himself, tell his child that his parents had died long ago? That would be the easiest solution, but he knew already that he would not be able to do it. The lies and omissions of his own parents had distorted his life. But if he were to tell the truth, that he had sailed away from the country of his birth more than a decade ago and had never looked back, what message would that give? That it was all right to walk away from family – that cutting yourself off from your mother and father was not such a terrible thing to do?

Returning to his truck, Matthew drove down the steep, sloping streets to the houseboat. The following morning he made for his office in Embarcadero, a cramped cubbyhole containing a battered metal filing cabinet, a desk, a typewriter on which Matthew one-fingeredly tapped out invoices, and a phone.

He estimated that it was around tea-time in England. He had bought a strong coffee from a nearby café to jolt his mind into gear. He found himself recalling sitting in the dispersal hut at Manston, waiting for the phone to ring. 'Get on with it, Reddaway,' he muttered to himself.

He took a scalding mouthful of coffee, picked up the phone and dialled the operator, asking to be connected to his mother's house in Oxford. During the long wait, during the whirrs and clicks and muffled voices on the line, he asked himself what was the worst that could happen. His mother might refuse to speak to him. She might put the phone down on him. But at least he'd be able to tell Susan that he'd tried.

The operator said, 'Putting you through, sir.'

'Oxford 791.' A woman's voice. 'Mrs Carstairs speaking.'

Startled, Matthew said, 'I was hoping to speak to Mrs Reddaway – I mean, to Mrs Godwin.'

'There's no Mrs Godwin here.' The tone short, displeased.

'She was living in the house in the late forties.'

'I'm afraid I can't help you. Was she the lady who died?'

The lady who died. Matthew said, 'I'm sorry to have troubled you,' and ended the call.

He sat for a moment, his heart hammering, staring out of the window at the network of cranes and pulleys spread along the docks. He slung the last of the coffee down his throat and then left the office, locking the door behind him.

Susan had a way of worming things out of him. There was that cliché about reading someone like a book, but his moods and preoccupations were written in three-inch-high typeface as far as Susan was concerned.

Matthew was showing her round the plot in Sausalito when she said, 'If it's too expensive, we can wait, Matt. We'll manage where we are or we can rent a house somewhere.'

'It's not too expensive,' he said. 'I mean, it'll be tight, but it's okay.'

'So it's not the land you're worried about?'

'No.'

'Matt?'

'I tried to phone my mother.'

Susan squeezed his hand. 'What happened? What did she say?'

Matthew was aware of the rustle of the breeze in the pine branches, and their resiny scent, which momentarily recalled to him the cliff path at Rosindell. 'She wasn't there,' he explained.

411

'My mother doesn't live there any more. The woman who answered told me she'd died. At least, I thought at the time that was what she'd said, but now I'm not so sure.'

'What did she say exactly?'

'She said, "Was she the lady who died?"' He peered at Susan, waiting for her response.

'It doesn't sound as though she was sure.'

'It doesn't, does it?'

'When you thought your mother was dead, how did you feel?'

Well, he thought, that's the thing. 'Shocked, to begin with. Disbelieving. And then a little bit relieved. I'm ashamed of that. But I thought it meant I wouldn't be able to let her down any more. I wouldn't be her golden boy and never living up to it. I wouldn't have to face telling her all the lousy things I'd done and see the expression in her eyes. But then I felt so sad. I wished I'd picked up the phone years ago and I thought what a fool I'd been, wasting all those years, not having the guts to find out whether she still thought of me at all.'

Susan had brought bottles of soda and they drank them sitting on the front step of the hut. Matthew said, 'If she's moved away, I've no idea how to find her. She and Dad don't talk any more, so there's no point phoning him, even if I could face it, which I can't, and even if he's gone back to Rosindell. And I can't see how he could have, because the place was a ruin.'

Susan said, 'Matt, you have a sister, don't you?'

Zoe was woken by a band of sunlight falling through a gap in the curtains on to the pillow. Light striped the white percale, and she discovered that she felt happy. A week ago she had picked Stephen up from school. The summer, with picnics, cinema trips and a seaside holiday on the Isle of Wight, lay in front of them.

She had not heard from Ben since he had walked out of her house. In the weeks that had passed since then, her emotions − guilt, regret, shame, embarrassment, a desire to see him and a dread of seeing him − had enmeshed her, tying her up in their complicated knots.

But today felt different. She glanced at the clock; it was almost seven, so she rose and went downstairs to make herself breakfast. As she waited for the toast to brown, it seemed to her that she had always been dogged by a sense of restraint. Only occasionally had she overcome her caution − that night in the Blitz with Reuben, and the evening in the pub when she had met Russ. Ben had once suggested that she was attracted to untidy people, but he had been wrong. What she needed was the company of the carefree, the open and optimistic, who could balance out the darker side of her nature and coax her out of her anxieties.

She unlocked the back door and, propping her plate of toast on the mug of tea, went outside. The sky was a flawless blue, promising another hot day. The garden was large for a city house. Russ had been a keen gardener and they had tamed it together.

The trouble was, she thought, as she sat down on Stephen's swing and rocked gently to and fro, she didn't know if she could do it again. Be carefree, latch on to someone else's optimism. *Cheer up, the worst may never happen,* people said, but it had happened, it had happened to her six years ago, and it had seemed at the time to justify every fear she had ever had, every single flicker of foreboding. They all had their ghosts, and hers would forever be contained within the night that Russ had died. You couldn't forget, and she had learned that neither could you arm yourself against fate. You might think you could fortify yourself with ritual, you might tidy your house and your life to perfection, but fate could still creep up on you in the worst possible way.

Yet she must keep going out into the world, however much she might sometimes prefer to hide from it, for Stephen's sake. Stephen was quiet and thoughtful and clever, and though Zoe might have chosen him to inherit Russ's sociable, outgoing nature, she knew he had not. But how to change — how to make some sort of pact with the world that would allow her to move on? And should that change include Ben? Many times since that extraordinary night she had thought of phoning him, but had held back. She might be capable of living with no man other than Russ. Ben might have regretted what had taken place; that might be why she had not heard from him. She felt no certainty about Ben. With Russ, from that first night in the pub, she had felt sure.

She looked up: Stephen was padding out into the garden in pyjamas and bare feet. His dark hair was tousled, his eyes blurred with sleep. He permitted her to kiss him.

'I'm making a chart,' he said. 'It's going to have one thousand, six hundred and eighty squares on it. That's all the days I have to be at school for the rest of my life.'

'Darling, if you don't like that school, then we'll find another one.'

'It's all right, Mum. It's a rotten dump, but I don't *hate* it.' He shot her a glance to see whether she'd tell him off for the slang, and then added cheerfully, 'It's going to be a humongous chart.'

Zoe made breakfast while Stephen dressed. The kitchen filled with the aroma of frying bacon. When Stephen was away at school, she had an apple and perhaps a piece of toast for breakfast. It felt celebratory to be cooking bacon, and she didn't mind about the spatters on the hob.

There was the thud of mail falling through the letter box. Stephen dashed off to collect it. Zoe served the bacon and eggs, then sat down and leafed through it. Bill, bill, a brochure from a supplier, a postcard from a friend, an airmail letter, another bill.

She looked at the airmail letter again. The handwriting was familiar; she froze. Then she turned the flimsy blue paper over to read the name and address on the other side.

She called her mother's house, but there was no answer, and she remembered that it was one of her Devon weekends. Her father didn't have a telephone, never having replaced the phone lines destroyed by the fire. She couldn't face calling her grandmother, who in old age had become very deaf.

In the end, she phoned Ben. Ben's friend Griffiths, a mild man given to sudden, unpredictable rages, answered. There was a wait while he fetched Ben.

'Hello?' Ben's voice.

'Ben, it's Zoe.'

A pause, and then he said, his tone neutral, 'How are you?'

'I've had a letter from Matthew.' She heard the shock in her own voice. 'He's alive and well and living in California.'

'That's wonderful.'

She felt his resistance through the phone line. She had hesitated too long; there it was again, her fatal lack of courage.

But she knew that she must take a leap into the dark, no matter what phantoms lurked behind the door, and she said, 'Ben, I have to go to Rosindell, I have to tell my parents about Matthew. Would you come with me?'

'Why, Zoe? What for? To drive the car — to keep you going when you're feeling blue?'

'Yes, all that.'

'Not sure it's enough, you see.'

She took a deep breath. 'It's not just to share the driving. Or because you keep me going when I feel low — though you do, in such a wonderful way. It's because I need you. I need you to come with me to Rosindell. You did once before, remember? And I need you again now, and what I've realised is that no one else will do.' She twisted the telephone wire round her fingers. 'Please come with me, Ben. Please.'

He took the train from Peckham to Kingston. Zoe picked him up from the railway station, and from there they headed on to the Guildford road. Stephen's presence, in the back seat of the car, curtailed the conversation that she knew they must eventually have. She described Matthew's letter to him – *married*, and a baby on the way! A building firm, and he's planning to build his own house! – but the thought of her brother, ten years older, ten years absent from them all, defeated her, and after a while she fell silent.

At Winchester, they stopped for coffee and sandwiches. Then they drove on, Ben at the wheel. He had not forgiven her, she thought, but the remnants of the optimism with which she had started this day clung to her, and she thought that they would work something out. As they sped through woodland where dusty dark green trees sagged in the heat, and as the high chalk plains of the south-west rose against a burning blue sky, there was a sense of homecoming.

Another stop by the roadside, the coffee muddy now and the orange squash lukewarm. Zoe drove again, and Ben and Stephen car-spotted as they crossed the Devon border. After the aridity of London, the lushness overwhelmed her: the knee-high grass and the buttercups in the meadows. What was it in this beauty that produced in her such apprehension? Was it their proximity to Rosindell, that place of magic and terror, of childhood protection and adult treachery? Five months had passed since she had last been there. She knew that her father missed her, and still she stayed away.

Another stop: Stephen felt sick. Zoe dropped eau de cologne on to her handkerchief from the little bottle she kept in her handbag and bathed his forehead, then confiscated his pencil and notebook. 'Mum,' he protested, at both these things.

Back in the car, all the windows open, Ben driving slowly

416

through the dizzying, narrow lanes, Zoe said, 'I don't know how to tell them. I'm afraid Dad'll have heart failure.'

'Gently. Give them time.' Ben cranked round to Stephen in the back. 'Not too long now, kid.'

'I'll make sure they're sitting down. Maybe a glass of whisky.' She was folding Matthew's airmail letter into a tight square, each fold making it smaller.

Ben put his hand over hers. 'It'll be fine,' he said. 'I promise you, it'll be fine.'

'I often think that it was the war that shaped us,' Devlin said to Esme.

They had planted the shrubs round the newly built terrace, she prising them out of their pots, he digging the holes, his shirt glued to his back in the heat. Then they had gone to the house and fetched a tray of lemonade and biscuits, and – a whim of Devlin's, this – the portable gramophone and a handful of records.

He played 'Always True to You in My Fashion'. He said, 'What I mean is that it was *only* the war that shaped us. That it made us what we were, and that afterwards we were no longer capable of change. An entire generation ruined, one way and another. All those men – Eddie Hutchinson, and Richards and Vickers, in my platoon, and so many others, that chap Sheridan at the nightclub – all dead, so long ago. And for what? For another war, twenty years later. The mud of Flanders *made* Hitler. It created the monster.'

Esme said, 'You survived.'

'A part of me survived. Perhaps not the best part.'

'You think too much,' she said gently. 'You always did.'

'Even Camilla . . . I wonder, sometimes, how different she might have been, if she'd grown up at some other time. She once told me that when the war was over, she would just have fun.'

'And she did,' said Esme drily. 'For rather a long time. My

417

mother had a letter from her. She was asking for money. Apparently she's living in Mexico now, in some sort of religious community.'

Devlin snorted. The music rattled on, singing of love and betrayal. Esme was wearing a blue skirt, rather muddy round the hem, a white shirt and ragged plimsolls, her customary garb for gardening. Her hair, which had turned from amber to silver a long time ago, tumbled out of the combs and clips that were supposed to contain it. He thought how beautiful she looked.

He said, 'I've always loved you, you know.'

She smiled. 'Not always. Not when I was a silly little girl, getting lost on the road to Rosindell.'

'Perhaps even then.'

The song had finished; he took the record off and chose another one. The opening chords of 'Every Time We Say Goodbye' shimmered in the cool green shade. He put down his glass and held out his hand to her.

'Devlin,' she said.

'One last dance. To make up for all the dances we missed.'

'We were such fools, weren't we?' she said, as she rose and he took her in his arms.

When he closed his eyes, it was as if they were young again, dancing on the terrace at Rosindell, and he breathed in, along with the scent of the pines and the sea, the perfume of roses. The years fled away and they were together again, he and Esme, and the future was ahead of them, golden and full of promise.

The sound of a boy's high-pitched voice made them both pause and look up.

'It's Stephen,' said Esme.

Stephen was leaping over the rocks and plants that bordered the stream, running towards them. Not far behind him was Zoe, also hurrying.

'Goodness,' said Esme. 'She'll think we're being undignified, you and I, Devlin. Did you invite them?'

418

'Granny, Grandad!' cried Stephen.

'Mum!' Zoe called out. 'I've had a letter!' Devlin saw that she was clutching something in her hand, a pale blue scrap of paper that she waved like a banner. 'I've had a letter from Matthew!'

That evening, in the cove.

He had said, 'I'm thinking of going back to Malta,' and she had said, 'Ben, you can't.' And a prickly argument had ensued as they had paced up and down the beach.

She would never think him good enough for her. What rubbish, she said, it was the other way round, and she found it hard to see why he would put up with her.

Well, he said, if you put it like that . . . but she saw the glint of humour in his eyes, and she gave him a little push and he pretended to fall into the sea.

'But we have always rather *grated*,' she said. 'You have to admit.'

'I don't think so.'

'You see, we can't even agree about that.'

'A lot of the time I'm in awe of you.'

'*Ben.*'

'It's true. You run your business, you've brought up that terrific kid. You managed to keep going through what must have been the worst thing in the world. Why wouldn't I be in awe of you?'

'I'm fussy. I'm irritable. Sometimes I'm not brave enough.'

'Rot. You're the bravest person I know. No wonder with you there was always someone else. I suppose I got used to it. That political fellow, Clive—'

'Cleeve.'

'Then Russ.'

'I'll never not love Russ.' She was tired; it had been a long, exhausting – and wonderful – day, and she was becoming ungrammatical.

'He was your husband. He was the father of your son. Of course you'll always love him.'

She had slid her sandals off and was walking where the sand gleamed, polished by the shallow waves. Each wave, slowed by the heavy heat that had transfixed Rosindell that day, left a lacy fringe of foam.

She said, 'I hate to think of you just walking away again. Going off to one of your islands for years and forgetting about me.'

'Come with me, then.'

'Ben, I can't.'

'Why not?'

'Stephen. The shops . . . my house . . .'

'Stephen would love it. He'd be seeing history. You could sell the shops and let the house out.'

'Camping,' she said, ticking off on her fingers. 'No proper bathroom. I suppose you'd expect me to wash my clothes in a stream.'

'Just an idea.'

'It's a terrible idea,' she said bluntly. 'If you think I'm the sort of person who could live in a tent, then you don't know me as well as you think you do.'

'Okay then, forget the tent.'

They had reached the rocks that fringed the arms of the bay. Zoe sat down on a rock and Ben sat beside her. He said, 'That day, a month ago, when you stopped your car and stuck your head out and called out to me, I was happy again. It had been a tough few months, but just then I was happy again. But I realised that you didn't feel the same. That for you I was an interruption to your routine.'

There was an element of truth in what he had said. She tried to explain. 'I like routines. Routines suit me. They make me feel safe.'

'You *are* safe.'

'Am I?' She twisted her mouth to one side. She could have

420

cried; she shoved her sunglasses further up her nose so he couldn't see. 'If you tell me that Russ would have wanted me to be happy, I'll throttle you.'

'Russ would have wanted to live. But he didn't, the poor bastard.'

She remembered how, as a child, she had liked to swim across the cove, and how there had always come a point, halfway between the safety of the shore and the islet, when she had felt frightened, knowing that she had a long way to go and was running out of steam.

She whispered, 'So I've got to live for him?'

'You might as well, mightn't you?'

'But what if something awful happens?'

'Well, it might,' he conceded. 'But if it did, wouldn't it be better to face it with someone at your side?' And then, before she could respond, he went on, 'You see, I've loved you from the first moment I saw you.'

'Not the first moment,' she said, remembering. 'Surely not. I was horrible to you.'

His eyes crinkled. 'You were, weren't you? I offered you a coffee and you gave me the brush-off. Stalked off, nose in the air. But it was as if you'd left an after-image. You know how, when you look at something very bright and there seems to be a trace of it left behind. And then you told me about Clive—'

'Cleeve.'

'It was obvious to me the guy was an idiot. And finally you gave him the heave-ho, so I hung around, hoping. Eventually I realised that it was me who was the idiot.'

'Was that why you didn't come to the wedding?'

'I'm not a masochist, Zoe. I got the message.'

'I'm not sure I can face looking after someone else again. Stephen's enough. I worry about him all the time.'

'Couldn't we look after each other?'

'And you're so untidy!'

'I'll change. Anyway, you're far too fussy about that sort of thing. What's wrong with a bit of mess?'

'And what about your work? You're away most of the time.'

'I wasn't suggesting marriage,' he said, and she, embarrassed, looked away.

'Of course not.'

'Zoe, I know that for you, marriage was Russ. You and me, we have to be different. But maybe we don't have to be less.'

She gave a gasp. 'I thought I'd got my life under control again! And now Matthew, and you, all this!'

'I know.' She linked her hands round his neck as they kissed. 'It's a bitch, isn't it?'

Chapter Twenty

1962

She saw her first in the window of Liberty, in the October of 1962, her reflection shifting in the glass. There was a moment when she thought she might walk away, but it passed, and she turned.

'Camilla? It is you, isn't it?'

'I knew you straight away,' said Camilla. 'I followed you all the way down Regent Street.'

There was an awkward kiss – it seemed necessary: sisters, who had not seen each other for more than thirty years – and then Esme found herself saying, 'Have you time for a coffee?'

'A drink would go down frightfully well.'

They went to the Bricklayer's Arms, just behind Liberty. Camilla ordered a gin and tonic and Esme a lemonade. Camilla made a show of looking in her handbag. 'I seem to have come out without my purse.'

'Let me,' said Esme.

'Thank you, darling.' This murmured in Camilla's old, familiar purr.

Camilla offered a packet of cigarettes to Esme, who shook her head. Camilla lit one, inhaled, and blew out a thin column of smoke. 'You look well,' she said.

'Thank you.' Because she had always found it hard to lie,

and so could not say the same to Camilla, she filled in the space by adding, 'Country life agrees with me.'

'Where are you living?'

'A little village in Berkshire. I thought you were in Mexico.'

'Mexico? Not for ages. Too divine, but some of the people there were rather unkind to one. I went back to Los Angeles for a while, but then I was rather unwell.'

'I'm sorry to hear that,' said Esme politely.

Camilla waved her cigarette. 'I'm fighting fit now. Let me freshen our drinks.' She waved her hand at the barman. Esme took a ten-shilling note out of her purse. 'That's only a dribble, darling,' Camilla was saying to the barman. 'Two fingers of gin. Something that hits the spot.'

Camilla's long white coat, with its collar and cuffs of dense blond fur, looked, Esme thought, overly warm for a mild autumn day. The fur cuffs, grubby and matted, hung over her gloved hands in greyish tendrils. Beneath her coat Camilla was wearing a low-cut black dress. Her hat, close-brimmed and black in the style of the 1920s, did not flatter a complexion that had darkened and seamed in the American sun.

Camilla must have caught her looking, because she gave a raucous laugh. 'What a pair of old crones we've become! I have to say, Esme, that you've weathered a great deal better than I have.' She raised her glass. 'Chin-chin. Virtue is its own reward, they say.'

'Though I've never felt that to be true,' said Esme.

Camilla shrugged. 'I wouldn't know. How are the family?'

'Mummy's rather frail now and terribly deaf. Tom keeps an eye on her and I go to Dartmouth once a fortnight.'

'So dutiful.'

Esme felt a flicker of distaste.

'I imagine Tom fat and florid, playing golf,' said Camilla.

This description was, in fact, quite accurate, but, defending her brother, Esme said, 'He still sails. He taught his three boys to sail. He's commodore of the yacht club.'

Camilla cackled. 'Good Lord, how dreary. What about your girl, that sweet, dark little thing?'

It had been years since Zoe had been a sweet, dark little thing, but Esme said doggedly, 'Zoe's very well. And my grandson, Stephen, is twelve years old, and very clever, doing marvellously at school.'

'And . . .' Camilla flapped her fingers. 'Your son . . .'

'Matthew? He has his own construction company in San Francisco.'

Camilla's thin, arched eyebrows raised. 'So he went to America, then, like me?'

No, thought Esme, nothing like you, Matthew has nothing at all in common with you. She said, 'He's married and has a little girl, and there's another baby on the way.'

'Do you go there often?'

Esme shook her head. 'Just the thought of flying terrifies me.' This was true. She could not imagine finding the courage to step on the plane. Would she panic, thousands of feet up in the air? It was unreasonable of Matthew to expect her to travel all that way.

'Then why not sail?' Camilla was suggesting. 'I remember when I first sailed to New York. It was on board the *Queen Mary*, back in 'thirty-six – or was it 'thirty-seven? Peggy Cavendish bought us both first-class tickets.' She chortled. 'We shared a cabin, it was such a hoot. We had a bun fight in the Starlight Club, made such a frightful mess . . .'

Camilla had not only aged, thought Esme spitefully, as her sister's reverie on times past lengthened; she had become a bore. When she paused to swallow the last of her gin, Esme said:

'You know I can't sail. I was always a bad sailor.'

And Camilla seemed to latch on to a truth, and said, 'Perhaps you feel Matthew should visit you here.'

'I have my responsibilities,' said Esme coldly. 'Mother and Zoe, and Devlin hasn't been well.'

It felt strange saying Devlin's name in front of Camilla. But then, all that had been so long ago.

'Children are thankless,' said Camilla. 'Melissa hardly ever comes to see me.'

'How is she?'

'Oh, a busy little bee as always, writing books or something.'

'She has a daughter, doesn't she?'

'Yes. They hardly ever visit. Most of the time I'm on my own, except for that dreadful Jane Fox. She will insist on hanging around, even though I've tried to dismiss her hundreds of times. She's a bad-tempered cow and she steals my things.'

'Surely not.'

Camilla's bloodshot blue eyes fixed on her. 'You can't trust servants. It's all yes madam and no madam, and then they spit on you behind your back.'

Esme began to wonder whether Camilla was entirely sane. She was going senile, perhaps. Or maybe – her sister was ordering her third gin and tonic – she had pickled her brain with alcohol.

She glanced at her watch. 'I have to head off, I'm afraid. I'm meeting some friends for lunch.'

'Toodle-oo, then. We must, we simply must keep in touch.' Camilla hunted in her handbag, drew out a compact and lipstick, and began to scrub at her face. Drifts of powder scattered on to the fur collar of her coat.

'I'm rather short of cash,' she said, pausing as she drew a scarlet Cupid's bow on her mouth. 'Some wretched muddle with my American bank account. You couldn't lend me a few bob, could you, Esme?'

I would pay a hundred pounds, Esme thought, never to see you again, never to hear your voice again, with its self-pitying whine, outdated slang and American drawl.

She took two ten-pound notes from her purse and handed them to Camilla, who tucked them into her handbag. Then they parted, and with a feeling of immense relief, Esme headed out to the Tate, to meet her friends for lunch and an exhibition.

Devlin had been prevented from taking his walk in the afternoon by a visit from the doctor and a phone call from Zoe, so he started on his circuit in the early evening.

He felt the coming storm in the air as he headed across the fields. A slab of low, dark cloud was suspended over the sea, and where the rain fell, the sky shimmered silver and charcoal. Since he had left Rosindell the wind had whipped up and was now swirling and stirring the grass in the field on which stood the octagonal tower. The structure had been built during the previous century to aid ships navigating the Channel. As he crossed the field, Devlin found himself avoiding stepping in the tower's black shadow. He remembered that when he had been a boy, he had been afraid of this place; that its empty, echoing interior had frightened him.

The weather was deteriorating, so he quickened his pace. Reaching the cliffs, he stood for a while watching the sea gather and hurl itself at the rocks below. He saw how its bruised surface, laced with white foam, rose into peaks and dipped into troughs as the wind sometimes hollowed out and sometimes whipped up the water, and he heard a booming sound, like a great bell being tolled beneath the waves, echoing off the cliffs; a dense, clamorous noise that brought to mind the artillery barrages on the Western Front. A gust of wind screaming over the headland threatened to topple him over the cliff, so he walked on.

Often, taking this walk, he would imagine that Esme was beside him. He felt her presence vividly now, could almost, as he turned his head, see her long amber hair, darkened by the rain, flaring back from her face as the wind buffeted her. He reached

427

out his hand, as if to take hers. 'I'm *soaked!*' he imagined her crying, and heard her laughter.

In the cove, needles of rock pierced a sea that was now and then the olive green of bottle glass. As he watched, a succession of waves built up into one great wave that cast itself on to the shore, seeming to pit itself against the solidity of the land. Esme was still beside him, peering over the cliff with him, watching the waves. When he closed his eyes, he was sure that he detected it, the scent she always wore.

He took the path beneath the trees. Heavy drops of rain tumbled from the pines and oaks. The latch on the gate was stiff, and as he gave it a shove, he felt a sharp stab of pain in his chest. He leaned against the gate, his hand to his heart, breathing shallowly. *Not far to go now*, he heard her say. Ahead of him, he glimpsed the terrace they had made two summers ago. They had sat there on her last visit, talking of this and that. It remained miraculous to him that during these two years, at his age and after so long and bitter a separation, they should have rediscovered love.

The pain had retreated, but Devlin knew that it was still there, poised like a predator, waiting to leap and tear at him. He was soaked now; if he caught a cold, Esme would scold him for going out on such a night. Yes: better now. He walked on.

But as he limped down the valley towards the house, agony gathered like the storm clouds, obliterating his awareness of the ache in his leg. He saw Rosindell, deformed and damaged like himself, rising black against an iron-grey sky, and he put his face up to the rain, hoping the cold needles might revive him.

The house was only a few hundred yards away, but he knew now that he would never reach it. He fell to his knees on the wet lawn, his hands clawing at the soil. *Esme*, he murmured, and he seemed to feel her consoling touch as he closed his eyes.

* * *

An ending.

Esme is at the cottage hospital in Dartmouth, where they took Devlin after Mrs Adams found him unconscious in the garden at Rosindell. She holds his hand as his breath spaces itself out, a longer and longer gap between each filling of the lungs, during which she waits, holding her own breath. Eventually he does not breathe again, and she presses her lips against his hand and then bends forward, as if unable to bear the weight of all the memories, resting her forehead against his arm while she weeps.

She realises that she thought him elemental, as indestructible as the sea and rock and sky that nurtured him.

Zoe arrives, and they fall into each other's arms. She is thankful now of Zoe's neat, efficient nature, because it is Zoe who fills in the forms and makes the phone calls while she sits on a hard wooden chair in the little room that the hospital puts aside for the bereaved. And anyway, it is Zoe who is Devlin's next of kin, not her. She has no claim on him.

Zoe insists her mother has something to eat. Esme, who cannot remember when she last ate and does not think she will ever want to eat again, allows her daughter to lead her out of the hospital and along South Town to St Petrox Lodge. But every step contains a memory as sharp as a knife: the hairdresser who bobbed her hair when they quarrelled; the ferry and all the journeys they took together; and this road. Nineteen years old, she looked out of her bedroom window and saw him. And so her story began.

Her mother has gone to bed, thank God. Esme sits at the kitchen table while Zoe makes toasted cheese. But when the plate is put in front of her, she covers her face with her hands and sobs.

When, at last, her tears run out, Zoe says, bewildered, 'I didn't think you loved him any more, Mum.'

And Esme looks up at her clever, practical daughter. 'Darling,' she says, 'I don't think I ever really loved anyone else.'

*　　*　　*

The funeral was a week later, at the church of St Thomas of Canterbury in Kingswear. Sitting between her mother and Stephen, waiting for the service to begin, Zoe craned her head to look back along the pews. At the front of the church sat the family: Tom and Alice and their three boys, along with the wives of the two eldest and Tom and Alice's two grandsons, and Zoe's grandmother, in her wheelchair and a little vague about who was to be buried that day. Then there were the Langdon cousins and second cousins, and the tenants of the farms, and friends – Robert and Thea and Miss Fawcett among them – and men and women from the boatyards. And, it seemed to Zoe, the entire population of Lethwiston, Foxes and Adamses mostly, and a great many people that she did not recognise at all, shoved up tight on the pews and crammed into the nave and the back of the church.

So many people, she wanted to say to her mother. But, overcome, she could not speak, and she looked down at the floor as she dug her teeth into her lower lip.

Zoe said, 'All those military men with moustaches.'

It was late afternoon and the family were in the kitchen at St Petrox Lodge, clearing up. There was that sense of relief that follows a funeral, of having got through an ordeal.

Zoe's mother dried a dish. 'The older ones fought with your father in the Great War. And some of the others were from the Admiralty. Something to do with boats that Langdon's made for the navy during the war.'

'Motor torpedo boats,' said Stephen. 'They were super-fast.'

'Dad was horrified when Devlin first suggested Langdon's make speedboats,' said Tom. 'I think he thought they were beneath us.'

Zoe said, 'Who was that young woman in the purple coat?'

Tom snorted. 'Fred Martin's wife. His second wife.'

'Fred Martin?'

430

'The publican at Lethwiston. She's half his age. Big scandal. Lucky bastard, that's what I say.'

Esme said, 'Why don't you take Stephen and the boys along to the castle, Tom? They could do with some fresh air. Alice, we're just about finished here, I think. You run off home and have a bit of a break.'

'If you're sure, Esme.'

'Perfectly. You've done so much, I can't thank you enough.'

Tom herded up his grandsons and Stephen and ushered them out of the house. His three sons went with them. Alice and her daughters-in-law put on coats and hats, and at the front door kisses and hugs were exchanged and promises to call soon.

After she had closed the door behind them, Esme sighed. 'Tom drinks too much and then he is so hopelessly tactless. And poor Alice still isn't all that well after her operation.'

'Shall I make tea, Mum?'

'Please.'

They drank the tea in the drawing room, collapsing into Annette's soft flowery sofas.

'Lovely that Sarah came,' said Zoe.

'Wasn't it?'

'I'm sorry Ben couldn't be here.'

'Where is he just now?'

'Malta.' Ben's first book on the Neolithic tombs of Malta and Gozo, published the previous year, had cemented his reputation and earned him a visiting professorship at London University.

'I always think Malta sounds so romantic,' said her mother. 'You know, the Knights Templar.'

'He wants me to go out there.'

'Why don't you, darling?'

'Well, the shops,' said Zoe, slightly irritably. 'They won't just run themselves.'

This was not a subject Zoe cared to go into; it was she who

had written to Ben, telling him not to come to the funeral – the expense, the disruption to his work – and yet today she had regretted it. She would have liked him to be standing beside her in the church that morning. She would have liked him to drive her and Stephen home tomorrow, distracting her by rattling on about Neolithic tombs.

'Wonderful beaches, they say, in Malta,' remarked Esme vaguely. Then she said, 'I wish Matthew had come!'

'Mum, his wife's just about to have a baby. I'm sure he'd have been here otherwise.'

'Well, he'll have to come home now,' said Esme, rather sharply.

'What do you mean?'

'Because of Rosindell, of course. Rosindell belongs to Matthew now.'

Did her mother seriously think that Matthew would abandon the life he had made in America, and with wife and children in tow cross the Atlantic to play lord of the manor in the ruined remains of the family home? Zoe was horribly afraid she did.

'He won't want it.' The words came out more bluntly than she had intended, but her mother had to face reality.

'You don't know that.'

I know Matthew, she thought. Even if it's years since I last saw him, I still know him.

'Mum, he won't,' she said gently. 'I'm sorry.'

'I want him to come home!'

There were tears in Esme's eyes; Zoe covered her hand with her own. 'You'll go and see him now, won't you?'

'I can't.'

'You mustn't worry about the flight. I'll take you to the airport, I promise. I'll buy the ticket and help you organise everything.'

'But *he* should come *here*!'

Maybe he should, Zoe thought, but he won't. She had wondered whether Matthew was afraid to come home. Or whether he preferred the reunion to be on his own territory.

'After everything,' her mother was saying, her voice tremulous, 'after all that time when we didn't know whether he was alive or dead – all that time when Devlin and I both blamed ourselves! He should come here!' Then her voice flattened. 'It makes me wonder whether he wants to see me. He says he does, but does he really?'

'Mum, just *go*.'

Her mother looked exhausted, pale and, for once, older than her years. She looked at Zoe. 'Do you think I should?'

'I think you must.'

'I would so like to see Lucy.' Lucy was Matthew and Susan's daughter, now two years old.

'I'll phone BOAC,' said Zoe, 'find out about flights.'

'If Matthew won't have Rosindell, then you'll have to look after it, Zoe.'

She stared at her mother. 'Mum, no.'

'You must. There isn't anyone else.'

'I couldn't.' She felt a familiar resentment that her mother should do this to her, that she should propose to disrupt her life at a time when she hardly had a moment to herself anyway, and land her with a thankless white elephant that she had detested for a long time now.

'Mum, I can't, I've far too much to do.'

But her mother, with the knack that she had perfected over the years, seemed to consider the matter settled, and said, 'I don't suppose you'd want to live there, but you could speak to Robert Hendricks and I'm sure he'd find someone to keep an eye on the house for you.'

'Mum—'

'Till Stephen comes of age, at least.' Esme squeezed out the last few drops of tea from the pot. 'Did I ever tell you that your father proposed to me in this room? He wasn't at all romantic.

433

He more or less told me that he needed a wife to run Rosindell. I remember that he said he admired my fortitude and perseverance. I thought at the time that he might have chosen qualities that were more modern, more *dashing*.' She passed Zoe her cup. 'Your father looked the romantic hero, but he wasn't at all romantic really. He was a very practical man. Whereas your Ben is a true romantic.'

'Oh Mum, he isn't,' said Zoe.

'Of course he is.' Esme gave her daughter a clear-eyed look. 'Didn't you know?'

Two months later, Esme stepped out of the Boeing 707 at San Francisco airport, her relief that she was still alive after hours of nauseating turbulence over the Rockies tempered by a measure of apprehension. What if she did not recognise him? What if she and Matthew's wife, Susan, did not get on? Dazed from travelling and having lost track of the time of day, Esme hauled her suitcase through Immigration.

And saw Matthew, with a little black-haired girl in his arms. She would, of course, have known him anywhere. If fifty years had passed and had they been separated by universes instead of oceans, she would always have known him.

They embraced; tears were shed. She was introduced to the petite young woman who stood beside him, and to her granddaughters, two-year-old Lucy and the new baby, Esme Catherine, who would be known as Mimi, to distinguish her from her grandmother.

Ahead of her, light flooded through windows and Esme found that she was curious to see the city. I shall have coffee and pancakes in an American diner, she thought. And I shall swim in the Pacific.

She stayed for four weeks. The house that Matthew had built perched on the steep slope like some long-shanked seabird.

The rear of the building slotted into the hillside while the terrace at the front jutted fifteen feet over the garden, supported on stilts.

It could give you vertigo. The house swayed a little in the wind. A certain amount of movement was necessary, Matthew said. You need a bit of give, especially in an earthquake zone.

The living quarters were on the ground floor, above the basement, which was used for the motor cars, laundry and storage. There was a room that Matthew and Susan called the den, with a dartboard and Lucy's tricycle and Susan's sewing machine. Much of the front of the upper storey of the house was made of glass. Esme felt that it was rather like living in a department store. You could sit on the terrace and lose an hour watching the boats in the bay.

It pleased her that Susan was a gardener, like herself. Matthew would have left the plot to its wild luxuriance but Esme and Susan plotted something more remarkable. Terraces with bougainvilleas and plumbago spilling from one level to the next, grasses whispering on the stony outcrop to one side of the house. And roses – 'Like an English garden,' Susan said.

Esme found it hard to imagine an English garden finding a place in San Francisco. The steep hills and valleys were too open, too bold, too confident. Though when the fog rolled in in the evenings, extinguishing the lights and blurring the outline of the bay and beading the leaves with droplets of moisture, sometimes, disorientated with jet lag and exhausted by the insomnia that had dogged her since Devlin's death, she found herself thinking of the clifftops at Rosindell.

Things lay between her and Matthew, unspoken. She knew after a day that they would never speak of them. Their relationship was too fragile, and besides, his allegiances had changed. You needed a bit of give, especially in an earthquake zone.

*   *   *

A December evening, but still warm enough to be sitting on the terrace. Susan was cooking dinner. Though Esme knew that she must speak of Rosindell to Matthew, she had already accepted that Zoe had been right and that he would not want it.

'You may change your mind,' she said. 'One day you might want to come home.'

'This is home. San Francisco is home.'

But my grandchildren, she thought. How can you ask me to grow to love them and then allow me to see them only once or twice a year?

She murmured, 'But it's so far away!'

'Then come and live with us, Mum.'

He was standing at the railing, looking out over the bay. He was thicker round the shoulders than she remembered, and his hair was starting to thin at the temples.

'Matthew, I couldn't.'

'Why not?'

'I wouldn't impose myself on Susan.'

'Susan would love you to. We've talked about it. I was going to add some more rooms on to the house anyway. You could have a separate apartment so you could have some peace when you needed it.'

She had been discussed, she realised — his mother, now growing old, a problem for which a solution must be found.

'You'd see Lucy and Mimi every day,' he went on. 'You'd see them grow up. You'd like that, wouldn't you?'

This was the nub of it: those two little girls, one dark, the other fair. Her namesake.

'Think about it, Mum,' he said. 'It'd be a new life. An exciting new life.'

And for a moment she saw it. She would eat picnics on beaches in November. She would walk under the giant redwoods. She would buy her clothes in San Franciscan stores — 'pants' instead of trousers, 'undershirts' instead of vests – and would learn to eat Chinese food. She would get to know her grand-daughters. She would meet them from school, take them to the park, buy them ices. She would be a part of their lives.

She understood completely what she was giving up, and it appalled her, and it was a moment before she was able to say, 'Matthew, it would be wonderful, and I can't thank you enough for thinking of it, but I can't. I have my own life back in England.'

'If you came to live with us, you'd have a family.'

He thought her existence barren, she realised. In coming to San Francisco, though, she had also recognised a truth, a truth that almost broke her heart: that Matthew no longer needed her.

But Zoe did. 'Darling,' she said, 'I'm deeply touched, but I can't live here, it isn't my home.'

He let out a breath. 'If you change your mind . . .'

'You'll be the first to know.'

He put an arm round her shoulders. 'Good long holidays then, Mum.'

'Good long holidays, for as long as I can bear that dreadful journey. I shall learn to be a long-distance grandparent. And you'll come and stay with me in England, won't you?'

Matthew frowned. 'I can't, not yet. There's a lot I feel responsible for.'

'None of it,' she said carefully, 'was your fault.'

'Wasn't it?' His mouth twisted. 'I was a mess when I came here. There are things I've done, things I don't think I'll ever be able to face telling you about. I'm helping Kevin O'Sullivan build a youth club for the church. Giving my labour for free. It means long hours, but I'm trying to make up for things. I've a lot to make up for. I guess I'm trying to do good.'

Stars pinpricked the sky and the lights of the houses and boats delineated the water's edge far below them. He said, 'Do you ever hear of Melissa?'

437

'She writes to your grandmother several times a year. She married a Frenchman but they divorced. She has a daughter, Coral. She sent your granny a photograph – a pretty little thing, fair, like Melissa.'

'But she's happy?'

'Oh yes, I think so.'

'Good,' he said. 'I'm glad.'

Part Four

Restoration

1974

Chapter Twenty-One

Summer 1974

Coral Desrosiers saw Rosindell for the first time in a photo-graph in her grandmother's flat. She had offered to go to the flat while her mother went to the hospital to visit her grandmother, who had suffered a stroke five days earlier. The flat, four rooms in a mansion block in Highbury, already smelled musty. Coral opened windows and picked up the fragments of broken glass, casualty of her grandmother's collapse, from the living room floor. In the fridge, milk had separated and solidified. Blue mould sprouted in the bread bin and beneath the sink were fifteen empty Gordon's gin bottles. Coral carried them down three flights of stairs to the dustbin.

Her mother had instructed her to find nightdresses, so she went through the drawers in the bedroom until she found a grubby ivory satin and a frayed eau de Nil silk. Neither seemed suitable for a woman in her late seventies who was paralysed down one side of her body, but Coral folded them anyway.

There was an empty chocolate box containing photos; while she had a break and ate a packet of Maltesers, she took off her glasses, polished them, and then leafed through the snapshots. Several were of a fair-haired woman, sometimes in a group, sometimes posing in evening dress or in a bathing costume on board a yacht. Coral guessed the woman to be her grandmother.

There was a photograph of a rather mysterious-looking house, trees to one side of it, gardens to the other. Coral stuffed the nightdresses and the photos into her bag, locked up the flat, and went to meet her mother at Fortnum's.

'How was she?' asked Coral.

'Just the same.'

'I'll come with you, if you like, next time.'

'There's no need.' Melissa poured tea. 'Did you find any nightdresses?'

'These.' Coral took them out of her bag.

Her mother made a face. 'I'll go to Marks and Spencer.'

'I found some photos. I thought you might want them. She was beautiful, wasn't she?'

'My mother was the sort of woman who lived off her looks. I don't think she ever worked for her living.' Melissa's deepest disdain was reserved for the idle, the cadger.

'Do you know where this is?' Coral showed her the picture of the house.

A shake of the head. 'I've no idea. You can get rid of those.'

'Don't you want them?'

'No, not at all.'

Then her mother put down the teapot and said wearily, 'Coral, she may have been my mother, but she spoiled things. She always spoiled things. That was just how she was.'

Coral had graduated in 1972 from a new university with a respectable degree in music and French. Oil crises, miners' strikes, power cuts and threats of three-day weeks had helped give the impression that the country was on the verge of anarchy. Coral's working life − she hesitated to call it a career − had been similarly fragmented. Shop jobs, pub jobs, office jobs, a month picking grapes in the south of France, a long, seasick month as a stewardess on a North Sea ferry. All had been temporary, little had engaged. Since September, she had been working for a string quartet based in London, making bookings and organising tours. She enjoyed the job, but suspected it would not last much longer, due to a shortage of money and a falling-out between the two violinists.

Three months after her grandmother fell ill, she was at the dentist, waiting to get a tooth filled. The dentist was running late and Coral was leafing through a copy of *Country Life*. *The Honourable Miss Josephine Watson, daughter of Brigadier General Sir James Watson, on her engagement to Mr Peter Ferrers*, beneath a photograph of a girl in pearls. An article on salmon fishing in the Tay. Not really her thing.

She glanced at the clock, flicked a page. And there it was, the same house as the one in her grandmother's photograph, heading an article entitled 'Lost Houses of Devon'.

So she knew the name of the house now: Rosindell. She turned another page and saw a photograph of a family group. She read the caption: *Mrs Esme Reddaway and her sister, Mrs Heron, at Rosindell. The children in the foreground are thought to be Mr Matthew Reddaway, Miss Zoe Reddaway, and Miss Melissa Heron.*

Mrs Esme Reddaway and her *sister*, thought Coral. The receptionist called out Coral's name. Coral went into the dentist's surgery and endured half an hour of poking, prodding and drilling. On her way out, her face puffy and numb from the anaesthetic, and seeing that the waiting room was empty, she slid the magazine into her bag.

Melissa had never been called Melissa Heron – there the journalist had been mistaken. Once she had been Melissa de Grey, and now she was Melissa Desrosiers. This much she knew about her slippery, evasive parent. She had a flat in Paris, in the eighth arrondissement, and a small manor house, a *gentilhommière* called Beaumanoir, in the Vallée de Chevreuse. She was a literary translator and often installed herself at Beaumanoir while she was working on a text. She was there when Coral next went back to France, armed with the magazine.

It was a warm late spring day, and her mother met her at the railway station. They kissed, and Coral put her bag in the boot of the Citroën.

'Darling, how was your journey?'

'Excellent,' said Coral.

'And your string quartet?'

'David' – one of the violinists – 'has been offered a season in New York. A solo season.'

'You should find a career that has more of a future. Why don't you make use of your languages? I could have a word with Thierry, if you like, I'm sure he'd have something interesting for you.' Thierry was her mother's editor.

'I like my job,' said Coral stubbornly, and changed the subject. 'How's Laclos?' Her mother had been commissioned to write a new translation of *Les Liaisons Dangereuses*.

'Slow. So hard to find the voice.'

'Is Papa coming to dinner?' Coral's father's weekend home was only a few miles from Beaumanoir. Sometimes he managed to escape from his current girlfriend, a cold, possessive woman, to dine with Coral and her mother.

'He hopes so.'

Coral waited until they had unloaded the car and were sitting on the terrace with a glass of wine, before showing her mother the article in the magazine.

'Oh yes, that's Rosindell,' said her mother, uninterested.

'So you know it?'

Her mother shrugged, that dismissive Gallic gesture she had perfected over the years. 'Once. It burned down a long time ago.'

'Part of the house is still standing, it says so here.'

'Does it?'

'Who are they?' Coral pointed to the family group. 'Why were you visiting them? And is it true that this woman, Esme Reddaway, was my grandmother's sister?'

'Yes, it's true.'

'So these children – Zoe and Matthew – are your cousins? Where do they live now?'

But something closed off in her mother's eyes, and she said crisply, 'I'm afraid I can't remember.'

A lie. Coral knew.

When she went downstairs after unpacking her bag, her father was in the courtyard, trying to stop her mother destroying the dovecote.

'But *chérie*,' he was remonstrating, 'you can't knock it down. It's a hundred years old.'

'The drains need to be replaced, Philippe,' Melissa said. 'The dovecote is in the way.' She gave the structure a hard blow with the axe.

This was her mother. No *sentiment*.

Because her father had, after his divorce, remarried several times, Coral had a great many French relations, stepmothers and half-siblings. They had all been of a type, her father's subsequent wives, thin, elegant, beautiful and empty-headed, as if he couldn't bear to be serious after Coral's mother had left him.

On her English side, the de Grey side, hardly anyone. A great-grandmother in Devon, whom Coral had never met and who had died in 1962. The Herons in Wiltshire, who weren't really relatives at all. And the grandmother whom she had seen at most half a dozen brief times during her childhood, and who now lay speechless and paralysed in a nursing home near Guildford.

Once, when she had been twelve years old, her mother had taken her with her on a visit to London. She had been

445

left with her school books in the imposing public room of a hotel while her mother had disappeared upstairs. Sitting in a leather armchair, Coral had memorised her German verbs while men snoozed over their newspapers and women poured tea.

Half an hour later, her mother reappeared, accompanied by an older woman wearing a black frock and a pale blue feathery hat.

'Darling, how you've grown!' said the woman in the feathery hat.

Her mother, tight-lipped, said, 'Coral, say hello to your grandmother.'

Coral murmured greetings.

'So lucky, to have inherited the lovely hair,' said her grandmother. 'But surely you don't need those frightful spectacles?'

'Mother, she can't see without them.'

'Here,' said her grandmother, pressing something into Coral's hand. 'A little present, darling. Buy yourself something splendid. Now, why don't we all have tea?'

'Mother, we have to go, I'm afraid.'

And Coral had been hustled out of the hotel. In the street, she had opened her palm and seen the two-shilling coin that lay inside it.

How was it that at twenty-three years old she was finding out for the first time that she had English relatives? What had her grandmother done to make her mother so determined to keep them apart?

Back in London, crises intervened. Coral's job folded, the first violinist having left and the financial position of the quartet, precarious for many months, having become untenable.

And then, Andy. She had met him at a folk club. He had a sweet voice and a beautiful, angelic face framed by golden-brown curls. They sang well together and she could have looked at that face on the pillow beside her for ever. Though Andy read *Private Eye*, and sometimes, when he could be bothered, *Socialist Worker*, and though he sported a 'Ban the Bomb' badge and sometimes dropped his aitches, he had been educated at a public school and his parents had bought him his Chelsea flat. Andy was pursuing, when he could be bothered, a career as a musician. It was the not bothering that had begun to grate during the three months that Coral had been living with him. He could spin out the newspaper to last the day, and a couple of joints got him through the evening. He had a way of sitting around until Coral made him a sandwich, and he left the washing-up until it teetered out of the sink and there were no mugs left. Coral, who you could not have called house-proud, did what had to be done.

She spent a day trawling the employment agencies on foot. It was raining, and there was a bomb scare and she had to endure half an hour standing in a crowded Underground carriage while the train came to a halt between Victoria and Sloane Square, trying not to think about what might happen if it wasn't, this time, just a scare. When she returned to the flat, Andy was sprawled on the sofa. Coral, who was starving, cooked fish fingers and peas, all there was in the freezer.

Afterwards Andy said, 'What's for pudding?'

She found herself looking at him and knowing then that it wouldn't do, that beauty wasn't enough. She put the plates in the sink, then went to the bedroom that she and Andy shared and began to stuff her belongings into her holdall.

'What are you doing?' He was standing in the doorway.

'Packing,' she said.

She felt a pang, remembering long nights making love in the bed in this room. Then she grabbed her guitar and coat and left the flat.

Perhaps she shared some of her mother's ruthlessness after all.

A phone call to a friend and she was offered a sofa to sleep on for as long as she needed. Back in an Underground train, heading for Notting Hill and the friend's flat, she thought: so, no job, no boyfriend and nowhere to live. What was she going to do?

See if she could trace those relatives, she thought. Find out what she could about the family her mother didn't want her to know.

Zoe said, 'I'm thinking of selling the shops,' and Esme said, 'Are you, darling? I think that's a wonderful idea. You work far too hard.' And saw immediately that that was the wrong thing to say.

They were in the kitchen of Zoe's house in Kingston upon Thames. Ben's friend Griffiths was sitting in a corner of the room, a large mongrel dog beside him, its head in his lap.

Zoe said, 'I haven't made up my mind yet.'

'No, of course not,' said Esme soothingly.

'It's not an easy decision.'

'Have you talked it over with Ben?'

'Not yet.'

'Why not?'

Zoe glowered. 'Because he'll say, just like you, that I work too hard and it's a wonderful idea.'

Well then, thought Esme, bewildered.

'Have you thought any more about your birthday, Mum?' asked Zoe, changing the subject.

It was Esme's seventy-fifth birthday in the middle of September. 'I'd quite like to ignore it,' she said.

'Mum, you can't. A little family dinner, I thought.'

Esme was saved from responding by the doorbell ringing. A few minutes later, Zoe, looking flustered, came back into the kitchen, accompanied by a young girl. The girl had long blond hair and gold-rimmed glasses and was wearing jeans, a faded pink T-shirt and a denim jacket.

'Mum, this is Coral Desrosiers.' Adding — as if she was senile, thought Esme — 'Melissa's daughter.'

Esme held out her hand. 'Hello, Coral. How unexpected — and how lovely to meet you. I'm Esme Godwin.'

'Esme?' The girl fumbled through an overstuffed cloth bag and drew out a purse, a make-up bag, a paperback edition of *Under the Volcano* and finally a copy of *Country Life*. She leafed through it and thrust out a page. 'Is this you?'

Thunderous footsteps on the stairs and the door flew open. Ben came into the room. 'Has anybody seen my notes on Skorba? Hello, Griffiths, are we looking after you?'

'Rex has a thorn in his paw.'

'Poor old Rex.'

'I put them on the sideboard in the front room,' said Zoe. 'Ben, this is Coral Desrosiers. Coral, this is Ben Thackeray. Coral,' she explained, 'is Melissa's daughter.'

'Melissa?' Ben's frown cleared. 'That Melissa? Matthew's Melissa? Is there coffee? Shall I make coffee?'

'I'll do it,' said Zoe. 'Do you think your dog might like to run round the garden, Griffiths?'

'Not with his bad paw.'

'The hairs,' muttered Zoe.

'The fresh air might be good for him.' Ben clicked his fingers. 'Rex? Rex?'

The phone rang. 'I'll get it,' said Ben.

'Mum?' said Zoe.

Esme was looking at the photograph in the magazine. Forty years had fallen away, and it was summer, and she was back in the garden at Rosindell and Camilla was visiting, looking wonderful in her white linen suit, while she herself was wishing she'd changed out of her plimsolls.

'Mum, are you all right?'

'Look,' said Esme. 'You looked so sweet in your gingham frock.'

Zoe put on a pair of reading glasses and peered at the magazine. 'Is that me? Such a sullen little thing.'

'Stephen!' bawled Ben from the hall. 'Phone!'

Esme took another look at Coral Desrosiers. Could she see Camilla in her? The colouring, of course, the white-gold hair. But the child's eyes behind their gold-rimmed glasses were a deep and lovely sea green, not Camilla's hard, crystalline blue. Esme was aware of an irrational flicker of fear.

'How did you find us?' she asked.

'There was a photograph in my grandmother's things. A photo, I mean, of the house.'

'Of Rosindell?' said Zoe.

'Is she dead?' said Esme. 'Is Camilla dead?'

Coral looked stricken. 'No – no, I'm so sorry, I've given you a shock, haven't I? I thought you'd know.'

'Mum, sit down. Ben, make Mum some tea.'

Esme sat down in a wicker chair. 'Where is she?'

'In a nursing home in Guildford. She had a stroke in February. I'm afraid she's very ill.'

Camilla was in Guildford, only a half-hour's drive away. Why did that knowledge so unsettle her, making her stomach churn and her mind rush round like a bird trapped in a room?

She made an effort to speak firmly. 'I'm not upset, Coral. Camilla and I never got on and we haven't been in touch for many, many years.'

'I hardly knew her. I didn't know about Rosindell or any of you till I found the photo.'

'Rosindell?' Stephen came into the room. His right arm was bound up in a sling. 'What about Rosindell?'

'I went there,' said Coral. Then, quickly, as if to pre-empt any more interruptions: 'I just peeked through the trees. The man in the pub told me the house belonged to you, Mrs Russell, and that you lived in Kingston upon Thames. So I looked you up.'

'It's mine, actually,' said Stephen. 'I'm Stephen Russell. Who are you?'

'Coral Desrosiers.'

'Melissa's daughter . . .'

'So we're some sort of cousins,' said Stephen. He looked pale, Esme thought, and his dark hair was tousled and untidy. 'Are there any aspirins, Mum?' he said. 'I've run out. Hello, Gran.' He kissed Esme's cheek.

She squeezed his good hand. Stephen was an absolute favourite of hers. 'Is it feeling any better?'

'Yeah, better, definitely.'

'I'll get you some aspirins, darling,' said Zoe.

'There was only one Mrs Z. Russell in the phone book,' explained Coral. 'I hope you don't mind me turning up like this.'

Did she? Esme wondered. Did she mind? She was afraid that she did. She feared old griefs and quarrels coming up to the surface once more, like Ben's fragments of pot and bone.

'Here's your tea, Esme,' said Ben, putting a tray on the side table beside her chair.

'I'd always assumed Camilla had gone back to America,' Esme said. But was that true, or was it that she had preferred to think that Camilla had gone back to America? Nicely out of reach, her malevolence an ocean away.

Coral said, 'I wondered whether you remembered when the photo was taken.'

'Aspirins,' said Zoe, coming back into the room.

'Thanks, Mum.'

Esme was still looking at the photograph. 'Nineteen thirty . . . or was it thirty-one? Camilla's husband took this. I can't remember his name.'

'James Heron,' said Coral.

'He was a handsome man . . .'

'I'm going to have to go down to the house,' Stephen said.

'That was Joe on the phone. From the pub,' he explained to Coral. 'He thinks someone's been camping out there.'

'Darling, you can't,' said Zoe. 'Such a long journey. I'd go myself, but we're doing the stocktaking this weekend.'

'I'll be fine. I'll take the train.'

'But you'll get *jostled*. Ben? Can you drive Stephen to Rosindell?'

'Tuesday,' said Ben, looking up. 'That's my first free day. That do you, Stephen?'

'I don't want us to end up with squatters.'

'I'll drive you,' said Coral.

Everyone stared at her. She shrugged. 'I'm out of work and I've nothing to do at the moment. Why not?'

Stephen said, 'You can take my car, if you like.'

'What is it?'

'An MGB.'

'I think I'll stick with my Hillman Imp.' Coral was bundling the magazine and the rest of her belongings back into her bag. 'Tomorrow morning at eight suit you?'

'Sure,' said Stephen. 'Thanks.'

'It's okay.'

In the doorway, Coral spoke as if the thought had just occurred to her. 'I thought it was beautiful,' she said. 'I thought it was such a beautiful place.'

And Esme found herself looking at the girl and remembering, and feeling a resentful apprehension at the possibility that she might disrupt the comfortable unreeling of family life.

Stephen Russell was, Coral guessed, about her own age, tall and slim and athletically built. His straight, so-brown-it-was-almost-black hair tumbled over his high forehead, and his eyes, which were dark brown and framed by black brows, had bruised shadows beneath them.

When she picked him up in the morning, he apologised

452

for the stubble on his chin. 'Bloody difficult to shave left-handed.'

He sat in the passenger seat of the Hillman Imp, the map on his lap, directing Coral through the tangle of roads from Kingston to Staines.

'Does it hurt?' asked Coral, glancing at the sling.

'Yes, rather a lot. But I'll go nuts if I'm stuck at home much longer.'

'What have you done?'

'Fractured my shoulder playing rugby. Ridiculous game, I should give it up.'

'What is it that you do when you're in one piece?'

'My PhD at Bristol University. Low-temperature physics.'

'Very cold things?'

'That's right,' he said. 'Incredibly cold things. What is it that you do when you're not unemployed?'

'Lots of different things. Secretarial work, mostly. My mother insisted I get a secretarial qualification after I left university. I read music and French, so people aren't exactly queueing up to offer me exciting jobs. I'll probably end up as a bilingual secretary.' She shrugged. 'That's okay, I'd like to travel a bit.'

'Which languages do you speak?'

'French and German. I was brought up in France and my mother said I should learn German.'

'Do you always do what your mother says?'

'No, not always.' Coral changed down a gear. 'Why "Matthew's Melissa"? Did your father mean Matthew Reddaway?'

'Yes. And Ben isn't my father, he's my stepfather; my unofficial stepfather. He and Mum aren't married. My father died when I was four.'

'Sorry.'

'S'okay. Look out for that van.'

'My parents are divorced. My father's latest girlfriend throws crockery at him. Limoges crockery.'

They both sniggered, and Coral felt a certain complicity.

He said, 'How much do you know about the sordid Reddaway family history?'

'Hardly anything at all. Is it sordid?'

'Pretty much.'

'Your grandmother and my grandmother are sisters.'

'And we share the same grandfather.'

Frowning, she flicked him a glance. 'Next right,' he said, peering at the map. 'The Camberley road. My grandmother, Esme Reddaway, who you met yesterday, was married to Devlin Reddaway, who had an affair with your grandmother, Camilla Langdon.'

Coral whistled. 'No wonder she dislikes her.'

'And then, later on, there was something between your mother and my uncle Matthew.'

'My mother . . .' she said. 'But they're—'

'Half-brother and sister. One assumes they didn't know at the time.'

Coral was starting to understand why her mother hadn't introduced her to her Reddaway and Russell relations. *You see, I fell for my half-brother . . .*

'The family tree gets a bit knotted at that point,' said Stephen. 'I don't think there was anything *incestuous*.'

'Glad to hear it. I was starting to worry about my DNA.'

'First love, my mother says. I imagine,' Stephen added with a cynical smile, 'lots of staring into one another's eyes while making vows of undying passion. The good thing is, whatever I do, whatever hopeless or unsuitable girlfriend I bring home, they can hardly criticise, can they? Which kind of frees me up.'

And that was when she began to like him. That was the moment when she knew that he saw things in much the same way as she did.

*　　*　　*

He said, 'Doesn't this thing go any faster?' They were on the A303, halfway between Andover and Amesbury.

'This thing,' said Coral, offended, 'is doing nearly fifty miles an hour.' Lorries and vans thundered past them. 'How come you own an enormous house *and* an MGB? Are you just filthy rich?'

'Not exactly. I bought the MGB a few years ago when I was twenty-one, with some of the money my great-grandfather put in trust for me. And Rosindell's mine because no one else wants it. It should have been my uncle Matthew's, but he lives in the States and never comes over here. And my mother hates it.'

'Does she? Why?'

'She thinks it's haunted.'

'Seriously?'

'So does my grandmother. I try and give them the rational side of the argument, but they don't listen. It's been quite a while, over ten years, since anyone's lived in the house. It's gone a bit damp and mouldy.'

'Do you want to live there?'

'Not possible at the moment. I have to be in Bristol, tending my cryostat. But yes, I'd like to one day. I've been trying to do it up, repair some of the plaster, fix the gutters, that sort of thing. I have this dream about getting it back to what it once was.' He shifted in his seat; Coral wondered whether his arm was sore. 'You see, I love it there,' he said.

At Stonehenge, they stopped and drank coffee from thermos flasks. While they made a circuit of the standing stones to stretch their legs, Stephen told her about the Reddaways, about their grandfather Devlin Reddaway, who had died in 1962, who used to take him down to the beach and help him look for crabs and sea anemones in the rock pools.

'He had a limp because he was injured in the First World War,' said Stephen, 'and he was burned rather badly in the fire.'

455

Coral remembered the *Country Life* article. 'The fire at Rosindell?'

'Yes. Some madwoman burned it down.'

Then he told her about the others. About Devlin's father, Walter Reddaway, a less charming character, a recluse, not above taking potshots at trespassers and poachers. And Walter's grandfather, also a Devlin, who had squandered the family fortune at the gaming table. And another Walter, further back, who had gone mad and ended up in an asylum. 'They seem to have alternated,' added Stephen, shaking the last drops of coffee on to the grass before screwing the cup back on to the thermos, 'the owners of Rosindell: a mad one and then a reasonable one.'

'Which are you planning to be?'

He grinned. 'Not sure yet.' They headed back to the car.

They reached Rosindell just after three o'clock. There was the chained and padlocked gate that Coral had climbed over on her previous visit, and which she helped Stephen unlock. The drive swung sideways and then sloped down through the trees. The house was at first a flicker of grey slates between the tree trunks, and then it was there, grey-gold and ancient, with an odd appearance, as if one side of the building had been sliced off with a knife.

Coral parked the car in the courtyard and they both got out. Dark green fingers of ivy crawled up the front of the house, covering some of the windows. The crunch and crackle of their footsteps on the gravel seemed to echo in the silent valley. To the far side of the building, the ground was tussocky and uneven. The newer part of the house had once stood there, Stephen explained, the rooms designed by the architect Conrad Ellison. Now all that was left were the grassy hummocks of the overgrown foundations.

Stephen unlocked the front door and they went inside. Ahead, a broad staircase swept up to a galleried landing.

'It's cold,' Coral said, and went back to the car to fetch her Levi jacket. When she returned to the house, Stephen had gone into an adjacent room. Heavy wooden beams supported the high roof of the great hall. He was walking round, running his eye over the sparse items of furniture.

'Some yobs broke in a while ago,' he said. 'Rampaged through the place, smashed some of the windows. I've been more careful about locking up since then. Joe from the pub comes and walks around a couple of times a week.' He peered into the grate. 'I don't remember there being so much ash. I thought I'd cleaned it out.'

More rooms: a library, where the books on the shelves were spotted with mould, and a dining room with a vaulted stone ceiling, ice cold and patched with shadows.

In the kitchen, the surface of the ceramic sink was flecked with a spider's web of crackles. A tablet of green soap, seamed with grey lines, stood on its rim.

Stephen touched it. 'It's damp. Shouldn't be damp. The roof lets in water in the attic, but this room's dry.'

'Condensation,' she said.

'Perhaps.'

They searched the house, every single room. There seemed to be dozens of alcoves and funny little corner cupboards. Hidden beneath the eaves in the attics they found a sleeping bag, rolled up and tied with twine, and a small plastic sponge bag containing a razor, toothbrush and toothpaste. Stephen grimaced and swore under his breath, and Coral took them out of the house and stuffed them into the dustbin.

He said, 'Let me show you the best bit,' and they walked down the valley, then through a wood carpeted with pine needles. They came out of the thick, tangled darkness to a cliff above a semicircular bay. Far below them, silky turquoise sea lapped at pale sand. A rowing boat, tied to a metal stanchion, was reduced by the height of the cliffs to a brown insect bobbing on the water.

'Wow,' said Coral.

'The beach isn't Rosindell land, but the people who walk this path don't tend to notice the steps down, so most of the time we get it to ourselves.'

'If you're worried about the house,' she said, 'I could keep an eye on it for you.'

Stephen slitted his eyes in the bright light. 'You mean, stay here?'

'If you like.'

'I have to go back to Bristol. Are you sure you'd be okay here on your own?'

'Because of the ghosts, you mean?' Coral made woo-hooing sounds, and he grinned.

'Wouldn't you be lonely?'

'I'll cope.'

'And there's no electricity or water.'

'There's a sea to swim in and a pub down the road.'

'If someone's been sleeping in the house . . .'

'Then I'll lock up carefully.' She thought the matter settled and said, 'We should eat something. Why don't we go to the pub?' And they headed off through the trees.

Later, they argued over who should sleep where. She should have the bed in the pink room, he said, because the sofa in the great hall was too bloody cold at night. No, he must have the bed, said Coral, because he was the one with the broken shoulder. And anyway, she was smaller and would fit on the sofa better.

She won. She unrolled the sleeping bag she had brought with her on to the sofa and snuggled into it. She heard owls calling as they swooped round the house, and fell asleep imagining their jewelled eyes and outstretched marbled wings.

But he was right, because the cold woke her in the middle

458

of the night, a gnawing cold that you might almost think the house had accumulated over the centuries. So she padded upstairs to the room where Stephen slept, and crept into the bed beside him.

In the morning, he opened dark, sleepy eyes, and said, 'Hello.'

'Hello,' she said. And then they kissed.

Almost all gone now, Esme thought, in the taxi. Twenty-five years since her father had died, twelve since she had lost her mother. Dear Tom had passed away the previous year – heart failure – and his eldest son, Christopher, now lived at St Petrox Lodge. All of them gone, the family of her childhood. All except Camilla.

The nursing home was on the outskirts of Guildford, beside a school playing field bordered with sycamores, which swashed their heads in the breeze. Esme didn't drive any more and hadn't been able to face the changing of trains so had hired a taxi, an enormous expense but a luxury she was thankful for because, apprehensive of this visit, she had slept little the previous night.

The taxi dropped her off outside the nursing home. It must once have been someone's rather grand family house, Esme thought as she followed a nurse through corridors decorated with the speckled paint deemed appropriate to institutions. Though it was early June, radiators blasted out heat and the air was clotted and warm.

'We think Mrs Hadley has lost some of her vision,' said the nurse. 'And I'm afraid her speech is very poor. But I'm sure she'll be delighted to see you. She doesn't have many visitors, only her daughter when she's able to travel from France, and a gentleman who takes the train down from Manchester once a month.'

The small room was furnished with a bed, bedside table and metal chair, on which Esme sat down. The nurse, arranging in a plastic vase the lilac and mock orange that Esme had brought with her, explained to her that Camilla was paralysed down the left side of her body. Her left arm was tucked beneath the covers, emphasising its uselessness.

The nurse left the two of them alone. Esme murmured a greeting. One of her sister's eyes had fixed on her; the other was masked by a drooping eyelid. A lock of thin grey hair had fallen across Camilla's face; Esme brushed it gently back. The rattle of trolley wheels in the corridor faded and the room was silent apart from the strained rasp of the sick woman's breathing.

'Poor Camilla,' said Esme. 'It's a rotten way to end up. I'm sorry for you, truly I am. But I came here because I wondered whether you would tell me why you did it. After all, it doesn't matter any more, does it? Devlin is dead and I don't suppose either of us has all that long to go. Was it because you loved him, or was it because you hated me?'

No answer. Just that fierce, glaring eye. Esme gave a little sigh. Camilla had never showed contrition. Even when they had been children, it had always been someone else's fault.

What she had once possessed had been the capacity to inspire passion. This was a gift, Esme believed, like any other talent or aptitude. Camilla had been beautiful, but it had been more than that – magnetism, chemistry, whatever name you gave to that combination of sexual availability, daring and wilfulness that men – and women – had found irresistible.

All three of her marriages had been disastrous. You had to compromise to make a marriage last, and Camilla had never compromised. Faithfulness, too, would not have been a quality that she admired, or even considered. Had she loved them, those men who had betrayed their wives and abandoned their children for her? Perhaps. But with Camilla, love had never lasted. Esme wondered whether, as her sister had grown older, she had minded that – whether perhaps in the end her life had disappointed. Her friends would have grown older, many settling for marriage and children. However lovely she had been, sooner or later she must have realised she was no longer the centre of attention. She would have found that hard to bear.

Yet Esme found herself recalling Camilla in her pale blue dress, dancing at her engagement party in the drawing room at St Petrox Lodge, and years later in her white linen costume, walking through the garden at Rosindell with James Heron.

From the twisted mouth, a sound. 'What?' said Esme, rising. 'What is it?'

But the effort of speech seemed to exhaust her sister, and after several moments her shoulders slumped and her eyes closed.

Esme's head ached and her bad hip throbbed. The futility of this journey, with its waste of spirit and expenditure of strength. Camilla would keep her secrets to the end.

'There,' she said. 'I have to go now.' She patted Camilla's hand, gathered up her bag and gloves and left the room.

As the weeks passed, Coral relaxed into Rosindell's dreamy heat. She read novels and played her guitar and sometimes just lay in the garden in her bikini, soaking up the sun. On the meadowland between Rosindell and Kingswear she discovered, hidden in a grassy fold, flowers whose curiously shaped lower lips resembled bees. She recalled seeing a wild flower guide at Rosindell – Stephen's presumably – and looked them up and learned that they were bee orchids. Other finds followed: tiny sea pinks whose ragged petals shivered on the slope of the cliffs, and helleborines, pale and secretive in the woodland.

She phoned Stephen, who had gone back to Bristol, from a call box three or four times a week. He'd come down when he'd caught up with his work, he told her. There was a promise in his words. She remembered the surprise and pleasure in his eyes when he had woken in the morning to find her in his bed, and the tenderness of his mouth and the heat of his skin.

Sometimes, walking through the grounds, she had the sensation that someone – something – was watching her. A prickling on the nape of her neck, a movement of the branches of the trees. Shadows licked across the grass, and in the evenings she found herself glancing up to the attic windows, where the reflection of the clouds on the glass seemed to conjure up movement. Though there were no broken windows or forced doors, she began to notice things: a gate left open that she thought she had shut, a dark path trodden out of the pale dew in the early morning. The publican, Joe, perhaps, checking out the house.

One afternoon she walked to Kingwear, where she bought postcards, stamps and spare batteries for the torches. On her way back, she scrambled down the cliff path that led to Rosindell Bay. Reaching the beach, she took off her shoes and socks and padded along the sand. Though the tide was out, waves threw themselves at the rocks beneath the spurs of the cliffs. The rocks and the deep, swirling sea made it impossible to walk from this beach to the next, which meant that the cove was only accessible by the cliff path.

Time passed as she squatted, studying the white curves of shells, and sea anemones like shiny plums clinging to the rocks, and a tiny pale green crab, a fragment of jade, slotting itself into a crevice. When she had finished looking in one pool, she went on to the next. An hour passed, and only the hot sun, scorching her shoulders, made her straighten and move into the shade.

She took off her jeans and placed them on a rock before wading into the sea for a swim. The water soothed her burned skin. Emerging after twenty minutes, she dressed and started up the path. She was halfway up when she looked up and saw that a man was standing above her, on the clifftop.

As she reached the summit, he said, 'Glorious view.'

'Isn't it?'

He was older than her, thirty perhaps, and was wearing jeans, a white shirt and a corduroy jacket. His eyes were masked by sunglasses and the breeze tugged at his short light brown hair. A pair of binoculars was slung round his neck. Coral was aware of her wet T-shirt – had he been watching her swimming in the bay?

'I hope I'm not trespassing,' he said.

'No, not at all.'

'Isn't this Rosindell land?'

'Rosindell's back there,' she said, pointing. 'Do you know it?'

'I've heard of it, that's all.' He offered her his hand. 'My name's Justin Shawcross.'

'Coral Desrosiers. Are you on holiday?'

'That's right. What about you? Are you on holiday too?'

'Sort of.'

'Staying nearby?' He gave a disarming smile. 'I'm sorry, you'll think I'm nosy. I'm spending a few weeks at the Royal Dart Hotel, on my own, and I've hardly talked to anyone for days.'

'Actually, I'm staying at Rosindell.'

'In the house?'

'Yes.'

'Just you?'

'At the moment.'

'Do you own it, then?'

She laughed. 'No, I'm afraid not. It belongs to someone else, but I'm looking after it for him. They've had trouble with squatters, you see.'

'Really? That's appalling.'

She glanced at the binoculars. 'Are you a birdwatcher?'

'I'm trying my hand at it. How long are you planning to be there?'

'I'm not sure.'

'Perhaps we'll run into each other again.'

He headed off along the path towards Brixham. Coral went into the woods. Her head ached and her sunburned skin scratched against the seams of her T-shirt.

When she reached the house, there was a letter waiting for her. Sitting on the front doorstep, she slit open the envelope and read through her mother's note. And so found out that the grandmother she had hardly known, the grandmother who had betrayed her own sister, had died three days ago.

There was a service in a church in Guildford, near the nursing home, and then Camilla's remains were to be cremated. The mourners divided into three groups: the matron from the nursing home and one of her nurses; family – Esme, Melissa, Coral, Zoe, Ben and Stephen; and two elderly men in raincoats and trilbys – friends, presumably, of Camilla's.

During the hymn, a thready rendition of 'The Day Thou Gavest', Esme noticed that the taller of the two elderly men had several times to break off from singing to blow his nose and wipe his eyes. He seemed, Esme thought, the only mourner truly affected by the occasion. A former admirer, perhaps. Melissa, stylish in a black skirt and jacket, had a remote air, as if she was thinking of something else. Coral, almost unrecognisable in similarly well-cut funeral blacks, sang out the hymn in a clear and attractive voice as if to make up for the poor musicianship of the rest of them. The second elderly man had a coughing attack during the final verse of the hymn and had to sit down.

Esme's gaze drifted back to the taller man. A prickle of recognition – was he familiar to her, or was she imagining it? At her age, she often encountered people who reminded her of faces from the past. Did she know him, and if so, who was he?

*　*　*

464

In the taxi, driving from the crematorium to the hotel, Coral squeezed her mother's hand. 'Only the lunch to get through.'

'Yes, thank goodness.'

'I wondered whether Papa would come.'

'He's in Rome. Some business negotiation.' Her mother took a powder compact out of her bag and checked her face. 'I don't want you to go back to Rosindell, Coral. I didn't tell you the truth before. A long time ago, when I was very young, I knew Rosindell well. When I look back to that time, it seems like a dream – or a nightmare, I've never been sure which. But I've since come to think that all that loveliness beguiles and enchants and stops you seeing clearly.'

The compact snapped shut and was replaced in the Chanel handbag. 'I've always felt ashamed that my mother didn't love me.' Melissa had turned to the window and Coral could no longer see her expression. 'As if it was my fault. Why is that, do you think?'

At the hotel, there was a buffet lunch and an air of getting things decently and quickly out of the way. The two nurses from the home left after a cup of tea and a sandwich. The shorter and rheumier of Camilla's old admirers was carried off by a chauffeured Bentley soon after he had squeezed Melissa's hand and told her what a great gel she was.

The other elderly man was now standing on his own to one side of the room. Esme introduced herself to him.

'Good afternoon, so good of you to come. I'm Mrs Godwin, Camilla's sister.'

'Denis Rackham.'

Denis Rackham. Though she could not place the name, Esme knew that she had heard it before.

'Damnable way for her to go,' said Rackham. He took a whisky flask out of his trouser pocket and topped up his glass with a shaking hand. 'Forgive me, but I feel so damnably low. Help you to some?'

'No thank you, Mr Rackham.' He was, she realised, very drunk. 'Had you known Camilla long?'

'We were old pals. Met her in 'twenty – or was it 'twenty-one? – at Cannes, when she was still married to that fool de Grey.'

Esme remembered. Herself, a young woman, at Rosindell, talking to Victor de Grey while Camilla flirted with this man, Denis Rackham. That disastrous dinner where the guests had not gelled and she had discovered that Devlin had once been engaged to her sister. Though his muscular frame had turned to fat, and his once handsome face had become jowly and pendulous, with the purple veining of the seasoned drinker, Esme recognised Rackham as the man whose raw, dominating sexuality had once attracted Camilla.

She said, 'You came to Rosindell, years ago.'

'Rosindell?'

'My home.'

But he was uninterested in her reminiscences, and looked away. 'Bloody awful to see her in that terrible place. She had such life. I used to tell her she had more life than the rest of us put together. What a girl. Such parties . . . everyone knew her, all the writer and painter chappies, they all adored her. That photographer chap, American, lived in Paris, funny name – Man Ray, that's it – he took her picture, y'know. Do you know why I adored her? It was because she wasn't afraid of anything. Was on a yacht with her once and there was the most fearful storm and we had to fight to take in the sails, but Camilla just laughed. I thought we were going to capsize, and all the time she was laughing.' Rackham slopped more whisky into his glass. 'She'd do anything, anything at all, and she didn't care a fig what other people thought. "I don't give a damn, Denny," she'd say to me. Never any other woman to touch her. I asked her to marry me so many times, but she only laughed at me.' There were tears in the pouchy, bloodshot eyes. 'She'd have been hell to live with, but at least I'd have been nearer my daughter.'

'Daughter?' said Esme. 'Where was your daughter, Mr Rackham?'

But he seemed to sober up, and flicked a glance across the room to where the rest of the mourners stood, and when he looked back, his expression had changed. He turned away, mumbling, 'Have to go. Forgive me. Train to catch.' Then he put down his glass and stumbled out of the room.

Stephen's arm was out of the sling. He and Coral were on the terrace behind the hotel, having escaped the buffet and its limp circles of cucumber and flakes of sausage roll and the tired guests looking at their watches and wondering whether they could decently go. The grey day had turned to drizzle, which clung to Stephen's dark hair.

'I wasn't sure you'd stick it out,' he said. 'I was afraid you might disappear back to France.' He ran his hand along the sleeve of her black jacket. 'I like the outfit. Sophisticated.'

'Do you prefer me sophisticated?'

'I like you any way at all.' And they kissed among the hydrangeas in pots, and the sound of the rain, as it gathered force, rattled in the metal ashtrays on the garden tables.

'When are you going to come to Rosindell?' she said.

'Soon,' he said. 'Listen, Coral, there's something I'd like to talk to you about—'

The door to the terrace opened and Zoe came out. 'Stephen, we're heading off now. You must come out of the rain, you'll get soaked.'

'Mum, have you thought any more about your birthday?'

Esme was in the passenger seat of Zoe's saloon car as they headed back to Kingston upon Thames.

'I don't want any fuss.'

'Mum,' said Zoe patiently. 'Seventy-five's important.'

'Seventy-five is ancient. Best forgotten.'

Esme looked out of the window at the row of passing semis. *She'd have been hell to live with, but at least I'd have been nearer my daughter.* What daughter? Who had Denis Rackham been referring to?

Because there was a terrible possibility. Esme shivered.

'You okay, Mum?' said Zoe.

'Just a little tired.'

'Ben, where's the travel rug? Mum's cold.'

Though she tried to calm herself, the thrum of the rain and the rhythmic movement of the windscreen wipers became a drumbeat, a chorus of agitation that underpinned the horror of her suspicions. She stared out of the window at the glazed grey ribbon of road. Could Camilla have lied? Would she?

Chapter Twenty-Two

Summer 1974

The pines were motionless, black against the early morning light. As Coral opened the gate that led from the garden into the grove of oaks and birches, she saw a flicker of movement in the undergrowth. 'Who's there?' she called, and the figure turned and she saw that it was Justin Shawcross, the man she had met on the cliff a couple of weeks ago.

'I thought I saw a green woodpecker,' he said. 'I hope you don't mind.'

'Of course not.'

The binoculars were slung round his neck. As they emerged from the darkness of the wood into the bright light of the cliff path, Coral noticed the yellow tinge to the collar of his shirt and the threadbare pile at the cuffs of his jacket. His watch was a scratched Timex and his shoes were scuffed and creased. He was wearing his holiday clothes, she supposed. Or he was one of those absent-minded men who always looked as if they had slept in their clothes.

'Still here, then,' he said, with a smile.

'Yes, still here.'

'Did you know that the house is haunted?'

'Rosindell?' Coral shrugged. 'Someone said something, but

I don't believe in that stuff, ghosts and ghoulies and things that go bump in the night.'

'You shouldn't make fun,' he said. There was a touch of anger in his pale green eyes. 'It's true. My mother told me.'

She looked at him sharply. 'Your mother knows Rosindell?'

'Knew it. She's dead now. She used to work there.'

'When was that?'

'After the war. There were always stories about the house.'

Coral, suspecting she was about to be bored by some tale of the paranormal, changed the subject. 'Are you birdwatching today?'

He nodded. 'I thought I'd head on up the cliffs, see if I could find anything interesting.'

They parted and she walked on. Just before the path turned away, she looked back and saw that he was standing on the cliffs above Rosindell Bay, the binoculars loose in his hand.

Esme was on stage, in a school production of *The Pirates of Penzance*, but she had forgotten the words of the song. When she looked down, she saw that instead of the crinolined gown she was supposed to be wearing, she had on her gardening trousers. She tried to edge to the wings, but an invisible force was pushing against her, and her feet moved on the spot as if she was treading water.

She woke up and looked at the luminous hands of the clock. It was not yet three. She put on her dressing gown and slippers and went downstairs to the kitchen and ran herself a glass of water. She had always regretted a little the replacement of the well in the back garden – so inconvenient, and yet such sweet, cold water.

She'd have been hell to live with, but at least I'd have been nearer my daughter. What if the daughter to whom Denis Rackham had been referring was Melissa? What if Camilla had lied all those years ago to Devlin, and it had been Rackham who had fathered her child?

Many years ago, when Camilla had first returned from France with her baby daughter, Esme had assumed Melissa to be Denis Rackham's child. She remembered him as a young man on the night of the dinner party at Rosindell, strong and sexually confident, enjoying his humiliation of Victor de Grey. Rackham had had straw-coloured hair and blue-green eyes. Both Melissa and Coral were fair, and both shared the same eye colour, a deep greenish-blue.

She would never know. The realisation tormented and exhausted her. Camilla had taken her secrets to the grave. As always, she had had the last laugh.

In the middle of the night, Coral was woken by a door slamming. In the time it took for the pounding of her heart to subside, she persuaded herself that she had *dreamed* that a door had slammed. But then, a pulsing sound: footsteps. Someone was walking along the corridor. Her limbs seemed pinned to the mattress by the pressure of air on them, and she stared into a darkness in which the denser patches formed by the furniture took on a limitless and menacing quality. She was unable to distinguish the patter of footsteps from the raw in and out of her breathing.

She felt for the torch she had left on the floor beside the bed and slid the switch. Nothing happened. She gave it a shake, tried again. Her hands were damp with sweat as she unscrewed the base to check the battery. The compartment was empty. She swept her hand over the bed to see whether the battery had fallen out without her noticing. No, it was not there. Yet she had slotted in a new one only the previous day; she remembered doing so. Her gaze moved in the direction of the door. No, she could not go downstairs and fetch a spare battery from the kitchen drawer. Feeble of her, but she couldn't.

She wished she had inherited her mother's skill as a translator, her knack of making sense of the incomprehensible. She

471

lay in bed in the pink room, waiting for the light, trying to render the sounds of the house into something reasonable. As the grey dawn filtered through the windows and the sounds became what they must have been all along – the old house settling on its foundations and the wind swirling down the chimney – she told herself that she had muddled up the two torches and put the new battery into the one that Stephen kept in the hall.

Drifting off into a deep sleep, she was woken by the hot sun pouring through the windows. She glanced at her watch: it was nearly ten o'clock. She pulled on jeans and a T-shirt. Her head ached and she felt sluggish and crumpled.

She locked up carefully before leaving the house, then drove to Kingswear, where she parked the car. Waiting by the slipway for the ferry, she watched the waves slosh on the stones and the yellow-brown pods of bladderwrack bob in the water. In Dartmouth, she did some shopping, then ate a sandwich, sitting on a bench near the harbour, hoping that the sunlight and the crowds would erase the jitters of the previous night.

Afterwards, she went to a phone box and dialled the number of Stephen's flat. No answer – he must be at the lab – and she was about to put the receiver down when someone said:

'Hello?'

A girl's voice. Coral said, 'Is Stephen there?'

'Who's speaking?'

'Coral, Coral Desrosiers.'

'Are you the girl who's staying at Rosindell?'

'Yes. Who are you?'

'I'm Ingrid, Stephen's girlfriend.'

Coral was aware of the hot, thick smell of the phone box, of the traffic noise and the cry of gulls. And of disappointment and humiliation and a shrinking of the day into something ordinary and effortful.

'Yes?' said Ingrid impatiently. 'Can I take a message?'

'It's not important. It can wait.'

'Good, because he's awfully busy. Goodbye, then.' The phone was put down.

Deadheading roses, memory pricked at her.

Her meeting with Camilla, a decade and a half ago, in Regent Street. They had gone to a pub – the Bricklayer's Arms, just behind Liberty – and she had bought her sister a gin and tonic. Several gin and tonics. What had Camilla said to her? Something spiteful, recalled Esme.

Most of the time I'm on my own, except for that dreadful Jane Fox.

Jane Fox had worked as a lady's maid for Camilla. A lady's maid tended her mistress in bedroom and bathroom. A lady's maid knew her mistress's secrets.

Sarah Fox, Rosindell's former housemaid and Jane's elder sister, had been Sarah Trent since she had married her sweetheart, William, during the war. Esme exchanged cards with Sarah every Christmas.

She put down the secateurs and went inside the house, her plimsolls leaving dusty imprints on the tiles. Opening her bureau drawer, she took out her address book. A telephone number was listed beside Sarah's name. Esme picked up the receiver and dialled the number.

What an idiot she had been, thought Coral as she drove from the Kingswear ferry up into the high ground of the peninsula. Stephen had kissed her because she'd climbed into his bed. What man would not have done the same? There had been no liking, no particular attraction. It hadn't meant anything to him at all.

Back at the house, the rooms seemed gloomy and overlarge. Coral felt the chill, the damp. The tape in her cassette player jammed, and as she sat in the great hall, disentangling the glittering brown ribbon from the spools, she heard the sound again: footsteps, coming from the floor above.

Both Stephen's mother and grandmother believed Rosindell was haunted. That man on the cliff path, Justin Shawcross, had told her the same. Coral didn't think the house was haunted. *Someone's come to retrieve his sleeping bag*, she thought. *And he's messing with my head.*

The torch gripped firmly in her hand, she went upstairs. Footprints on the dusty wooden floorboards – hers, or someone else's? The trouble with a house like this was you could never know what went on in every corner of it. A student bedsit, you were familiar with every inch. Entire families could camp out at Rosindell, and if they were quiet, you wouldn't have a clue. And when you looked at the house closely, shining the torch into dark corners where floorboards rotted and mildew blossomed over walls, you saw the impossibility of the task Stephen had set himself. *I have this dream about getting it back to what it once was.* That was all it was, a dream. The man was lying to himself. Just as, presumably, he had lied to Ingrid about Rosindell's current tenant, Coral Desrosiers.

She went downstairs, finished unthreading the tape from the cassette player, put on Fairport Convention and went to make a cup of tea. Approaching the kitchen, she heard a whistling, rustling sound.

She had to steel herself to open the kitchen door. Her relief that the room was empty was tempered by a feeling of foolishness, but then she caught the whiff of scalded milk and saw the saucepan on the camping stove. The milk inside it had almost burned dry. Coral wrapped the handle in a tea towel and dumped the pan into the sink. Drops of water spat and hissed on the hot metal.

Had she put on a pan of milk and forgotten about it? Had she been so distracted thinking of Stephen's girlfriend, the presumably lovely Ingrid? Or was someone trying to spook her, to make her leave the house? The thought disturbed her.

She should go, she thought. She had no reason to remain

here; she was wasting her time. She would write to Stephen and tell him that she was planning to leave by the end of the week. She would make some phone calls, find a job and somewhere to live, and try to work out what she wanted to do with the rest of her life.

Sarah said, 'Jane went into service with Miss Camilla – Mrs Hadley – when she was thirteen years old. She retired four years ago.'

Esme was having tea with Sarah in the garden of the Trents' detached bungalow in Walton-on-Thames. The wooden table was in a shady corner, out of the afternoon sun. Sarah's husband, William, was pottering in the greenhouse.

'Such a long time,' said Esme. 'Was she happy in her work?'

'Very. She went everywhere with Miss Camilla, all over the world. France, America – all sorts of places. Milk, Mrs Godwin?'

'Thank you. Do please call me Esme.'

'I think Jane felt that some of the glamour rubbed off on her. She liked the high life, Jane, she liked nice things. She saw places she'd never have seen if she'd stayed at home like me. Not that she would ever have stayed at home.'

'Why not?'

Sarah paused before speaking. She had filled out in old age, but the lineaments of the pleasant, rosy-faced young girl who had welcomed Esme to Rosindell more than fifty years ago were still visible.

'Home life wasn't what you'd call happy. Our Jane couldn't wait to get away.'

'But you stayed.'

'I was the eldest. Someone had to look out for our mum and the little ones.'

'So Jane never married?'

'She was never the marrying sort. Never even had a boyfriend, as far as I know. She adored Miss Camilla. She'd have done anything for her.'

475

'My sister was good at that,' said Esme, rather acidly. 'Inspiring adoration.'

'I'll take Will some tea, if you'll excuse me,' said Sarah. 'He lives in that greenhouse.'

'Is he the gardener?'

'He does the garden, I do the house.' Sarah smiled. 'He knows I couldn't bear him messing up my house.'

When Sarah returned to the table, Esme said, 'So Jane always worked for my sister?'

'Not always. She was at Rosindell to begin with.'

'Rosindell?' Esme frowned. 'I didn't know that.'

'It was before your time, while old Mr Walter was still alive.'

'Why did she leave?'

'She was never happy there. She didn't like the house. It's funny, though, even though she said she hated it, she knew Rosindell like the back of her hand, all its twists and turns. I always said she could have found her way round it blindfolded.'

A slice of Sarah's excellent sponge cake lay on Esme's plate, but she had lost her appetite. She said, 'After she left, did Jane ever come back to Rosindell?'

'Oh yes, lots of times, to visit me.'

In the greenhouse, the shadow of William Trent moved behind the glass. A suspicion had formed in Esme's mind, too momentous to be immediately scrutinised. She folded her hands in her lap to disguise their tremor.

She said, 'And Jane's still alive?'

'Yes. She's living in Lethwiston, in our old cottage. Mr Devlin sold it to Will and me after the war. Mum stayed in it after Dad died, and then we kept it on after she passed away. We used to go down there for weekends. Will's made it nice and Jane had nowhere to live when she left Miss Camilla, so we offered it to her.'

Jane Fox was living in Lethwiston, less than a mile from

Rosindell. When she looked up, Esme recognised the unease in Sarah's expression.

'Mrs Godwin, why are you asking me all these questions about Jane?'

'I think she might be able to help me with something.'

'Are you planning on calling on her?'

'Yes, I think so.'

Sarah pressed her lips together. Then she said, 'I should warn you that even if Jane could help you, she might not. She hates the Reddaways, you see. Always has done, for as long as I can remember.'

On her last morning at Rosindell, Coral walked down the cliff path to the bay. In the windless early morning the sea looked flat and hard and crystalline. On the strand, light flashed on the wet pink stones.

She walked from one end of the horseshoe-shaped bay to the other. She had become familiar with it, knew the best rock pools for shrimps and sea anemones, had looked up the names of seaweeds and shells. She thought of London: the litter-strewn streets and overflowing dustbins, the howl of police sirens and the way the tall buildings trapped the hot air.

Later, she drove to Kingswear to buy provisions to replace those she had used – soap, washing-up liquid, a packet of flour and tea bags. Before driving back to Rosindell, she went into the Royal Dart Hotel. She asked the receptionist whether Justin Shawcross was still staying there.

'Shawcross?' The card index was riffled with a painted finger-nail. 'No, we have no guest of that name.'

Leaving Kingswear, Coral discovered that she felt relieved. She had sensed in Justin Shawcross a fascination with Rosindell that had begun to unsettle her. She was glad that his holiday had ended, and that he had gone back to wherever he came from.

Back at the house, she spent the next few hours cleaning, scrubbing floors and sweeping out grates. She was coming downstairs carrying a bucket of dirty water when she heard it again: a scrabbling, rasping sound, as if someone – something – was clawing at the front door, trying to get in. One hand clutching the banister, she stood motionless.

Then a voice called out, 'Rex! *Rex!*' and Coral heard a dog bark. Putting down the bucket, she opened the door and saw Stephen.

He said, 'I got your letter.'

'You didn't have to come.' She stood aside to let him enter. 'I was going to leave the key with Joe.' The dog was racing in circles round the gravel. 'Is that Mr Griffiths' dog?'

'He's not supposed to keep pets and his landlord found out. I offered to have Rex while Griffiths finds somewhere else. He hates the car. He howled the whole way from Bristol.'

'I've cleaned up a bit. Nothing's broken or missing.'

Stephen frowned. 'Coral, I haven't come here to check up on you.'

Might this be the last time she saw him? Easier if he hadn't come. Easier if she had just left Rosindell and never seen him again.

She said, 'Why *are* you here, then?'

'Your letter – it was rather sudden. I hadn't realised you were planning to leave.'

'I can't stay here for ever.'

'No, of course not.' He was scowling. 'I just thought . . . Is it the house? I wondered whether you'd get fed up with it, alone here.'

'I don't mind being alone.' Coral thought of the footsteps, the pan of milk. 'Really,' she said, 'the problem's been the opposite.'

'What do you mean?'

'It's a funny thing . . . It's as though I've been sharing the house with someone I never saw.'

'I don't understand.'

She tried to explain. 'Once, when I was in London, I rented a flat with a nurse who worked nights. Days would pass and we wouldn't see each other at all, but I always knew she'd been there. Warm water in the kettle, a damp towel in the bathroom, that sort of thing. That's what it's felt like these past few weeks, living here.'

'You think someone's been in the house?'

'Maybe. I'm never sure. Perhaps I'm imagining it.'

Stephen looked up the stairs to the landing, as if expecting to see the sway of a curtain, a movement in the shadows.

'I'm not talking about *ghosts*,' she said.

'I didn't imagine for a moment that you were. But perhaps it's just as well that you're leaving.'

His last words made her feel so miserable, she was afraid he would read her feelings, written in her eyes, so she went into the great hall, where her belongings stood by the sofa.

He said, 'Where are you planning on going?'

'Paris.' Until she said it, she hadn't known that she had made the decision. 'I'll get some translation work,' she said. 'My mother's been telling me I should for years.'

'Is it what you want? Is that what you care about?'

Her back to him, she zipped her guitar into its case. 'It'll do for now.'

'And you'll settle for that?'

'Yes.' Turning, she saw criticism and disappointment in his eyes. She looked around. 'I think that's everything.'

'What about that?'

Her cassette player was on the mantelpiece. She tried to stuff it into her holdall, but the zip jammed. The dog, Rex, chose that moment to bound into the room, pull a trailing scarf out of her case, and run off with it. Stephen yelled at Rex; Coral yanked at the zip.

Stephen came back into the room and held out her scarf. 'I'm sorry, he's made rather a mess of it.'

The silk was wet with drool. Rex was sulking in a corner of the room.

'It doesn't matter.'

'I'll buy you another one.'

'Stephen, it's not Chanel or anything, it really doesn't matter. My blasted bag . . .'

He knelt down on the floor beside her and fiddled with the zip, knitting the teeth back together. He said quietly, 'I understand why you have to go, but I'll miss you.'

She felt angry with him, partly for mending the zip so quickly, but mostly for his duplicity.

'Will you, Stephen? Really? What about Ingrid?'

'Ingrid?'

'Yes, Ingrid. Your girlfriend Ingrid. *That* Ingrid.'

'You spoke to her?' he said sharply.

'I phoned your flat and she answered the call.'

She gave up trying to fit the cassette player into the bag and stuffed it under her arm, then picked up the holdall and the guitar.

She heard him say, 'She's not my girlfriend.'

'She was in your *flat*, Stephen.'

'She's got a key. I gave her a key when we were living together. I keep asking her for it back, but she always claims to forget it. It's a rented flat, so I can't change the locks.'

'If you were living together . . .'

'It went sour for me months ago. I tried to finish it. And now she just turns up. I know she goes to the flat when I'm not there, because she moves my things. She denies it, but she does. I'll move out as soon as I can. I'm sorry you had to find out like that, Coral. I meant to talk to you about it when we met at your grandmother's funeral, but there wasn't the opportunity. That's why I didn't come down here. I thought I should get it sorted, make a clean break first.'

First, she thought. And then? She said slowly, 'But if you've really finished with her, why don't you just tell her?'

'I did, and she tried to kill herself.'

She stared at him. 'Stephen, how awful.'

'She had to have stitches in her wrists and they sent her to see a psychiatrist.' He let out a breath. 'There's this horrible part of me that thinks she didn't try *that* hard, and that she was just trying to get attention, and then I hate myself for thinking that. What a mess, what a bloody mess.'

He looked so unhappy she put down her luggage. Chewing her lip, she studied him. 'How long had you been together?'

'Six months. She wanted us to live together and I gave in. I shouldn't have; I was an idiot. She wanted to be with me all the time – and I mean *all the time*. She even came into the lab, though it must have been as dull as ditchwater for her. I had to get some space. Anyway, we had a row, a bad row, and I said we should call it a day. I tried to do it kindly, but . . .' He grimaced. 'If you're dumping someone, then you're dumping someone. I'm not sure kindness comes into it. Anyway, she went into the bathroom and eventually I realised she'd been in there a long time, so I knocked on the door. She didn't answer, so I went in. There was blood everywhere. She'd cut her wrists with my razor.'

'Stephen, I'm sorry.'

'I haven't told my mother, anyone in the family. I'm not proud of myself.'

'It wasn't your fault.'

'Wasn't it?' His eyes were bleak. 'I could have handled it better. I should have seen what was coming. And she's still around, and I can't get angry with her just in case . . .'

'In case she does it again.'

'Yes.'

'Do you think she would?'

He stared out of the window. 'Probably not. They weren't all

481

that nice to her in the hospital, made her feel she was a tiresome nuisance. As soon as I've finished the experimental work – and I'm almost there – I'll get away, leave Bristol, bury myself somewhere so that I can write up my thesis.'

'Here, you mean?'

'I thought so.'

'Just as well I'm going, then,' she said with a lightness she did not feel. 'You wouldn't want me in your way.' And she picked up her bags and walked out of the house.

She was halfway across the courtyard when he called out to her.

'First time I saw you, in the kitchen at home, it was as though I recognised you. As though I'd known you a long time and then I'd forgotten you, and now here you were again, at last. Don't go, Coral.'

The breath seemed to leave her lungs in one long, loud sigh. She stiffened, hearing his footsteps on the gravel.

'Don't go.' He slid the cassette player out from under her arm. Then he took the bag and the guitar and put them down and wrapped his arms around her, and she rested her head against his chest and closed her eyes.

They took the dog for a walk. It seemed a good idea, all things considered, and anyway, Rex was nuzzling between them, making yelping sounds.

They talked about: where Coral would live when she went back to Paris (she would rent a room on the Left Bank, not in the stuffy eighth); their favourite writers (his Asimov, hers John Barth or John Fowles, she couldn't decide); their families (Coral's parents both with apartments in the same arrondissement and weekend places only a few miles distant – 'Unconventional,' said Stephen. 'Difficult,' said Coral – and Stephen's living half the year apart); whether they preferred cats to dogs; what Stephen was going to do after he had written up his PhD, and

482

his worries about Rosindell. She told him about the footsteps, the milk pan. 'Hippies,' said Stephen. 'There's a dozen of them camping on the headland, near the old gun battery.' He had his old-fashioned side, she thought fondly.

And whether it mattered that they were cousins. 'Half-cousins,' said Stephen. 'No, of course it doesn't matter.' They had gone back to the house by this time and were in bed. She was lying on top of him and his hand was running down her spine and then curving up to her bottom.

'A bit pervy, perhaps,' he added.

'Do you think so?' She kissed him.

'Mmm.' His hand slid further down. 'Yes, definitely.'

Coral woke in the middle of the night. Moonlight filtered through the uncurtained window and she remembered what Stephen had said about Ingrid, his mad girlfriend, and the keys. Ingrid had a key to his flat. *I know she goes to the flat when I'm not there, because she moves my things.*

She had assumed that Justin Shawcross had booked out of the Royal Dart Hotel, but what if he had never been there at all? What if he had been lying about that but telling the truth about his mother? What if his mother had worked at Rosindell, and what if she had kept a key?

There were half a dozen ways you could get into Rosindell. The front door, of course, but also back doors and side doors and servants' entrances and the door into the cellars, which, Stephen had told her, led beneath the house before coming up to a trapdoor in the floor of the oldest part of the building.

Could Justin Shawcross have been camping out at Rosindell? And could he have returned to the house after she had come to stay here? Coral pictured his scuffed shoes padding through attic rooms and corridors, slipping into the kitchen when her back was turned and putting a match to the burner beneath a pan of milk.

What had her mother said? *All that loveliness beguiles and enchants and stops you seeing clearly.* But she had been wrong. Solitariness, Coral had discovered, had allowed her to learn to observe and to understand. Rolling over in bed, she studied the curve of Stephen's jaw, the shadows like thumbprints beneath his eyes, and she felt herself changing, a covering of skin sloughing off, leaving her raw, tender and exposed.

Waking early in the morning, she went to the window and looked out. *Is it what you want? Is that what you care about?* Stephen had asked her the previous day. Sometime in the night the answer had come to her. *This* was what she cared about. The bee orchids in the folds of grass, the jade-green crabs on the shore. The shadowed trees in the valley, blue-grey in the curling mist, and the spikes of thistle and nettle piercing the vapour like reeds in a pond.

Something glinted among the trees that masked the cliff, a small, revealing flash of light. Sunlight on a piece of broken glass. Or on the lens of a pair of binoculars.

Stephen was still asleep. Coral pulled on jeans and a jumper and brushed her lips against his forehead before she left the room. Emerging into the courtyard, she breathed in the cool air and squinted at the brightness of the sun. Damp blades of grass brushed against her legs as she walked down the valley, towards the sea.

To either side of the path that led from the gate to the cliff was dense woodland. In high summer the leaves formed a canopy, letting in only chinks of light. Nettles and briars masked the trunks of the trees, and the entwined, whiskery fronds of old man's beard scrambled over the vegetation. But when she looked closely, she was able to make out broken branches and trampled leaves and, on the soft ground beneath the oaks, the shadowy hollows of footprints.

The sticky threads of spiders' webs clung to her face as she scrambled through the undergrowth and clambered over a fallen log covered in gleaming orange bracket fungi. As she pushed between the billowing forms of box trees into a clearing, a yellow powder rose into the air.

In the clearing stood a small khaki tent. To one side of it were the blackened remains of a bonfire, a water bottle and a plastic washing-up bowl. The front of the tent was looped up. Squatting, Coral looked inside and saw a sleeping bag, a rucksack, some cans of soup and a tin-opener.

'What are you doing here?'

His voice made her jump to her feet. Justin Shawcross was standing on the edge of the clearing, the binoculars around his neck.

'This is Rosindell land,' she said.

'I know.' He came towards her. 'What of it?'

'You're trespassing.'

'Not me. It's you who shouldn't be here.'

Something about his smile and the glitter in his gooseberry-green eyes disturbed her.

'Is was you, wasn't it?' she said. 'You were camping out in the house.'

'I've been living there for months.' He had moved from the perimeter to stand beside her. 'And then you came along.'

Close to, his clothes smelled stale, and she could see flecks of dandruff on the shoulders of his jacket. She said, 'You've been trying to scare me off.'

'You should have gone, Coral. You should have taken the hint.'

'You came into the house – you've been watching me.'

He laughed, and for the first time she felt afraid. 'Of course I have. I've been there all the time. We've been living together, you and I. I've watched you wash your hair and cook your dinner. I've watched you while you sleep.'

'You have to go.' But her voice was unsteady.

He shook his head. 'Plenty of room for us both, some might say, in a big old house like that, but I don't think so. I gave you plenty of chances. You should have taken them. You don't belong here, Coral.'

'I'm family.' And for the first time, she meant it, felt it. Reddaways, Langdons, Russells and Desrosiers: linked together in a cobweb of connections.

He reached out, touched a strand of her hair, and she shuddered. 'Rosindell should have been mine. It was meant to be mine.'

'Because your mother was a servant here?'

He hit her across the face then, and she cried out, falling to her knees.

'My mother was never a *servant*. My mother was engaged to be married to Devlin Reddaway. But he was a liar, a liar and a cheat. That's your *family*, your rotten, lying family. He made promises to her and then he broke them.'

His blow had knocked her glasses off; though she felt for them on the grass, she could not find them. When she put her fingers to her mouth, they came away tipped with blood.

He hunkered down in the grass beside her, and she breathed it in again, that stale, sour smell. 'I was fine before you came,' he said. 'But now you're getting in my way.'

He grabbed her wrist, jerking her roughly to her feet, and she cried out again. What did he intend to do to her?

'I'll go,' she whispered. 'I don't want Rosindell, I never have. I'll go, I promise, and I'll leave you alone.'

'I don't believe you. You're a liar, like the rest of them.' He was dragging her out of the clearing.

'I'm sorry . . . I didn't know . . . I didn't know about your mother.'

'Oh, she got back at him.' Suddenly he paused, yanking her to a standstill. 'She didn't let him get away with it.'

'What do you mean?'

He mimed striking a match. Again he smiled. 'Only takes one.'

Somewhere close by, a dog barked. Justin Shawcross's head whipped round, and in that moment Coral ran out of the clearing. Thorns dragged at her clothing and nettles whipped her legs, and the woodland was a myopic blur of green and brown, the trees crowding together, confusing her, barring her way, trapping her in their darkness.

Ahead she saw sea and sky and she knew that she had reached the cliff. Her throat was tight and she could hear the sobbing of her breath as she ran along the narrow path.

And then he was there, in front of her, barring her way.

Something woke him — a cry — and the dog was standing head low, nose pointed, ears pricked.

Coral wasn't there. Stephen flung on his clothes and ran out of the house. Another cry, from the woods — what the hell was going on? Rex hurtled ahead, barking. The gate was open, and to his right he could hear someone running through the woods. Stephen took the quicker path through the pines.

He saw her as she tumbled over the cliff. The graceful arc of her fall, her arms flung into the air and her silver-fair hair flaring out against the blue of the sky. Stephen roared out her name and threw himself at the man standing on the cliff path, knocking him to the ground and punching him over and over again.

A fist struck his shoulder, where the break had been, and he heard himself scream. Another blow, to his head, and his vision was reduced to a kaleidoscope of tree and grass and sky. *Dear God, he's going to kill me.*

And then a furious growling and he was half smothered by a brownish-grey mass of fur, and this time the scream wasn't his.

* * *

487

The phone rang. Zoe answered it.

'I've decided what I want to do for my birthday,' her mother said. 'I'd like to have a party.'

'Are you sure, Mum?' Her mother wasn't a party person.

'Everyone is to come. You and Ben and Stephen, of course. And Matthew and Susan and the girls.'

'Matthew? I'm not sure—'

'You must *make* sure, Zoe.' Her mother, familiarly autocratic. 'After all, it's my seventy-fifth birthday and I may not be around much longer.'

'Mum, I'm sure that's not so.'

'And that girl, Coral, and her mother.'

'Melissa? You want Melissa?' Her mother had gone mad, Zoe thought.

'Yes, Melissa must come. That's most important. And I want the party to be held at Rosindell.'

'Mum . . .'

'At Rosindell,' repeated Esme. 'Nowhere else. I want to have one last party at Rosindell.'

They were in the drawing room of Christopher Langdon's house, St Petrox Lodge, in Dartmouth. The police had not yet found Justin Shawcross, and it was thought unsafe for them to return to Rosindell.

'He'll turn up in some casualty department, the police think,' said Stephen. 'Rex made a mess of his leg.'

'How's your arm?'

'Okay. Just a bruise. How are you?'

'A bit sore.' She hurt all over from her fall.

Maureen Langdon came into the room with a plate of egg sandwiches, which she put on the coffee table. 'In case you get peckish.' When she left, Stephen slid the plate to Coral.

'I couldn't.'

'The police found newspaper cuttings in his rucksack,' said

Stephen. 'Old newspaper cuttings about Rosindell and the fire. He must have been obsessed with the place.'

Coral couldn't bear to think about it. She couldn't bear to think about falling down the cliff, slipping on scree and vegetation, reaching out for something to hold on to and finding nothing: her terror. If she didn't think about it, maybe she wouldn't remember it.

He said, 'Maureen says we can stay here overnight.'

'I'm catching the London train.' She glanced at her watch. 'There's one leaving in half an hour. While you were getting your shoulder X-rayed, I phoned my father. He's meeting me at Paddington.'

'Coral,' he said softly.

'Look at us, Stephen!' She had never found her glasses and tears were blurring her vision, but she could just about make out the marks that Justin Shawcross's fists had left on his face. Her own arms and legs were covered in scratches from the gorse that had eventually arrested her fall.

She looked down. 'I just want to go home,' she whispered.

'And home's France?'

She nodded. 'I'm sorry.'

She stood up, gathering her things. A policewoman had fetched her bag and her jacket from Rosindell; everything else could wait.

He said, 'I'll see you again, won't I?'

At the door she paused. 'I don't know.' She closed her eyes, trying to find a scrap of courage. 'I hope so.' And then she pressed her lips against the hollow at the corner of his mouth.

Chapter Twenty-Three

September 1974

At ten minutes to three, while Esme is trying to remember where she has put her reading glasses, Zoe's car draws up outside the house.

Zoe bustles inside, kisses her mother, finds Esme's spectacles on top of the toaster, and tells her off for the mouldy crusts in the bread bin.

Esme says, 'Where are Ben and Stephen?'

'They went to the house early, to get things ready.'

'And Matthew? Have you heard from Matthew?'

Zoe is dusting crumbs from the work surface into the bin. 'You know what he's like, Mum. I'm lucky if I get two letters a year.'

'What if he doesn't come?' Esme feels anguished. 'He *has* to come.'

'Mum . . .'

'I don't mean,' says Esme, remembering the shadow of favouritism that has sometimes fallen over the family, 'that it isn't equally wonderful that everyone else will be there.'

'We're all longing to see Matt and Susan and the girls. It'll be fine, honestly.'

Zoe glances at cooker switches and windows, picks up her mother's bag, and they go outside. Zoe watches as Esme locks the door — *just checking*, she thinks — and feels a rush of affection for her considerate, conscientious daughter.

As they climb into the car, Zoe says, 'What are you wearing tonight?'

'My black.' Zoe looks dubious, so Esme adds firmly, 'You can't go wrong with black. And anyway, I feel the cold.'

She imagines the walk from Rosindell to Lethwiston, along a road that has never been surfaced, and is glad that she has packed a quilted jacket. She is assailed by a rush of apprehension. Rosindell has a dangerous magic. Has she made a mistake in insisting that her birthday party be held there? She has never rid herself of her ambivalence towards the house. She remembers the baby she lost, and Devlin's betrayal of her, and the fire. And of course, that much more recent horror.

She says to Zoe, 'Have they found him yet?'

'Justin Shawcross?' Zoe shakes her head. 'No, I'm afraid not.' She glances at her mother. 'Try not to think about it, Mum. It's your birthday. It'll be a great day.' She starts the car.

But as they head through the village, Esme feels no confidence that any good will come of what she intends to do this day. Jane Fox might refuse to speak to her. Matthew might decide not to travel to the house he has not seen in more than thirty years. Her family might squabble and fall out, as it so often has, or she might falter at the last moment and her strength fail her.

Her ghosts are with her as they set out on the journey to Rosindell.

Coral said, 'What time shall I book the taxi for?' and her mother replied, 'I thought we might walk.'

'Walk?'

'Along the cliff path.'

They were drinking coffee in the reception room of the Royal Dart Hotel, where they were to stay overnight.

491

Coral said, 'Mum, I don't want to.'

'I know, *ma chère*. But I think we should. It takes about an hour, doesn't it?'

Coral frowned. 'You know it?'

Her mother smiled. 'Oh yes, very well.'

Coral was afraid that every time the path turned a corner, she would see Justin Shawcross, born Trevor Gresham, the son of the woman who had burned Rosindell to ashes, barring her way, hatred in his pale green eyes.

'Mum, I can't.'

'You can, because I'll be with you.' Her mother rose, smoothing down her navy skirt. 'You won't be alone. You see, you mustn't let him win. Now, it's half past six. We should get ready.'

Three-quarters of an hour later they were on the cliff path, wearing their party dresses and walking shoes. Melissa's high-heeled shoes and Coral's wedges were in Coral's bag. The sun was lowering itself over a dark turquoise sea, and inky shadows spilled across the path and waves crashed against the rocks in the inlets.

They passed the old gun battery at Froward Point and started on the last stretch of the coast that led to Rosindell Cove. Her mother looked at her and said, 'Shall we go on?' and Coral nodded.

'I used to walk along here each morning,' said her mother, 'to meet Matthew on the beach. You'd think, wouldn't you, that after so long you'd forget, but I remember every step. It brings it back, how happy I felt, how certain I was that I'd met the man with whom I was going to spend the rest of my life. I thought I'd never feel lonely again. After Matthew, I always kept a part of myself back. I was afraid of falling in love. I endured deprivation and danger during the war, but I was never as afraid of them as I was of human closeness. So I gave my life to my work instead. I'm proud of what I've achieved and I have few regrets. Philippe is the man I've loved most, and I believe he knows that. But I've missed something, and I don't want you to do the same, Coral. Memory can paralyse, or it can spur you on.'

Coral said, 'Stephen's my cousin.'

'Half-cousin.' Her mother picked a strand of goosegrass off Coral's plum-coloured Biba frock. 'The only thing that matters is that you love each other.'

'But I don't know.' When she looked back, what had passed between her and Stephen that summer seemed so fragile, so temporary. Easier, in many ways, to let it go.

As they rounded the final bend in the path, Coral nerved herself to look into the woodland. The undergrowth had been cleared away and she could now see between the trunks of the oaks and pines as far as the green glitter of the garden at Rosindell.

They went to stand at the top of the steps that led down to the beach. Coral looked down to the cove, to the sand and the swarming sea, so far below. With her mother's arm linked through hers, she did not fear falling.

She understood the effort that her mother, a reticent person, had made both in coming here and in speaking of the past, and she said, 'I don't know what Stephen feels about me. We never talked – we never talked of love.'

'Then talk,' said her mother. 'And then at least you'll know.'

So much easier, thought Zoe, as she drove the last few miles of their journey over the Kingswear headland, if her mother had not insisted on holding her birthday party at Rosindell. Why haul everyone across the country to that dreadful old ruin when they could have had a lovely party in Kingston, or even Little Coxwell? All the organising, and the trouble they had had to go to, cleaning the place up to make it look respectable. Zoe had had to search out a gardener prepared to mow a decent-sized patch of the horribly overgrown lawn, and caterers who would drive out into the wilds along unmade roads. And one could only pray that the fine weather held so they could dine in the garden and were not forced indoors.

All this when she had so many other worries. The business, of course, and the decision she had struggled to take, so difficult and momentous; and poor Ben had had a miserable August suffering from some horrible summer flu, and could have done without a week of hauling furniture around that mausoleum of a house. And Zoe still went cold inside whenever she thought of what might have happened to Stephen, what Bonnie Gresham's son might have done had Griffiths' dog not attacked him.

After Bonnie's imprisonment, Justin Shawcross had spent much of his childhood with foster parents or in children's homes. He had idolised the mother he had only occasionally seen, inheriting both the newspaper cuttings she had kept about the house she had longed to possess and her resentment of the Reddaways. A loner whose short temper and impulsive nature had prevented him from settling to anything, he had adopted the surname of a clergyman who had fostered him in his teens, swapping 'Trevor' for the more fashionable 'Justin'. The police suspected that he had been living rough at Rosindell for some months before Coral had moved in. After the attack on Coral and Stephen, Shawcross had never been found. The rowing boat moored in Rosindell Bay had gone missing, and it was thought possible that, weak with loss of blood from the savaging of the dog, he had drowned.

Though Stephen's physical injuries had healed, the ordeal had changed him. He had lost some of his carefreeness. He denied that he was unhappy, but Zoe suspected he was. As for her mother – Zoe glanced at Esme, sitting beside her – she looked exhausted, pale and fragile. Beyond Amesbury Esme had

494

dozed off, lulled like a toddler by the rhythm of the vehicle, to wake blinking at Totnes, where they had stopped for a cup of tea. Such a long journey to put herself through at the age of seventy-five, to insist on going back to a house that must hold unhappy memories. It was incomprehensible.

But as they reached the turn-off to Lethwiston Zoe found herself distracted from her thoughts by the familiarity of the landscape, the downward slope of the road and the luminescence of the sky ahead, which seemed to reflect the shimmer of the sea. As they approached the village, she noticed that one of the barns was in the process of being transformed into a house. And then the tarmac petered out and they were rattling along and the trees that marked the perimeter of Rosindell land lay ahead of them.

They saw a pinpoint of light, and then, as the car passed through the gates, another. Zoe gasped.

A necklace of lanterns lit the drive down to Rosindell. Zoe whispered the word for them: *flambeaux*.

Zoe parked the car and Esme got out. There was a long table, covered with a white cloth, on the lawn. Candles flickered in jam jars and pink and apricot roses spilled from glass bowls. Music was playing and paper lanterns were slung from the trees, and there were pots of scarlet geraniums by the steps. A banner saying *Happy Birthday, Esme* festooned the front door.

Guests had gathered on the lawn. Esme's eyes flicked over them. There was Ben, and Stephen. Oh, and Christopher, William and Gary Langdon, Tom's sons, and their families. And a whole host of Langdon cousins and second cousins. And Thea's sons and daughters-in-law – dear Thea – and many, many other friends from Lethwiston, Kingswear and Dartmouth.

But her gaze still moved, searching for the face she longed to see. No matter, she tried to comfort herself; I shall write to him.

And then a young fair-haired girl ran out of the house and Esme's heart swelled. Then Matthew's roar: 'Mimi, come back here! Mommy needs to do your hair!'

But Esme's granddaughter, that other Esme, ran on down the combe, her amber-coloured hair streaming out behind her. And Matthew, emerging from the front door, said, 'Mum,' and Esme burst into tears.

'I was afraid you weren't coming.'

'Of course I came. Wouldn't have missed it for the world. We wanted it to be a surprise.'

'You've been *plotting*?'

'All of us, yes.' He enfolded her in his arms. 'Okay now?'

'Yes, Matthew,' she said humbly.

'Now where's my wretched daughter? She never listens to a word I say.'

And they walked arm in arm across the grass.

Zoe found Ben in the kitchen. Bottles of wine were cooling in the sink.

He said, glimpsing her, 'I had a tramp round the cellars to see if I could find any Château Margaux or Mouton Rothschild hidden away in a dark corner, but no luck, I'm afraid. Hello, darling. How was your journey?'

'Long,' she said, kissing him. 'Ben, you've done a marvellous job.'

'Stephen did most of the work.'

'How is he?'

'Twitchy. And Esme?'

'Very happy to see Matthew and Susan and the girls. Is everyone here?'

'Pretty much, I think.'

'Ben, I need to talk to you.'

They went outside, heading away from the lawn. Matthew's girls were playing beside the stream.

She said, 'When are you planning to go back to Malta?'

'End of the month, perhaps.' He ran a hand over his hair, which was white now; if not cut often enough, it flared out from his head. His mad professor look, she called it. 'Come with me, Zoe.'

He always asked her, every time he went back. But this time she said, 'All right.'

'What?'

'I'm coming with you.'

'Seriously?'

'Seriously.'

'What about the shops?'

'I'm selling the shops.'

'Zoe, you don't have to do this. Not for me.'

'It's not only for you, it's for me as well. I'm tired of it, Ben. I used to love it, but I don't any more. I hate the clothes now – so inelegant, and the colours are so garish. And every year the same problems, but I don't find them a challenge any more. The young people, Jason and Emma, I can see they find it all so exciting, but I don't, I don't feel it here.' She put her fist to her heart. 'So I think it's time to go.'

He said gently, 'And Russ?'

Zoe thought of Russ, and how much she had loved him and how much she had missed him and had wanted to carry on his legacy.

'I think he'd have been proud of me,' she said. 'I did what I had to and I know I did it well. I've found a suitable buyer, someone who understands the location and will care about the shops and look after the staff. And anyway . . .' She took his hand, turned it over, saw the shadowy line that crossed his palm, the legacy of the time he had cut it on the baked bean tin. 'I think I need to become more adventurous,' she said. 'I've never found it easy, being adventurous, and if I don't start now, when will I?'

497

'So, then,' he said, kissing her. 'Malta and Gozo. I'll buy a bigger tent. I'm joking. We'll buy a flat in Valletta and we'll live there half the year. Zoe, you've made me so happy.'

'I've been steeling myself for sleeping bags and camping stoves.'

'There'll be a bit of that. But not too much, I promise.'

'And there's another thing.'

'What's that?'

'If you wanted to marry me,' she said, 'nothing would make me happier, Ben. Nothing at all.'

'I wasn't sure whether you'd come,' Stephen said. 'I wasn't sure whether you'd ever come here again.'

'Neither was I,' said Coral. She studied him, found him changed, and tried to explain. 'I had to find out who I was, what I wanted, first. I couldn't' – and she softened it with a smile – 'run off into the arms of the first nice man who came along.'

'And have you? Have you found what you wanted?'

'Yes, I think so. Stephen, I've got a job, a proper job.'

'Congratulations. What are you doing?'

'I'm working for an environmental group. We try and stop ancient woods being car-parked over, that sort of thing.'

'No more paving Paradise?'

'Yeah, that's it. I love it. I feel as if I'm doing something useful at last.'

'About what happened . . .'

'I'm getting quite good at not thinking about it. Sometimes, when I'm working and my mind's on other things, a whole morning goes by.'

'Coral,' he said softly.

But Matthew was chinking a fork against a glass, and champagne was being poured, and Zoe and Ben herded them all back to the table on the lawn, where toasts were proposed, speeches made, and 'Happy Birthday' was sung.

*　　*　　*

An hour later, when the party was in full swing, and after claiming to need a short lie-down, Esme headed up the drive. The music became fainter as she entered the darkness of the trees and was lost by the time she passed through the gate. It was chilly, and she was glad of her quilted jacket and the torch she had thought to bring with her.

The lights of Lethwiston lay ahead. She turned by the barn, and then she was walking along the row of cottages until she stopped outside the end of the terrace.

She rapped on the door. No answer. Perhaps Jane Fox was away. She felt a mixture of relief and distress. And yet a light showed through the curtains.

She was about to knock again when the door opened. A voice said, 'If it's about your wretched cat . . .'

The woman who spoke was a head shorter than Esme. Age had whittled her wrists and ankles to sticks, but she still held herself upright.

'Miss Fox?' said Esme.

'Yes.' Suspiciously.

'I'm Mrs Godwin, Mrs Esme Godwin. I used to be—'

'Mrs Reddaway. I know who you are. What do you want?'

'To talk to you.'

A silence, and then, anguish in her eyes: 'My sister told me she was dead.'

'Camilla? Yes, I'm afraid so. She died three months ago.'

'Did she suffer?' The words were raw with pain.

'Not too much, I don't think. May I come in?'

Jane Fox stood aside, letting Esme pass into a sitting room comfortably furnished with a small chintz-covered sofa and matching armchairs.

'I should have been there. I would have taken care of her.' Jane Fox made a quick gesture, indicating that Esme should sit down. 'Did she ask for me?'

'I'm afraid that at the end, my sister was unable to speak.

But she was well cared for. You mustn't upset yourself, Miss Fox.'

'Upset myself?' A flash of anger. 'What would you know?' The maid's voice lowered to a whisper. 'She needed me. I would have known how to make her comfortable. I knew how to soothe her when she had one of her headaches or when she was in a temper. "Come and hold me, Foxy," she'd say, if she felt blue, and I'd kiss her and caress her. "What would I do without you, Foxy?" – she must have said that to me a thousand times. No one else knew her like I did, no one. None of those fools of men, and certainly not you.' There was derision in Jane Fox's eyes. 'I'll never forget what she said the day you married Mr Devlin. "He'll be bored within a week", that's what she said to me. And he was, wasn't he?'

Such contempt. 'Devlin loved me,' said Esme.

'Love?' said Jane Fox scornfully. 'Miss Camilla had only to look at him and he came running. What man would have given you a second glance when *she* was around?'

Esme opened her bag and took out the photographs she had brought with her. She spread them on the side table. 'I came here to ask for your help,' she said.

A mistake, that. Jane Fox's sneer was visible. 'Why should I help *you*?'

'Were you with her then?' Esme showed Jane a photograph of a beach party at Cannes.

Emotions flitted across the old woman's face as she studied the snapshot: longing and regret and pride. 'Yes, I was. I went everywhere with her.'

Esme pointed to one of the other bathing-costumed figures. 'That's Denis Rackham, isn't it?'

'I can't remember.'

'Camilla was angry with Devlin for marrying me. She tried to break up our marriage. In the end, of course, she succeeded. I've always wondered why she minded so much. Was it simply

500

that she resented him forgetting her and turning to me, her little sister? Or did she feel something for him?'

A silence, then: 'You took what should have been hers.'

'Camilla would only have married Devlin if he had given up Rosindell. And Devlin was incapable of giving up Rosindell.'

A hiss. 'He loved her long before he even looked at you! I saw them kiss, I watched them, all those years ago, in London!'

The maid's upper lip had curled in disgust and another piece of the jigsaw had clicked into place. Esme said, 'You were jealous of him, weren't you? Because you loved her.'

'What if I did?' said Jane proudly. 'None of the rest of you could hold a candle to her.'

But in the end, thought Esme, Camilla let you down. After more than fifty years' service she left you destitute.

She said slowly, 'But Camilla got back at Devlin. She made him suffer for what he'd done. She told him that Melissa was his child, when in fact she was Denis Rackham's.'

Another silence. A pulse thudded in Esme's throat. It was still possible that the maid would guard her mistress's secrets even after death.

But when she looked up, she saw a wild and triumphant laughter blaze across Jane Fox's features.

'Where did you think those eyes came from? Miss Camilla always said that Mr Rackham was as thick as a barn door, but she adored his sea-green eyes. Miss Camilla was pregnant before she went with Mr Devlin. A lady's maid knows these things. Besides, she told me everything.'

Esme felt no relief, no sense of victory in the revelation, only sadness. Love – love for a woman, a man, a house – had torn them all apart.

Jane Fox was looking down at a snapshot of Camilla as a young woman.

'She was horrified when she found out she was expecting.' Now she seemed to speak half to herself. 'She'd got rid of a baby before, visited some butcher, and she couldn't face going through that again. We tried everything – hot baths, gin, pennyroyal – but nothing worked. Doesn't matter whether you're a maid or a mistress, the same rules apply.'

The air in the room seemed fetid with old jealousies and tainted love. Esme longed to leave. But she picked up another photograph and held it out to Jane.

'That's you, isn't it?'

It had been taken before the First World War, in Devlin's father's time. A dozen servants were lined up in the courtyard at Rosindell to welcome their master back to the house. Two of the white-aproned maids were mere children: Sarah and Jane Fox, local girls from Lethwiston.

Jane glanced briefly at the picture. 'Yes. That's me and Sarah.'

'Sarah told me that when you worked at the house, you knew it like the back of your hand. And I've wondered – I've wondered whether you came back there, and if so, what you did when you returned. You see, I can't remember seeing you there.'

'But you wouldn't, would you?' Jane Fox's cold green eyes rested for a moment on Esme. 'I was a servant. People like you, you don't even see servants. But I saw you.'

Such dislike in her voice. Hatred, even. Esme said, 'You stole from me, didn't you? You came to my house and you took my things.'

'What if I did?'

'But why?'

'I deserved them. I worked hard enough.'

'So you took them because they were valuable? Or was there some other reason?'

'I told you,' said Jane. 'You stole what should have been hers.'

Such devotion. The theft of a silver hairbrush, a bracelet, a pair of earrings. And the theft of a husband.

But Jane's admission had given her some relief, explaining events that had haunted her throughout her life, and Esme rose, picking up her handbag.

'There never were any ghosts, were there?' she said. 'It was always you. The night of the dinner party, when we played hide and seek, it was you I followed through the house, you who went into my room. It was, wasn't it?'

'What if it was?' muttered Jane Fox. But the fight had gone out of her, and she sank into a chair, a tired old woman.

As she let herself out of the house, she felt as if a weight had fallen from her. Devlin had been right all along. All was explicable: no bad luck or evil apparition had ever haunted Rosindell. The witches' marks on the fireplace were leftovers from more superstitious times, that was all. No poltergeist had stolen from Rosindell, only Camilla's light-fingered maid.

Esme walked briskly back down the narrow street and turned on to the road to Rosindell. But as she reached the trees, the strength seemed to go from her, and she leaned against the gatepost, shocked and destabilised by what she had discovered that night. There was a pain behind her breast-bone and she felt dazed and faint. The sound of the sea, with its rhythmic crash and rush, filled her head, louder and louder, insistent and demanding, leaving space only for horror, horror at the consequences of Camilla's actions: the tearing apart of Matthew and Melissa, her own separation from Devlin, Devlin's guilt and regret, and the ten long years during which she had not known whether Matthew was alive or dead. All these things could be laid at Camilla's door. She herself had always been mistaken: the house had never hurt her family; only Camilla had, through her spite, egotism and jealousy.

The sound of the sea ebbed, the pain faded and she could breathe again. Exhausted, she moved slowly down the drive. The mistakes and regrets of the past could never be repaired, but there was one last thing she could do for her family, and that would be to tell them the truth.

Later, they danced on the lawn. Coral was wearing a coat over her party dress because it was cold, and some old song was drifting from the record player.

'You see,' she said, 'this place. I wouldn't want to own it. Not because of what happened. It's just not my thing, owning stuff. It's too big, too heavy. A room's enough for me.'

Stephen's arms were round her and her head was resting on his shoulder and he was stroking her hair. 'I've been thinking about that,' he said. 'The house is falling to pieces anyway. I thought I'd see if the National Trust wanted it. The land – now something useful could be done with the land. A nature reserve, perhaps. Maybe you'd like to keep an eye on it, Coral. Or the NT, if you'd rather not.'

She said, 'But you love Rosindell.'

'I love you more. People are more important than houses, don't you think? And now that we're not even cousins any more . . .'

'Half-second cousins,' she said.

'Something like that. Disappointingly unpervy. But it kind of sets us free, doesn't it?'

She wondered, as they kissed, whether it did. With the saying of the words – I love you – the possibility of something lasting had flowered, and wasn't that a tie? Still, she thought, you couldn't run free for ever. Eventually you accumulated things: places and people and passions. And that wasn't so bad, was it?

The sound of the sea had been replaced by the music that wafted over the overgrown gardens and lawns, the music of the summer dance at Rosindell. They were playing a Cole Porter song, 'Always True to You in My Fashion', and now the years slipped away and Esme was dancing with Devlin in the garden.

I've always loved you, he had said to her that day, the day they had learned that Matthew was still alive. *Always*, he had repeated as they had danced together, one last dance. *Always and for ever.*

Houses crumbled, but love lasted. Love threaded them together, her and her family. From her vantage point on the grassy slope, Esme watched the dancers: Coral and Stephen, Zoe and Ben, Matthew and Susan. Her sprawling, complicated, disputatious family; their love for each other now extended halfway round the world, as strong as the ivy that clung to the walls of Rosindell. Her love for Devlin and Devlin's love for her would stay with her until the day she died.

In the end, what remained was love. Esme walked down the lawn, back to her family.

The wind ripples through the grass and murmurs over the overgrown ruins of loggia and terrace, where decades ago other lovers once danced. It rustles a heap of dead leaves, making them skirl and scatter, and it reveals a glint of gold – a bracelet or an earring perhaps, lost by someone long ago.

The breeze finds its way into the house and a window rattles. There is an echo of laughter, though no one is there. A door opens and closes, and then the house becomes quiet again.